THE WAR
OF THE BOULD

Robert C. Thomason

iUniverse, Inc.
Bloomington

iUniverse books may be ordered through booksellers or by contacting:

iUniverse
1663 Liberty Drive
Bloomington, IN 47403
www.iuniverse.com
1-800-Authors (1-800-288-4677)

Because of the dynamic nature of the Internet, any web addresses or links contained in this book may have changed since publication and may no longer be valid. The views expressed in this work are solely those of the author and do not necessarily reflect the views of the publisher, and the publisher hereby disclaims any responsibility for them.

Any people depicted in stock imagery provided by Thinkstock are models, and such images are being used for illustrative purposes only.

Certain stock imagery © Thinkstock.

ISBN: 978-1-4620-1369-2 (sc)
ISBN: 978-1-4620-1370-8 (hc)
ISBN: 978-1-4620-1368-5 (ebook)

Printed in the United States of America

iUniverse rev. date: 09/30/2011

For McKenzie,
My sweet treasure,
and for my dad,
gone too soon

TABLE OF CONTENTS

NOTES ON PRONUNCIATION

M ost of the place names and character names in this story are drawn directly from the language of Tor, or from one of the Kingdoms of men that rule the lands of Aegea. All of these languages, excluding that of Nefala, are syllabic tongues, with each written character acting as a syllable rather than as an individual letter. Thus, rendering the names into English is difficult, and some explanation is necessary to ensure proper pronunciation.

Vowels

The vowels of Aegea each carry only one unchanging value, and are never silent.

A-always carries the value of a short A in English, as in *CAT.*

E-always carries the value of a short E in English, as in *NET.*

I- always carries the value of a short I in English, as in *LIT.*

O-always carries the value of a long O in English, as in *BONE.*

U-always carries the value of a double OO in English, as in *BOOT.*

Additionally, every vowel, no matter its placement within a word, or whether or not it is paired with another vowel in a diphthong, holds its value and must be independently annunciated. Hence:

1) Gladue is pronounced *Glah-`doo-eh*

2)Tolone is pronounced *Toe-`low-neh*

3) Bould is pronounced *`Bo-oold*

Consonants

There are some letters in English that have no equivalent in the language of Tor, or are unnecessary:

C- Always carries the value K, as in *KITE,* except when coupled which an H, in which case it is pronounced CH, as in *CHURCH.* In the dark lands of Sindus, K is used frequently, as well as C, and both carry the value of K. It is also common to join the letters CHT in a syllable. In this case, the CH is pronounced like K, as in the German word *nicht. (Nicked)*

G-always carries the value of G, as in *GET.* Therefore, Aegea is pronounced *Ah-eh-geh-ah.* There is no sound in the language of Tor that corresponds to the English J, as in JEEP. The tongues of Andesha and Gladue, alone among the kingdoms of men, use a J sound in their speech.

NOTES ON AEGEA

Some astute readers may notice that the dates provided do not seem to match up very well. The answer lies in the fact that although Aegea has a 365-day year like our own, they have arranged their calendar in a different way. Each of the twelve months of the year has thirty days, no more or less. The disparity is made up by the five-day "harvest festival" that took place between October and November every year. Once every twenty years, this festival was extended to ten days, making a correction that we currently alter with leap years. The years of these extended festivals were called "Tor Years", and the long period of rest was designed to allow all willing at least one chance in their lifetime to make a pilgrimage to the Temple of Tor in Rubia.

The continent of Aegea itself is quite small, about the size of the southeastern United States, and along with its several small, coastal islands, represents the entire known world at the time of this tale. The land lay in a temperate region of the world, and experiences seasons that flow with steady predictability. The extreme south, in the lands of Tolone and Nefala, the winters are less harsh, but otherwise the weather is uniform.

Over the long centuries, beginning with the time of Tor on the earth and including the millennia since his imprisonment, men had altered the lands as they could, building roads and carving paths through the mountains. An impressive transportation system was in place by the time of these events, connecting the major capitols and larger settlements. The cooperation between the kingdoms, even before the rebellion of the Norsa, was possibly the greatest achievement ever accomplished by men, and the results were a land full of wonders in construction and advancements in tools and weaponry. A flourishing trade of thoughts and resources allowed each kingdom to specialize and focus their energies on that which they did best. As a result, the standard of living for most people was high compared to others in a similar state of primitive existence, and the gods were wise, allocating resources throughout Aegea in an even way. While some kingdoms made furniture or seafaring craft from the abundant timber within their borders, others made steel of the highest quality. Some grew plentiful fruits and vegetables, while others could produce some of the most impressive beasts of burden that could be imagined. The kingdoms were united in their stand against the dreaded enemy of the east and worked together to spread the best of what they had to offer through trade.

However, even with advanced ideas and profound freedom, there still existed pockets of empty lands, full of mystery and fabulous wealth that could upset this delicate balance.

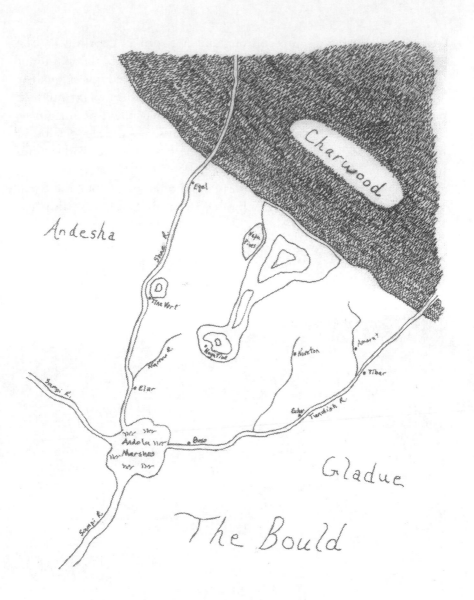

Charwood

Andesha

Egal

Shaul R.

High Trees

Tine Vert

Narrow R.

Main Tine

Noreton

Amarat

Tibar

Elur

Smargi R.

Edge

Tiendish R.

Andola
Marshes

Doso

Gladue

Sampi R.

The Bould

A PERILOUS DECISION

When Fordrun Noveton of Gladue announced to his family that he wanted to sell their holdings and move to a free homestead in the Bould, at first there was only stunned silence. Seventeen pairs of eyes stared back at him with shocked amazement. A moment passed in which the patriarch of the household could hear the cattle rustling and stamping their feet in the pasture forty yards away. The stems of the rose bushes outside the window scraped against the glass, softly swaying in the early spring breezes. The tiniest sound came to Fordrun, as audible as shrill speech, noises that even his diminished hearing could detect. Then, as if on cue, everyone seated around the large dining table began to talk at once. Men, women, their grown children, and the adolescent grandchildren began to harp and warble, nudging and working diligently to make room for their own opinion. There was obvious disagreement over the wisdom of this decision, as there should have been, for moving to the Bould was no easy chore, and weeks of hard toil were promised to anyone that sought to undergo such an adventure.

As Fordrun listened to the heated chatter of his household, he could discern the lines along which the debate would divide the home. The lines fell much as he had predicted they would. Overall, the males were in favor, while the females tended to be against it. In addition, the older members of the family were against moving, while the younger persons and the children were excited about the prospect. The only exception to both of these broad groups was Lendum, the youngest son of the house. At eleven years of age, such a venture should have held the promise of great feats, worthy of tales and song. However, instead of wide-eyed dreams of excitement at the idea of something new and different, Lendum felt only great apprehension about living in the Bould.

"I'm not afraid of moving," he would say later to his father in private. "It's the idea of moving to *the Bould* that I fear. There is evil there, if the tales are true; an evil that is dressed in satiny lace and speaks with the voice of an angel. I think going there of our own accord is madness. It's like putting the noose around your neck with your own hands."

Fordrun would snicker at that image, late at night with his most tender child sitting close to his knee in the dark, the single lamp casting a pale light across his son's face, making him seem thin, feeble, and so very young. Later he would laugh aloud at the memory of that talk, especially after the discovery of the mine, the words seeming more and more like the craven counsel of a frightened youth that cannot appreciate the rich rewards to be harvested from risk. Nevertheless, as time passed at their home in the Bould, Fordrun laughed less and less, and he came to realize that his youngest son was not a fearful little boy, but wise beyond his years.

At present, however, Fordrun heard nothing but the relentless chatter of conflicting desires.

"What if we get lost?" said his wife Marle. "There is nothing there, nothing at all to guide us."

"There is no law there," said Deana, his oldest daughter. "We would be entirely on our own."

The oldest son, Seleus, a wise man with forty summers, was leery of moving, but the possibilities did pique his interest. "I hear that the soil is black, and that grass grows even on the rocks." His eyes danced as he spoke, dreaming of the fertile lands.

"We could certainly profit from the free acreage," said Antion, the second son, "though the labor could be inhuman."

After several weary moments, Fordrun sat down, forced his aged knees and hips to bend, and laboriously crossed his legs. He plucked an apple from a nearby wooden bowl, and leisurely began to eat it. He sat there, chewing thoughtfully, his blue eyes that had refused to dim with age focused on nothing. The wrinkles around his saggy cheeks flexed and released as he chewed, making his face appear as a butterfly that could not quite muster the strength required to take to the air. The debate continued unabated, and Fordrun had resolved to hear it out until the end, though the words he heard began to run together and form an unintelligible goop. He had started this by making his pronouncement, and now it was his part to endure the aftershock by hearing the resulting discussion. This he did with good humor, especially considering that the debate was pointless. An argument over the merits of a particular decision ignores the fact that *a decision has already been made*, and as such, arguing the finer points is useless. After a time, Fordrun realized that his loving wife, twelve years his junior and whom he still found beautiful beyond measure, had disengaged from the talk and was looking at him intensely with an odd combination of fear and trust. She smiled weakly, offering her husband a support that was perfunctory at best. She, more than anyone, recognized that her husband had made up his mind already. If there had been the slightest sliver of doubt in his mind, he would be quarrelling with a passion along with everyone else. He was not. He was only sitting, calmly eating his apple, the light of the flickering flames of the hearth making dancing colors in his shoulder-length hair. Any debate was futile.

Fordrun had spent his life, as all people must do at some point, following the decisions of others. Now the time had come when others must abide by his decisions, and he had already decided. They were moving to the Bould.

⇒ ⇐

Lendum, though young, knew a great deal about the Bould and its history. His grandsire had obsessively devoured tremendous amounts of lore, and Fordrun had been the beneficiary of that accrued knowledge. He, in turn, regaled his children with all of the history he had learned, and Lendum more than any other would sit in rapt attention, taking in every word. The tale of the Bould was one of the most enticing, for not only was the land tantalizingly close, but it was also a tale that was going on still.

The Bould was a triangular-shaped piece of land that bordered three kingdoms: Andesha to the west, Gladue to the southeast, and the forbidden realm of Nactadale, domain of the dark lord Sindus, to the northeast. The frontiers of the Bould were evident. The Shae and the Tundish rivers lined the boundaries with Andesha and Gladue, respectively, until they met, flowing together to make the point that was the southern extreme of the region. The forest line of Charwood marked the border with Sindus. A backbone-like ridge of hills and plateaus ran through the center of the area, flattening out to grass-covered plains as one came closer to the life-giving rivers. The area was a massive spearhead, the point of which was plunged deep into the perilous Andola Marshes, a swampy, stagnant bog that covered several thousand acres. Cut off by large rivers and flanked by mighty powers earned the area its name. In the language of Tor, the Bould literally means, *the between*.

At one time or another, both of the bordering kingdoms of men had laid claim to the Bould, but neither had seen fit to dedicate a portion of their strength to defending it. Such an acquisition would add more miles of frontier with the dreaded dark lord Sindus of the east, who craved only to maim and destroy. The land of the Bould was rumored to be good for farming, with soil that was rich and untouched, but aside from that little else was in evidence to warrant the additional expenditure required to hold this small piece of Aegea. There was no gold or silver, no mines of copper or iron or tin, no great herds of wild animals to harvest for meats or hides. The few explorers that had examined the region found no wealth whatsoever, except for the bounty of the earth, which was little inducement for pioneers to risk their lives and fortunes. Because of this, no one moved to inhabit the Bould, and the monarchs gave their people no motivation to do so. Therefore, the hordes of Sindus came to have dominion over the area, and would often use it to cross into their hated enemy's territory, wherever the rivers got low enough to cross.

So it was for many generations, and many centuries, until the Famine.

In the year 542, a long, frightfully cold winter swept away thousands of unfortunate souls and animals from the treeless plains of Andesha and Gladue. Hunger spared not a single household the loss of a loved one, or horses or oxen or sheep. People welcomed the thaws of spring with joyful praises to the gods, but the gods are temperamental, receiving praises awkwardly. When the sowing of seeds came (for those that had animals well enough to pull the plows), a late frost came that killed most of the year's planting in the ground. Farmers with enough seed defiantly planted again, only to see their humble fields succumb to devastating heat and drought. Harsh winds blew the resulting dust away in massive throat-clogging clouds, killing anything left that was growing and green.

The Famine nearly destroyed the two bordering nations of the Bould. There was almost nothing to eat. Ravenous folks slaughtered surviving beasts of burden, and even household pets, for meat. Out of desperation, men fished the rivers and lakes known to hold the dens of the dangerous rompu, and for such recklessness, many found themselves in the belly of one of the great beasts. Women and children were found dead in their homes, their mouths and tongues green from trying to eat boiled grass and hay. There were tales of men eating the heavily seasoned leather of their boots and satchels. Spouses came up missing, their husbands asserting that hunger had claimed them, while it was obvious no such thing had occurred. The Famine was a terrible thing, a misery with no precedent, and there was no relief from any quarter. The other kingdoms of men sent what provisions they could, but it was simply not enough, and in any event, the donated foodstuffs that arrived went to those in the cities. There was no way to get the precious provender to the homesteads, where the suffering was most acute

The following year, a King's council was held in Farshton, the second such council ever called in the history of the world, the first being more than 500 years earlier after the rebellion against Tor. The kings agreed that one of the ways to ease the suffering of the Famine was to open the Bould to settlement. A unanimous agreement was reached that would allow Andesha and Gladue joint occupation of the territory, and all of the seven kingdoms would dedicate soldiers to the task of cleansing the Bould of the minions of Sindus, and guarding the border along the eaves of Charwood. The Council offered free homesteads to any that wished to move to the area, provided they would use their lands to produce food and would pledge a tithe of their produce to the common good.

Thus, the next spring, there was war in the Bould for the first time. Righteous men armed with deadly weapons spilled blood on its innocent soil, marking sites of great valor and loss. The men of the kingdoms of the earth swept across the surface of the Bould, flushing rokul from their holes and shooting kaitos from the skies, until the ominous trees of the Charwood stood before them, the servants of Sindus all but eradicated from between the rivers. They made the land clean.

In the year 547 A.R., pronouncements came from all of the kings of Aegea; those who were willing could go forth and be welcomed in the Bould. They were invited under the terms reached at the King's Council, and with the full understanding that there would be no guarantees for their safety, and no protection under the law. There was no way to institute a rule of law in a land with no settlements, and under the joint jurisdiction of two kingdoms.

Nevertheless, pioneers did come. Those that had lost so much during the long famine saw new hope in the rolling virgin lands of the Bould. They came from Rubia and Anafaline, riding in horse drawn carriages bearing all of their possessions. They came from Nefala, Tolone and Hashana, holding the precious seeds that would make the earth come alive with growing abundance. Mostly they came from Andesha and Gladue, the two bordering nations of men that held such close kinship through their royal houses (On at least three occasions, the ruling kings of the two lands and been brothers). Farms sprang up along the rivers, and every home had at least one boat that could provide a quick escape in the event of danger from the east. Every household was armed, and every boy of age (and in some cases every girl) could wield bow and blade with skill. For many decades, the population grew slowly, with Andesha and Gladue having about an equal number of settlers. These pioneers lived mostly by the lifelines of the rivers. The interior of the Bould, so full of uncertainty and peril, was virtually uninhabited, and would remain so for centuries.

This uninhabited region was precisely where Fordrun intended to settle his large family. At the time of his decision, several decades had passed with no news of any activity among the agents of Sindus, either along the forest or the rivers. The dangerous rompu, who more often than not shunned men when given the choice, had descended the rivers and taken up residence in the marshes. No one had seen one in the waters along the Bould since time out of mind, and now children would splash and play in the cool, flowing water with no fear, while their mothers tended the wash or gathered wild herbs and berries.

The people of the Bould had melded into a unique race. Most of the folks living there could speak Andeshan and Gladuese, as well as the language of Tor, and this fact alone set them apart from the other peoples of Aegea. They intermarried, producing children that had no single nationality, and loyalty to no single monarch. Over time, they gave their first allegiance to the Bould itself, and secondly they considered themselves subjects of faraway kings. Soon, no allegiance existed to any king whatsoever, and although this could have been problematic for the kings of the Bould, they overlooked this quirk of the people, because the Bould became prosperous, more so than anyone could have imagined. Every year, tons of grain and live animals crossed the rivers, on their way to feed thousands of hungry people. The best course of action, it was agreed, was not to upset this spectacular production by antagonizing the residents. Demanding loyalty to the crown was something that the royal heads sacrificed to keep the valuable carts full of tithes coming from the wilderness.

Therefore, the people of the Bould grew hardy in labor, deeply attached to their freedom, and enjoyed many, many years of peace. Many more years of peace they would have enjoyed, were it not for the arrival of Fordrun Noveton.

⇒ ⇐

The month following the divisive family meeting was March, and as the winter frosts peeled away, the Noveton family labored strenuously, preparing to depart. Eight wagons, heavily laden with goods and supplies purchased from the sale of the farm, made a little caravan prepared to journey into the west. Fordrun had sold the farm to a neighbor that was not hindered from showing his distaste for Fordrun's decision to leave.

"You're a damned fool!" he had proclaimed, the deed to the two-hundred acre farm still in his hand. He scrunched up his nose as if he smelled something foul, making him look a bit like a mole. "Why a man nearing seventy would want to risk his neck for some young man's dream of ambition is beyond me. Why do you not stay here, and enjoy your last days in peace and leisure? Bould folks are not like us. They only look after themselves, not outsiders. You'll be utterly alone."

"That's precisely what I want," Fordrun thought, but only replied that he would be careful, and that his boys were big enough to watch out for him. He made his farewell from his longtime neighbor, and with a considerable amount of money in hand (rumor was that it was some thousands, perhaps *several* thousands), he turned to look once more at the farm that he had inherited from his father. For six generations this tiny patch of the earth had sheltered and fed the Noveton family. The whole farm was crisp and ready to do work, but at the same time, the spirit of life that had been so pervasive for so many years was gone. The farm carried the feeling of bereavement, an oncoming loss that seemed too soon.

Fordrun felt a tear well up in his eye. For the slightest moment, he could sense a twinge of doubt bore its way into his mind. Guilt weighed on him heavily, for he was risking not only his own life and fortune, but also those of everyone and everything he loved. The journey itself would be hard enough, but once there, the circumstances would force them to carve a home out of the wilderness, and time was pressing. They had barely six months before the onset of the first of the winter's frosts, which would then turn into a bitter cold that could claim lives without four walls and a good fire to battle against the chill. "Could this be a mistake?" he wondered. "Should I not do this?"

He forced such thoughts from his mind. He could afford no second-guessing. The memories of the farm were sweet, but the soil had grown bitter. Yields had been falling the past few years, and profits with it. There was less and less to take to market, and soon it would be hard to feed themselves. The answer was to allow a plot or two to lie fallow for a season so the soil could grow rich again, but they could not permit land to lay idle, lest they go hungry. Though they had some means, it was hardly enough to sustain them for several seasons. Yes, he had seen it coming for some time; the farm was dying, and to stay and cling to it out of some misguided sense of duty or loyalty was to invite disaster. They needed new lands. Cheap lands. Virgin lands. Larger lands. Only one place in Aegea could provide all they needed: the Bould.

= =

The journey would be a long one. Nearly 150 leagues separated them from the Tundish River. From there, Fordrun hoped to cross into the region, following the river until they struck a smaller stream they could follow into the interior. With luck, they could stake a claim and have new holdings by the beginning of summer.

They departed on the second of March, in the year 1102. Fordrun sat in the leading wagon, the charter given by King Frondus granting their homestead clutched tightly in his hand. At present, the charter was one of the most valuable articles in his possession. Within its words the crown guaranteed a three-hundred-acre patch of the earth in perpetuity, with a promise that the king of Gladue shall never hinder or repossess the gift. In exchange, Fordrun had sworn to give the crown its tithe for as long as he or his family inhabited the claim. Fordrun looked forward steadily, the rocking of the wagon causing him to sway. Lendum sat next to him, looking backward, unable to peel his eyes away from what they were leaving behind.

They made slow progress, for not only were there eight wagons, loaded heavily and pulled by teams of lumbering oxen, but dozens of other animals were being led as well; goats, horses and sheep. None of the travelers, Fordrun included, had had any experience with this kind of trek, and movement was maddeningly slow. They made only 8 miles the first day, and all were surprised to learn how wearying it could be to sit in a wagon all day. Mundane tasks like gathering wood for the evening fire and boiling water for broth seemed more tiring than anything that could be conceived. Lendum ached all over, and the act of bending his back and stretching his limbs was troublesome. He kept a positive attitude, but the distraught faces of his family members were disheartening. He went about his chores lethargically, tending to the animals and unpacking needed provisions. They ate their meals in silence, and after the first dinner eaten out of doors under the clear night sky, the family lay down to sleep. The night turned cold, and men, women, and children tossed and turned under their blankets, their bodies protesting to lying on the frigid, unyielding earth. Lendum could hear women and children weeping in the night. The men suffered in silence, but they were equally miserable.

However, the days of travel became easier and more productive as their skill improved. Cooking without a stove became easier, and unsaddling the beasts of burden every day was done quickly. By April, they were covering more than fifteen miles a day. The angry flesh of their bodies ceased grumbling as they became accustomed to repose outdoors. The flavor of campfire cooking became more satisfying, filling their bellies with refreshment that they could not have believed was possible. Lendum could feel his body becoming tougher, the muscles growing even tauter under his pallid skin. He smiled more, and occasional he would sing songs to pass the time. More and more often others would join in, the atmosphere growing lighter as the burden became less arduous. Their pace quickened, as they learned to do the monotonous duties of packing and unpacking with greater swiftness and agility.

On the fourth of April, they struck the Tundish River, and after traversing the eastern bank for half a day, they came upon the one bridge that connected Gladue to the Bould. They crossed, and found themselves in Ghar, a tiny village of folks that mostly claimed Gladue descent. Lendum was very pleased to encounter this group of people. In his mind, Lendum had assumed that the family would be completely removed from any other persons, but it seemed that the Bould was not as deserted as he had believed. Not only were these folks available to give aid, they were civil and friendly, eager to help. They addressed them with intimate monikers, and smiled with genuine gladness. Neat little rows of cylindrical structures lined the dirt streets, small round windows showing the modest interior. The people had built their homes of clay brick, lined the walls with woven branches, and conical, thatched roofs spouted thin plumes of smoke into the sky. Fordrun bought supplies from a local merchant, they refilled their barrels with fresh water, and the family camped on the outskirts of the village.

That night there was genuine happiness. They had made it to the Bould! They sang songs and told tales, the flames of the fire glinting in every eye. Children played silly games, as the adults smiled wistfully at their antics. They laughed heartily at old memories and ate food that tasted sweeter than any they had eaten before. A sense of true accomplishment filled the thoughts of all. Fordrun was mindful of their good fortune. They had come a long way, and no one had been injured or ill. The journey was not yet finished, but that did not reduce the contentment that the family felt. They slept that night as if on feather beds with down pillows.

The next morning they turned west, following the flow of the river. The land was completely untamed, and the wagons swayed and creaked as they traversed the hilly countryside. Lendum liked the lands he saw. A pure, green country met his eyes everywhere he looked, and there was absolutely nothing at all that resembled settlement. There were no houses, no barns, and no smoke on the horizon. Nothing but pristine beauty was evident. The traveling was more difficult over the broken terrain, but Lendum found it infinitely more enjoyable. After five days, they happened upon a stream coming from the north that flowed into the Tundish. They turned north and Fordrun told Lendum to pay special attention. Somewhere along this lazy course of clean water they would build a new farm: the foundations of many more generations of this family.

After six days of following the stream, Fordrun found his claim. A little valley opened before them, the tiny river threading its way through the hills like a walkway. A small grove of pecan trees stood near the bank, and broad, flat acres stretched in every direction. Tall grasses swayed in the breeze, weighed down with nutritious seeds for hungry animals. The setting sun made everything seem rich and golden, a tranquil paradise for weary wayfarers.

"This is it," said Fordrun to Lendum, placing a strong arm around his son's shoulders. In his mind's eye, he could already see the layout of his new holdings, his vision stirring up emotions that he had long since forgotten. "Here it is, and nothing could be better. We will stop here."

⇒ ⇐

For the next two years, the family labored almost ceaselessly. Out of the wilderness a civilized order emerged, and in every way, it was superior to their previous life in Gladue. Nearby timber provided all the free lumber they could use, so instead of one large home for all, ten separate dwellings were constructed, each with its own little garden for herbs and vegetables. The houses were log constructions, with low, dome-shaped thatched roofs to deflect the winds of the plains. They built two barns, and fenced two pastures, one on each side of the stream, and the animals feasted and grew fat on the plentiful grasses. Additionally, two large plots were broken and sown, one on each side, and to the great pleasure of all, the soil was very fruitful. The trip back to Ghar after the first harvest brought four wagons of grain, which covered the tithe to the crown and produced a profit greater than anything that could have been hoped. The grain was so bulky that Fordrun decided to build a waterwheel mill, utilizing the never-ending energy of the stream, to grind flour for their use, as well as to sell at market. Lendum helped build this in the fall and winter.

The next season brought even greater rewards with less work. The bountiful earth seemed so very eager to laugh forth with a harvest at the mere tickle of a plow. There was plenty for all, both from their own fields and from the natural production of the land. The pecan trees that had so attracted Fordrun to this location were a boon that all enjoyed with unrestrained delight. Lendum especially cherished the early mornings he would spend with his father; walking amongst the trees, searching for the most desirable pecans to put in pies, sprinkle on dishes, or to eat right from the hull. He and Fordrun would usually eat more than they retrieved, and the walk back to the house was always slower, full bellies protruding before them.

Nothing could be seen on the horizon that could tell of troubles ahead. Fordrun was happy, and he laughed as he had not laughed in ages. He felt full of vigor, and his energy brought a sense of reclaimed youth. All were pleased at Noveton Farm, and no one suspected that seven day's ride to the north would bring them to the realm of creatures so fearsome that they would slay themselves at the sight.

FALLING INTO TREASURE

Lendum was born on the twenty-fifth of March, well past the prime of his father. Fordrun was fifty-five when Lendum was born, and though he felt apprehension at having a child so young, he came to love the boy just as he loved his other children. "You are my proudest accident," he would often say, his face split into a boyish grin that conveyed his jest.

Twenty-five years separated Lendum and his oldest brother, Seleus, but the differences were greater than mere age. While all of the children of Fordrun had his dark hair and eyes, Lendum was born with a flash of white hair, so light that sunlight caused it to disappear before watching eyes. As he aged, his locks took on a darker hue, a sandstone blonde that undulated like the dunes of the desert. In this way, he was much as his mother had been. Lendum was more like his mother in look and manner than any of Fordrun's other children. Since she was born in Andesha, the gods had blessed Marle with the light hair and pale skin common in that land. Perhaps this resemblance to his beloved wife made Lendum more precious in the eyes of his father, but Fordrun was unaware of it. To him, Lendum was a beautiful boy, and his advanced age brought an increased joy that had been absent when Seleus was a child.

Lendum enjoyed a softer father than his siblings had endured. Fordrun already had grandchildren nearly the age of his youngest son, and the years that had added gray to his hair and wrinkles to his skin had made him less quick to take up the rod when Lendum misbehaved. The boy and his father were more friends than anything else, talking for many hours about whatever came into their minds, passing the time in a most pleasing way.

However, Fordrun was not overly lenient. The children of the farm had to work like everyone else, and Lendum was no exception. They were saddled with fewer duties, for Fordrun deemed education as important, and most of the children were not only fluent in three languages, but were literate as well. The family rose at dawn, and after breakfast every person was busy performing all manner of chores around the farm until it was time for the midday meal. After the refreshment the adults went back to work, but the children attended their studies for two or three hours, learning numbers or letters, hearing history, or learning skills like sewing or weaving, or even learning the skills of the sword or the spear. After this study time, the children were released from all tasks, and were free to run amok and play until dark. Lendum especially liked this time. Now fifteen and nearly a man, his period of adolescence was nearing an end, and sweetest is that which we are about to lose.

He would spent his free time exploring the outer reaches of the Bould farm, usually alone, singing songs quietly to himself or repeating the day's lesson so as to cement it in his head. Often he would carry his sword with him; an old, rusted thing with a cloth wrapped wooden hilt, short and broad, the style commonly used by the pirates of Anafaline as an off-hand weapon of defense. He would daydream of slaughtering the enemy, swinging his blade at ghosts, the harsh swish of cut air strident in his ears. Repeating his lessons, he would rout is imaginary foes, bringing his weapon to bear with deadly precision and making his adversaries flee in cowering fear. Always he was triumphant (as we tend to be in our own minds).

On a beautiful day in April, he carried his sword, and was so full of energy that he thought he might explode. Spring had arrived in full, and he had spent all morning helping his brother Seleus plow the western field. In the afternoon, Seleus, by far the best swordsman in the household, had given a superb lesson to his little brother. Seleus had learned a great deal of the art of *atum rah,* a highly efficient fighting style that focused on perpetual offense. Every movement of a fighter's weapon was intended to turn into a strike against the opponent. Each parry turns into a thrust quickly and with deadly hurt. All of the sword was a weapon, not just the blade. The hard pommel slammed into the forehead, or the unforgiving hand guard striking the teeth, could cause as much damage as the edge of any steel. The constant barrage was designed to keep an opponent on the defensive from the very outset, and Lendum relished the art. His time with Seleus learning the ancient techniques was most enjoyable. After a particularly vigorous session, Lendum took to the fields, spending the remaining daylight repeating what he had learned. With the setting sun warm and bright in the west, he turned eastward, chasing his long shadow, waving his sword wildly in his play. He smote his pretend enemy with brute strength and screamed taunts at the top of his voice, the sound ringing out across the plains. He was so engrossed in his fiction that he failed to notice the buildings of the farm shrink behind him. He failed to notice the direction he was running. He failed to notice that he was farther from the farm that his father allowed. Under his feet was a portion of the world where no man had walked since the creation of the world.

Lendum was thinking how foolish he had been to advise his father against moving here. This place was fantastic! He was happier than he had ever been in his life. Sweat rolled off him from his exercise, tiny droplets accumulating in the cleft of his chin. His hair hung lifeless across his brow. He felt unstoppable, his confidence reinforced by the superb surroundings that he called his home. The land was rich, pure and clean, untouched by man, and no blemish but that which the Norsa had made.

With his joyful thoughts still fresh in his mind, the ground opened up beneath his feet, and he was falling. He fell for what seemed a long, long time, and then...*splash*! Ice-cold water was flowing all around him. He quickly got to his feet, coughing and sputtering, shaking his limbs and head like a wet dog. Once he opened his eyes, he found himself in almost complete darkness. Only the opening through which he had fallen provided any real light. To his eye, the hole seemed absurdly small to have permitted his entry.

"Could I have fallen through that?" he asked himself. The hole was only about eight feet up, but even so, any hope of boosting himself up to it quickly fled. He was not getting out the way he had come, at least not without help.

After a few seconds, his eyes adjusted to the dark. In the failing light, he could see that he was in a tunnel, almost perfectly round, with a little stream coursing its way along the bottom. The passage must have been cut to its present size by the relentless flow of this underground stream, casually making its way along its path for eons. Once Lendum had his bearings, he took time to examine himself, and was relieved to find himself unhurt. He shouted for help towards the surface a few times, but even as the words left his throat, he knew they would be fruitless. Even to a person standing near the opening his voice would sound muffled and far away, and no one was near, he was sure.

An enormous fatigue settled on him, and he sat down to rest. The bank of the stream was narrow, but by crossing his legs beneath him, he was able to keep his feet out of the water. The rocks under him crunched under his weight and ground into the woven fabric of his breeches. His breathing became more regular, and suddenly he felt an incredible thirst come over him. Lendum licked his lips as he listened to the sound of the trickling water. He reached out from the gathering dark (night was coming on more quickly with each passing moment), until he felt the cool wetness of the stream flowing between his fingers. He wondered briefly if the water was safe to drink, but decided that he was going to drink it in any event. He felt so thirsty, and the notion of crisp water running down his parched throat was too much to resist. He cupped his hand, scooped a handful of the liquid and hastily poured it into his mouth.

He spat it out immediately. The water tasted terrible, bitter. Lendum leaned his back against the wall of the cave and let out a heavy sign. The enormity of the situation hit him abruptly. He had no food or water, no light or heat, no one knew where he was, and night was upon him. He tried to get a sense of his location, but it was useless. He could not remember how far he had run during his mock battle against evil. How close was he to the farm? Had he run a half mile? A mile? Could he have left any tracks behind? Was there anything at all that could lead his family to where he was? He was not sure, but he could not think of a single thing that could. All he knew was that he had been running eastward, chasing his shadow across the plains. He became frightened, and panic seized him. His heart began to pound, making the blood course loudly in his ears.

Lendum took several deep breaths, trying to calm himself, forcing his lungs to work evenly and loosening the tightness in his chest. As he did so, the last of the day's wavering light vanished, leaving him in total darkness. His family would miss him soon, if they had not already, so he strained his ears, hoping to hear his name called. He could hear nothing. A long time could pass before anyone found him, possibly days. Suppose he was not alone in this subterranean passage? What if a network of these caves spread all over the Bould, and still housed the dark creatures he had heard of so often in tales?

He struggled to force such thoughts from his head. The idea was probably preposterous, and in any case, thinking about it was less than helpful. He was already in a bad enough bind without adding invented demons and red-eyed wraiths with which to do battle. Besides, he was not defenseless. He had had some training, and his sword, while rusty and blunt, could serve to…

Then he realized his sword was gone, lost from his grip during the fall into the earth. His breaths became shallow and raspy as panic seized him. He felt all around him like a blind man, searching feverishly for something his heart already knew he would not find. He crawled over the rocks on the bank, the small stones cutting sharply into his knees and palms, fingers grasping fruitlessly. He searched the bed of the stream, limbs growing numb from the coldness of the water, but he found nothing. It was hopeless. His sword was gone, most likely on the surface, flung from his hand as he collapsed. There it could rust away to nothing before anyone found it.

Lendum returned to his place on the bank of the shallow stream. His situation was now worse. He had no food or water, no light or heat, no one knew where he was, he could not get out, *and* he was unarmed: unarmed in the Bould.

"Well," he said aloud, "at least I can try to rest." His voice sounded very loud in the cavern, and he told himself not to speak aloud any more unless there was some hope of being heard from above. He was probably alone in the cave. *Probably.* However, *probably* alone was very different from *certainly* alone. There was no need in taking the risk of alerting greedy ears to his presence.

Lendum removed his leather shoes and placed them under his head. As he lay on his back, he stared into the nothingness, trying to imagine the ceiling of the tunnel. After a few moments, he felt cold, as the night began to grow deep. His wet clothes stuck to his body, and he began to shiver. He drummed his fingers against the supple leather of his vest. He tried to think of anything other than the cold, or the hunger, or the thirst, or the fear. After a time, he felt himself drift away, enclosed within a troubled sleep.

═ ═

Lendum awoke on his side. There was a shaft of light coming from the opening above his head, striking the wall of the tunnel on the far side of the stream. He hoisted himself up slowly, his every muscle protesting even this minor request. His right calf especially cried out. It had withstood the worst of his fall, and now that it had been given a few hours of repose, it ached with a constant throbbing that pulsed with his every heartbeat. Lendum forced himself to his feet, wincing from the hundred needle pricks that came from a night sleeping on the rocks. He rolled his head, trying to loosen his stiff neck.

Even with the bright sunshine coming through, the cavern was still quite dim, but at least he could see a little now. He was surprised to see that the stream was little more than a creek, barely five feet across. He squatted down and splashed some of the water on his face, careful not to get any in his mouth. The water was cold and invigorating, and it eliminated any lingering traces of sleep, leaving him fully awake and alert. He put on his shoes, and began to pace back and forth, a slight limp favoring his right side, never straying from the edge of the light. After a time the exercise began to make his body feel less bruised, but a hunger that he had never known before fell on him. He had not eaten since his lunch the day before. He guessed the time to be about eight o'clock, so about twenty hours had passed since he had had any food. He was famished, but he focused his thoughts on searching his surroundings. Eager eyes scanned every inch exposed by the morning light, but Lendum saw nothing but stones and dirt. The floor and walls of the tunnel seemed to sparkle in a peculiar way, but there was little else of any interest. He had hoped to find his missing sword, but such hopes were in vain.

Wanting to do something other than sit, he continued walking around the shaft of light, crossing to the far bank of the stream and then back again, testing the depth of the water in several places. He noticed that there were no stones along the bed of the stream, which he thought a little odd, since the banks were so littered with the crunchy little rocks. For more than an hour, he walked back and forth, crossing the little creek, until the cold of night departed and his body felt warm and loose. His limp became less pronounced, and soon a gleam of fresh sweat graced his forehead, as the exercise drained what little strength he had. He sat down again, waiting for whatever would come, breathing hard and ignoring his growling stomach.

Hours passed as he sat, and dread began to work its way into his mind. Undoubtedly, his family was now searching frantically for him, but he had not heard anything from above, only the gentle gurgling of the creek. He would have thought that some one would have found him by now, and fear grew like a tumor in his chest. He must have run much farther that he had reckoned, making his rescue take much longer than he had supposed it would. He resolved that once he was free of this subterranean prison, he would be less reckless.

The circle of light that cascaded from above moved down the wall of the passage as time slipped away. Once it reached the far bank, hundred of little twinkles blinked in the light, as if numerous tiny jewels were reflecting the sun's rays from finely cut facets. Lendum was about to look more closely when he heard something. Cocking his head, he listened hard, not daring to breathe. Soon he heard it again, and then again. Someone was calling his name!

He sprang to his feet, grimacing from the aches and pains that had returned in his idleness. He shouted, "Here! I am here! I am here!"

Over his head, he heard, "There! A hole!" A second later, the face of his brother Seleus emerged. The sunlight formed a perfect corona around his face, making his countenance seem god-like. At that moment, Lendum thought that he *was* one of the gods, or at least an angel.

"Boy, what are you doing down there?" Seleus asked in a voice that somehow conveyed both scolding and relief. "Mother is beside herself and Father hasn't stopped looking for you since you missed supper."

"I was running and the earth just opened up and swallowed me. It all happened near sundown yesterday."

"Well, I need to fetch some rope to pull you out. Need some more muscle to help me, too. You're not as small as you once were, brother." Seleus made a little smile, but them it was gone. You could always count on Seleus to be serious, whether it was necessary or not. "Are you hurt?" he asked with genuine concern.

"No, just hungry," he answered. Lendum swallowed hard before he asked his next question. "You don't have anything to eat up there, do you?"

Seleus' head disappeared for a moment, and then reappeared with a hand near his right ear. "Here. Catch this." His hand released what Lendum readily recognized as a drawstring sack full of pecans. "I'll be back soon," Seleus said, "and I'll bring help. You'll be out of there in a half hour, okay?"

Lendum nodded, but did not speak. He was already chewing a large mouthful of pecans. Seleus disappeared, and Lendum continued eating, chewing and swallowing with dangerous speed.

⇒ ⇐

In less than a half hour, three heads poked over the opening of the round hole in the earth. The bag of pecans was empty, folded twice and stuffed into Lendum's pocket. Though his hunger was sated, a vicious thirst replaced it that made his parched tongue stick to the roof of his mouth. A voice called out.

"Hello down there, you rascal!" called his brother Antion. "Find anything useful during your adventure?" he said, adding a hearty laugh.

"We could use a few bats or newts. I've a mind to do some conjuring!" He laughed again, as was his nature. Antion was always quicker to laugh than do anything else, especially since he was clearly overjoyed that the fall had not harmed his little brother.

"Could you please just lower the rope?" Lendum asked, exasperated but laughing in spite of himself. "Those pecans have left me so thirsty that I feel I could drink the Tundish dry."

"Aye, me bucko!" Antion responded, still laughing. A coil of rope descended into the hole, and Lendum made it fast around his waist. A few moments later the strength of his three brothers brought him off the ground and in seconds grasping hands were pulling at his clothes, pulling him to safety. He stood in the clear light of day, blinking like a newborn pup. Grasping hands embraced from all sides, and in that moment he actually felt like crying, though he fought it with every fiber of his being. Lendum knew that his family loved him, but to have it expressed so openly was rare, and the emotions of the moment were a little overwhelming.

"How did you find me?" he asked, sniffing a little.

"Well," said Antion, "*that* is not normally something we see on the plains." He gestured to the right, and there, stuck into the ground near the opening of the tunnel, was Lendum's short sword. The sunlight twinkled off its surface. "Seleus saw that from a hundred yards, and sure enough, you were nearby. You never go anywhere without it, which we all know very well." Panelus retrieved it for his little brother, and Lendum held it for a long, pensive moment before replacing it in the tiny scabbard at his waist. Then the hugs began anew, with even more laughter and love.

After his brothers had said their welcomes, Fordrun, his father, stood before him. He was walking with the aid of a cane, and the single night Lendum had been away had seemed to age him many years. His cheeks were blotchy, and his shoulders were stooped, as if heavily burdened. His face was expressionless, and for a minute Lendum was terrified that he was about to receive the scolding of a lifetime.

"Come here, son," he said with an even tone. "Let me get a look at you."

Lendum took a few cautious steps forward. Once he was close enough, he found himself in the embrace of a bear. Fordrun had never hugged him so fiercely before.

"I feared we'd lost you, boy." His voice broke during the sentence, and Lendum realized that his father was crying, which was an event that had not occurred before, at least to his knowledge. Fordrun held him tight for what seem a very long time. Rough whiskers scratched at Lendum's cheeks, and the dusty smell of his father's clothes was welcome and very pleasing. When the father released his son, he placed his hands on his shoulders, and looked into his face. His eyes were wet, ringed with red circles.

"Are you injured?" he asked. "Are you cut or bruised or broken in any way?"

"No, father. Fortunately, the fall was not very far. I am not hurt."

Fordrun took a quick glance at his son's body, only to reassure his troubled mind. As he did so, a quizzical look came over him. "What is this dust all over your clothes?" he asked. "Why, it's embedded in the very fabric!"

Lendum looked at his attire. He had not been able to notice in the dark, but his father was right. A white, powdery dust covered him from head to toe. Closer inspection revealed small pebbles stuck in the stitches of his pants, in his pockets, even sitting loose in his thick, curly hair. "I don't know, father," he answered. "I couldn't really see."

Fordrun plucked one of the small stones from a groove of Lendum's brown leather vest. He rolled it gingerly between his thumb and forefinger, squinting at it with extreme concentration as if it were a valuable jewel. He brought it to his nose a made a couple of quick sniffs, but his face revealed that the smell answered nothing. Finally, he stuck out his tongue and slowly placed the pebble there. His eyes grew wide. His excitement was palpable.

"It's salt!" he proclaimed. "Good gods, you found salt, boy!" Fordrun turned to his other three sons. "Fetch the lamp from my cart. You are going back down there with a little light. Let's see exactly what our little explorer here has discovered."

After a few moments, Antion and Panelus were down in the tunnel, a bright oil lamp showing them much more than Lendum had been able to see during his confinement. After some minutes, they shouted back to the surface.

"It's everywhere, father!" Panelus yelled. "There is salt lying on the ground wherever we lay our eyes! We've walked forty yards in both directions, and it lies around us like diamonds!" His voice was so excited that he was chirping his words like a small bird.

Lendum remembered how horrible the water had tasted. He had thought that it was spoiled to the point of horrible bitterness, but it was not so. It was only salty. Very salty. Almost like brine.

Fordrun interrupted his thoughts by throwing a heavy arm across his shoulders. He was smiling broadly. He looked young again.

"Son," he said, "you've just secured this family's future for many, many years."

Throughout Aegea, and especially in isolated areas far from the sea, men ate meat with rarity. Most people ate bread and assorted fruits and vegetables every day. Besides what could be grown, the average person supplemented their diet with whatever the land provided; nuts, berries, wild green leaves, and sometimes, if you were lucky, a small furry animal, or perhaps a fowl that was tender and nutritious. Any animal that was consumed was typically small enough to be eaten at one sitting. Meat was uncommon as a daily source of food because of its propensity to spoil. In fact, the slaughtering of most animals took place in the winter months, the hope being that the cold temperatures would help keep the meat fresh. Even then, the slaughter of an animal as large as a cow or a goat was reserved for the butcher of a large population, or for festivals or celebrations where a large group of people gathered to guarantee that nothing went to waste. One can eat an apple whist doing no harm to the tree, but it is impossible to roast a ham without killing the hog. The only way known to preserve meat was through drying, or by packing it with salt.

Salt, however, was also very rare. Most of the salt used in Aegea was harvested from the seas, and by the time the commodity reached the center of the continent, its price was high indeed. Almost no salt was used in the Bould, because it was as far from the ocean as you could get in any direction, except through the Charwood, but that was not a place for honest men. Nearly all of the animals raised to be sold were marched to the rivers and loaded live onto boats to be sent south. Therefore, unless a wedding or the harvest festival brought several hungry people together at once, farmers in the Bould could rarely enjoy the meat of their own herds. Fordrun himself had wished on many occasions that he had a nice cut of pork or a thick steak to fill his grumbling belly, at times when oat porridge and plain black bread had lost its charm. However, it could not be so, even for a man like Fordrun Noveton, who had modest means, and was considered wealthy by Bould standards. In remote areas like the Bould, the value of a pound of salt was greater than a pound of gold.

≡≡ ≡

Over the next several days, while Lendum rested and recovered from his ordeal in the cave, the sons of Fordrun did much work with great enthusiasm. A ladder made access to the salt quicker and safer. Lamps and torches were mounted on the walls of the tunnel to give a great deal of light. Further explorations showed nothing but the salt. They found no living thing. In a curious twist, the salt that attracted so much attention from men seemed to repel everything else. Explorations revealed a few other passages, and they were equally filled with salt. Fordrun dared to dream of a supply of salt large enough to support the grandchildren of his grandchildren, and in truth, there probably was enough to realize such ideas of grandeur. It glittered everywhere one looked.

Once Lendum had regained his strength (and finally convinced his mother that he was all right), he joined his brothers in their labor. The sons of Fordrun would descend the ladder into the tunnel and shovel bucket after bucket of the raw salt. They hauled these buckets to the surface by a rope and dumped them into a waiting wagon. The first week alone, with their time split between the mine and the fields, the Novetons harvested five wagonloads of raw salt from the unassuming hole in the earth, with a value greater than three-years-yield from the fields. Fordrun laughed often with restless excitement.

Once back at the farm, in a small shed that could shield them from the sun, the women and young children would sort the stones, separating the rocks, mud, and other debris from the salt rocks. Then the salt was ground into a fine powder, ready to use. The work was tedious and tiring, but the amount they generated from their toil was staggering. A full twelve barrels of processed salt sat alone in a barn, aside from the portion the family intended to use themselves, and the earth continued to yield its bounty. After a few day's time animals were being killed and the flesh packed in the salt and then crated for the trip to Ghar. There, Fordrun knew he could sell the meat to the locals and sell the twelve barrels to the merchants at the river docks. With the money from the sale of these goods, he could buy gifts for the entire family, a happening he had always desired but had never achieved in his long life.

After two weeks of diligent labor, a wagon was loaded down with goods for the trip to Ghar. The day Fordrun intended to depart dawned bright and fair, with long, lazy wisps of cloud smeared across the sky. Fordrun sat in his tiny kitchen, eating his breakfast; biscuits with fresh butter, clean water from the stream, scrambled eggs and bacon. He chewed the bacon slowly, savoring the taste for as long as he could. The early morning light came through the window, falling across the table and bringing welcome warmth to the room. Nearly a year had passed since the last time he had tasted bacon. Nothing could be compared to its flavor. It was ecstasy.

Lendum was outside, having finished his meal quickly. He was brimming with excitement, for he, as well as Seleus and Fordrun, was to go to Ghar, and the trip, while long and tiring, would be a welcome break from the monotony of the farm. He could enjoy many days without feeding hogs, gathering eggs, milking cows, or weeding the garden. The morning was cool, especially for late April, and as he ran amongst the animals in the south pasture, he could see his breaths escaping his lips. Dew flew through the air as he ran, kicked airborne by his energetic feet. He left a trail of moistened footprints in his wake.

The rising sun appeared very bright this morning, a white globe in the sky. Looking directly east was difficult, in not impossible. For this reason, Lendum did not see the approaching stranger until he was very close.

A man was coming from the direction of the Charwood. He rode a horse that was pure white, and sat upon a saddle that was of quality make, but was completely unadorned and ordinary looking. The man was tall in the saddle, and dressed completely in black, from his boots to the hooded cloak he had draped around his shoulders. His dark hair was shoulder-length, and pulled into a short ponytail that exposed a large forehead.

Lendum saw the stranger and stopped in his tracks. A lump rose in his throat, and his heart, already beating fast from his play, somehow beat even faster. He saw nothing in the man's appearance that would warrant fear, but he was apprehensive all the same. His years in the Bould had taught him that solitude was to be expected, even cherished. Anyone that threatened that solitude was to be viewed with skepticism, if not outright suspicion. He could not remember anyone ever being at the farm outside of the family, and that fact alone made this stranger unique, and worthy of wariness. He decided to wait for the man to arrive, instead of trying to run to the house. Lendum carried his short, rusty sword, and felt confident enough in his skill to use it if the need arose. Besides, the man probably had no foul purpose, and it would be rude to run away at the mere sight of a visitor.

Presently, the man approached. Without a word his horse stopped, about twenty feet from where Lendum stood. The man gave a sign of salutations common in the Bould; both hands open with the thumbs pointing outward, exposing the palms.

"Greetings, little brother," the man said, and he smiled broadly. Lendum felt all of his fear leave him. The voice was so agreeable, so enchanting, that Lendum could not imagine any aggressive behavior coming from the owner of such a voice. His hand, which had drifted to his hilt, returned to his side.

"Happy days to you, good sir," Lendum replied, bowing at the waist. "Could I persuade you to dismount, and partake of our humble hospitality?"

The man threw his head back and laughed with pleasure. "Such a polite young man, yes you are!" he exclaimed. "I would be honored. However, meaning no disrespect to you, I should prefer it if the master of the house were to invite me. I would feel better about my encroachment."

"As you wish, good visitor," Lendum said, bowing again. "If you please, wait here, and I shall summon the master at once."

The man nodded briskly, and Lendum set off at a run back to the house, more than eager to report this unexpected development.

Fordrun sat at the table, his right hand tucked into the belt of his pants, an empty plate before him. Marle scrubbed a skillet feverishly with a stout brush as she disapprovingly watched her husband pick his teeth with his knife. When Lendum burst in, nearly taking the door off its hinges, Marle yelped in surprise, dropping the skillet to the wooden floor and making a terrible racket. Fordrun jumped at the surprise of it, pulling his hand from the waist of his trousers with amazing speed.

"Confound it, boy!" he blurted out, throwing his knife on the table in disgust. "What's all this, then?"

"Father," Lendum panted, "there is a visitor here. He has asked for you."

Fordrun leaned forward, his eyes narrowing into slits. "Asked for me, did he?" he asked low, almost to himself. "He knows my name?"

"No," Lendum answered, still breathing hard. "At least, he didn't ask for you by name. He asked to see the master of the house."

"I see." Fordrun sat back in his chair, considering a moment. "Is he armed?"

"Not that I saw," Lendum replied. "In fact, he carries nothing at all; no satchel, no pack, and no saddlebags. He is riding a beautiful white horse. He came from the east."

Fordrun cut his eyes sharply at his son after hearing that. He was clearly suspicious before, but now he had a sense of foreboding. He sat quietly for another full minute, Lendum almost ready to explode with nervousness. Marle retrieved her skillet and dutifully began to clean it again, already losing interest in the news. She had no room for gossip or excitement when there were chores to be done. The harsh sound of bristles against iron filled the small room. Finally, Fordrun spoke.

"Let's go and see him, and have him depart as quickly as courtesy allows. We have important business today." He rose from the table, and father and son went to see the mysterious stranger.

The man remained where Lendum had left him. The horse stood perfectly still, not bending to eat at the tall green grass, or even stamping a hoof in protest. The man was still smiling.

Once Fordrun was close enough, he shouted, startling Lendum slightly, who had not expected it. "Greetings, stranger!" he called out, which was a little rude. "I am Fordrun, master of this farm. Who are you?"

The man's smile did not falter. Either he did not perceive the slight, or he chose to ignore it. "May I dismount, good sir, that we may be properly introduced?"

Fordrun staggered a bit when the man spoke. Then his face split in a friendly grin. Lendum was grinning also. He was overjoyed to hear the man speak again.

"But of course, Brother," replied Fordrun, using a much more proper term of address.

The man dismounted with the agility of a cat. Lendum noticed that even though he must have traveled many miles across the Bould to stand before them, he had no dust on his boots or clothes. Neither, for that matter, was the horse dusty. The man showed no signs of fatigue, but rather seemed fully rested, as if after a full night's repose.

The man bowed very low, so low that Lendum feared his back would snap. When he rose, he held his cloak out, and then wrapped himself tightly in it. "I have many names in many lands", he said, "but it would please me very much if you would call me Trand, and I am honored to stand before the master of this household, who undoubtedly is noble and generous beyond the worth of one such as myself."

Fordrun bowed low, and Lendum did again as well. "You honor me and my house with pleasant speech," replied Fordrun. "Come, Trand, and break your fast with us, or at least share our ale, and we permit your horse to refresh himself on our grass."

Trand said something to the horse that Lendum could not understand,

and the animal broke his statue-like posture and began to eat. "He is a good beast," said Trand, "and serves me with steadfastness and affection. His name is Dampe, and he is grateful for your hospitality." Trand bowed again, not as low this time. "I accept your gracious offer, Fordrun. I would speak with you while we eat, if that is to your liking."

"It is indeed to my liking." Fordrun smiled like a child. His desire to rid himself of this guest and be on his way to Ghar was apparently forgotten. "Let us go inside, and we can have ourselves a nice talk."

In the kitchen, Marle busied herself making another batch of bacon and eggs for their visitor. She moved with grace around the tiny kitchen, an effortless display that was the result of years of repetition. Her round figure made plump by the years was covered by a broad indigo apron. The apron was clean, and the flour on her fingers was the only evidence of her labor. Fordrun apologized to Trand for not joining him, but explained that he had already eaten. Lendum had also already eaten, but was prepared to have a second go with Trand, who so intrigued him.

Marle placed a heaping pile of food before Trand. "For you, Brother. May it strengthen you for the toils ahead."

"Thank you, Sister. I hope that the sun always rises with the same beauty that I see in your eye."

Marle blushed-*actually blushed*-then made a little curtsey like a schoolgirl. She exited quickly, not explaining her abrupt departure. Fortunately, no explanation was necessary.

Trand lifted his fork. "With your permission, master." Fordrun nodded his assent, and Trand hurriedly began to eat. He kept perfect decorum, but nonetheless finished in a matter of minutes. Lendum tried to keep pace, but it was useless.

"Delicious!" he exclaimed, wiping his face with his napkin, even though his face was quite clean. "Most delicious! How rare it is to have fresh bacon in these parts. You humble me with your generosity. Are you so giving to all of your guests?"

"Well, in truth, you are the only guest, either invited or unexpected, that we have ever received since we moved to the Bould three years ago."

Trand nodded as if this did not surprise him in the least. "Mankind is scarce in this part of the world. Do you have time for a little talk? I would like to exchange a little news, and take some leisure before Dampe and I move on."

Lendum expected his father to politely decline, saying that they were just leaving on errand of there own, but his response both shocked and delighted him.

"Yes, a little news would be most welcome. Lendum, run and tell Seleus to carry on with the chores as usual. We shall not leave until tomorrow."

Lendum was off without replying. He hurried out the door and ran all the way to his brother's house across the river to deliver the message.

Seleus seemed a little put out by the news, but he took it in relatively good humor. "So be it," he said sullenly. Evidently, he was also looking forward to a few days reprieve from the farm. "I suppose one more day's wait couldn't hurt. Why the delay?"

"He is hosting a guest," Lendum said, still out of breath from his run. "A man arrived just this morning. They are speaking even now."

And I wish to get back at once, he thought, but did not say. He reasoned that Trand has a good deal of knowledge of the world, and he very much wanted to absorb every word that he could.

Seleus knew his little brother and could nearly hear his thought. "Well, go on then. It is clear you would rather be there than here. But know this: The instant this man departs I want to see you in the north fields, breaking the sod. Understand? Panelus will be pleased to know that he will not have do it alone, so don't keep him waiting any longer than necessary."

Lendum nodded and was off again, running as fast as his legs would carry him, his boots kicking up little pieces of dirt with each footfall. The sun shone down on him, and his exertion made him begin to sweat again. The day was beginning to get broad, and a little hot.

In moments, he stood outside the back door of his house, panting harshly, trying to get control of himself. For some reason, he did not want to appear fatigued in front of Trand. After a few minutes, his breathing slowed, and he could feel his heart return to a more normal rhythm. He wiped the sweat from his brow with the sleeve of his shirt, and opened the door.

Lendum had never seen his father so enthralled. He was paying such rapt attention to Trand's words that he barely noticed his son's return. Trand continued speaking, ignoring Lendum as he regained his seat at the table.

"And," said Trand, waving his hand as if speaking to a large crowd, "I am sure you are aware that King Frondus of Gladue has passed, and been succeeded by his son, Jonas." Trand sat back in his chair, his legs crossed comfortably before him. He seemed quite at ease.

"Is that so?" asked Fordrun. "A pity. King Frondus was kindly and wise, if the rumors are true. It was by his grace that we came to own the charter for these very lands."

"He was indeed kindly and wise," replied Trand. "I was in his service for a time, and he thought of his people first and foremost. His son is very different. The young king is fiery and brash, as quick to grab the sword as the goblet, and his youth makes him intemperate. He barks to show he can bite, and often bites to prove that he has teeth. Perhaps time will cool his temper and shrink his ego, but will we be allowed the time?" Trand looked at nothing, his thoughts swirling in his head.

"You served King Frondus?" asked Fordrun with raised eyebrows. "You seem so young, begging your pardon, to be entrusted with such duty."

"I was his advisor, in a manner, though seldom did he truly need advice. He took great pains to avoid crushing his subjects underfoot, knowing that a small misstep by a monarch could have lasting ramifications. He often thought excessively over an issue before finally making a decision. My voice was reassurance that his proposed course of action was correct." Trand looked at Lendum with bright eyes. "True kings-*good kings*-are not the pampered royalty that most people believe. Good kings, and Frondus was one of them, are slaves. Their arms and legs are free, and they call no one master, but their hearts and souls and minds are enchained to the realm, and they are required to serve, as are the rest of us."

"You seem well traveled," remarked Fordrun, "and appear to have a good deal of knowledge of the world's doings, Master Trand."

"Call me not master, if you please," Trand retorted. "I have stood in the great hall of all of the seven kingdoms of Aegea, and have shared thoughts with some of the greatest minds of the world. But I am master of no one, not even myself, and have no hearth or bed to call my own."

Lendum was listening on the edge of his seat. He had never met anyone like Trand before. His father had always seemed the wisest man conceivable, but now this wandering loner had stolen that title, and in less than a morning's time. Indeed, even Fordrun was so enraptured by his talk that he deferred to Trand even in his own house. Lendum grew bold enough to ask this visitor a question that had been on the tip of his tongue for several minutes.

"Have you seen any monsters?" he asked, at once sounding afraid and irrepressibly willing to know. Fordrun started like a man coming out of a trance. He had not noticed that his youngest had returned until that moment.

Trand looked at the boy with kindness, a gentle smile on his lips.

"Yes, I have seen monsters; monsters so fearsome and full of malice that your blood would turn to ice in your veins if they were to cast their gaze upon you. The rokul of the mountains and the forest, the willing servants of Sindus, still roam the wide world, and can be found if one is foolish enough to go looking. They are an abomination, so enveloped in their hatred that they would slaughter their own kind for just the chance to taste your flesh."

Lendum shivered, but did not interrupt. He was fascinated.

"These creatures are lizard men, slimy and disgusting, going about on two feet like men, yet burrowing in the earth like loathsome beasts. They are altogether wretched, and unfortunately, wholly beyond redemption. They test the air with their forked tongues, and slither through the trees of the forest and boulders of the mountains in search of prey. Their flattened heads hold what little wits they have, which allows them little more than the basest of urges. They will carry their anger for all time, unwilling, and perhaps unable, to turn their efforts to honorable uses."

"They sound horrible," Lendum said softly.

"They are horrible, but they are not the worst there is."

Lendum's face betrayed shocked disbelief. "What could be worse than these vile beings?"

Trand's face suddenly grew very grave. "There are many monsters in this world, young master, and you have seen them yourself, though perhaps you knew it not. The rokul, at least, cannot be mistaken. On sight, even a dullard would know that they are nefarious, so they are incapable of trickery. Nevertheless, not all evil goes about on limbs of flesh and bone, causing mischief. Some are buried deep in the earth, waiting. And when they are exposed, their veil of innocence is left intact, as others do their unspoken bidding." Trand, his face still as grave as death, shifted his dark eyes to Fordrun. The old man could see himself reflected in those eyes. "Many things that appear to be great treasures come with a high price, a price that oft is not easily paid. These things are better left buried, forgotten, lest many suffer for the actions of one man."

Fordrun swallowed hard, so hard that Lendum heard it. Trand sat unmoving, his eyes locked on his host. A silence filled the room that seemed to weigh heavily on the occupants. After several awkward seconds, Fordrun spoke.

"You are more than you seem, are you not? It appears that the discovery I fancied to be so secret is not so secret after all, eh?" Fordrun leaned back in his chair with resignation. Trand had dashed his dreams with just a few sentences, and the spellbinding effects of his voice were now lessened. "Do you wish to advise me counselor? I am not so stubborn as to deny a wizard his say. Proceed, if you will, and I shall listen."

Lendum was dumfounded. A wizard? He could not fathom what was happening, so he merely continued listening, more anxious than ever so soak up every utterance.

"You have a good life here, do you not?" Trand asked. Fordrun nodded his head weakly, but did not speak. "The Bould has provided for you and yours in abundance. Do you really require this additional boon that the earth has put forth?"

Lendum interrupted. "How do you know of this?" How *could* you know of this? Less than a fortnight has passed since we learned of it ourselves, and we have told no one."

"There are many things of which I am aware, Master Lendum, including that great riches betray honest men." Lendum thought that he saw a red sparkle in Trand's eye. His skin took a on a more pallid hue, and he appeared to grow sickly. He turned his attention back to Fordrun. "I beg you, Fordrun Noveton, keep this discovery to yourself. You cannot begin to understand the misery you would unleash. Please, leave it be. Cover it, fill it with earth, and forget that you know of it."

Fordrun sighed deeply, considering. "I shall think on this, good Trand. I have, I must admit, been carried away like a reckless youth." He laughed suddenly, reflective. "At my age I should be content with my chair and my tankard, not dreaming of the power of great wealth. You have brought me back to the earth, and for that I am thankful, dear guest."

"Then there is little more I can do to persuade you. It is enough that you have given ear to this stranger. And now," he said, getting to his feet, "I am afraid that I must depart. There is urgent business in the south that requires my attention, and time is short. I thank you again you sharing your food and lending me your mind." He bowed again, and Lendum was struck by how limber the man seemed to be.

"Come," said Fordrun. "We will escort you outdoors."

The three men walked through the house, exiting by the front door. They walked together until they were amongst the pecan grove. The sun was now almost to the ten o'clock hour, and the heat of the day had chased away the morning mists. The water of the stream trickled over rocks, making soothing songs as it made its way to the Tundish.

"Lendum," Fordrun said, "run and fetch Brother Trand's horse."

"No need for that," said Trand. He placed two fingers in his mouth, and with a small intake of air, he whistled sharply four times. Lendum cringed at the starkness of the sound. Toward the north, they heard a neighing that was almost human in response. Looking, Fordrun and Lendum were amazed to see Dampe galloping through the meadow, swimming in grass that nearly reached his flanks. His line did not waver, for he was traveling as fast a loosed bolt toward his master. He did not slow until he was within feet of Trand. He nuzzled his snout against Trand's shoulder, a sign of unmistakable love.

"Shh," he said to the horse, stroking his forehead. "We are leaving. I hope you have eaten well, and used the time to rest, for the miles are many and long, and I would not have you exhaust yourself needlessly."

Dampe gave a mild snort in response, and Trand mumbled something indiscernible back. With a final pat on the horse's face, Trand hopped in the saddle with the smoothness of fluid.

"Good days to you, gentlemen. I pray that the gods show you favor, and heed my words." With that he was gone, heading due south with a speed Lendum would never have believed possible, even by an animal as majestic as Dampe. They watched Trand ride away until he was nothing more than a speck on the horizon, then he was gone.

"Interesting fellow," Fordrun said conversationally. He reached up and plucked a pecan from a nearby branch. "I believe he could have spoken for many days without repeating himself. Full of lore, that one is, and wisdom. I'm sorry to see him go."

"I'm sorry, too," Lendum agreed, "but part of me is glad. He frightened me a little, but it was more a fear of respect than a fear of harm. I never felt unsafe in his presence, but his words filled me with dread, if you understand me."

Fordrun snickered quietly to himself, as if remembering some fond memory. "I certainly do understand, for I felt the same. I will think hard on his advice. He offered no proof, but he was so persuasive." The pecan cracked in his aged hands, and Fordrun began to pick the nut from its hull.

"Do you think we will see him again?" asked Lendum, gazing in the direction their caller had gone.

"I don't know, son, but I think not. He's a wanderer, and he will not likely pass this way again." Fordrun popped the pecan into his mouth, chewing as slowly as a cow. "It's a shame," he said, the words subdued by his mastication. "I rather liked him. So very polite and proper he was."

"Yes," Lendum agreed. "I liked him, too."

They stood there, under the welcome shade of the trees, father and son, looking southward with forlorn expressions. At length Fordrun broke the silence.

"You best go now and get to your chores. We have already spent half the morning idle. It wouldn't do to let the other half pass so as well."

"Yes, sir." It required obvious physical effort to turn his gaze away from the south. He headed toward the north fields, walking this time rather than running. Driving a team of horses that would be pulling the plow was not something he was desperate to begin.

Fordrun stood several minutes more under the trees. "He asked that I heed his words," he said quietly. "Perhaps I shall." Then he went back to his home for a short midmorning nap. He never saw Trand again.

⇒ ⇐

Over the next two days, Fordrun Noveton found little rest. The decision he had to make plagued him, and weighed on him more heavily than he could have imagined. He could not deny that he did not need the wealth. He had received a large sum of money for his old farm, and had used none of it to purchase his current holdings. Furthermore, he was in his seventies, a very advanced age for a common man, and he knew that he would have little use for treasure in the unknown. In fact, when the time came for him to follow Miro, his children would be able to live off their portions of his riches for many years, and remain at leisure while doing so. There was no need for him to embark on this venture, either for himself or for his children.

However, as his thoughts progressed, the wisdom of Trand began to make less and less sense. He started seeing past his children to his grandchildren. How many did he have now? Thirteen? Yes, thirteen. Moreover, more were certain to come along in the future. His family was ever growing, and the proceeds necessary lay under the earth, a few hundreds yards away. It would be foolhardy to cover it and pretend it does not exist on the word of a smooth talking stranger, no matter how cordial he had been. "He spoke vaguely," Fordrun would say to himself in the small hours of the morning, unable to sleep. "He spoke of suffering and high prices, but what does that mean?" He would toss and turn, his broken dreams filled with stacks of gold coins piled to the heavens. When he would awaken, grasping at the air, he would deceive himself.

He did not long for the treasure on his own account. Goodness no!

He yearned to make things easier on his family. This hole in the earth could yield enough wealth to allow his grandchildren's grandchildren to live in splendor.

On the morning of the third day after the departure of Trand (the words of the visitor a very distant memory), Fordrun made his own departure from his home. Seleus, Antion and Lendum joined him. They drove two wagons, each pulled by very strong horses. Loaded onto each wagon were twelve barrels of finely ground salt, ready for market. Fordrun expected to make more profit from the single venture that he had the whole previous year. He was not disappointed.

The travelers returned home two weeks later, both wagons laden with goods. There was new china, cutlery, high quality oil lamps, shirts and breeches of finely woven fabric, soaps, perfumes, spices, and toys for all of the children. In addition, a substantial amount of gold remained, which he shared equally with all eleven of his children, for they had all labored to create this huge quantity of wealth.

Two months later, they repeated the trip, this time with three wagons. As Fordrun and his sons rolled into Ghar for the second time in less than a season, the whispers began. Wide eyes watched as Fordrun made his transactions, and folks in Ghar spoke of him long after he was gone. On his third appearance, the nature of the looks he received changed. Before they were full of only amazement, but they altered into ones of envy and hateful jealousy.

However, it was nearly a year before they found someone encroaching on their land. The ejection of interlopers became a weekly occurrence, to the point where a thorough search of their acreage was the morning ritual. Homes popped up just off Fordrun's property, with men and women digging frantically, hoping to strike a vein of this rumored endless mine of salt. So many squatters took up residence around the farm that it took on the look of a small village. Folks began to refer to the area as Noveton, a clever joke full of both derision and merriment, because Noveton literally means, *New Town*.

Rumors flew wildly. The mine was an enormous cavern. The mine was small but stretched for miles, a labyrinth under the earth. Fordrun Noveton was a warlock, making salt from the mousegrass of the plains. People came calling every day, wanting to see the mine like folks on holiday. It became such a nuisance that Fordrun hired twenty men from Ghar to begin the rather ambitious work of fencing in his *entire* three-hundred acres. Since the proposed fence was intended to keep people out rather than animals in, he wanted it to be twenty feet high, with a walkway allowing sentries to view the surrounding plains. The lumber for this enormous undertaking was not available in the Bould, or even in Ghar. It had to be imported from Gladue, which took the news even farther, to more hungry ears.

The work on the fence began on the first of April: one year after the discovery of the mine. As the high walls went up, the whispering advanced into open talk. Folks called Fordrun a skinflint and a penny pincher, so afraid to lose a grain of salt that he wanted to turn his home into a fortress. This was, of course, not true. Fordrun merely wanted to return to the days of peace and solitude he had enjoyed before the salt had made him famous as well as wealthy. He was also no skinflint, for he was generous with his money, always dealing locally when he could, and he was never heavy-handed in his negotiations. The men that came to work for him learned to love their employer, making a very good living and voluntarily giving their loyalty to the master of Noveton Farm.

However, for all of his good will and fair dealing, nothing could squelch the speculation and idle talk. For the first time, Fordrun could feel the heavy burden of fame, and he found it disagreeable to say the least. Nevertheless, he was happy. His family was whole and safe, and they now enjoyed material goods that fate had never allowed before. If the price for their comfort was intrusion and gossip, then so be it.

By the end of the second year, when Lendum had become tall and handsome, and long after the wooden fence had made Noveton into a fort, the murmuring and grumbling of jealous townsfolk became so loud that it reached the ears of powerful men, far away.

THE AMBITION OF KINGS

King Jonas of Gladue heard of it first. He was very young, a boy king, and his inexperience did much to flaw his reasoning. He was also unmarried, which was fortunate, because the newly crowned monarch was not a handsome man, and most of the eligible ladies of his court silently prayed that they would not be the one he would choose to wed. Thin hair graced his head, and his face was heavily pockmarked with scars, relics of his constant battle with skin blemishes. He was thin and sickly looking, and dark sacks perpetually hung from his eyes. Even on his best day, Jonas appeared haggard, weak, and not long for the world.

The news of the salt mine in the Bould was tantalizing. The young king was skeptical, but he reasoned that there was no harm investigating the matter, to discover if there was any truth buried within the rumors. He sent a single, unadorned scout (in other words, a spy) to the Bould to learn what he could of the infamous 'Lord Fordrun of Noveton Manor'. When the scout returned with a handful of salt and a story of a large, wooden keep in the wilderness of the Bould, the young king began to dream of annexation, and his councilors heartily endorsed such a move, especially his chief advisor, the crafty Motte.

"My Lord," he would say, "that man could be making his fortune from resources that by right should be held by the kingdom of Gladue. Have we not made our claim many times in the past only to have our ambitions thwarted by lesser men with inadequate proofs? That land is your birthright! It should belong to the nation that has paid for it with so much of her blood and valor! Will you not claim it and make it your own?"

The young king, wallowing in his own importance, was filled with images of large regiments of soldiers, each full of stamina, refreshed from the salted beef and pork carried in their satchels. With the revenue from the mine (not to mention all the other produce of the Bould), he would outfit his legions with shining chain mail and high helms, and the sun would shimmer on a thousand spearheads moving in unison like the flow of a river. The shields of his warriors would sparkle like polished gems, and would endure the blows of the hated enemy of the east, Sindus, ensuring peace along his borders and safety for his people.

So Motte swayed the king to his own manner of thinking (though in truth it took little more than a nudge), and Jonas dispatched an official delegation to the house of Fordrun Noveton, to discuss the possibilities of a peaceful seizure of his property. Fordrun was, after all, a subject of Gladue, and was responsible for doing the bidding of his liege regardless of his location. That was, at least, the point of view of Jonas.

Jonas also sent a full delegation to Grindal, the King of Andesha, and he sent emissaries to all the other kingdoms of Aegea. Their instructions were simple: Gladue gave notice that her participation in the settlement of the Bould was renounced. She rescinded all previous treaties regarding the joint occupation of the area. The Bould was to become the sovereign territory of Gladue, and the edict demanded all other monarchs vacate the territory within six months. The same day that he sent his ambassadors, Jonas mustered a battalion of troops, four-thousand men, fully armed. Within a week, they began the march to the Tundish. Motte had assured his Lord that the mere presence of such force would make the claim legitimate, as well as filling the void created by the departure of the soldiers of the other kingdoms. Jonas never believed that he would need to fight a war to defend his claim, because he had good legal standing, as well as a sympathetic base of citizens (more than half of the Bould's residents were from Gladue or could claim Gladue descent). He also had history on his side. Though there had been isolated rebellions and insurrections during the time of men, a full-fledged war between kingdoms of men had never occurred. However, war was a possibility he should have considered, for the news that reached his ears from across the Tundish River found its way across the Shae River as well.

⇒ ⇐

King Grindal was also young, and even more aggressive than his counterpart in Gladue. Newly come to the throne and a bachelor, he was impulsive, curt with his servants, highly competitive, and overly concerned with his legacy. Upon hearing the news of the salt mine of the Bould, he did not wait for confirmation from scouts, did not consult with his advisors, and did not waste time pondering what course to pursue. He *immediately* mustered a force of two-thousand horsemen, and ordered them to ride to the banks of the Shae and await further instructions. Only then did he dispatch ambassadors, but only to Gladue. To his mind, this matter was of no concern to the rest of the world.

Grindal suspected that his distant cousin Jonas would make a bold move once he learned of the mine, and he longed above all else to not lose the area and this fabulous windfall by being outmaneuvered to the goal. His motivation was more a desire to beat a rival than to secure wealth for his kingdom. The ego of the bearded monarch was such that he would routinely reprimand his jesters for being too funny. The members of his hunting party missed their targets on purpose, and only Grindal would bring home a trophy at the end of the day. No one overshadowed the king of Andesha.

Grindal reasoned that military strength positioned within the territory would settle the dispute faster than any real negotiations. He did not believe it would be necessary to fight for the Bould, and assumed that overwhelming force could dictate his aims without any actual combat. Grindal had cherished his time in the army, and fancied himself a superb soldier and strategist, but he was a poor interpreter of the motives that govern the hearts of men.

A discovery made by a young boy had set the armies of kings in motion.

⇒ ⇐

Fordrun would have been most distressed to learn of these developments. In fact, if he had known that he was the cloth between the blades of the scissors, he would have packed up his things and left at once. Unfortunately, he was unaware of the approaching armies and the wishes of the ruthless kings that they served. He had other, more immediate, concerns. The issue of the trespassers had escalated from simple nuisance to genuine threat. An armed man had somehow gotten inside the walls, and once discovered, had to be forcibly removed from the property. He kicked and fought, screaming at the top of his voice about how his children were starving, and Noveton should share his good fortune with the impoverished. Fordrun agreed, but the man had completely lost his wits, would not listen to reason, and had nothing to say but threats and acidic vulgarities. After a few wearisome minutes, Fordrun had the man removed, without any satisfaction. Following this episode, Fordrun hired twenty trusty, hearty men to patrol his grounds, keeping an eye on things. The men he hired came from Ghar, and each had a deep respect for the Noveton family and for Fordrun in particular. Their loyalty was unquestioned and very strong. The guards were a good precaution, and well intentioned, but sadly they proved to be inadequate.

Fordrun was walking in the early morning, going to fetch pecans. Marle wanted to make pies, and since pecan pie was a favorite of the elderly patriarch, he was willing to do the task of bringing in and hulling the nuts. The sun had just crested the horizon in the east, and the whole world was bathed in light as red as blood. Light breezes kept the chill of evening alive during this mid-summer morning, rustling the leaves and making the grasses sway back and forth. Fordrun paused in the thick of the grove, taking the cool air deep into his lungs. He sighed with contentment. His last thoughts were that he could endure all of the troubles that came with wealth and fame if idyllic mornings like this were his reward.

Fordrun was being hunted.

Crazed eyes watched him through the trees. An evil heart silently cursed him for being blessed by the gods and given such good fortune. Murderous thoughts had poisoned his mind and had formed his passions into a single point of malicious intent. The hunter patiently awaited his target, not moving, not even breathing, his every muscle tensed and ready to pounce.

Every step brought Fordrun closer to his doom. He unhurriedly continued to pick pecans, depositing the ones he judged best into a worn burlap sack. His aged joints popped and crackled audibly as he made his way deeper into the grove. He had just noticed a bough heavily weighted with large pecans when he caught movement from the corner of his eye. Thinking that Lendum had chosen to join him as he so often did, he turned, and the dagger pieced his heart. The pain was enormous, and he lurched forward, falling into his assailant. He craned his neck upward, and his eyes locked with those of the man that he had ejected the month before. Fordrun saw insanity in those eyes; insanity and hatred.

"The gods curse you, gold hugger," the man hissed. "You deserve this for letting my family starve for the price of a pound of salt."

Fordrun could not reply. He gurgled, then fainted, and fell on his face. He was dead, having followed his sires into the unknown.

"The rich man is dead!" the man screamed with a voice that was shrill with madness. "Now I am the rich man!" He began to jump around in his glee, covering the fallen with the dust from his boots.

The man heard a noise like the buzzing of a fly before the arrow plunged into his throat. The force of the strike knocked him on his back, and he began to writhe and kick, his hands grasping the shaft, blood seeping from his between his fingers. Then he lay still.

Mercifully, Lendum had not witnessed his father's murder, but he did recognize the man, and even from fifty feet could see the bloody dagger in his hand. To his own amazement, he did not feel anger or grief as his mind slowly understood what had happened. He felt an increased awareness come over him. Coolly he notched his arrow, and with disturbing calm, he drew back the string. With unflinching hand and unblinking eye, he found his mark. Apathy released the string, and remorselessness guided the bolt. When the target was struck, Lendum felt no joy, no sorrow, no pain or guilt or hatred. He felt nothing. He would mourn his father in time, but for now, there was nothing but the task at hand, and that was enough. The release of that arrow killed both a murderer and what remained of a boy's innocence.

=⇒ ⇐=

Fordrun had been buried three days when the messengers from King Jonas arrived. The party contained fifteen men, most wearing the green tunics of soldiers, and armed with blade and bow. The ambassador carried no weapon. Any sword or mace would clash with the gallant air he was trying to emanate. The crown of his helm was lined with the fur of sable, and he wore a large medallion of silver around his neck, reflecting his status. The standard-bearer bore aloft the regal flag of their country; a great eagle with open wings clutching a silvery fish in its talons, embroidered over a field of emerald green, trimmed handsomely with gold.

Seleus went to meet them once he was informed of their arrival. By the legality of their charter, and by custom, he was now the master of these lands, by virtue of being the eldest son. He had given some thought on what to do now that such wickedness had occurred, stealing away Fordrun at the height of their success, but no real decisions could be made during the period of mourning. It would not be proper.

Seleus met the delegate outside the southern gate. He did not invite them in after seeing their weaponry. His brothers joined him, as did a couple of nephews. Lendum stood near the back, the coldness once again in his eye. He did not like the ambassador on sight. The man almost reeked of pomposity. That initial impression would soon be reinforced with irrefutable evidence.

"Greetings, gentlemen," began Seleus politely. He did not bow or salute. "What can I do for you on this fine day?"

The ambassador stirred in his saddle, not answering for a brief yet discernible moment. Apparently, Seleus paid him less respect that he thought he was due. "I am Tillus, ambassador for King Jonas of Gladue. I have come to speak with Fordrun Noveton, master of this estate and holder of the royal charter creating it. Would you summon him?" Tillus sniffed as he spoke, a clear sign that he was bored with this exchange, and judged it beneath him. It did not go unnoticed.

Seleus swallowed hard before he answered, dealing with the rage he felt rising within him. As Fordrun's eldest child, time was quickly making him an old man. He had exceeded his fortieth year, and joints now grated together where once they had been fluid and smooth. Gray hair had invaded to join the black that covered his head, and he had noticed that the long hours spent doing hard labor took a greater toll on his body, requiring more rest to recover. Despite all of this, his blood still ran hot, and controlling himself took a great deal of effort. Finally he said, "Regrettably, Fordrun Noveton has been murdered, three days past, and this house is in mourning. We would ask that you follow custom and honor the dead, who was a good and decent man, and allow us our bereavement undisturbed until we have completed the time of sorrow." The time of sorrow was twenty-one days. Seleus was asking the messenger to wait eighteen day's time, which, under the circumstances, was a reasonable request, considering the violence that had ended Fordrun's life.

Tillus huffed with exasperation. "I'm afraid that is most impossible. I have come on a matter of the highest import and must insist that I speak with the head of this house at once."

Seleus clenched his jaw in anger and sucked air between his teeth. His muscled forearms bulged beneath his white shirt as he balled his hands into fists. His large knobby knuckles turned white. He wanted to smite this arrogant man to the death, but that would make him even more disrespectful to his father than this haughty ambassador. Instead, he took several deep breaths. When he spoke, his voice was even.

"I am Seleus Noveton, the eldest. Title has passed to me. Speak."

Unaccustomed to being spoken to in such a curt manner, Tillus hesitated a moment, his eyes wide with shock from the lack of cordiality. Some of the soldiers in the party murmured under their breath. Nevertheless, Tillus, a seasoned diplomat, quickly regained his composure.

"King Jonas has decreed that the original charter creating this homestead has been hereby revoked. The King offers full compensation for your lands and grants you an allowance and six months time to move to another homestead, or wherever you might wish."

To his credit, Seleus was fully prepared for this, an insistence made by his father. Arguing was actually something he did quite well, since he enjoyed it so. "Sir," he began, "the charter you refer to was granted by King Frondus, not his son, and as long as we remain in compliance with the requirements stated therein, King Jonas has no legal standing to alter it in any way, much less revoke it entirely.

"Furthermore," he continued, his voice rising ever so slightly in volume, "the Bould is a territory under joint jurisdiction, and no king of Aegea may impress any of its residents, or make any demands of them, without the approval of the full Council of Kings. Has King Jonas acquired such approval prior to issuing his decree?"

Tillus wavered, casting his glance away for a moment, unable to meet the steady eye of Seleus. He did not respond. It was clear that such approval had not been granted.

"I see," Seleus said, as if Tillus had answered the question. He continued. "Thirdly, and most importantly for your lord, the allegiance of this house to the king of Gladue died with my father. No one living at this farm has sworn an oath to any king, and as such we owe no debt to any crown."

"Oh, come now," Tillus scoffed, waving his hand at such nonsense. "Don't be absurd! If your father was a subject of our king, then so are you, and each member of your house. Surely you can see this, even here in the wilderness." He spread his hands, showing Seleus the unsettled lands all around him. "You are your father's son, are you not?"

"Indeed I am sir, and proud to be so," he answered, standing tall. "But I am also my mother's son, and she is from Andesha." The murmuring of the soldiers began anew, and with more vigor. Tillus let his mouth drop open, his surprise overcoming his sense of propriety. "Are we to split our deference to two monarchs, or should we slight one to honor the other? Since I find it distasteful to do either, I choose to do neither. I recognize no authority behind the decree of which you speak."

Tillus was undone by this unexpected development. For a moment, he considered accusing Seleus of lying, but it was clear he was not. Each member of the House of Noveton had split bloodlines, and in legal tradition, Seleus was right. The kings of the earth had always allowed the children of mixed nationalities the right to choose which monarch they would serve. Once sworn, these 'border children' would live out their lives as subjects of their adopted kings. Choosing neither had never been an option, except on the one spot of the earth where they now stood: the Bould. Inhabitants of the Bould were exempt from military service. They were exempt from all forms of taxation. They were under no obligation to come forth when summoned, or even to face prosecution for crimes. If they paid their tithes, then their charters remained intact, and the King's council honored their claims. Tillus was on shaky ground, and he suddenly realized that the sight of a few spears and a banner were not going to weaken the resolve of the man that stood before him. Nevertheless, he felt compelled to fulfill the will of his lord, even though inspiring fear in this stout fellow seemed quite unattainable.

"Am I to understand that you refuse the rightful decree of our sitting king? I would urge you to consider the peril of such action and think of the consequences of your decision."

Seleus showed no signs of intimidation, though inside his chest his heart thumped so hard he could feel the blood coursing through his ears. He was extremely nervous, but his answer betrayed no fear. "I would advise your king to consider his own peril, for the world will frown upon a single man trying to change the governing rules of an entire region to satiate his own greed."

Tillus was now beside himself. He had never heard such insolence coming from a commoner. *Only in the Bould,* he thought, *can a man speak so of a king and remain free.* The soldiers of his party were aghast. Hands strayed to hilts, and offended soldiers leveled spearheads at the men blocking the gate leading into Noveton. Horses whinnied, expecting action to come from such movements.

Seleus stood his ground, placing his hands defiantly on his hips. His brother, who was so obviously willing to courageously die rather than submit and besmirch his father's memory, inspired Lendum. He found even more reason to love him.

The soldiers of Gladue, enraged by the insult to their king, without orders began to advance. They were in a land with no laws, and the slaughter of a whole family would attract little attention, if anyone noticed at all. Certainly no reprimand would be coming from their lord, who had made it quite clear that he desired these lands above all else. They could act with virtual impunity, which is a heady tonic for doing evil to otherwise noble men.

Just then, the sergeant of the detachment saw movement along the wall. Twenty men stood there, bowstrings pulled taut and lethal points aimed at the hearts of every soldier. They were outnumbered, and any attack would lead only to their own demise. "Halt!" he ordered. "Stay your weapons!"

The men did halt, but did not lower their steel until they saw the force arrayed against them. Slowly, with great reluctance, the men of Gladue sheathed their swords and pointed their spears back towards the sky. "Who was this Noveton?" the sergeant wondered. "How could a man inspire such fealty?"

Seleus still stood, out at the elbows, resolute. "You are answered, sir," he said, still polite. "Go now and tell your lord what has transpired here, and let him know that the men of the Bould will not yield their goods or their homes at the behest of a distant king that fancies himself a tyrant."

Tillus attempted to look shocked all over again, but he had not the energy. The ploy that he had believed so sure to be successful had unraveled before his eyes. "I hope His Highness receives you message in good humor, or it may prove ill for you."

Seleus said nothing. When Tillus saw that no reply was forthcoming, he turned his horse to depart. All of his party followed suit, each staring with hateful intent at the man that had shown their lord such impertinence. Seleus met each glare without lowering his eyes.

The party broke into a gallop, heading southwest, back to Gladue. When they were out of sight, Seleus breathed a deep sigh of relief. He had run a dangerous gambit, but had emerged victorious, for now. He called for Antion, and sent him to Ghar to hire as many men as were willing to help defend the homestead. Seleus guessed that the next time the young king sent representatives, they would not come to negotiate, and they would come with many more spears. Furthermore, they would come soon. In less than a fortnight, Jonas would learn that his ploy had failed. In another fortnight, more soldiers would be at the gate of Noveton. He had one month to prepare, or all would be lost. He had even less time than he reckoned.

⇒ ⇐

Events unfolded quickly. King Grindal spoke with the ambassador of King Jonas, and learned that his worst suspicions were justified. Gladue had claimed the Bould, and any hesitation would lead to disaster. He sent word for his army to enter the Bould, "to protect the sovereignty of the province and maintain order in the area, as well as protect the subjects of Andesha and their property." This order, and its high-sounding phrasing, was an obvious scheme to allow Grindal a pretext for sending his men to the region. However, as the horsemen crossed the bridge at Tine Vort and entered the Bould, they did not move to defend the lives and property of their fellow citizens. They headed toward Noveton, toward the mine, riding as fast as could be, closing the distance with every beat of a horse's gallop.

At the same time, and contrary to what Seleus had believed would transpire, Tillus crossed the Tundish back into Gladue, and there met the encampment of Jonas' army. He told the captain to begin his march to the farm, and to secure the salt mine for his lord. They carried out their orders with speed and alacrity, especially after word spread that the master of the mine had been so very rude to the representative of the king.

The ambassadors of Gladue came in time to the other kingdoms, and their messages were heard. The reactions from the other monarchs were quick, and universally unfavorable. None of the other kingdoms recognized the authority of Gladue or Andesha to claim the territory as their own without a full council of kings to discuss the issue. The charters issued by the other crowns continued to be held in full force and any attempt to seize the territory claimed by subjects of another realm amounted to invasion of sovereign lands and equaled a declaration of war. All the kingdoms warned that they would meet any aggressive move with full embargo of trade and possibly by military intervention. The king of Rubia went a step further and prepared an army for action and issued a decree that all loyal citizens should abandon their homesteads and return to Rubia for their own safety. However, all such attempts to forestall were too late. Both armies had already crossed into the Bould and were marching towards each other with all haste.

⇒ ⇐

Lendum lay in bed, looking into the ceiling, thinking. He could not sleep. The night was clear, and bright starlight streamed through his window, bathing his room with angelic luminance. The house was enduring the last night of the time of sorrow, and tomorrow there would be a feast dedicated to his father's memory. It was the memory of his father that troubled his slumber.

He recalled the night he warned his father that moving to the Bould would be perilous. Fordrun had laughed, but he was not laughing now. Now, he was doing nothing at all. Lendum would have given anything to hear that robust cackling again, but that voice was forever silenced. He missed his father terribly. Lendum felt like what little remained of his boyhood had been stolen from him. Never again would he run aimlessly over the plains, fighting invisible foes, engaging in fierce battle and suffering no injury. He had not the will to do so. The joys of childhood now seemed a frivolous burden, worthy of being cast aside like chaff. Any future battles would be fought with real adversaries, wielding keen blades and employing them to do deadly hurt. For better or worse, Lendum's childhood was over.

After a few hours of fruitless tossing and turning, Lendum arose. He could not shake the feeling he had of impending calamity, as if the earth could open and swallow him at any moment, just as the mine had done. He decided that he must seek comfort somewhere, if he could not find it in his warm bed. He opened the door and crept down the hall to see his mother.

Marle lay on her side, facing the window, her husband's scarf held tightly against her breast. Lendum could tell that she was deep in slumber from her breathing, but he knew that he would wake her up anyway. His heart ached from his worries and his grief, shattering whatever remained of the protection the cocoon of boyhood had provided. His only hope of solace lay with his mother.

He knelt by his parent's bed, now only half-used. She looked very old in the pale light, but peaceful, without all of the troubles that surrounded her in the waking hours. The light of the stars made her hair seem as golden as it had been in her youth, erasing the gray of the years. Lendum must have seen his mother dozens of times in repose, but he could not remember her looking so lovely, and he chastised himself for wanting to deprive her of the rest she so deserved.

"Mother," he whispered. The sound was very loud in the quiet room, but she did not stir. He reached out and touched her shoulder, shaking her gently. "Mother," he repeated, louder this time. "Mother, wake up."

Marle inhaled deeply, trying to respond and keep sleeping simultaneously. After a brief struggle she spoke.

"Fordrun, what is it?"

Lendum felt his heart break. He wanted to leave the room, but he could not move. His knees seemed rooted to the floor, as if his body refused to leave until his soul had received some peace. Only a mother could give him the tranquility he needed.

"Mother, it's me, Lendum."

She stirred once more, and then abruptly opened her eyes, waking with a start. Once she recognized her son's face in the white light of the stars, she relaxed. "What is it, son? Are you okay?"

"Yes," he said. "Well, no, actually. Not really, no." He wanted to confide in her, but did not know what to say. "Were you dreaming?" he finally asked.

"I think I was, but I can't remember," she said sleepily. "I'm glad I've forgotten. My dreams have been troublesome of late." She sat up on her elbow and rubbed her eyes.

"Could you have been dreaming about father?" he asked.

Marle smiled. "Most likely," she answered. "I dream of him quite often, both in my sleep and during the daylight hours. Why do you ask?"

"You said his name just now, as I tried to wake you."

Marle continued smiling, though the pleasantness drained from her face, leaving only sorrow behind. "Your father gave me his whole life, and I will miss him until the day I follow him. I know that he loved me. He loved all of us, and would have done anything to protect us. You know that, don't you?"

"Yes, I know."

"He had a good long life, full of healthy, productive years, and was surrounded by ones that cared about him very much. The memories and life lessons he passed down to you and your brothers and sisters will be remembered and handed to his grandchildren, making him able to survive death. By any measure, his life was a success, despite how it ended. Do you agree?"

"Yes, mother. I believe that with my whole heart."

Marle reached out and touched her son's face. "Then what troubles you, my youngest?"

Lendum hesitated a moment. He was not sure how to express the feelings within him. He knew what he wanted to do, but was at a loss to explain why he wanted to do it. "I know father loved us," he began. "I never doubted his love for me, not once in my whole life. But he has passed on, and his troubles are over. I hope he finds rest."

Marle said nothing, but a tear escaped her.

"My worry is for the rest of us. We should leave, mother. We should leave the Bould and go somewhere else, anywhere else. I feel a dread I have not known since we first set out to come here. If we stay, it will prove ill for us."

"That decision is not yours to make, dear. This is your brother's household now, and if he decides to go, then we will go. If not, then we will stay. It is the way of things. You could try to persuade him, but in the end, his decision will stand."

Lendum cast his eyes to the floor. "He will not leave father's bones, not after Jonas tried to take this land. He will die defending it." His voice dropped to less than a whisper. "And he won't be alone. We will all suffer for it. His pride has been ruffled, and he will stand his ground in sheer terror."

"You have always been wise beyond your years," she said. "Your father believed you to be too cautious, but caution is most often the course of wisdom. Speak with your brother. Tell him your concerns. He may yet hear you, and find you sensible." She did not speak it aloud, but Lendum could tell that his mother also wanted to depart. There was such anxiety in her tone. "You mention this to him tomorrow, but for now, get to bed. If you cannot sleep, then practice your speech. Seleus will respond to well-crafted argument, and things will appear less menacing in the light of day."

Lendum hugged his mother fiercely. When he released her, his eyes were wet. "Thank you, mother. I love you."

"I love you too, son." She caressed his face once more. "Go on now. To bed with you."

Lendum stood and exited. As his bare feet carried him across the cold floor toward his own room, he realized that no real words of reassurance had been exchanged, but he felt better all the same. That is the power a mother wields.

Back in his own bed, Lendum did as his mother suggested. He made every point in favor of leaving that he could think of, and then countered every argument that he could conceive being used against him. After an hour of internal debate, sleep finally stole over him. He dreamt of legions of soldiers, all weary and bloody, marching in four columns. On either side of the battle-tested men swarmed horrid creatures in the darkness. They squealed and mocked the soldiers, shouting evil things and curses upon the footsore men. He did not know where they were going, but Lendum knew that they were heading into dire peril. Most of them would never see their homes again.

The dream troubled Lendum, but thankfully, he did not wake. He was granted a bit of rest, the last rest he would ever have in that house.

The next morning Lendum was awakened by the sound of herald trumpets. The noise was far off, but unmistakable, and even over the long distance the music seemed harsh and cruel. After the trumpets faded away, a voice carried across the farm, but Lendum could not make out the words. Hurriedly he arose and dressed, donning his sword and quiver, and ran out of the house heading south. He was sure that the emissary from Gladue had returned, this time with more soldiers, and he would be needed if the confrontation came to actual fighting. He did not think to check on his mother before he left. He would regret that oversight.

As he ran, the coldness felt upon him again. It felt comfortable and strengthening. His fear during the night seemed like folly. Why should he fear? At the very worst, he would follow his father into the unknown. At best, other men would fall, and Fordrun could have his vengeance on their spirits, if he chose. They were worthy of revenge, for trying to seize that which was not theirs. In his current state, Lendum was not afraid to die, and he was not afraid to kill. At this moment, Seleus was the bravest man in Aegea, and the wisest. Lendum was a fool for doubting his brother's counsel.

Just then, the trumpets sounded again, and Lendum came to a sudden halt, listening. He was confused, because the sound came not from the southern gate, but from the north, from the gate the faced Andesha. He turned and ran in that direction, heading for the tiny bridge, his quiver bouncing on his back and the sheath at his hip slapping against his thigh. His breaths were deep and fulfilling, and his muscles felt loose and ready. He realized that he actually wanted a battle. Death was the worst possibility he could conceive, and that was acceptable. He ran faster.

When he arrived at the gate, every man of the farm stood waiting. Seleus was there, directing the small band of followers that had pledged their honor to the Noveton family. He seemed to have aged ten years since the day before. About forty strong men stood near the gate, each one armed and capable, but also listless and full of dread. Each face was grave and hopeless. The very air seemed saturated with despair.

"Seleus!" Lendum cried out, and his brother looked up. His face was worn and wrinkled, and his eyes were sunken. Lank hair hung in his eyes, saturated with sweat from the heat of the morning. He extended his arms to his little brother. When Lendum approached, he embraced him so violently that he forced the air from Lendum's lungs.

Still holding him tightly, he whispered in his ear. "Take mother and the women and the little ones and lead them south. Pack as much food as you can carry and depart. We are undone here. I will give you as much time as providence allows, but it is likely to be just a few moments. Go while you can."

"No!" Lendum protested, and began to struggle. "I want to fight! I am not helpless! I can slay a man as well as you!"

Seleus released his brother, but then slapped him across the face. Hard.

"Listen to me you little fool!" he demanded. "There can be no victory here. To stay here is to die."

Lendum did not speak, but his face betrayed his disbelief.

"Look for yourself," he said, and walked to the gate. The trumpets blared again, very loud so close. Seleus opened the viewing slot in the door and shoved Lendum up to it. When Lendum looked, he gasped, and uttered a groan.

Outside the gate was a multitude of men on horseback. Lendum could not guess their number. They were dressed nearly identically in dark brown tunics, made from very shiny leather. Heavy plate armor covered their arms and legs, and each man bore a sword, spear and bow. Wooded shields covered the horse's flanks. These men were not from Gladue. They had lighter skin, and Lendum noticed that most of them were blonde or redheaded. They all appeared very grim. Lendum could not see a single tooth as he scanned their ranks. The herald and the standard-bearer stood together in the front, along with a man Lendum assumed to be the captain of this regiment. He alone had a tall plume of white feathers sprouting from his helm. A horrid scar ran down the right side of his face, an injury that had maimed his eye and left it milky and useless. His face was contorted with an evil smirk.

"Open this gate in the name of Grindal of Andesha, who has taken possession of these lands!" the herald cried out. "You have one hour to comply!"

"You see?" Seleus whispered behind him. "You must escape and save as many as you can. We cannot hold, and we cannot rely on their mercy. A king does not send an army to negotiate. He sends them to slaughter, and we have little protection."

Lendum could see that some of the men of Andesha had dismounted, and were stoking fires on the ground. His father had never intended the wooden walls to hold off a determined army, and they would burn away easily enough. Apparently, that is exactly what this army intended to do if Seleus refused to open the gate. Lendum knew his brother was right, but still refused to flee.

"Can't one of my nephews do this duty? I do not wish to leave my father's bones."

Seleus looked at his brother with pity. "You honor our father, and that is good. He will know of it. But you are the youngest of his children and the charge is yours to save who you can. I will wait for half an hour, and then try to speak with them. You should be gone before then. Now go, and do your duty."

Lendum did not cry, but felt his heart break. He was about to tell Seleus that he loved him when herald trumpets broke the silence again. However, these horns sounded far away. To the south.

"Tor help us, what now?" burst out Seleus. "Antion, go see what that is." Antion jumped on his horse and sped away toward the south gate. Meanwhile the herald outside the gate began to scream at once. Evidently, he had heard the trumpets as well, and thought them ominous.

"Noveton!" he screeched. The noble sound of his voice was now gone. "Noveton, open this gate at once!"

Seleus motioned for the men around him to climb to the walkway. Silently they did his bidding. "What do you want?" he asked with a tone full of oblivious innocence.

"Open this gate in the name of the lord of this land, King Grindal of Andesha! This is your last warning!"

"Go," Seleus said to Lendum. "Save who you can, hide if you must, but be quick about it."

Lendum briefly considered arguing some more, but knew that it was a waste, and would devour precious minutes. He ran back towards the houses, bound to save his family from the imminent threat.

Seleus turned his attention back to the herald outside his gate. "This land has no lord, unless it is me! I will not open this gate until you state your business!"

"Archers, make ready!" the one-eyed captain ordered, and Seleus knew they were all doomed.

Just them Antion returned. He rode up hard, and dismounted with a quick leap. "A great host approaches the south gate, brother. Soldiers of Gladue. We are besieged."

"How many?" he asked.

"Some thousands, all on foot. They come to make war, or I am a fool.

Perhaps you were too short with the ambassador, brother." Antion smiled at the memory. If he was afraid, he did not show it.

"If they want war, then let us do our best to give it to them." Seleus could see from the gate that a line of cavalry archers had taken position and were ready to draw. Each had arrows notched with flaming heads. At any moment, the walls of Noveton would be burning.

"Oh captain!" Seleus cried out in his most mocking tone. "I fear you are too late! Your competitor has arrived, and he is ready to meet you on the field!"

The Andeshan captain paused, the tall feathers of his helm fluttering in the breeze. He had heard the trumpets in the south, and thought them nothing but villagers come to help a neighbor in need, or perhaps men hired to fight on behalf of the Noveton family. Now he paused, considering the possibility that Gladue had come to seize the mine, just as he had. Could there be an army coming from the south? He did not believe that Gladue could bring an army this far so quickly. He blinked as he thought, stupidly. The useless eye was as bleary as a pearl. Indecision plagued him, and it was at this moment that Seleus chose to strike.

There were thirty-five men along the wall, each wielding a bow. With a wave of his hand, Seleus ordered them to fire. They were few, but they were accurate, and their targets were very close. Projectiles flew straight and true, and wherever they struck, flesh was torn.

Each man had fired twice before the captain came to his senses. He had already lost nearly seventy men, but that was not a tithe of his command. "Loose!" he cried, and five-hundred arrows responded. Within minutes, everything was in flames, and a thick, acrid smoke rose to the heavens. The men along the wall that had survived the initial onslaught had to withdraw because of the heat and fumes. After only a few moments, the battle was over, and still men of Andesha continued to fire.

⇒ ⇐

Lendum was still close enough to hear the captain give the order to fire. After that, it was amazing how quickly things turned to utter chaos. Screams filled the air as the members of his family not directly involved in the fighting lost their wits and became like beasts in panic. The animals began to stamp and bleat, full of fear and trying to break out of their fences. Lendum tried to gather some of his family, but no one paid him any heed. He did notice that everyone seemed to be fleeing to the south gate, and that was good. If there was any safety from this disaster, it would be to the south, or so he believed. All of his sisters, his nieces and young nephews, and his mother were now scampering in a huddled mass that direction, weeping and wailing as they went. All of his brothers and nephews of fighting age were defending the wall, which was already a lost cause. Lendum knew they would all perish. All he could do was help the women and children escape.

For that, they would need food.

Lendum ran into Seleus' house, which just happened to be closest. In the kitchen, he rifled through the cupboard, where he found a few loaves of bread, a jar of pickles, and several slices of dried meat. There was not much, but it was better than nothing at all. Perhaps there was enough to get them to Ghar. He crammed all of the food into a pack that he slung over his shoulder. He grabbed a full waterskin and slung it over his other shoulder. In his brother's bedroom, he found a small bag of gold coins that could sustain them for a very long time if they could reach the river.

From outside a resounding crash came to his ears, and then the terrifying sound of galloping hooves. "Find the mine!" a voice cried out. "Find and secure the mine!" Lendum ran to a window and saw that the north gate and a large portion of the wall had collapsed. The remainder of the wall was in flames and teetering. All of the grass around the area was black and smoking, but the disciplined cavalrymen of Grindal had galloped ahead and risked their lives for their lord.

"There!" the captain screamed. "After them! They mustn't escape!"

Lendum ran to a window that faced the front of the house, and his heart sank. Women and children, his closest kin, fled away from him, but were pursued by the brown-clad warriors. They were struck down with no regard, screaming and crying for help that would never come. In the little dirt path that ran from the bridge to the southern gate, he saw Marle, his mother, knelt down in a posture that begged for mercy. Her hands were clasped before her chest, and she gazed up at her assailant, looking delicate and powerless. The captain of Andesha rode up to her, looking down upon her like an executioner. Marle was weeping, but her emotion and pleading did nothing to soften the heart of the Andeshan captain. He ran her through without speaking, allowing her body to crumple into the dust before seeking another target.

Insanity clenched Lendum's soul. The youngest son of Fordrun drew his sword. He knew he was going to die. Just as his brothers and sisters, just as his nieces and nephews, just as his mother, he would die. Nevertheless, he would take as many of the treacherous men of Andesha with him as he could. He looked at his blade. It twinkled brightly in the sun, like a polished mirror, except for the edge. Antion had sharpened the blade on his sixteenth birthday, and it was dull with keenness, as if light could not penetrate it.

Lendum started towards his doom, ready to walk headlong into the unknown, when he heard his father's voice, far away in the back of his head, as if coming through a pane of glass.

"No, son," the voice said. "Run and hide, that you might live, and bring justice for your family on another day."

Lendum squeezed the hilt of his sword tightly. He did not want to flee. Such action seemed the course of a coward. In addition, he knew that his grief was in check for now, but soon it would come upon like a storm, and the pain would be too great. He would rather die now, brave and without tears, rather than later, wallowing in his craven heartache. The voice responded to his thoughts.

"What can you do to solve this by yourself?" the voice asked. "Your family is slain. What service do you do for them by dying today?"

Lendum had no answer. He knew that the voice spoke wisdom, and his passions cooled. The coldness descended on him, and he could think clearly again. "Where am I to hide?" he thought aloud. "Surely they will search and burn every building. Where can I stay out of sight?"

The voice did not answer, but instead Lendum had the vision of a great battle. He was watching very close to the ground, as if only his eyes stood above the grass. Two armies of men were engaged in close combat, men of Andesha and Gladue, and Lendum could see them far off, and he could hear their screams of agony. When he could stand no more he sank into the ground, and he was plunged into darkness.

"The mine!" he said. Just then, there was another crash, this time to the south. Angry bellowing filled the air, and soon the unmistakable din of parrying steel rang out across the farm. The War of the Bould had begun.

Lendum crept out of the house, staying low, and looked south. He could see no soldiers near him, but far off he could see the green tunics of Gladue, and the horsemen of Andesha rode to meet them. There was no parlay or negotiation: just war on sight. The two groups of men clashed and then disintegrated into a thousand tiny battles. The twangs of bowstrings filled the air with dreadful music. Men were dying, dying for salt. Lendum kept as low as he could and ran to the east. The mine was not marked, and was nothing more than a hole in the ground. He could be safe there for a long time. The sounds of the battle were getting farther and farther from his ears. Soon he came to the mine, and he nearly cried at the sight of it. Could it be possible that everyone he cared for had been murdered so some king could take possession of this puncture in the earth? It seemed surreal.

The ladder was there, and he slithered down. He stole a last glance at the battle, and he saw the men fighting, just as he had in his vision. Arrows flew with abandon, cutting the air with spiteful song. He heard dreadful screams of agony and wails of anguish. The pained screeches were so frequent that they overlapped each other, trebling their intensity. Men were hewing at each other with vicious strokes, creating examples of the worst kinds of bloodshed. The renowned cavalry of Andesha rode bravely into the battle, putting forth resistance in the face of impossible odds. Their horses were gifts from Tor himself, and were tireless, courageous, and steadfast in despair. Dozens of men had fallen, never to rise again. Blood stained the ground, red as the setting sun. The scene was altogether horrible, assaulting all of the senses equally, and proving thoroughly barbaric, inhuman, and cruel.

"This is madness," Lendum said quietly. "Madness has engulfed the men of the world." Lendum could endure no more. He descended the ladder, and the earth swallowed him. Once at the bottom, he pulled the ladder down into the cavern with him. With good fortune, he could stay down here until nightfall, and he could make his way south past the regiments, and then to safety.

Lendum felt very tired suddenly. He sat down, and as his body began to rest, the resolve of his will weakened, and his grief overtook him. He wept. He wept for his family and for his home. He wept for his stolen future. He wept for the hours he had spent in this place, happy and carefree, now gone forever. Mostly he wept because he had been right. He wished more than anything that he had been wrong, but he had not. Coming to the Bould had cost his family everything. Lendum wept his last tears as a child. He wept until he lay asleep on the hard ground of the tunnel, the salt getting into the fabric of his clothes.

Andesha had a more maneuverable force, and could accurately engage the enemy at range, but there were simply not enough of them to carry the day. King Jonas, more through luck than by any real gift of strategy or foresight, had sent twice as many soldiers. The defense by Seleus had not made much of a difference numerically, but Andesha had lost some strength because of it, and the morale of the men had been reduced by a greater degree than the actual loss warranted. After three hours of combat with the men of Gladue, their numbers declined substantially, the horses were footsore, and no more could be endured. By comparison, Gladue had lost barely five-hundred of their four-thousand. They were not nearly as tired, being able to stand and fight without traveling huge distances around the buildings of the farm.

Therefore, Andesha surrendered, and offered to exchange prisoners. The captain of Gladue, who was aghast by what had just transpired, graciously accepted, and not only returned prisoners on a one-for-one basis, but also allowed his enemy to collect their dead. At the end of the day, Andesha could count six-hundred with no hurts at all, and almost one-thousand wounded. Four-hundred had given their lives for their king. Gladue had won the first battle of the Bould, the first battle ever between armies of men.

As word spread, the majority of the men of the world hung their heads in shame, disappointed and grieved that such a thing could happen. Alliances had been shattered, and old kinships that had endured long centuries of troubles and toil were forgotten.

However, in the east, hidden deep in the black forests of Achtwood, secure behind jagged mountains and safe in his mighty citadel of Kan Chatuk, Sindus smiled, and plotted his treachery.

REBIRTH

Lendum was dreaming. Once again, four columns of men were marching to war. Each column of warriors had different helms, and each bore different styles weaponry. All around the files of soldiers evil creatures swarmed in the darkness, Lendum could hear them speaking in their vile tongue, cursing and showering scorn on the columns of soldiers. Lendum could hear their laughter, hissing with pleasure at the measure of men's folly. The sound was grating to the ear.

Lendum was brought closer. He could see that all of the men suffered wounds. Some were cut about their faces, leaking blood into their eyes and mouths. Others carried more serious hurts; arms missing, horrible burns on their chests and backs, or arrows sticking from their bodies like quills. Some of the men had pallid faces, made white from disease or poison. On and on they marched, relentless, going to war, continuing to fight no matter what their bodies endured. Always there was the terrible, screeching laughter of the mysterious creatures in the darkness.

＝ ＝

Lendum woke with a start. The night had come. He could smell small traces of smoke, and somewhere, far away, songs rang out into the night. "A victory song," he thought bitterly. "Whoever won is singing about their victory on this day." Bile rose into his throat. The idea that anyone could celebrate what had happened on this day made him sick. He felt angry tears come to his eyes, but he forced them away, as well as the feelings that created them. He needed to concentrate, and emotions so strong could only distract him.

He stood up in the complete darkness. Only the stars overhead provided any light at all, and that was negligible. Now was the time to make his escape, if he could. Quietly he placed the ladder back upright, and climbed the rungs one by one until he was back at the surface. The smell of smoke was thicker now, and Lendum could see why. Fires burned all around him. All of the buildings he and his family had built were ablaze, as well as the remnants of the wall. Campfires dotted the landscape in every direction, with several dozen men grouped around each fire. They sang as they ate their evening meals and drank their beverages. Clearly, they were not on duty, but even so, their senses were not so dulled by victory that they would not notice a farm boy dressed in homespun clothes walking amongst them. There was no way for Lendum to escape. He would never manage to slip past unseen.

Dejectedly, he descended the ladder once again. He stood at the bottom, the salty water running just inches from his feet. He placed his hands on his hips and thought. How could he get away? There must be a way.

"Follow the tunnel, son," his father said to him. "They do not yet know the location of the mine, and you could get quite far before they realize you were here, if they ever realize it at all."

Lendum looked at the nothingness before him. Each direction showed nothing at all, and betrayed no hint or clue of what lay ahead. "Which way do I go?" he asked aloud in a hoarse whisper. "Where does it lead? I think that this tunnel is evil, and I do not trust it."

"What feeds all life?" the voice asked. "Follow the water, and it will show you the way. Fear not the earth. It is neither good nor evil. It just is."

Lendum found comfort in that. The soft trickling of the little stream was suddenly very soothing. This passage must emerge somewhere, and he would eventually get there, provided he did not starve before he reached the end. He had food and water, and he had rested. If he was going to go, now was the time. He only lacked one thing; light.

Yes, he would certainly need some light if he were to attempt to traverse this passage. Many, many miles could lie ahead, and without some way to see, it would be slow going indeed, not to mention treacherous.

Several oil lamps hung on hooks along the wall of the mine where he and his brothers had labored, but he had no way to light them. He had his flint rocks in his pack, but he thought it unwise to shoot sparks into a bottle of oil. He needed something that he could ignite with the flints, that could then be used to light the lamps.

He began to pace around, thinking furiously. After several minutes, he stubbed his toe on something so hard that he nearly fell over. He clamped his hand over his mouth to stifle a yelp. Reaching down with cautious fingers, he felt for the obstruction.

The ladder lay at his feet.

It was nothing more than a few sturdy boughs held together with some rope. The wood was of little value, but the rope would serve nicely.

He drew his sword and began to cut at the rope holding the ladder together. He took great care in the darkness, separating the fibers of the rope from the wooden rungs and keeping them in a neat pile between his knees. As each wooden component came apart in his hand, he tossed it with a splash into the stream, to be carried away from him for all time by the unstoppable water. After twenty minutes of diligent, careful work, the ladder was no more and Lendum had a good pile of fibers.

Next, he brought out his flints. He struck them repeatedly, each strike creating sparks as bright as a supernova in the blackness of the cave. Very few moments passed before a piece of the rope caught and sent up a tiny finger of flame.

Lendum ran to the wall of the cavern and snatched one of the lamps from its iron hook. It was only about half full, but there were others, and he could harvest a good deal of oil from them. He ran back to the miniature fire he had started, picked up the burning coil of rope, and gingerly touched it to the wick of the lamp.

It was as if the sun itself had descended into the earth. The sudden onset of light struck Lendum blind, stabbing at his eyes like a thousand needles. He shielded his sight with his hand, giving himself a moment to let his eyes adjust to the brightness. After a few seconds he could see very well, and was amazed at how the wall and the water twinkled in the light. He had seen it many times before over the past couple of years, but he still greatly admired its beauty.

"Snap out of it!" he said, scolding himself. "Time to move, and put some miles between myself and this accursed place." He gathered up all of the rope ends and stuffed them into his pockets, making them bulge. Next, he collected all of the oil lamps he could find and brought them back to his luggage. There were four of them, in addition to the one he had already lit.

"Don't need to bring them all, just the oil," he said aloud. He thought frantically. He could feel time ticking away. Daybreak could be in three hours, or in thirty minutes. He really had no idea. All he knew for sure was that at dawn the soldiers above would begin searching for their prize, and it would not take them long to find it, and find him.

Suddenly he lit on an idea. He rummaged through his pack, and brought out the jar full of pickles. At the sight of them, he felt very hungry, and he quickly ate four of them before putting the rest into his pack. He poured out the brine, and then carefully poured the oil from each lamp into the jar, and sealed it. Every available drop of oil went into his pack, along with the wicks from each lamp. Lendum thought there was enough to last many hours, perhaps as long as two full days.

Lendum gathered up all of his belongings, eating two more pickles as he did so. The rumbling of his stomach had been antagonized by the first bit of food rather than satisfied. Soon, he was ready to depart. He lifted his burning lamp, and turned it as low as it could go, just bright enough to see the next few steps. He began walking, following the flow of the water.

⇒ ⇐

None of the men of Aegea, whether directly involved or merely observers, actually believed that the dispute over the Bould would lead to war. Most found it inconceivable that men would kill each other over something as mundane as a supply of salt, regardless of its value. However, all were wrong in their beliefs, and now that war had indeed erupted between nations of men, the miscalculation was compounded by the assumption that the war would be a short one, if not already concluded. In truth, many thought that the battle of Noveton Farm had settled the matter, with Gladue emerging victorious.

Such beliefs denied the pride and determination of the belligerents. King Jonas, though heartened by the win, was deeply troubled. He had not wanted to fight, and he found the unexpected combat unsettling. He suspected that Grindal would counterattack, so he reinforced his army in the Bould, bringing the number of his effective strength to seven-thousand. Two-thousand were to remain at the mine for protection, while the remainder marched to the Shae to defend against further encroachment from Andesha. While these measures were strategically sound, Councilor Motte warned that they were not enough.

"We are at war, my Lord," he said, his voice low yet still filling the hall. "To guard our spoils is prudent, but it is less prudent to believe that it is the only precaution we need take. We share a long border with our enemy, and we cannot assume that horsemen will not cross into our lands at some point other than the Bould. We must defend it all."

"Great Tor!" the young king cried out. The suggestion distorted his ugly face into a mask of utter disbelief. "That would take a force of forty-thousand, and even then they would be spread so thin that they would be rendered ineffective in battle. We do not even have that many men sworn to service. *No* kingdom has. No army of that size has existed since the days of Menduval."

"Be that as it may, we have little choice in the matter," Motte responded, full of guile. "Our enemy is mobile and speedy, and could quickly encircle us and destroy our regiments piecemeal. We risk utter ruin by allowing Andesha the chance to cross the Sampi unchecked. If the number of soldiers we have is insufficient, then they should be conscripted."

"You're mad," said the king, but with little conviction. Beads of sweat rolled down his face, and matted his scraggly beard to his face. Even in the palace, the summer heat was stifling. "Any attempt to impress men to service will foment a rebellion."

"I think not, my Lord," answered Motte. "Once word has spread that Gladue has been attacked and that men have died defending our soil, I think it likely that volunteers in plenty will be pledging themselves to the crown. We may yet fill our ranks with the willing and eager."

The king thought a moment. Motte could see that his argument had won the king over, but Jonas needed to make it seem that the idea was wholly his. Such was his pompous nature. The infantile fool had no idea that he was little more than a puppet.

"I think my subjects will rally to our cause, once they know of the treachery of Andesha," he finally said. "We will need no conscripts, for anyone that can carry a weapon behind our flag will be coming forward with little prompting."

"A most astute observation," Motte said, lowering his head humbly. His expression did not change, but inwardly he was smiling. "Your Majesty knows his people very well."

Jonas nodded, completely swallowing the false flattery. "Send riders in every direction, spreading the news that one of our pioneer families has been slaughtered and that the brave men of Gladue have been slain in their defense. Summon every willing, able-bodied man to Ashtone that we may marshal our strength, and defend our borders against further unprovoked malice."

"Should we make any plans for conscription, my Lord, in the event that our people do not rally?" Motte's face was full of feinted concern.

"Not yet, no," the king replied with an air of finality. "Let us see how the common folk respond to the call before we force men from their homes."

"As you wish, my Lord," said Motte with deference. He bowed low, and then turning on his heel he shuffled out of the room, going forth to do the will of his lord.

$$\Longrightarrow \Longleftarrow$$

Lendum was a prisoner under the earth. He slept fitfully.

There was no way to tell how far or for how long he had walked. The absence of the alternating sun and stars made time something that was without meaning. He relied solely on his body to make decisions that hitherto had been at least partially dictated by the time of day. He would eat when he got hungry, and drink when he had thirst. In the cavern, mealtimes were a foreign concept. When he was weary from his effort, he would sleep, and whether or not the sun was showing on the surface was of little consequence. Lendum would simply lay his head on his pack, extinguish his lamp, and rest on the bank of the stream, listening to the bubbling creek beside him. When his body was refreshed, he would awaken, and whether it was day or night was of little consequence, for the sun held no sway under the earth.

Because he could not know the time, Lendum began thinking of his journey in terms of 'cycles'. He would awaken, walk as long as he could, rest, walk as long as he could again, and then sleep. That was one cycle. So far, he had traveled for four cycles, and there was no end in sight. He had encountered nothing else alive: no creatures, no roots from overhead flora, and no insects. There was nothing but the tunnel, and it went straight and true, no breaks in the walls or branches to either side. Lendum had the impression that he was moving lightly downhill, but for the most part, he seemed to be traversing level ground. The water trickled ceaselessly.

"What if the end is beyond my reach?" he would ask aloud, alarmed at the sound of his own voice echoing against the walls. The pickles were gone, and the only food left to him was some dried meat and a loaf of bread, a little stale but still edible. He had been very careful with his water, taking only a few sips at a time, but even so, his skin was more than half-empty, and despite the moist air of the cave, his throat felt perpetually parched. Overall, only three 'cycles' worth of provisions remained, and he feared that it would not be enough.

Lendum awoke. It was the beginning of the fifth cycle. He used his flints and lit the lamp. Thankfully, the oil for the lamps was something he had in plenty. He would be able to lie down and starve with plenty of light, if it came to that.

Once he could see, he broke off a piece of bread, wrapped it around some meat, and began to eat his breakfast. He chewed with great deliberation, letting his teeth break down the food as much as possible, because he did not want to use the water to help him swallow. After he had eaten, he took one large mouthful of water, swishing it vigorously before swallowing. Then he gathered his things and he began another arduous period of toil. Another cycle had begun.

Lendum sang to himself as he walked. Fear was his constant companion, but he kept it at bay by singing. Yet another unwelcome visitor had begun to force its was into his mind that was immune to the songs; sorrow. With nothing more engaging to occupy his mind other than where to place his next step, Lendum was more apt to begin crying all over again. With great effort, he turned his mind to inane songs and poetic verse, just to make the waking hours pass. As the cycles passed, his mind changed his fear and grief into quiet anger and vengeance. These thoughts were more acceptable somehow: less troublesome. The Andeshan captain, the tall man with the misshapen eye and the hideous scar, was the focus of his ire. The man was not human. How could he be? He had skewered Lendum's mother as she begged for mercy in the dust. He could feel his muscles relax as he daydreamed of making the man pay for his deeds. His coldness became something hard and cruel, almost a thing he could touch, and he felt in total control of himself, as if he could stop the very beating of his heart at will. Each step down the long tunnel brought him more into the mold of a warrior: not a frenzied lunatic bend on dealing death, but a calculating commander willing to sacrifice without pause to achieve an objective. His objective now was revenge on the heartless captain, or from his point of view, justice. There was nothing else in the world for him to crave.

He had walked about five hours when he perceived that the character of the tunnel was changing. The water began to flow with more speed, indicating the greater slope of the passage. The walls began to constrict, to the point where Lendum could touch the ceiling with an outstretched hand. After another hour, the stream no longer ran in its bed, but touched the walls of the cavern. Lendum had water past the ankles of his boots, and it was rising with every step. Another hour passed and the water was past his knees, and he kept his head ducked to avoid hitting it against the roof. The walls began to undulate, losing their smooth character. Lendum imagined walls not of rock, but of living tissue, pulsing with contractions, trying to force him out. He was no longer welcome.

Soon the choice was either swim or go back. There was barely enough room for him to hold the lamp aloft over the flowing water, and the strength of the current made it next to impossible to walk. He expended more energy keeping his feet than in making forward progress.

"Follow the water," he heard his father's voice repeat. "Follow, and see where it goes."

Realizing that he had no real choice in the matter, Lendum knew that he must discard his belongings and take to the stream, which was now more of a river. To go back meant death. By now the soldiers had certainly found the mine, perhaps even knew that he had escaped into the tunnel. Soldiers possibly pursued him, and even if they did not, he would die from thirst or starvation before he could get out. The options were certain death or probable death, so he chose the latter.

Lendum opened his pack and hastily ate the remainder of his food. Then, without thinking about it anymore, he drank all of the water. For a small moment, he allowed himself to enjoy its cool refreshment, until the last drop was gone. Finally, and with the greatest hesitation, he blew out his lamp, and put it in his pack. Now in darkness, he lifted his feet, and let the current carry him, saving his energy as much as he could.

For hours, he floated along, using his outstretched arms and legs to keep him as close to the center as he could manage. The water was not that cold, but even so, he felt chilled to the bone. Over the noise of the rushing water, he could hear his teeth chattering. Soon his feet were no longer able to touch bottom, and what remained of the cavern above water was right above his head. Breaths began to come intermittently, as the water sloshed across his face, filling his mouth and nose. The taste was still so salty that Lendum always spat it back out before catching a quick breath. The sound of the rushing water grew deafening, roaring in the tiny space, and Lendum could tell that the speed of the current was very great. The end of air was near. With his hands, he could feel that mere inches existed between the ceiling and the water, and each attempted breath of air risked smashing his head against the unyielding rock.

Then all at once, the air was gone, and Lendum kicked with the current, aiding it to carry him as far as it could before he drowned. He opened his eyes pointlessly under the water, but the briny fluid hurt so much that he shut them immediately. Jagged rocks bit at his hands, mocking him, calling him a simpleton and a fool. His chest burned. His lungs cried out, begging for air.

"Let my body find the sun," he prayed. "Though I die under the earth, let my body be warmed by sun once more, so I may be found and laid to rest with respect."

The current went faster. The water turned Lendum over repeatedly, losing his direction. It seemed that a great, white light appeared before him, though his eyes were still shut, and then he was falling.

≫ ≪

King Grindal was furious.

His pride was very developed, and to have suffered defeat at the hands of his cousin across the river demanded a response, even if nothing more was at stake. His councilors all urged diplomacy and patience, but Grindal would have none of it. He dismissed his entire council, and surrounded himself with eager warriors, all of whom demanded blood. The greatest of these was Quereus, the Grand Marshal of Andesha, commander of all armies of the realm. Only Grindal himself held higher military authority in Andesha.

"The Bould," Quereus said, "can be won if you desire it my Lord, but we must be crafty. Our strength is in speed, for we can circle our enemy and strike unawares to their rear. I would avoid any direct assault if possible."

"I agree," said Grindal as he paced around the mighty hall. His silk robes trailed behind him and twirled each time he turned his body. "What strength do you believe we shall need to ultimately secure the area?"

"That depends on what course we take," he replied. The late afternoon sun coming through the window reflected like crimson jewels off the armor attached to his torso. "I suggest that we use a good portion of our strength to perform a feint."

The king stopped pacing. "Do you indeed?" asked Grindal with curiosity. "Go on."

Quereus cleared his throat, giving himself a moment to organize his thought before he spoke. "Our scouts have told us that Gladue is marching to the Shae with some five thousand troops. Since this a force too weak to invade our country, Jonas means to secure the spoils and prevent our entering the area. I think we should send a force to the Shae as well, though for a different purpose than our adversary. We can win the mine by deception."

"Ah, yes. The mine," said the king. In his lust for revenge, he had nearly forgotten the original objective of his campaign. "How many do you require for this plan?"

"Five-thousand for the feint and ten-thousand for the flank. All in all, three full regiments and five companies, all of which are fully assembled and ready to ride."

Grindal cocked an eyebrow at this news. "I gave no such order to muster our men. How is it that they are prepared so?"

Quereus bowed low, suddenly very contrite. The wavy hair swayed into his brown eyes as he ducked his head. "Forgive me, my Lord. I took it upon myself to issue such orders, once I received news of your intention to enter the Bould. I feared that being unprepared could lead to disaster."

"Are there any other orders you have issued that I should be made aware of?" asked the king, his indignation bubbling just beneath the surface.

"No, no my Lord." Quereus knew that his sovereign was already enraged from his loss, and needed just a little antagonizing to unleash his anger fully. "I beg your forgiveness. My actions were taken with your kingdom as my chief concern."

"You are forgiven, this time," answered Grindal, his voice ominous. "See that you do not overstep your authority again, or I will remove you from your post. You'll be a commoner outside royal graces, and you'll live out your days as a cobbler or a tanner, or worse." He said this loudly, so that all of the other captains could hear.

"I understand, my Lord," said Quereus. Inwardly he was fuming, but he let not a shred of it show on his face. His job required him suffer indignity now and again, and it was something he had learned to do with great patience, even though being denigrated by a stripling of a king was as demeaning as anything that could be imagined. He did what he did because he loved his country, not its monarch. Kings came and went, but the land was there for all time. If he needed to be spanked in front of his men from time to time, then so be it.

Grindal was blissfully unaware of his Marshal's internal conflicts. He only nodded, acknowledging his subordinate's groveling. "So be it. We will do as you suggest, Quereus. Tell me your plan in full, and I will provide you with everything you need to succeed. The Bould will be ours!"

"Lunacy!" burst out Trand. "Absolute lunacy! What madness comes over men to make them such slaves to their egos?" Such rhetoric went completely unanswered.

Trand stood in the King's Hall of Farshton, at the very pinnacle of the citadel. He had just been given the news that not only had a battle taken place between Andesha and Gladue, but steps were being taken that could only escalate the conflict. Troops were on the move, and both sides thirsted for combat. Aegea stood on the brink of the first full-fledged war between kingdoms of men.

"We must do something," he pleaded to his audience, which included three kings, eight army commanders, and a handful of other important men, ranging from governors to magistrates. "Surely you cannot plan to sit idly by while the alliance crumbles."

The group of men looked at one another, but not at Trand. It was evident that they had planned to do exactly that.

Trand threw up his hands in frustration. "Two nations are lining up to destroy each other and you do nothing!" he scolded. "Has the whole world forgotten the menace of Sindus in the east?"

"What would you have us do?" asked King Duras of Nefala. "As distressed as we are over this turn of events, we cannot overlook our responsibilities to our own people. Their safety comes first, and I will not allow my brave soldiers to die in the Bould at the hands of other men. My men are clothed in rokul skins, and it is their bodies I would rend and destroy, not the flesh of my brothers." The other kings in attendance, King Ralus of Anafaline and King Poce of Rubia, nodded at these words, giving their whole-hearted agreement to the sentiments.

"I would have you do what you have always done," answered Trand, his dark eyes blazing with righteousness. "I would have you defend your realms by helping your neighbors defend theirs. If there be no other course, then march your armies as one into the Bould and demand a cessation of this foolish conflict at once."

"Now that is madness," said Duras. "The dam has broken Trand, and no effort can hold back the river. Any man that stands stubbornly in the way will be swept away by the deluge."

"Indeed," said Ralus. "What responsible King would send his subject into the jaws of the wolf?"

"A king that knows that death is coming, either sooner or later. Mayhap it will come sooner for some, but it will come later for all." Trand suddenly seemed very tall, like a king himself, though he had no one to command. "Please, I beg you, use what strength you have to put an end to this catastrophe in the north, lest this calamity engulf the whole world."

A silence filled the great hall. No one spoke, and the slightest movement or breath of air could be heard. The soft clink of chain mail that reverberated as men shifted their weight rang out like crashing cymbals. Finally, Duras stood, his necklace of kaito horns swinging back and forth in front of his exposed chest.

"As king," he began, "I am bound by the law of my people to partake in no battle in which I would not be willing to spend my own son. I can assure you; this venture does not merit the wasting of my son's life."

"Perhaps your son should be the one to answer the question of what merits his blood," Trand retorted. The listeners ignored the interjection.

"I will not participate in this," Duras continued. "Furthermore, I am withdrawing my portion of the border guard. If Andesha and Gladue wish to fight over the Bould, then let them defend it as well. As it is, no Nefalian blood will stain that soil."

"I must concur," said Ralus, standing next to his fellow king. "I also am withdrawing all of my strength from the Bould, to better hold my own borders and remove them from danger."

Poce of Rubia nodded in agreement, but said nothing. He had already issued such orders, and most of his men had already left the area. He was actually willing to do what Trand suggested, but he would not do it alone. Unilateral action would make no difference. In fact, it would complicate matters, because instead of two kings fighting, you would have three.

Trand looked around the large room, holding each man's eye for a fleeting moment before moving on to the next. His black garb stood out in stark contrast to the white marble that made the greatest part of the room. He had his hands on his hips, as if inspecting small children before sending them off to school. Finally, he said, "Do as you will. I will waste no more time here." His disgust was conspicuous. "I can see that my past counsel and aid give me no credit for the future." He turned and made for the door.

"Where are you going?" asked Poce.

"I go to war, since that is what must be done, and I go alone, since I have no aid from the kings of men." Then he was gone.

≡ ≡

Lendum was sure he was falling to his death. The light grew brighter as he tumbled, the water crashing all around him, a constant assault on his ears. At last, he fell into a great pool, deep enough to accept the plunge without injuring him. Quickly his feet found the bottom, and as his every muscle ached for him to breathe, he extended his legs with the last of his energy, and forced himself upward. The light became brighter and brighter as he rose to the surface, a brilliant radiance that penetrated even his closed eyelids. Just when his lungs could endure no more, his head broke the top of the water, and he encountered the sweetest air he had ever experienced. Lendum coughed uncontrollably, but still managed to take in several deep breaths between the spasms of his chest. Slowly the tension in his muscles dissipated, and he felt better. He tread water for several seconds, the waterfall crashing down behind him with significant power, making him bob up and down in the pool. Scarcely able to believe that he was alive, Lendum at last opened his eyes to see the midmorning sun shining down on him. The pool he was in was no more than twenty feet across, and much less salty than the stream that had coursed through the cave. Ahead of him, he could see that the stream continued at a very lazy rate, probably eventually making its way to join the Tundish. After resting for a few moments, he kicked his legs and dogpaddled to the nearest bank. He pulled himself onto the ground, and fell face first into some very soft grass. Abruptly he turned on his back and let the sun warm his pruned flesh. The day was already very hot, and his skin dried quickly, making the cold leave him. Suddenly he laughed. He laughed long and hard, filled with a joy that he had not known before. He was alive! He had risked unknown peril, and he had survived.

"Thank you!" he cried out, not knowing for sure whom he was thanking. "Thank you! Thank you! Thank you!" Soon he was on his feet and dancing about, his damp, limp hair swinging around his head, droplets of water flinging wildly from his clothes. His boots squished with expelled water with each hop.

All at once, he stopped his merriment. Something caught his eye in the grass. A pale, opaque blanket of discarded skin lay amongst some large stones not far from the water. Lendum took a cautious step forward for a better look, and what he saw confirmed his suspicions. He had seen one of theses before, when a traveling carnival stopped near his home in Gladue. They had had one on display, and the adults and children alike had flocked around it, each having paid a farthing for the privilege of viewing it. Everyone had gasped in astonishment at the sight of this thing, which seemed so foreign and horrendous that it brought excitement because of its repulsiveness. This thing made nightmares, but it was terrifyingly real, and Lendum was not excited, but horribly frightened. This was no carnival show near his home, but the wild lands of the Bould, and this thing so close to him carried with it the potential for a gruesome death.

A molted rompu skin lay near the rocks. The creature had come from the water, and rubbing its snout on the rough stones had broken its scales and shed the old skin, from which a new creature emerged. This skin looked to be about ten feet long, which meant that the monster that had shed it was now twelve feet or more in length. The empty eyes stared at Lendum, still carrying a threat that was palpable.

"I must get away from this water," he thought, and ran toward a cluster of trees several dozen yards away, his pack bouncing against his rear end. The trees were packed together tightly, and it would be difficult for a beast as bulky as a rompu to enter.

Once within the safety of the grove, Lendum could see that the waterfall that had delivered him to this spot was really two. A surface stream flowed several feet above the pool, depositing its water as it had for time beyond measure, but its cascade hit the opening to the cavern that Lendum had traversed. That is why the saltiness of the water was so diluted in the pool, and why rompu could tolerate this particular body of water. Rompu tended to avoid briny waters, preferring the freshwater of lakes and marshes.

Lendum took a moment to assess his situation. He still had his sword, which was good, but his bow and quiver were gone. The pack he was carrying was empty, the contents lost to the water, so there was no more lamp or oil. He was glad he had eaten all of the food, but he was at a loss as to how he would acquire more. He also had the waterskin draped over his shoulder, though it too was now empty. The stream was available, but the evidence of rompu made drinking from it full of great danger. He had several cuts and scraps on his hands and knees, but none of them were serious, and in any event, the saltiness of the water had cleaned and closed the wounds. He was without food and water, he did not know where he was or even the date, but he was whole and healthy, and most importantly, not drowned.

He decided to head southeast, along the course of the little river, that being the most logical choice. He needed to find people, and if he was right about this stream being a tributary of the Tundish, then the settlements along that large river offered the best chance of finding help. He still had his bags of gold coins, and he could find a soft bed and a hot meal in the villages of the river.

He began to walk, keeping the stream a stone's thrown to his right, and avoided the tall grasses. Rompu would most likely not venture this far from the water, but it was too much of a possibility to let down his guard. One second in the jaws of one of those monsters would render all of his toil for naught.

He walked for some hours, until the sun passed the noon and began its slow descent into the west. The sun beat down on him, and the heat that he had found so pleasant before now made him quite uncomfortable. His clothes, dried out of the water of the pool, began to remoisten with sweat. His belly protested its emptiness, and his mouth cried out for water.

"I could drink from the stream," he pondered. "The taste would be sweeter now, and some drink could even fill my aching belly, tricking it for a little while." He had just decided to risk the rompu for this, when he saw something that made his heart jump for joy.

A tiny tendril of smoke rose in the distance to the south, right in his path. The line of smoke was quite narrow, and Lendum reckoned that it did not originate from a campfire, but from a chimney. He was near a homestead, and possibly near salvation.

He forgot his plan to drink from the stream. Lendum slung his waterskin over his shoulder again, and ran with all of his speed toward the plume of smoke. After a half mile, he could see it; a small cottage made of stone. As he drew closer, he could tell that the home was nice and well maintained. Thick, burgundy curtains covered the windows, trimmed with lovely white lace. Carved characters that Lendum did not recognize decorated the dark, wooden door. The roof was thatched with thick bundles of grasses from the plains, and a very high chimney of stone belched the smoke that he had seen from afar. Behind the house was a small barn, connected to a tiny corral that held two lethargic horses that grazed leisurely on the thick grass. All around the small dwelling the wilderness was cut away in a neat circle, and lovely flowers grew here and there, making this entire sight seem quite out of place amidst the unsettled plains. Were it not for the smoke, Lendum might have easily passed right by this place without ever knowing of its existence.

Tentatively he approached the broad front door. A plank porch stretched the width of the house, and held a small chair, a washtub, and several logs of wood. A pair of blue cloth shoes sat side by side next to the doorframe. A coat of arms hung over the door; a golden haired man with a hand full of five stars. The words of the motto were written in the same characters that graced the door.

Lendum put his ear to the door, listening for any sound coming from within. There was an occasional thump or scrape, but no voices. He felt apprehensive, but he knocked on the door with three quick raps.

After an incredibly short period, the door swung open, and there stood an elderly woman. She wore in an ill-fitting dress of homespun fabric, but it was very clean. Two embroidered roses covered her chest, the stems of the flowers crossing over her heart. A white apron with frilly lace edging covered her thighs. Her hair was uniformly gray, and very long, done up in a great bun about her head. Rosy cheeks complemented her face, flanking a round, cute nose. She had lines on her forehead and around her mouth, telling of a lifetime of daily laughter. Indeed, she laughed now, a robust, joyous sound that made Lendum smile.

"Greetings!" she said loudly, and then laughed again. "Would a weary traveler wish to rest his feet and refresh himself in my humble home? I would be most happy to invite you."

Lendum bowed low. "I thank you, Bould-mother," he answered, very proper and demure. "I have been traveling for many days, and would cherish the lady that would offer such a timely relief from my toil."

The lady clapped her hands together and jumped up and down with excitement. "Most welcome traveler, my name is Amarut, and with open heart I bid you enter. Leave your troubles at the door, and come in that we might talk a while."

Lendum quickly stripped off his luggage, including his sword, and placed them by the door. Next, he slipped off his leather shoes and set them on his pack. Amarut stepped from the doorway, motioning for Lendum to enter. He stepped into the house with a feeling of welcome and complete calm.

The interior of the home was immaculate. There was little furniture, with only a small table with two chairs, a long bench with cushions along the wall, and two additional chairs near the hearth. A small hutch fit neatly into the corner, full of perfectly stacked plates and bowls. Four windows let the light enter from the outside; two on each side of the fireplace, and two others set into the opposite wall. The curtains that Lendum had noticed as he approached graced all four of the windows. The walls were paneled with wood, and were richly carved with writing and objects of beauty, showing no pattern or any discernible nuance. Another door led into the back of the house, which Lendum assumed was the bedroom. Everything was clean and tidy, without a speck of dirt or a crumb of food anywhere. On the table sat a vase with fresh flowers, golden and glistening in the dim light of the fire. Their aroma was invigorating. Lendum felt most at home, comfortable and wanted.

"You have a lovely home, Bould-mother," he said with sincerity. "My name is Lendum, and I am pleased to know you, and am honored that you have welcomed me into your house."

Amarut giggled again. "Please sit, kind sir, and I will prepare a little something to eat. It is near the supper hour, and you must be hungry as well as weary."

"Indeed, and thank you," he said, taking a seat. Amarut began to move around the room, fetching crockery and comestibles for their supper. Soon there were plates and cups, knives and forks, a platter of food, and a pot of hot beverage arrayed on the table. Lendum noticed that all of the crockery matched perfectly, without a chip or a fleck of paint missing.

The platter had a good, round loaf of bread, a block of ripe cheese, and some small, oblong berries that Lendum did not know. Amarut soon joined him at the table, and poured liquid from the pot into the two cups. It was brown, hot and steaming. "Let the drink cool a bit before you drink it," she warned. "It is enjoyable hot or cold, but the heat of the day may make it disagreeable to sip a warm beverage." The steam brought the smell to Lendum's nose, and he found it refreshing. He felt his hunger lurch forward.

"Eat, guest," said Amarut. "There is no need to be too polite or formal. Satisfy your needs as if this was your own house, and then we can have a good talk."

"As you wish," said Lendum. Those were the last words he spoke for some time. He was unsure whether the food was of exceptional quality, or if his hunger was exceptionally great. In either case, it was the best meal of his young life. The bread was soft and sweet, melting in his mouth. The cheese was faultless, tangy and firm, delectable. Lendum picked up one of the berries with curiosity. It was cool to the touch, deep purple in color, and squishy between his fingers. He popped it into his mouth and bit down. The sweetness that erupted from it was so sudden and overwhelming that he winced. Juice dribbled down his chin.

"Are you alright, dear?" asked Amarut.

"Yes, Mother," he answered, coughing the words as he spoke. "Pray, what are these berries? I've never eaten them before."

Amarut smiled with pleasure. "They are a mouthful, yes? They are grapes, and they are quite common in my homeland south of the mountains. I seeded them here in the Bould, and was most pleased when they grew tall and plump."

"Where are you from, may I ask?"

Amarut smiled kindly, showing her deep dimples. "Eat now. You are so thin. We can talk all you desire later."

Lendum did as she bid. Not much encouragement was required. He finished his plate, and without any prompting, he refilled and finished it again. He drank three cups of the strong beverage. The liquid was soothing to his stomach, and seemed to relieve his aches and pains. He wanted to ask about it, for it was as foreign to him as the grapes, but he resigned to wait until his hostess was more prone to discuss it.

When the meal was over, Amarut deftly cleared the small table. Lendum rose to help her, but she dismissed the notion as pure nonsense. "I will handle this. No need to worry yourself. Please, have a seat by the fire and be comfortable. Rest. You must be tired."

With a full stomach and a feeling of safety for the first time in days, Lendum did feel a sleepiness steal over him. He sat in the wooden chair by the fire, sinking into the cushions, and placed his bare feet on the small stool before him. Instantly he felt his eyelids grow so heavy that they seemed to be made of iron.

"I feel safe," he thought. "I'm safe for the first time in days. How many days, I wonder?"

"Mother, what day is this?" he asked groggily.

"Why, it's the fourth of August, the first day of the sign of the warrior."

"Five days," he thought. "I was in that tunnel for five days." Then sleep took him.

＝ ＝

When Lendum awoke, it was dark. The fire was burning brightly, fighting the growing chill of the night. Amarut sat in the chair next to him, watching him intently. The very moment he opened his eyes she asked, "Would you like some more tea?"

Lendum put his feet on the floor and sat up straight, fixing his posture.

"Tea," he said. "I thought that it was tea, but was not certain. I had heard of it, of course, but had never had it before."

"Do you like it?" she asked, concerned. "If not, I can make you something else."

"I like it very much. I would be delighted."

Amarut's face broke into a great grin, making her cheeks dimple again. Quickly she pulled the kettle from the fire and poured a cup, then handed it to Lendum. He thanked her, and then eased back into his seat, sipping the tea in silence.

Suddenly, Amarut became very serious. The laugh lines in her face smoothed out, which oddly made her seem older. "You have suffered a great loss, and now must endure hardships too bitter to be pressed upon one as young as you."

"You have a keen eye, Bould-mother," but he said no more.

"You may stay here as long as you wish," she said hopefully. "I could care for you, if that would please you." Her eyes reflected her earnest desire for companionship: to see to the needs of another.

Lendum considered her offer briefly, but knew he could not stay. The soldiers could be looking for him, and to remain here put this kindly woman in jeopardy. "You are very kind, but I must go, and soon." He paused for a moment. "In truth, you should leave as well. This land has grown dangerous."

Amarut looked sidelong at her guest, a faint smirk on her lips. "There is nowhere else I want to go. My husband has been with Miro three years come September, and I have no children. This is my home, and I will not leave it, no matter what threats bear down on me."

"War has come to these lands," Lendum mumbled. "A war between men. In such circumstances, there can be no guarantees of safety. You should come with me to Ghar, and then make your way to a new home, so you may live out your days in peace."

Amarut laughed suddenly, the flames of the fire dancing in her eyes. "I know there is war," she said, "and I know from whence you came, Lendum Noveton." Lendum's eyes grew wide at the sound of his full name. "I have been expecting you, though I must say your arrival is much later than I anticipated."

"Expecting me?" he said, flabbergasted. "How could you know...?"

"Trand," she answered before he finished. "The wise wanderer. He told me you would be coming, and that I must help you when the time came. That was more than two years ago. I was beginning to think that you weren't coming."

Upon hearing this, Lendum thought that he must be dreaming. This story was preposterous, but Amarut seemed so sincere that he doubted his rational mind. He certainly remembered Trand; how mesmerizing he had been, how he had warned them to forgo the mine and all of its wealth, and how he had correctly predicted the very events that had transpired. Was it really so outrageous that the man could have foretold of his coming to this house in the middle of the uncharted lands? His mind said that it was indeed outrageous, but his heart was not so sure.

"If you know there war," he finally said, "then why do you stay? You have provided me with assistance, as you were bid, so now staying is needless."

"Trand told me that helping you would lead to my own safety," she said matter-of-factly. "I need not fear war or weather, man or beast."

She laughed again, a loud, raucous burst of merriment that seemed to rattle the walls. "How glorious!" she exclaimed. "You have come, and now I can live out my days in peace and plenty! And all for nothing more than displaying kindness I would have gladly shown you anyway!" She clapped her hands together with pure joy.

Lendum was somewhat baffled by her blind belief. Nevertheless, he decided to let her have her faith without debating the matter. "What else did Trand say? Was there any message for me?"

"Yes," she said, still smiling. "Stay away from Ghar. The people there know you, and they may find you out. Instead, make for Tibar, farther up the river. It is a closer destination, only five days from here."

"What am I to do once I get there?" he asked.

"I know not. He said nothing more."

Lendum took a sip of his tea. He had been in Ghar several times, often with his father, making very large, noticeable purchases. Furthermore, as the major settlement along the riverbank, at the site of the only significant bridge across the Tundish, Gladue was likely using it as a staging point. The village would be teeming with soldiers, more likely as not. Trand was wise as well as foresighted.

"Are you to leave on the morrow?" Amarut asked with concern. She clearly did not wish him to go.

"Yes, Bould-mother. I am afraid I must. It seems my presence here could be putting you in danger."

"Then sleep now, and rise rested and ready to undergo the beginning of your trials."

Amarut had prepared a bedroll on the floor near the fire. Lendum drained his cup of tea and rose to go to it. Amarut stopped him by placing her soft hands on his face. "You are very young to be a man, but a man you are, all the same. I know you will make me proud." She hugged him gently, and Lendum was a little surprised when he hugged her back.

"Thank you, Bould-mother. I am blessed through you."

Lendum then lay down and fell into a deep, dreamless sleep.

⇒ ⇐

The next morning Lendum awoke feeling refreshed. A washtub full of clean water and a towel was nearby, as were his boots, scrubbed clean and even polished. Another kettle of tea bubbled over the fire, and the aroma of fresh bread filled the room. Although Amarut was obviously out of bed, she was nowhere to be seen.

Lendum washed his face and hands in the tub, and dried them with the towel. He then put on his boots and opened his pack. It was stuffed with food, much more food than he would need for his five-day journey to Tibar: dried grapes, fresh bread, a little salted beef, a quarter of cheese, apples, nuts, and even a jar of pickled eggs. Lendum was repacking this food when Amarut walked through the front door.

"Good morning, Lendum!" she almost sang. "Did the night treat you well?"

"Very well, thank you. You seem to have been very busy this morning," he said, gesturing to the goods at his feet.

"Oh, that was nothing. The real chore was getting Timo saddled and ready to ride, but the task is done."

"You're giving me your horse?" asked Lendum in disbelief.

"Well, to be perfectly honest, he was my husband's horse, but he no longer needs a horse in the unknown, I reckon!" she said with another burst of laughter that made Lendum smile.

"You are too generous. Let me pay you some gold for these provisions."

"Nonsense!" she said, shaking her head. "I have plenty. Trand told me to treat you as if you were my own, and kin don't take money from kin, lest they reap bitterness." She moved quickly to the tiny hutch, bringing out dishes for breakfast. This time Lendum did help, and she did not protest.

Soon they were eating. The food was much the same as the night before, but Lendum did not mind. The taste was as good as he remembered, and just being in the same room as Amarut was soothing.

They cleared the table together after eating, speaking courteously to each other as they did so. When the chores were complete, the inevitable moment of his departure arrived, something they had both tried to postpone. Lendum gathered his goods, and started to walk towards the door when he realized that his sword was gone.

"Where is my sword?" he asked.

Amarut put both of her hands to her face, making a perfect circle of her mouth. "Goodness me!" she exclaimed. "I was nearly forgetting. Half a moment, please."

She went into her bedroom and immediately returned with not one sword, but two. "I fear your blade was ruined by the salt," she said apologetically, even though it was in no way her fault. "I wanted to polish it, but I cannot even pull it from its sheath. Perhaps with time I could repair it, but…" She trailed off, the rest being unnecessary. "I would like you to take this one, also my husband's, from his days as an officer in the army of Tolone."

Lendum began to say no, but could see from her expression that any argument would be in vain. Reluctantly he took the sword, and pulled it halfway from its sheath. An exquisite weapon, the blade was impressed with the same characters that he knew from the front door. The hilt was long, at least a foot, and was wrapped tightly in soft, black leather. A ball of steel that fit nicely into the palm made the base of the hilt, so the sword could be quickly directed from one side to the other, making the weapon easier to wield in close combat. An eagle with outstretched talons was embossed on the ball, a symbol of great strength and power. The blade itself must have been more than three feet in length, and it was heavy. The weapon was ideal for one that knew the *atum rah,* easy to turn and misdirect strikes while lashing out with a furious counterattack. He doubted that he could wield this sword as well as he could his shorter blade, but perhaps with time he could.

"Thank you." He could think of nothing more to say. She placed a hand on his shoulder and turned him, leading him gently toward the door. She opened it for him, and the light breezes of the early morning caressed his body, making him shiver briefly.

Amarut clutched him tightly. "You take care now, and don't be rash in your judgments. Remember that even though you have lost those closest to you, there are still people in this world that love you."

"I will remember," he said, and meant it. "Thank you for all you have done for me. I shall not forget it. Perhaps someday I can return to you, at a time when there is nothing pressing and we can spend a little time without the urgency of these days."

"I'd like that very much," she replied. She kissed his cheek, and with that, they parted. Lendum mounted the speckled horse named Timo, and rode into the southeast, following the flow of the water.

THE RETURN TO GLADUE

The commander of the Gladue Third Battalion, a veteran named Ione, had seen plenty of battles. He had personally slain more than forty rokul warriors, and had seen entire companies of them from time to time, but he had never felt as troubled as he did now. Andesha was assembling across the river. From where he stood, atop the hill at Tine Vort, he could see at least four full regiments, and more were almost certainly coming. A counterstroke was imminent. He had already ordered riders to head north to Egel to summon the men there to come and reinforce his position. That addition would give him four thousand men to guard this passage. Another thousand of his troops lie to the south at Elur, but he felt they should stay there, knowing that a cross at the marshes was much more likely than a thrust close to Charwood.

Ione was perturbed that he had so few men to guard such a long front. The job was easier by the fact that there were so few places to cross the river. Only three bridges spanned the Shae along the Bould, and perhaps two to five places existed where the water was shallow and tranquil enough to ford the river, depending on the season. Even so, five thousand men was a small force to spread, especially given that an attack was virtually assured.

For three days, Ione had watched the enemy assemble. They had made no move to seize the bridge, but it was only a matter of time. When the time came, many men would die, perhaps himself included. Fearless riders atop galloping steeds would stream across the bridge, breaking shaft and bone, bent on gaining the opposite bank with willful determination. Would the brave men of Gladue be able to stop them? Who could say? At present, his numbers could make an adequate defense, but if the force across the river continued to grow…

He put it out of his mind. There was nothing to be done about it but hope. He expected more men any day, but the Bould was a frontier, and the problems that could arise by simply crossing it were numerous. He would do the best he could to fulfill the wishes of his sovereign with the resources at his disposal, or he would die in the attempt. That was his duty, and he always did his duty.

≡ ≡

Lendum found his journey to Tibar most enjoyable. For three days, he had traveled along the path of the stream, and he had never regretted once the decision to go this way. The scenery was breathtaking. Hills rolled over and again, a vast sea of green surging ceaselessly. Random thickets of maple and birch dotted the hilltops or the valleys, faultless in their unspoiled beauty. After leaving the humble abode of Amarut, he saw no other signs of settlement: only the raw loveliness of an unadulterated countryside. The horizon seemed to go on forever, uninterrupted by anything greater than the tall, dancing grasses.

He had been ambivalent about taking the horse (not tot mention the saddle and bridle), but Timo was fast becoming an indispensable friend. Once free of the corral, the animal grew less lethargic, and could travel for many miles at an even trot without any rest. He understood commands, always behaved prudently, and gave Lendum an ear for his thoughts, which was invaluable for the long hours of solitude.

Lendum would speak to Timo often during his travel. He told him everything that had happened since coming to the Bould. He told him of his loss, his family, and his good fortune to be still among the living. Timo never answered.

"What am I to do?" he asked Timo as they trotted along, making good time through the waving grass. "I arrive at Tibar, but what then? Do I become an apprentice, learn a trade and live out my life earning my keep from my skill?"

Timo snorted, shaking his head in irritation, a gesture that seemed resoundingly negative. Lendum chuckled.

"Well then, friend, should I get my own farm, marry a comely lass and have fat, happy babies as my father did?"

Again, the horse snorted, shaking its head vigorously. This time Lendum did not chuckle.

"What else is there?" he asked Timo. "What am I to do with what is left of my life?" The horse did not respond, but his father's voice did.

"Remember us," it said, sounding so forlorn as to be pleading. "Remember us, that we may be avenged." The specter of the murderous captain's visage entered his thoughts, filling him with rising anger and hatred.

"How?" Lendum asked, but the voice was gone

His hand strayed to the hilt of the sword at his hip. He drew it, and with a metallic twang, the blade emerged and glittered in the failing sunlight, glowing like steel hot from the forge. Timo stopped his trot and whinnied, seemingly giving his approval. Lendum looked at the long weapon in his hand, and suddenly something came to him that had never come before; purpose.

"Soldiery," he said aloud, eyes still locked on the blade. "How else do I punish those responsible for the reprehensible murder of my innocent family? I will fight for Gladue, and make Andesha bleed for her deeds. Perhaps I can even the score before my own life is spent."

Timo stamped the ground with his hoof, but made no other sound. With great disinclination, Lendum replaced the sword in its sheath, but left his palm on the hilt. The feeling of the leather against his rough hand was right and comforting.

Lendum dismounted, deciding to make camp for the night. He unloaded his packs, and removed the horse's saddle, giving Timo the chance at a well-earned repose. He contemplated tying the horse to a nearby tree, but knew that it was unnecessary. They had established such a wonderful rapport so quickly that he felt that he could trust the animal not to wander off. He was correct. Timo never got more than a dozen yards from Lendum's bedroll.

Lendum sat and ate a leisurely meal while Timo munched on the plentiful grass. He lit no fire, fearing that he could set the whole countryside ablaze, and out of his desire to avoid attracting any attention to himself, though that possibility was unlikely. It seemed that this part of the world was utterly abandoned. As the sun crept slowly toward the western horizon, Lendum felt an indescribable sense of isolation come over him, accompanied by a sense of profound peace. His cold mind had found what it wanted; the purpose that would drive all of his future endeavors. His sleep that night was undisturbed.

Two days later Lendum stood on the northern bank of the Tundish River, just as the crashes of thunder reached his ears from a menacing storm approaching from the north. Darkness engulfed the area, making it appear like evening in the early afternoon. Lendum could see no activity in the village across the river, as if all of the people had scurried away from the hazard of the storm. Tibar had closed itself against the impending tempest. Lendum feared that he might be forced to wait out the storm exposed to the elements, for no one appeared that could bring the ferry to his side.

There was no bridge here, and there was no other place to could cross for miles. Save swimming, his only options were to wait or travel south to Ghar, which was what he hoped to avoid at all costs.

"Oy!" he shouted into the wind. "Oy! Ferry master! Are you there?"

"Aye!" answered a grizzled voice. "What want ye?"

Lendum could see no one, but he assumed the voice he heard came from the small structure near the dock. The raft-like ferry bobbed with the current, held in place by a thick rope. Lendum made his response in that general direction.

"I wish to cross, of course! Hurry now! The storm is nigh!"

"It's s silver piece to cross!" the voice cried out. "Show it to me! I shan't get soaked for any less!"

Lendum sighed audibly. He dug into his pocket and plucked a single gold coin from the bag there. He held it above his head. Even in the dim light, it was obviously gold.

The door of the dock house creaked open, the rusty sound of the hinges brought to Lendum's ears by the rising gusts of wind. An old man shuffled out and made straight for the ferry. He moved with care, but with reasonable speed. He was evidently determined to get his gold *and* avoid getting soaked.

A small area on the bank had been cut away to allow the ferry to dock on the Bould side of the river, and Lendum went down to it, leading Timo by the reins. There he waited patiently for the old man to bring the ferry. He was obviously a river man, for he handled the ferry with little difficulty, despite the current and the rough water caused by the wind. A guide rope as thick as a man's wrist was strung across the river, looped through an eye hole attached to the ferry, but the line was never drawn taut, since the man's skill kept the simple craft on such an even course. As the raft slid up to the bank on Lendum's side, the first drops of rain hit splattered on the deck.

"Come on, boy," said the ferry master. "Mustn't dilly-dally. Load up and let's be gone." Lendum led Timo onto the raft, who handled the circumstances better than most horses would. Once aboard Lendum turned to see the ferry master with his hand outstretched. "Let's have it, young master." He had crooked joints, and a back that was curved into a terrible hump, but Lendum also noticed the glint of steel that hung at his belt, barely concealed beneath his weathered cloak. Even old men went armed in this part of Aegea.

Without pause, Lendum placed the coin in the man's gnarled hand.

Aged fingers snapped closed, and nimbly placed the piece in the breast pocket of the ferry master's cotton vest. A delighted smile passed over the old man's face, revealing a mouth that held few of the teeth Tor had given him. "Eating well tonight, I am!" he proclaimed as he covered his balding head with the hood of his cloak. Agilely he began to pole the raft away from the bank, until the wooden craft was at the mercy of the current. Only the skill of the handler kept them on an even keel, across the river rather than with its flow. The rain began to fall more frequently, large droplets that crashed sporadically along the floor of the raft. Lendum placed his own hood over his head.

"If I may ask, Master," Lendum said, his voice loud to eclipse the rising wind, "where will you be dining? I could use a reprieve from the monotony of my field provender, not to mention a warm bed, and perhaps even stabling for my animal."

"Aye, I would say you do, at that," the man replied, his voice even despite his struggle against the river. "There is a small inn, run by the good Master Alton, where many folk of the village come by of an evening to pass the time. Good ale is brewed by the Master, and I believe he would even be willing to stable your beast, provided you can pay, of course." A strong wind blew, making Lendum lose his balance for the tiniest moment. Timo splayed his legs, making himself sturdier against the gale.

"Where can I find this inn?" Lendum asked once he had reclaimed his footing.

"Folks call it the Old Mill, on account that we used to grind wheat there when I was a lad. 'Twas near ten year ago that Alton bought it and began hosting folks and housing travelers. You could see it from here, had the sky not been turned this unnatural dark." The rain began to fall in torrents, and lightening flashed overhead just as the raft pulled alongside the dock. The ferry master yanked himself up with surprising dexterity and began pulling the raft ashore with a strength Lendum would have thought impossible. Thunder crashed so near that the air was electrified, warning all fools to take shelter before the storm washed them away. Once up the bank the rain was falling so hard that Lendum could barely see the ferry master before him, and his voice seemed far away as he spoke.

"Follow me, and I will lead you to the Mill!" he screamed. "It's not far! Step lively!" Off he went at a trot, his boots throwing up strings of muddy water from the gathering pools. Lendum followed as best he could, leading the faithful Timo behind him. Small cottages lined a slender street, each with shuttered windows that let only the narrowest lines of light escape from the interior. Lendum guessed that Tibar was a quaint, riverside village, lovely to the eye and full of friendly, helpful people that were eager to share a tale or a mug of brew. However, in the ferocity of a summer storm everything seemed dark, dead, abandoned.

After some minutes, a stone path emerged that led up a small hill. At the top a great windmill stood, the cloth long since removed from its blades. Lendum could see that wooden additions were built all around the original stone structure, so now the whole building was quite large, easily able to hold several dozen guests. They followed the path right to the front door of the Old Mill, and Lendum tied Timo to the hitching post by the entrance. "Wait here boy. I won't be long," he whispered. Timo nodded his head slowly, enduring the storm but clearly in misery from the pelting rain. Lendum turned and followed the ferry master through the front door.

The light inside was dazzling after the darkness of the storm. The room they were in was circular, at least thirty feet across, with a vast, brightly burning fireplace built into the far wall. In the center of the room the huge gears of the windmill still stood, though the grinding stone itself had been removed. A dozen round tables were spread throughout the room, spaced evenly, each with a lamp and four chairs, and a basket of clean cutlery placed in the center. An elderly man and a boy sat alone at a table to the left playing Queens and Aces. The boy was barefoot, and the legs of pants were rolled up to the middle of his calves. He had a head of wavy blonde hair, and his skin was pale and freckled. The older man was barely animated, seeming to not even breathe, and moving only to play the chosen cards from his hand. Other than those two, no one else was present. The storm had made most folks decide not to brave the weather for any entertainment. The two looked up from their game for a brief moment, saw the ferry master, and nodded a rudimentary greeting. The young boy waved a hand at the expansive room, apparently inviting them to sit wherever they wished.

The ferry master sighed with exasperation. "Corce, you best snap to and see to this gentleman. He's got a horse to stable, if it hasn't yet been washed away."

The boy, Corce, never looked away from the cards in his hand. "How many days?" he asked, as indifferently as could be imagined.

Lendum was not sure. He did not know how long he could linger here, but he did know that a small break for the horse, not to mention himself, was warranted. He finally settled on an answer. "Two days."

"Can you pay?" Corce asked now, still not looking up. He played a card from his hand onto the oak table.

"Yes, he can pay," said the ferry master. "He's paid me, you worthless runt. Would you please see to the horse now, before I have Alton remove whatever hide you have left?"

Corce still did not move or look up. "Right after this hand. I'm really playing the game of my life."

The ferry master rolled his eyes. "Youth is wasted on the young," he grumbled, then realized that Lendum had heard him. "Beg your pardon, sir," he quickly added. "Didn't mean you in particular." Clearly, the lack of hospitality embarrassed him. "Let me fetch the master of the inn. He'll set things to rights."

The ferry master went through a door on the right, shuffling along with adroit speed. After a few moments, a very large man entered, just as a tremendous crash of thunder shook the building. The man had to duck his head to avoid colliding with the frame of the door. The ferry master followed him, looking like a child next to his prodigious girth. The man wore an old apron, stained from years of use, and the sleeves of his red and black striped shirt were rolled up past his elbows, revealing bulging forearms rippling with muscle. His pantlegs were tucked into his leather rain boots, and he carried a barber strap in his hand. His expression indicated that he was not against using it.

"Why is it," he said with a booming voice that could rival the thunder, "that the only son given to me must also be the laziest boy whatever walked the surface of the world?"

At the sound of that voice, Corce did look up. Cards fell from his hand and fluttered to the floor. Without speaking, he scurried toward the front door and flung it open, running into the storm coatless and hatless, neglecting to even put on his shoes. Such was the fear inspired by Alton the innkeeper. The door slammed shut after his exit, making the fire on the far wall dance with the wind.

"My apologies, young sir." The man approached and extended his meaty hand. Lendum took it without hesitation. "I am Alton, and welcome to the Old Mill. Elden the ferry master tells me that you require two day's lodging. Is this correct?"

"It is. My name is Lendum, and I think two days is as long as I can stay. I am going to Ashtone, and I have been already six days in the wild. I expect eight more days before I reach the capital. Is that an accurate guess?"

"Yes, I would say so, if the weather is kind. If I may, you come from the Bould?" Alton asked this with the tiniest amount of trepidation.

"I do," Lendum answered, not offering any further explanation.

"I know you are tired, and probably wish to take a little rest. But at supper, perhaps I could persuade you to have a little talk, and maybe give some clarity to some of the wild rumors we have heard over the past week. I would be most grateful. In fact, I would be willing to reduce the cost of your stay, if you would grant me this small courtesy."

Lendum considered a moment. Any talk of the Bould was potentially dangerous, but the offer of the discount was most tempting. He had very little money, and every opportunity to save was welcome. He finally elected to postpone the decision for the time being. He was weary, soaked to the bone, and he wanted above all else to simply be warm and dry, and to rest.

"Let me think on it for a time," he said.

"Yes. Yes, of course you should," Alton replied, seemingly unbothered by the delay. "Supper will be in a few hours. Come, and let me show you to your room. This way, please." Alton led him through the door on the left, down a narrow hallway with doors every few feet on both sides. At the end of the hall on the right Alton opened the last door with a key and led Lendum into a charming little room with a table and chairs, a small bed, a quaint fireplace, and a tall bureau in one corner. Thick curtains covered the room's only window, but Lendum could still see the flashes of lightening outside as the storm continued to unleash its fury. The hearth and the wall cradled a stack of dry logs, and Alton began to build a fire in the tiny fireplace. Soon he had a good blaze going, and the welcome heat did much to relieve Lendum's cold and discomfort.

"I hope this is to your liking, Master Lendum," said Alton as he made his way to the exit. "Supper should be ready around six, so you've a good four hours to rest before then. I'll send Corce when everything is prepared, to see if you'll take your meal in the parlor or in your room."

"Thank you, Alton. You have a fine inn, and I am pleased to be here."

Alton nodded with sincere gratitude. "You are too kind, sir. I apologize once more for Corce. Most of my business comes from local folk, and although that does not excuse rudeness, it does explain why he can be so lax in providing the service all of my guests deserve. Familiarity can be a curse, if you take my meaning."

"I understand, and please, think no more of it. You have shown attention to this stranger greater than he deserves. Thank you."

Alton nodded once more and then took his leave. Once he was gone, Lendum slid the lock on the door and put his luggage on the floor by the table. He slipped out of his rain-soaked clothes and spread them over the chairs, moving them as close as he dared to the fire. He then crawled into the soft bed and let his body sink into the feather mattress. He had barely begun to register how comfortable he was before he drifted into a deep sleep.

In the south, the desires of two kings were colliding with potentially dreadful results. The battle over the Bould was becoming a war as all chances for peace evaporated near the Andola Marshes.

Quereus was a gifted battlefield commander. His evaluation of field position and strength was unmatched by any in all of the armies of the world. His weakness lay not in tactics, but in overall strategy. The decisions he made were sound once the battle was joined, but his foresight was flawed. The enemy was not static, as they appeared to be in his own head as he formulated his plan. He had conceived of a plot to sweep south of the marshes and enter the Bould undetected. Never had he considered that his adversary might attempt a similar maneuver.

That is precisely what transpired. About four days from reaching their proposed crossing point at Boso on the Tundish, scouts returned in the early morning that reported a large host approaching their position. An army of Gladue, legions of infantry and bowmen, were coming toward them, about twelve thousand strong. Quereus commanded ten thousand men on horseback, and though he could give battle under most conditions, the terrain this close to the marshes was sloppy and unstable, and not conducive to the swift movements required to make his force the better. The one advantage he had, he presumed, was that his enemy was ignorant of his presence, and that would be gone in a matter of hours. Prudence demanded that he withdraw before he could be engaged, and allow his men the chance to fight another day.

Would that day come? Quereus already knew that the main crossing at Tine Vort was held against him, and attempting to cross there would be disastrous. The force heading toward him, if unchecked, would make any future thrust south of the Bould impossible. They could even invade

Andesha, and cause considerable damage before forced to withdraw. In any case, turning back now gave all of the initiative to the enemy, allowing them the leisure to strike where they wanted, whenever they wanted. Andesha would be on the defensive, perhaps permanently. The War of the Bould would be over, lost by Andesha not after a great battle worthy of song, but after slipping away like ashamed dogs, unwilling to endure hardship and risk.

Quereus could not face his liege after such a withdrawal. He spilt his force into two parts, sending the smaller south with orders to flank the enemy and strike from the rear. His main force was sheltered in a little valley hidden from view of his enemy for several hundred yards. Quereus hoped to let the men of Gladue march to him, and then charge into their ranks before they had time to position themselves for an adequate defense. Surprise was his best tool, and he would exploit it fully and do as much damage as possible.

Hours passed. The men grew restless. Horses bucked with nervous energy. The sun climbed in the sky, hidden now and then by wisps of clouds floating in from the east. At the crest of the valley, lying prone with two of his captains, Quereus could see a storm far off. Some time would pass before it would come upon them, and for that, he was thankful. The ground was already too soft for his liking. Attempting cavalry movements in the rain and the resulting quagmire would be more than foolhardy.

At last, Quereus heard what he had been waiting for; the unmistakable sound of marching companies. The rhythmic whump-whump-whump sound of thousands of men coming closer and closer made the heart of even a veteran like Quereus beat with a speedy pulse. He gave the signal for his men to mount their steeds and make ready. Silently seven thousand men climbed into the saddle, grasped spear and shield, and breathed deeply, calming themselves for what could be their last moments before venturing into the unknown that awaited them after death.

After twenty minutes, Quereus could see them. The heads of lines of men, bobbing in union with each step, crested the far hill and began to fill the valley before him. Quereus slithered out of sight, and then sprinted down to his men, his captains on his heels. He mounted his own horse, and gave the order to advance. The men of Andesha spurred their steeds, and with a light gait began to walk up the hill, going with open eyes into the waiting grip of death. Right before reaching the top, Quereus signaled his bugler, and with a mighty blast from his horn, the bold horsemen plunged into the valley with their enemy. Amid the awful ruckus of galloping hooves and screaming voices, the men of Gladue gasped and stared, unable to believe the force streaming towards them. The trap was sprung, and the surprise was complete.

Lendum awoke to the sound of Corce hammering at the door.

"Master Lendum, sir? Are you awake?" The voice was humble, perhaps making amends for earlier impoliteness. "The master bids me to ask you to supper, if that be to your liking."

Lendum sat up and rubbed his eyes. He had slept so soundly that he could barely remember where he was. The rain had ceased, and the fire had burned down to mere embers. He tried to answer, but the first attempt at speaking produced only grunting gibberish. He cleared his throat, and then said, "Please tell the master that I will be joining him in the parlor shortly."

"Very good, sir!" the boy answered with genuine excitement. Lendum could hear his footfalls as he scampered back down the hallway, eager to deliver the news.

Lendum got to his feet, stretching as he did so and opening his mouth in a wide, gaping yawn. He felt of his clothes, and was delighted to discover that they had dried almost completely. He began to dress, and all at once, he felt incredibly hungry. He had eaten a meager breakfast at first light that morning, but nothing since, and he was quite famished.

Lendum also decided that he would engage Alton in some talk. He could receive the discount and save some money that he desperately needed, but he could also hear some news that would be of great benefit. He had been out of touch for some time now and truly had no idea of how events had unfolded beyond what he had seen with his own eyes. A little more information could place him on a more enlightened path.

Lendum unbolted the door and stepped into the hall. The first thing that struck him was the smell. The mixed scents of various foods assaulted his nose, and his mouth watered. He could detect roasted meat, fresh bread, and something else that was akin to cinnamon. He turned and walked hurriedly toward the parlor.

As he got closer, he could hear voices. Many voices. The low murmuring of what had to be several men and women got louder with every step. A part of him warned that he should return to his room. The other part of him (the hungry part), forced his legs to make the last few strides that carried him into the main dining area.

Lendum could not believe his eyes. There were not ten people, which would have been reasonable, or even twenty people, which would have been possible, but no fewer than forty people crammed into the Old Mill. People lined the walls, sat upon the hearth, and squeezed shoulder to shoulder around every oaken table. One table was empty, and Alton stood beside it, looking quite beside himself. Corce and the old man that had been playing cards earlier were bustling all around the room, serving plates of food and pints of ale, collecting used dishes, and pocketing tips hand over fist. Sweat poured from their brows, and even Alton seemed a little winded.

At the sight of Lendum, the talking gradually ceased and folks stared. Forty unique faces with various forms of interested expressions watched shamelessly as Lendum stood and fidgeted. Lendum suddenly felt very guilty, though he had no idea why. Alton quickly came over and put a stout arm around his shoulders, pulling his ear close.

"I am very sorry about this, Master Lendum," he whispered. "That blasted Elden went and blabbered to the whole village and I reckon anyone with two feet and a heartbeat turned out to get a gander at ye."

Lendum looked around the room and against the far wall he espied Elden the ferry master. He raised his pint in greeting. From the glazed look in his eyes, Lendum figured that that pint was not his first. He nodded in acknowledgment.

"I completely understand if you wish to retire back to your quarters and have your supper there," Alton continued, sounding even more apologetic. "No man can relax under this kind of scrutiny, and a kind-hearted stranger like yourself certainly doesn't deserve this."

Lendum most definitely wanted to return to his room. All of the curious eyes on him made his heart flutter and his skin crawl. But to leave now would be rude, and would probably arouse more suspicion than sitting and being personable for an hour or two. The worst of the damage was done, he reckoned. Besides, he was still very hungry, and Corce was presently preparing what could only be Lendum's supper at the lone empty table.

"I will stay, and make myself available for questions, if that be the price of my time here." He put on the largest smile he could manage. "The smell of your fare has tempted me too greatly. I would be most grateful if you could find time to join me. I would rather not sit alone."

Alton's grin nearly spilt his face in two. "I would be honored. Please, this way."

Alton led Lendum to his table, and once there, the host served his guest a most splendid supper. Roast pork and potatoes, boiled carrots and cabbage. Lendum chewed every bite long and thoroughly, savoring every delicious morsel. The ale was as good as Elden had promised, even better, with only the slightest hint of bitterness. Alton dutifully sat at the table with him, watching his hungry visitor refresh himself on his well-prepared food. For half an hour Lendum spoke not at all, and soon he could feel fewer and fewer eyes on him. The residents of Tibar, apparently realizing that no juicy gossip was going to come forth during the meal, turned their attention elsewhere. Slowly the room returned to a collection of chatting locals rather than a silent mob bound to watch one stranger eat. A few games of cards resumed at some of the tables, and a few songs broke out here and there, making the atmosphere more festive. Lendum found this version of the Old Mill most enjoyable, unlike anywhere he had been in his life.

After an hour of undisturbed eating, Corce came with desert; hot tea with cakes of cinnamon and peaches, topped with a glaze of honey. Lendum found them to be the perfect end to the meal, not too sweet, and light enough to enjoy even with a full belly. After he had eaten two of the dainty cakes, Alton leaned close.

"Tell me, traveler," he whispered, "is there war in the Bould?"

The room began to fall silent again, and all of the people present inched closer, straining their ears to catch every word. Lendum felt the eyes on him once more, and a feeling of claustrophobia clenched his heart. He was a little frightened, but he pushed it away, forcing the butterflies in his stomach to settle. He summoned all of his will, and announced:

"Yes. War has come to the Bould."

That opened the floodgates. Questions came at Lendum from all directions with startling rapidity: not only Alton, but also from anyone that was bold enough to ask. Rarely could Lendum ascertain who had posed a query, so more often than not he would answer to a direction rather than an individual. What was the war about? Who was fighting? Who was winning? Where were the battles? How many had been killed? Was the war nearly over? Would it last for years? Lendum answered what he could, but usually the response was vague or unsatisfying, like 'I know not,' or 'I couldn't say,' or even 'No one knows.'

For two hours, Lendum was pounded with questions. Mercifully, persons seemed to be less interested in him than in the general condition of the Bould itself. He answered the questions that did concern him as simply and succinctly as possible: He was fleeing a homestead to avoid the conflict. He described his home as the same plot where he had met Amarut, and he made it clear that this was too close to the fighting to suit him. This explanation seemed to convince most people, as they could fully understand evacuating a war zone. Steadily the questions moved away from him, and became broader in scope. People asked the same things twice or even three times, but Lendum endured it all with admirable patience. In time, he rather liked being the focal point of so much attention; that all of these good-natured and curious folks could be so interested in the news brought to them by a single traveler. In fact, he realized that he felt better now than he had in many days. He was clean and dry. He felt rested and had a full belly. He did not feel that peril could come upon him unawares at any moment. He began to relax, and allow himself to become distracted. He grew so at ease that he did not notice the tall, hooded and cloaked figure snake through the crowd and make its way down the hall toward his room.

At 9 o'clock, the crowd began to thin. Men yawned and stretched, and spoke of the chores that needed to be done at first light. Elden the ferry master approached Lendum's table, his stagger giving elegant testimony to the amount of ale he had consumed. He smiled broadly, showing the gaps in his teeth, and slapped four silver coins on the table.

"I don't know about the rest of the wide world," he slurred, "but here in Tibar we generally trade five silver coins for one of gold. You overpaid for your crossing, and I'm pleased to give you the difference."

Lendum accepted the coins and looked at the old man with gratitude. "Thank you, Elden. You are an honest man, and skilled in your labor. I am better for having met you."

Elden slapped a bony hand against Lendum's shoulder and lurched for the door. Soon the other patrons followed, and then an exodus of customers led to the desertion of the Old Mill. All that remained were Lendum and Alton, and Corce, who was busy cleaning up dirty dishes and spilt ale.

"I must apologize again, Master Lendum," said Alton in a low voice. "Like I said, most of the folks I get in here are local, and the few travelers that stop are traders from the south or east, who spend one night and return the way they came in the morning. To have a traveler from across the river is rare." Alton suddenly laughed. "Ol' Elden hasn't been paid a fare in weeks upon weeks! No wonder he was so ripe for the ale tonight!"

"I understand the curiosity, I assure you," said Lendum, "and truly, no apology is necessary. Your hospitality has been most gracious, and the food was the best I've had for some time."

"You're too kind. I must say, the questioning you endured here tonight was no doubt a tiring labor, and though it grieves me greatly that you dealt with it, it has been a boon to me. Never have so many folks been packed within these walls, and for that, I am indebted to you. Allow me to make your stay here a gift to show my thanks."

Lendum could hardly believe his ears. "Are you certain of that? That is a very kind offer, and I do not wish to impose upon you in any way."

"I insist. The business your presence here has given me exceeds by a great amount the fees for your room and board, and the stabling of your horse. Consider it a trade if you will. You feed the ears of the gossipers, and I feed their mouths, for a price."

Lendum snickered. "So be it, Alton. I accept your proposal. I don't know how to thank you."

"No need," Alton replied, waving his hand. "Now, you must be tired, and I have many things I must tend to before I retire for the night. Will you need anything else this evening?"

"No, I am more than content." In truth, Lendum felt exhaustion flow over him. Answering questions repeatedly was strenuous work, he had discovered. "I think it's to bed with me." He stood, stretching as he had done when Corce had awakened his so many hours ago. "Good night, Alton. I'll see you in the morning."

"Night, Master Lendum," he said, and turned his attention to helping Corce clean up the bits of food and spilled drink that littered the dining hall. Lendum proceeded down the narrow hall, passing all of the doors until he came to his own. He opened his door, and was amazed to see Trand sitting at the small table, his legs crossed and his hands steepled in front of his face. The sword of Tolone, the gift from Amarut, lay on the table before him.

Lendum stood in the open doorway a moment, his mouth agape. Finally, Trand said, "Are you daft, boy? Get in here and close the door. If old Alton learns that I am here I won't get a minute's peace until I leave."

Obediently Lendum shut the door and latched it, and sat down in the other chair at the table.

"You've done quite well," said Trand, speaking like a mentor. "To have come so far is impressive, yet I fear there is much more you must face before your trials in this matter are complete."

"Who are you?" interjected Lendum with a fascinated tone of voice.

"Why, I am Trand. Do you not remember me?"

"I know your name. I guess what I mean to say is, *what* are you? You are not a man, at least not wholly. Who among men can see the future and show up at opportune times knowing things that no one else could know?"

Trand smiled with pleasure. "*What* I am is too great a matter for you, or for anyone. Some call me wizard or warlock, but these terms are off the mark, for I am greater than these are, yet at the same time even less. All you ever need know is that I can be trusted, as I hope I have already proved."

Lendum thought a moment. The same enchantment he had experienced when he had first encountered the mysterious Trand fell over him. He indeed wanted to trust Trand, and his heart told him that he could. His words were as sweet as honey, and felt as true as a pronouncement from the gods.

Nevertheless, his remaining independent thought cried out for rational consideration. What did Lendum actually *know?* Trand had made some accurate predictions, it was true, and he had seen to it that Lendum would receive aid when he most needed it out in the wild. Amarut had known he was coming, and had tended to him, giving him succor at a time when grief and weariness had nearly done him in. Trand had been responsible for these things, but was it luck, or deception, or genuine acts of trustworthiness? Lendum was not sure.

Just then, a familiar voice chimed in. He had not heard the voice for some days, but he knew it as well any. His father's voice spoke to him.

"Son, listen to him. Never has he given you reason to doubt him. He tried to warn us. Do you not remember? Before all of the hardship, death and destruction, he warned us to forgo the bounty and live in peace. He asked for nothing, and gave us wise counsel. Will you not hear him now? Will you not listen?"

Lendum decided that he would.

"You have certainly impressed me with your foresight," he said as noncommittally as possible. "Why are you here now? Do you not have bigger concerns other than my well being?"

Trand's face changed to one of utter disbelief. "Good heavens, no!" he exclaimed. "Nothing could be of greater import! You have been reborn, Lendum Noveton. Can you not see it?" Trand swiftly reached into his cloak and produced a rather large, round looking glass. He thrust it before Lendum's face.

Some time had passed since Lendum had seen his own countenance. He was astonished to see a stranger staring back at him. A man, whose features were drawn and grim, had replaced the thick-faced boy he expected to see. Whiskers graced his face, short but thick, and the light hair that had always been so short was now longer and lank, soiled from travel and toil. The most telling difference was the eyes. The eyes he saw in the mirror were ice blue, cold, and almost heartless. At some point while he was not paying attention Lendum had become a man, and a perilous man from the look of it. He tentatively placed a hand to his cheek, feeling the scruffy beard there with disbelief.

"Do you see?" Trand asked again. "The boy you thought you were is gone. A man has usurped him, and that man is destined to accomplish great deeds." Trand abruptly removed the mirror from Lendum's view and flung it into the fireplace, where it shattered and erupted into flames, igniting the kindling and starting a roaring fire.

"You may not be a wizard, but surely you do not fault those that think so," said Lendum, shielding his face from the bright light and intense heat. "Such magic earns you that reputation, no matter what you may be."

Trand said nothing. He only sat with the hint of a thoughtful smile on his lips.

"What would you have me do?" Lendum finally asked. "I had intended to go to Ashtone and join the King's army, but if you have another suggestion I will hear you out."

"My purpose here is not to alter your path in the slightest, but rather to offer help that will make your journey and duty less taxing." Trand moved his fingers rapidly, and suddenly a medallion appeared in his palm. It was silver, perfectly round, with a worn impression of the Eagle of Gladue embossed on its shiny surface. *Shama* was written in the characters of Gladue, a word loosely translated as captain. The talisman glittered in the firelight. "Keep this with you at all times. The officers of the army of Gladue are each issued one of these with their commissions, as a sign of their status. Show this to the recruiter, and tell him that it belonged to your father. He will think that he was a captain in his youth. This will speed your acceptance."

"Must I really use trickery to achieve my ends?'

"No, of course not. As I said, it will *speed* your acceptance. You could do well by your own merits, but time is short and we must go forth with all possible haste."

"Why the hurry?" Lendum asked with curiosity. "Less that a fortnight has passed since hostilities commenced, and I think perhaps it could already be finished, if there's any hope of mercy in the world."

"You're faith does you credit, but it is misplaced," Trand answered, all at once very grave. "This is not near finished, and in fact, it has grown larger while you have eaten and answered inane questions." Trand ran his long, pale fingers through his hair, placing his raven-black locks behind his ears. "I fear that on this day all hope of reconciliation and reason has fled. A battle has been fought, the casualties are great, and I am terribly vexed by the anguish of the fallen."

The room was silent for a moment. Lendum could hear the wind outside, giving its last breaths as the storm died. The fire crackled and sizzled, sending random sparks twirling about the hearth.

"I had planned to stay here two days, but if things are as bad as you say, I suppose I should go forth in the morning, and leave this charming place."

"Actually, I would ask that you leave at once, but you should take some rest while you can. You can leave at first light, or even earlier if you can manage it. If you can slip away without too many people knowing your doings, so much the better."

"Is secrecy that essential?" Lendum asked. "I am but a single soul traversing the earth. Who would care at all about my comings and goings?"

"There are some people with great power that would be very interested in your whereabouts," Trand said with a twinkle in his eye. "Do not forget that you are the legitimate heir of a vast fortune, and the name Noveton is well known in the halls of kings. They will be looking for you, for so long as you walk free in Aegea, you are a threat. They would stop at nothing to silence your voice and put an end to your claim."

Another moment of silence passed. Lendum heard the slow, steady breaths of his visitor. At length he spoke.

"Very well. I will depart on the morrow, and make my way to Ashtone with all speed. I will enlist in the King's army, and do my best to avenge my family." He paused, and then asked, "What will you do?"

Trand smiled as he replied. "Very little can I do directly, though it grieves me to be idle in such mighty matters. Rest assured that I will be pushing others into place, just as I have pushed you. Only through the deeds of men will this tragedy end, and if men come up lacking, then the kingdoms of Aegea will fall, one by one. Be mindful that there are greater concerns than your vengeance."

"Will I see you again?" asked Lendum, suddenly afraid. He was tempted to ask Trand to accompany him to Ashtone, but knew the chances of that happening were slim, if not laughable. Trand seemed one not to suffer the company of anyone for very long.

"You shall see me again," he replied, and Lendum's heart was comforted. "It could be a long while, but we will meet at some point, and the moment will be as opportune as this reunion has been. I hope that when the time comes you will be as accepting of counsel as you have been on this occasion."

"I will try," said Lendum, then he laughed. "In truth, I believe I will have little choice in the matter. Your words carry much weight. At times I feet enchanted."

Now Trand laughed, and clapped his hands together in his amusement. "So much the better!" He stood suddenly. "I am off. Much to do and no rest for Trand, not yet at any rate. Mind your business, and remember, do not speak the name of your father. The Noveton name carries peril, and you should bear it only in your heart. Farewell!" And then he crossed the room with amazing speed, spread the curtains, flung open the window and leapt out, leaving Lendum alone and rather breathless. Trand had been with him for scarcely twenty minutes, and already it seemed like a dream. Were it not for the open window and the smell of the rain-washed timber and cobblestones, Lendum would have believed it nothing but a hallucination.

He was all at once very sleepy. He returned to the main hall of the Old Mill, and informed Alton that he would be leaving before daybreak the next morning. He requested breakfast in his room, and that Timo be saddled and ready as well. Alton was visibly disappointed, because he had hoped for another night full of guests eager for food and ale and rumor. Nevertheless, he assured his guest that all would be done. Lendum said good night, returned to his room, and fell into the soft mattress of his bed. He was asleep almost at once.

A HERO EMERGES

Besides the element of surprise, Quereus had another advantage of which he was unaware. The army of Gladue, though formidable and made of the strength of three full regiments, was not an invasion force. They had orders to guard the Sampi at the three primary crossings of the river, each regiment given the responsibility of a different crossing. As such, a commander led each regiment, but the entire force had no overall marshal. As a result, when the horsemen of Andesha crested the hill two hundred yards away at full gallop, yelling with murderous rage and leveling their lethal weapons, the men of Gladue froze. When orders finally came, they were haphazard, uncoordinated, and contradictory. The battle was nearly over before the first man fell.

The horsemen crossed the open valley in seconds, and as they approached the green-uniformed ranks of their enemy, they slowed not at all. With unforeseeable malice and hatred worthy of a more deserving adversary, the lines of Andesha crashed against the brave men of Gladue, who stood their ground in the face of the onslaught. Arrows fired in haste and fear flew overhead, but sailed askew and rarely found a target. Wide swaths of carnage divided the army into pieces, until finally the entire force crumbled into pockets of dazzled soldiers. Hundreds died in the initial charge, pierced by spear, hewn by blade, or trampled by armored stallion.

Nevertheless, the men of Gladue were bold, and professional, and though their hearts were at first immobilized by fear, their sense of duty at last loosed their limbs. They formed circles of defense, and soon they had put aside despair, as the men in brown were unhorsed and slain. The battle waxed and waned, shifting from one side to the other, the advantage being passed from one side to the other and then back again.

After two hours, it appeared that the battle was a stalemate, but then the tactics of Quereus proved the better. The contingent he had sent to flank the enemy arrived, fresh and eager for battle, fell and perilous. Three thousand horsemen smashed into the enemy from the opposite side, and all of the defenses of Gladue were undone. Men ran from danger to danger, as Andesha slowly encircled the remnants of the enemy. At last, the men of Gladue began to throw down their arms, surrendering their weapons in hope of mercy. The Battle of Andola Marches was over.

Quereus, pleased that his courage and cunning had carried the day, ordered his men to stay their weapons. He rode to meet with the two remaining captains of Gladue. The third died while trying to rally his troops. The terms of surrender were thus: All remaining soldiers of Gladue were disarmed. They were allowed to return to their homes, provided they agreed to do the work of interring the fallen of both sides. At last, Quereus made a solemn oath that Andesha would never again cross the Sampi into the territory of Gladue, if Gladue made a similar oath.

This last condition betrayed the horror of what had just occurred. Dead men covered the floor of the valley, slain in every conceivable manner, a grotesque display of butchery that no man had ever witnessed before. Such appalling slaughter made Quereus realize that this war must be contained in the Bould. Trying to defend the entire border that the two kingdoms shared would be folly, and would invite even greater massacres that could dwarf the havoc already unleashed.

Seven thousand men lay dead on the field. The army of Gladue was decimated. The army of Andesha was victorious, but substantially weakened. The work of burying the dead lasted two days.

With favorable weather and a well-rested horse to carry him, Lendum made the journey to Ashtone in only six days. He passed the time talking to his reliable friend Timo, perusing his thoughts and speaking them aloud to gauge the reactions of the horse. The feedback was not frequent but often enlightening.

As he approached the city, he was awestruck. He had never been to Ashtone, and though he had heard stories of its beauty and grandeur, his mind could not appreciate the magnitude of its description. Even from far off, he could perceive the high walls and the castle beyond. As he got nearer, he passed fields of wheat and barley, tall and ready for harvest. Small cottages dotted the landscape, some of wood, others of stone, but each well tended and surrounded by busy persons performing tasks. The road widened as he drew closer, until he felt very small traveling within its breadth.

After some minutes, Lendum saw the gates of the city. The massive oaken doors were swung wide, but a dozen soldiers in full regalia stood at attention blocking the entrance. Lendum gave the reins the slightest tug and Timo checked his pace, slowing to an unhurried walk. The enormous walls loomed, at least thirty feet over his head. He craned his neck to see the top, where a parapet protected men patrolling the perimeter. If the evidence were not before his eyes, he would not have believed men capable of building such a marvel.

The city guard, which had stood as still as statues, took aggressive stances once Lendum got to within twenty yards. "Halt!" one of them cried. "Dismount and state your business!"

Lendum did what he was told, quickly and humbly. "I have come to offer my service to the lord of this land, King Jonas of Gladue."

"Approach," the soldier ordered. Again, Lendum did as he was bid. "How are you called?" he asked once Lendum stood before him.

"My name is Lendum Cetus," he replied as naturally as he could. The guard eyed him suspiciously for a moment, though Lendum surmised that this guard, by virtue of his duties, was suspicious of everyone, and was not alarmed by anything Lendum had said or done.

"You are aware," the guard said, "that a state of war exists between our realm and the Kingdom of Andesha, and any who volunteer at this time will almost certainly be thrust into battle, to spill blood or have his blood spilled for our lord?"

"I am aware, although the point is moot. I passed my eighteenth year last March, and the time of my service has come due. I have little choice, though I would choose to serve in any event." Lendum was an able liar. It was not in his character, but he showed a skill just the same. He had already deceived this man regarding his name and his age. He could be untruthful about nothing more fundamental.

"So be it," said the guard, who was well past his fortieth year. Guard duty was his reward for many years of faithful service, no doubt much of it in dire peril. "Go forth, and turn right at the stables. There you will find the mustering. Already many await inspection before assignment. Your wait could be long." The guard returned to his post without any more words.

Lendum led Timo through the gate and walked about fifty yards before coming to the stables. Capable of storing five-hundred horses within the city, this structure was another sight that made Lendum gasp in astonishment. The stables existed to hold the horses used by the king's message riders, his personal guard, visiting dignitaries, or other honored guests. However, during this time of hostilities, the stables were completely full, often housing two animals to a stall to make room for all of the extra beasts brought forth by volunteers.

Lendum left Timo with a stable boy that seemed busy to the point of being frazzled. After saying goodbye to his equine friend, he proceeded down the right hand alley as the guard had instructed, and soon came to an open courtyard, and a sea of men. Hundreds had gathered, and from the look of them, they represented every strata of society. Silk-clad gentlemen rubbed elbows with peons wearing ill-fitting homespun garments. The old mingled with the young, as the generations overlooked their differences to better unite for the common cause. An atmosphere of anxious anticipation engulfed Lendum. The willingness of men to kill and die for the crown was blatant.

The mass of men were fed into ten orderly lines, moving at a slow pace. Uniformed soldiers were doing the inspections, checking each recruit for physical signs of weakness or illness, asking questions that could help determine where and how and individual might serve, and separating those with experience from those with none. They measured strength, mental awareness and reaction, and asked about skill with blade or bow. Soldiers dressed in the dark green tunics of the palace guard moved through the crowd, directing men to this line or that, based upon their answers and appearance. Over an hour passed before one of them addressed Lendum.

"What is your name?" he asked curtly, feeling the muscles of Lendum's arm and shoulder.

"Lendum Cetus," he replied, offering no more.

"Were you born of Gladue?" he asked just as curtly. He now studied Lendum's eyes, holding them wide with his thumbs and forefingers.

"I am a son of Gladue, yes."

"Who was your father, and what was his trade?"

"My father was Seleus Cetus. He was in the king's army." Lendum showed the soldier the medallion that Trand had given him. The soldier's eyes betrayed surprise for the tiniest moment.

"A captain?" he asked. "How came you by this?"

"My father bequeathed this to me shortly before he followed Miro. I am his only son. His only child, in truth." Lendum was calm and convincing as he lied. The soldier did not doubt him in the least.

"Past the lines for you, and through the arch to the training hall." He pointed to the huge arch ahead as if Lendum needed directions, though only a buffoon could not realize which arch he referenced. "You are exempted from general inspection and may proceed to skill assessment." The soldier gave Lendum a white pebble and went on to the next recruit.

Lendum proceeded through the large courtyard, leaving the mass of men behind. He passed the long lines, and passed the tables covered with different colored stones, until he came to the enormous archway. Beyond this opening, there were large doors, guarded by two soldiers. Without any prompting, Lendum showed the stone to them, and they allowed him to enter without a sound. The doors creaked on their hinges, and Lendum walked into the training room.

Inside was an armory. The spacious room had high walls with wide gaps in the top to allow the entrance of light and fresh air. Dozens of styles of weaponry covered the walls. Spears and shields, truncheons of various weight and design, war axes and hammers, and dozens of swords were evident. On this day, however, the weapons were idle. Men sparred with wooden swords. At a hastily constructed archery range, men fired arrow after arrow into figures of men made of hay. Others threw spears at targets, or thrust them violently into bags of sand, measuring the depth their force had achieved. Recruits moved from station to station, performing acts of mock war while warriors of the crown were judging every stroke and shot, scoring each combatant by skill, endurance, and sheer brutality.

A soldier of great size accosted Lendum. "What training do you have at arms?" he asked with a voice so inherently menacing that Lendum could not help but shiver.

"Sword and bow," he answered succinctly.

"Do you use shield?"

"No. Only broadsword." Lendum gestured at the sword of Tolone at his hip.

"Have you ever been outfitted for armor, mail or plate?"

"No. Never."

"Very good. To that station, please. You begin with the sparring."

Lendum went where he was told. There a man took his sword, and gave him a wooden replica. It was light, and Lendum could handle it easily. He was matched against another recruit, a lad that appeared even younger than he was.

Lendum entered a wide ring, as did the boy. His opponent was obviously scared, and literally quaked with fright. Several others that were waiting their turn milled about, watching with great interest. Three soldiers stood evenly around the ring, ready to score the fighters.

"Score three hits to be victorious," one announced. "Leave the ring and you forfeit. If you lose your feet, you will be pointed. Do not strike a downed opponent. Do you understand?"

"Yes," Lendum said smoothly. The boy only nodded. His shoulders sagged under the weight of his sword and shield, as if they were made of Nefalian steel rather than pine.

"Begin."

Lendum felt no animosity toward this complete stranger, yet he attacked with vehemence. Once the battle began, he no longer saw the rosy face of a teenager, but the grizzled countenance of the Andeshan captain that had murdered his mother. Lendum swung his sword with all of the force he could summon, yet still kept his control and his footing. His adversary blocked the blow with his shield, but the power of the strike sent him reeling, until he stumbled across the cobblestones that lined the circle. With one swing, Lendum had defeated the boy.

"Match!" cried the soldier closest to the boy. "The victor stays."

Lendum next found himself against an older man, perhaps in his late twenties. The newcomer showed no fear, but Lendum still handled him easily. With grace and elegance, he bested his foe without yielding a single point.

Lendum faced five opponents in a row, the maximum a man could face during skill assessment. As the matches progressed, he felt more and more at ease, until the fighting became somewhat of a routine. This semblance to doing mundane tasks did not go unnoticed by the observers. Lendum garnered new respect as he dispatched each new fighter with ease. He did not tire or betray weakness. He was daring and fearless, or at the least, he controlled his fear, which was even more admirable. Every commander in the world wanted battalions full of men like Lendum; warriors that did their duty regardless of peril and could be counted on to perform their deeds with success due to their drive and ability.

Lendum made the rounds that day, performing acts of war at every station. The king's loyal warriors judged him at every skill, but his future was decided in the sparring circle. Lendum was to be an infantry soldier of Gladue. In addition, he was given a commission as company chief, due in no small part to his performance, and because of the medallion that he bore. Lendum would be in command of a hundred men before he had even bloodied his sword.

King Grindal was overjoyed to hear of the victory at Andola Marshes, costly though it had been. He was less pleased to learn that his chief commander had pledged to never again attack from the Sampi River.

"You have lessened our spoils by making me bound to honor this agreement, Quereus," the king scolded. "Now, what advantage we had is thrown away, and our men have died in vain. I should repudiate your actions."

"My lord, I do apologize, but our losses…they were so…" He trailed off. Quereus found it difficult to describe the repulsion that he had seen. "The horror of it haunts me still," he admitted. "That valley ran red with the blood of men from both sides, and I maintain that to venture that route again could only lead to more loss of life without making our objective any closer to achievement."

The king sat back in his throne, pondering.

"My Lord," Quereus stammered, "nothing more could I have done. Our army was made ineffective even with the victory, and I could not know if the enemy had reinforcements en route. To press on was not an option, due to our grievous loss of horses, and we could not hope to hold the field if set upon once more by our foes. Victory forced us to withdraw, and we had little hope of preventing invasion of our own soil even after our departure. I made arrangements that could spare the southern half of our country much misery, and now we need not deploy large numbers of troops to protect it."

Grindal said nothing. He was convinced that Quereus had done rightly, but he glowered at him anyway, trying to instill his marshal with a sense of fear. It was not working as he planned. Quereus was more than weary; tired from battle, from many days of travel in the saddle, and overcome with the anguish brought from such a terrible battle. The screams of the wounded and dying kept him awake at night, and the memory of the dead brought nightmares that disturbed his sleep even when removed from the din. If the king held him responsible for the losses and charged him with treason for palavering with the enemy, Quereus would count it a blessing. Then he would fall to the headsman, and the screams would stop.

However, Grindal had no intention of charging Quereus, or even reprimanding him. He had performed well, and his actions had improved the security of the nation.

"I suppose we have been fortunate," Grindal said grudgingly. "The enemy paid more dearly than we, and now we can concentrate our strength on the Shae. How do you propose we proceed?"

Quereus sighed deeply. He had not lain in a bed for two weeks, and not eaten anything but stale bread for five days. He was sore, famished, at the end of his wits, and he was not ready to concentrate on the next offensive while so many of his loyal men walked with Miro in the unknown. The king's expression was quizzical, and showed the smallest trace of impatience. Quereus could tell that he would receive no rest until he had satisfied his liege. He sighed again, trying to gather his thoughts.

"We can still flank the force at Tine Vort, if we can cross the marshes themselves."

Grindal's eyes grew as round as eggs. "That's ridiculous!" he bellowed. "There's no way a mounted force can cross those marshes. Half would be drowned or fall prey to rompu before they reached solid ground again. The journey itself would be so arduous as to make each man useless in battle."

"With good fortune, my Lord, our enemy will also think that." Quereus had learned a valuable lesson at Andola Marshes: Your opponent does not lie still while you move. He is also on the move, and deciding his next play. Think as he thinks, and the advantage is yours.

The king was not yet persuaded. "Even if they do think that unlikely," he said, "it helps us not at all, because they are right to think so. Our cavalry cannot cross the marshes."

"I completely agree. That is why which is why I am proposing to cross the marshes in boats, and leave our precious steeds behind."

Grindal's eyes seemed to grow even larger than before. "We are not foot soldiers! Every man that serves me values his horse as much as he does his own family, and would feel naked going into battle without them We may as well tell them to leave their swords behind as well."

"That is another reason I believe this will succeed. The surprise will be complete, and that is a tremendous advantage. Were it not for our ability to come upon Gladue unawares, the outcome of our previous engagement would have been ill for us."

Grindal continued to sulk, but there was no better plan in his own mind. To cross into the Bould required the bridge at Tine Vort, and as long as Gladue held the village then any assault would be beaten back with heavy losses without fail. They must go around. That meant either going through the marshes, or through the Charwood. Going through Charwood was madness. No one had even suggested it to the king, nor would anyone ever suggest it. When the time came, Grindal would think of that option all by himself.

But for now, the only options were crossing the marshes or admitting defeat. Grindal's ego was not yet ready to admit defeat.

"What do you need?" he asked, and Quereus began to speak.

= =

Lendum was in Ashtone more than a month, enduring intense training, being issued armor and uniforms, and getting to know his superiors and his subordinates. Though the physical demands were taxing, he relished the exertion because it made him feel more alive and in touch with himself than ever before. He enjoyed a feeling of sublime peace whenever he wielded his blade, and the men under his command quickly understood that their chief could carry the force of a hammer in his weakest whisper.

After weeks of preparation, the army that held Lendum's company finally received orders: They were heading for the Bould. News had spread that a great victory was won in the south, Andesha had retreated, and now the only territory in which soldiers could engage was the Bould itself, an area becoming known as "the bloody triangle." Three regiments, containing several veteran soldiers of the Andola campaign, were heading to Tine Vort to reinforce the troops already there. Many reasoned that the window was fast closing on the chances for Andesha to prove the stronger. After this new force arrived, the Bould would be virtually unassailable.

The army began its march on the first of October. It was a glorious morning, one that Lendum would recall with perfect clarity to the end of his days. The sun shone down brightly, reflecting a reddish glow off the helms of six thousand men, looking like the scales of a fearsome dragon. The cool air leftover from the autumn night fought against the coming day, but eventually lost to the warming rays. Thin layers of fog covered the landscape for miles around, an immeasurable blanket of moisture that would be gone within an hour. The road to the Bould lay before them like a ribbon, leading them to glory, or to their doom.

Lendum marched alongside his men, spreading words of encouragement and buoying spirits as best he could, though morale was very high. The men were rested, well fed, fully armed and confident. Many miles still lay between them and danger, and in the clear light of day the prospect of marching into the mouth of Kan Chatuk itself did not seem too daunting. Lendum himself felt a queer sense of elation, though he tried to crush it. Everything felt so right, almost festive. Many of the companies were singing songs as cadence. The uniforms were new and clean, never soiled by blood, sweat, or tears. The weapons were keen and glistening with oil, bound with flawless leather and held by solid hafts. The armor showed no scratches or dents, no stains, no defects of any kind. Everything was pristine, unblemished, and perfect. The only thing Lendum missed was his friend Timo. He had hoped that his sturdy companion would be able to join him, but alas, it was not to be. Only regimental commanders and men of higher rank rode horses.

The journey to the Tundish would take at least six days. Lendum would have assumed such a venture to take much longer, but he had never traveled with a military unit before. The men were in tremendous physical condition, and after they covered twenty miles the first day, Lendum was convinced that the full forty leagues would be behind them in less than a week.

The marches lasted from early morning until dark, with only a short break at midday to consume a quick meal. The men spent the evenings resting around campfires, telling stories and trying to unwind after a long day of labor. Lendum spent his time walking amongst his men, complimenting them on their performance and exhibiting pride in their achievements. In return, he received grateful grins and shy thanks.

It was on the evening of the second day that Lendum found something unexpected. As he walked around the fires, he saw a face that he recognized. For a few seconds he could not place it, but then he remembered.

"Corce!" he exclaimed, actually excited to see someone he knew, however remotely. "What are you doing here?"

Lendum could tell that Corce was having an equally hard time placing his face, but then dawning awareness passed over him. "Master Lendum!" he said, then noticed the two notches on Lendum's helm. Corce quickly got to his feet, and offered a salute. "I mean, Chief Lendum. It's good to see you again, sir."

Lendum returned the salute, and Corce seemed to relax a bit. "My father sent me south, after you left. He said that he had had enough of my foolishness." Corce's voice dropped to a whimper. "He caught me at the ale again. He claimed that the army could straighten me out. 'Tor knows I can't do it', he said. So here I am."

"How does the service find you? Is it to your liking?"

Corce's voice dropped another register, as if he wanted those near him not to hear. "Well, sir, to be honest, I don't care for it much. I am proud to serve Gladue, and to do my duty, but I do not know anyone here, and no one seems to like me very much. I miss Elden, and Old Bubo." He hesitated and added, "And my pa."

Lendum felt pity for the boy. He also missed his father, very much. He thought of him often, remembering all of the little things that make kinfolk so endearing. He remembered the way his knuckles would crackle as he hulled a pecan. He remembered the wrinkles that would form around his mouth and along his forehead whenever someone made a good jest. He could recall the long, warm evenings, just the two of them, watching the stars and guessing which one was Nisha and which was Herlion. Mostly he thought of the pride that he could see in Fordrun's eyes, even at the most humble of his youngest son's accomplishments. That was what Corce was missing: his father's proud expression. Before now, he had not longed to see it, but as he walked with this army, far away and heading to war, he did want it. Needed it. Lendum resolved to help him if he could, not only for Corce's sake, but also for his own. Secretly he longed for someone with which he could converse, no matter how shallow the history between them.

"If I can," Lendum asked, "would you like to join my company? Perhaps your days would be less grueling with a familiar face nearby."

Corce's broad smile answered before he spoke. "Yes indeed, sir! I'd be in your debt."

"Very good, then. I'll see to it." He slapped Corce in the shoulder and then continued his rounds.

Later that evening Lendum saw Corce's superior and made a formal request for his transfer. The request was granted. The captain seemed eager to get rid of Corce, though he gave no explanation why that was so.

The next day Corce joined Lendum's detachment during the march, and both boys found themselves less lonely. The feet of the men tramped in hypnotic rhythm, and songs broke out from cheerful throats. Only the men that had survived the battle of Andola marshes restrained their voices. They remained strangely silent.

The journey of six days to reach the crossing at Ghar went by quickly. Once over the river, the men were granted two days of rest and leisure. Lendum rarely left his tent, and when he did so his excursions were rapid and usually at night. Some of the men pondered at this, especially Corce, who found it quite odd. No one knew the significance of the small village to Lendum. He avoided the eyes of the townsfolk as often as possible.

After their days of rest, the men of Gladue continued their march, going at a much slower pace because the task became much more punishing. Once outside the perimeter of Ghar, civilization fled, leaving only the wilderness of the Bould. After the first day, there were no houses, no fences, and certainly no roads. Not even an oxcart path was evident. At times, the men were struggling through grass that was higher than their waist. Other times treacherous, rocky terrain threatened to twist ankles and strain knees. The songs of the men fell quiet, and before long, the yelps and curses filled the air instead. Fatigue descended on all, and when the first day in the Bould ended, scarcely anyone even bothered to light a fire. Hungry men ate cold meals, and fell to sleep with a growing dread of the coming day and the toil that it promised.

For over a week, the army traveled thus. The weather turned cooler, and for the first few hours of morning, the breaths of men hung over the marching ranks. The grumbling continued for some time, but eventually subsided, as it became clear that the incessant complaining did nothing to ease the passage.

At the end of the eighth day, the men bedded down with lighter hearts. The end was in sight. One more day of travel separated them from their destination, and once there, the duty would be something less strenuous than relentlessly marching through the wilderness. Everyone rested well, except for those unfortunate enough to draw the night watch.

Lendum was sleeping soundly when a horn rang out in the distance. It was the early morning, and the sun barely shone over the horizon, foretelling of its coming brilliance. He recognized the sound of the horn. The blaring noise came from a trumpet of Gladue, and it was sounding an order of retreat. Lendum quickly got to his feet, shouting orders as he rose.

"To arms! To arms!" he exclaimed, bursting from his tent and drawing his sword. Soon all of the men under his command assembled, shaking the sleep from their heads with astounding rapidity. By contrast, the other platoons were less swift in their readiness. Amazingly, some continued to sleep.

Lendum moved toward the sound of the horn, and his men followed, weapons at the ready. All around them confused and frightened men stammered and fidgeted, as ambivalence in motion.

Lendum continued toward the sound, the sun rising higher as he ran, making his sight better with every passing moment. All at once, he could see the source of the ruckus: A host of men of Gladue came towards them in total disarray. They came without any kind of formation, running madly, some without weapons or armor, others without even their tunics. They came with complete abandon, more as startled beasts than as men. At the sight of them, some of the other companies turned and fled as well, their fear getting the best of them.

At first Lendum could see no reason for the haste of the retreat, but then he heard a noise that froze his heart; hoof beats. Many hoof beats. A company of horsemen crested the far hill, several hundred strong, galloping hard, bearing down on the retreating soldiers. The thought of fleeing never entered his mind.

"Forward!" he ordered. "Forward, and save our countrymen!" Off he went at a run, and his men followed him. Corce ran beside him, matching his stride and screaming with a fearsome voice. Others not in Lendum's platoon, shamed by their cowardice or inspired by his courage, broke their own ranks to join his own. Other commanders and captains stood dumfounded, unsure what to do in such sudden circumstances. Most had new commissions, and the raw action of a battle had never been in their experience. The leadership fell to Lendum, made a de facto captain by virtue of his bravery.

Lendum led his men, his ranks now swollen to almost two hundred, until he reached the position he wanted: the top of a little dell that would force the cavalry to slow before they could slam into his lines. "Spearmen to the front!" he ordered. "Archers to the rear!" The men assumed their positions as quickly and calmly as they would during drill.

The horsemen of Andesha continued to close on their quarry. They paid no heed to the other force, most of which was as ineffective and confused as the one they were pursuing. The retreating men reached Lendum's line. Some stayed to join the vanguard, while others, lost in their own quest for survival, passed through and continued running as if their fellow soldiers were invisible.

"Make ready!" Lendum shouted. The archers fitted arrows and pulled the strings taut, aiming at the mass of steel and flesh stampeding towards them. Once they were in range, Lendum gave the order to fire. Bowstrings twanged like a massive harp as the arrows flew into the early morning air, cutting along their trajectory until they fell like stones into the advancing horsemen. Dozens fell with feathered shafts sticking out of their bodies. The cavalry checked their advance, slowing their pace significantly, but soon another volley fell into their ranks, and then another, until they realized that the very small contingent to their right was actually standing their ground and assaulting them. They charged at Lendum's position, determined to close the distance between them and render their archers useless.

Lendum, incredibly, ordered a charge of his own. "Down the hill!" he shouted, his voice steady despite the danger and mayhem. "Spearmen, run to meet them! Let them taste your steel!" At a run, Lendum raced down the hill, his sword high in the air, his men following without thought or question. Lendum looked back and was proud to see Corce running along with him, bellowing fearsomely. His eyes blazed with daring rage, and he bore his spear steadily. The bravery of his adopted friend was impressive, and a little surprising. The archers continued to fire, raining cold death from the sky. The lines of the horsemen were thinned considerably by the aerial onslaught, but a full two-hundred remained, and they rode heedlessly at Lendum's line, bent on avenging their losses. The riders of Andesha screamed as they approached, kicking up dust and shaking the very ground with the ferocity of their gallop.

Lendum stood in front of his heroic men, and watched the riders close in on him. In a curious quirk of mind, all of them slowly began to change. The face of every rider morphed into the face of the hideous one-eyed captain that had murdered his mother. Their expressions were obscene, and he could hear the curses that they threw down on him and his valiant followers. Hatred swelled in Lendum's heart, but it inspired no anger, or fear. Instead, the calm that he had experienced facing his father's murderer in the pecan grove filled his being and suppressed his baser drives, leaving only his cold lust for revenge.

When the men of Andesha were less than fifty yards away, Lendum raised the sword given to him and blessed by the kindly Amarut. He bellowed at the top of his lungs, "For Gladue, the mother of us all!" The men began to cheer, but Lendum's own voice was silenced when a broad shaft of light erupted from his blade, engulfing the oncoming riders with dazzling brilliance. Horses whinnied in protest, and the approaching lines began to crumble. The beasts veered off track, turned and fled, or simply stopped altogether. During this critical moment of turmoil, the spearmen of Gladue struck.

"Forward, men! Now is the time!" One hundred brave warriors crashed into the line. The confused riders were stymied by the uselessness of their beasts of war. Some attempted to dismount and fight on foot, but many others fought against the will of their steeds, trying in vain to force them to obey their commands. Bucking animals threw men from their saddles, giving injury or death in their madness. Even after the magical light was extinguished, the horses of Andesha were like a ship of war with no rudder; physically imposing but entirely beyond control.

The chaos of Andesha was offset by the professional deliberation of Gladue. Even with the fever of battle burning within them, they maintained their line, and once they reached their foes, they dispatched them with surgical precision and complete ruthlessness. Men were skewered by shaft and blade, and mangled underfoot. A very few threw down their arms and sued for mercy, but found none, not on that day. When all was done, every rider was slain. All that remained was Lendum and his courageous followers, all of whom had escaped the confrontation without injury.

After the battle, when all was again calm and under control, a battalion commander that he did not recognize accosted him. The man actually saluted before Lendum had an opportunity to do so.

"Greetings, Chief," he began, but with a subdued timbre. He was visibly fatigued and worn from his ordeal. His eyes sagged and the flesh of his face drooped, making him look a great deal like a hunting dog. "May I have the honor of your name?"

"Lendum Cetus, sir," he replied.

"Well, Chief Lendum, my name is Ione, and I owe you a debt of gratitude that I fear I will never be able to repay. My men and I were fleeing without hope when we saw your group, and our spirits rose at the sight, but almost immediately we were plunged back into despair when it seemed that our countrymen were not going to aid us. That's when your leadership brought forth men of courage and stood their ground against a foe that should easily have bested your handful of warriors, no matter how virtuous and heroic they may have been."

Lendum did not speak; only nodded his head.

Ione smiled. "I see that you are humble, as well as brave. All the better. I need officers that know how to make decisions in an instant, with no time to reflect or ponder alternatives. It is a rare skill, because no amount training can teach it. At times it can be learned through vast experience in combat, but that can take years to develop, and we have not years to cultivate more officers. Too many have died already." His haggard face showed a hint of bitterness. Lendum was unsure if Ione was upset at the loss of his men, or rather because they were lost at the hands of another kingdom. The conflict brought emotions hitherto unchallenged by the hearts of men. "You have demonstrated your ability," Ione continued, "and a man with your innate skills should be in a position of greater authority than that you have already been granted. I am the highest rank here, so

I assume command of this entire body, and my first action is to promote you to captain with a field commission. Now, instead of one-hundred men, you shall command five-hundred. Do you accept?"

Lendum did not need to think before he answered. His rank mattered not at all, as long as he could fight. He longed for vengeance. Nothing else drove him. "I do accept, with thanks, sir."

Ione nodded as if he had expected no different. "Very well. Be in my quarters at noon for the briefing. See to your men now, and then we shall discuss the doings of this war."

"Yes, sir," Lendum replied, and saluted. Ione returned the salute and then turned on his heel and strode away.

Lendum left to see to his troops, and pondered quiet thoughts of his future.

$$=\!\!=\quad=\!\!=$$

Sindus was a creature of complete malevolence. He literally hated everything in the world. He hated the sound of wind blowing through the boughs of trees, and he hated the sight of stars as they made their way across the nighttime sky. The smell of flowers made him sick, and soft grass under his feet brought forth sores. He even hated his own hatred, for it tormented him even as it gave him comfort.

However, more than anything else, he hated men, and the dominion over the earth granted to them by his former master. If Sindus could have one wish, it would be to extinguish the life of every man, woman, and child of Aegea, allowing him and his minions rule of the world with no restraints. Tor was imprisoned, and the other gods were forbidden from interfering in the doings of this world.

Because of his hatred, Sindus employed brutish monsters that shared his utter distain for humanity. For centuries bands of hideous rokul and squads of vicious kaitos had plagued men along the borders of Nactadale, moving swiftly from the forests to strike and then fleeing back to the sanctuary of the ominous trees. The servants of Sindus were little more than mindless beasts, and equally bent on the destruction of the world of men.

Yet, if the servants of Sindus were mindless, their master was not. He was crafty, cunning, and above all else, patient. All the long years had passed with no visible schism amongst the kingdoms of men, until now. When his winged messengers brought him news of the conflict in the Bould, Sindus sensed the opportunity that had evaded him for ages: a break within the alliance of men. Because of his nature, and his deliberate scheming, he did not order his slaves to attack, but rather their immediate withdrawal, not to the forests, but to the other side of the Smoke Mountains. He wanted no sign of his chattel within the view of men. As a result, thousands of rokul left their holes and vanished deep into their master's domain, there mustered until such a time as their strength could best be used.

That time was fast approaching.

With no obvious signs of the enemy, men soon forgot the threat Sindus posed. Border patrols grew weary of reporting no activity day after day. Frontier families would allow their children greater freedom to run across the plains, convinced that no evil creatures were present to cause them harm. The soldiers in the Bould had enough worries already, and scarcely considered the eastern lands and the terror they held. The borders grew lethargic and docile, and apathy replaced vigilance. The dark lord of Nactadale used this time of neglect to spin his most egregious web, and captured a follower that would prove more useful than entire legions of his nefarious henchmen. As a seed may be small and unassuming, with time and care it can grow to a large and cumbersome thing. The seed was now planted, and Sindus nurtured it with his despicable patience. Though it was in clear view, no one saw it for what it was. They perceived a rose where there was only a bramble of thorns and hemlock.

Sindus grew gleeful at these developments, and watched with his damnable patience for the inevitable mistake that such complacency would invite.

⇒ ⇐

Lendum arrived for the captain's briefing a little before noon. He left Corce, whom he had seen fit to promote to sergeant, in charge of his company. The boy had matured a great deal in the last few hours. He had found a courage that he barely believed existed, and now relished his service. He felt an inexplicable sense of gratitude toward Lendum, as if he would never had discovered his gift without his help. He did his new duty with enthusiasm.

The tent that was serving as Ione's quarters was large enough to hold several men, with a single guard stationed at the flap. Upon announcing who he was, Lendum was given a new medallion of a Company Captain, much like the one given to him by Trand. Time had worn this one, much more so than the one he had received from Trand, because it had been carried for years by another unfortunate soul that now walked with Miro. Lendum held it for a moment, cupping it in his palm, feeling not so much the weight of the thing as the weight of the responsibility that it represented. Hundreds of men would now be at his command, and to him fell the unenviable duty of ordering them to carry out deeds that could end with their demise. The medallion seemed to grow heavier as these thoughts passed through him. With effort, he put it out of his mind and slipped the silver chain over his neck, letting the round token fall upon his chest. He opened the tent flap and went inside.

Within the tent fifteen other men stood. Supply crates formed a crude table in the center of the tent, and a large canvas map of the Bould lay across it. Little clay figures of green and brown were scattered across the surface of the map, representing the forces of Gladue and her enemy. To his disbelief, brown figures, many brown figures, sat within the Bould, near Tine Vort, which had been their destination this morning. Lendum reasoned that something had happened to disrupt their march, and their destination was Tine Vort no longer.

The captains stood in small groups, gesturing at the map and murmuring to each other. When Lendum entered, most of them offered a nod of acknowledgement, which in reality was a display of high respect. Most of the captains present had witnessed Lendum's fearless charge while they remained frozen to the ground. They felt that his show of courage had not only saved lives and lessened the strength of the enemy, but had demonstrated his leadership and earned his right to be at this council, despite his inexperience and youth. They did not begrudge his presence.

Ione came to the edge if the table and raised his hands. "Gentlemen, let's begin. We have much to do and it must be done quickly." Thick whiskers covered most of his face, except for a jagged scar that ran down his left cheek. A rokul claw had maimed him in his youth. He had grown a beard to try to mask its effects, but it was still painfully evident. "First, we should reform companies, to allow for our casualties. I want a detailed, company by company list of strength, to know precisely where we stand as regards our manpower."

Each captain now reported the number of soldiers he had under his command. All of the companies on the march from Ashtone were at full strength, including Lendum's company. The men that had fled from Tine Vort were mere fragments of their former units. Ione assigned these men to the existing companies, and the figures revealed that seven-thousand and forty-two men were encamped at that spot.

Ione shook his head. "No, it will not be enough," he said to himself. He rubbed a rough hand on his chin while he thought. "We must remain here for a while." The other captains did not interrupt this one-man conversation, but remained quiet, listening with the disciplined patience that only soldiers can maintain.

Finally, Ione seemed to turn his attention back to his captains. "Gentlemen, two days ago our forces at Tine Vort were defeated." The small area of the tent was suddenly filled with sighs and pained groans. Lendum himself closed his eyes and exhaled heavily. He had already reasoned that this defeat must have transpired, but to hear it spoken aloud was still a heavy burden. "Soldiers of Andesha, having forsaken their steeds, apparently crossed the marshes and came upon us unawares. All our defenses were centered on holding the bridge, and I never considered this move to our flank." Ione paused a moment, feeling a pressing weight of personal responsibility. "Once our lines were broken, the horsemen across the river charged, and we were completely undone. I led a retreat, but once the crossing was secure, Andesha pursued us, and had we not encountered this host of our countrymen by sheer chance, I have no doubt that we would have met our doom. Andesha now holds all of the crossings of the Shae and already has a considerable force in this territory, several thousands at the least."

Ione paused another moment, letting the news sink in. No one spoke, and the silence was complete. All the captains stood rigidly still, listening intently to their commander, awaiting his orders.

"Captain Bereus," Ione spoke, "how many horses do we have ready for swift travel?"

"Only fifteen of our own, my lord. We captured twenty-two of our enemy, but several of these suffered hurts of some kind and will require time to heal. We could perhaps enjoy the speed of twenty-eight animals, if need be."

Ione thought briefly. "As soon as this meeting is concluded, I want riders sent to Ashtone, to report to King Jonas our losses and request instructions. Similarly, I want scouts sent to Tine Vort to monitor the movements of our enemy. If they move their forces from the river, I need to know about it. Also, send riders to Noveton, to warn them that our position is compromised. They should be as alert and cautious as possible."

Lendum started at the sound of his proper name. The burial site of his father was immortalized with his own surname. This was perversely comforting, after a fashion.

Ione continued giving orders. "Captains Larsh and Cane, march your companies to Noveton to support our troops already there. Our messengers will announce your coming. Move with all possible speed, and coordinate your defenses as best as may be. The enemy could come upon us at any time. Be on your guard."

Larsh and Cane nodded their assent, giving perfunctory 'Yes, sirs' as they did so.

"As for the rest of us," Ione continued, "our position here is too exposed, and too close to the enemy. They will be expecting the return of their riders soon, and when they fail to arrive, they will come looking for them. My heart yearns to avenge our losses and reclaim Tine Vort, but I know our numbers are too few. If they discover us in this place, they will destroy us, rest assured. We must withdraw, but to where? Suggestions?" His eyes scanned the canvas room, searching the faces of his captains. None volunteered his opinion, until finally Lendum broke the silence by clearing his throat.

"Sir, we are the only force in this part of the territory that can hope to give battle. We must remain in the Bould, and hold a point far from Noveton, forcing Andesha to best us before they can move to the mine." He pointed to an area of the map, at the very center of the Bould. "There is a ridge here that runs nearly to the Charwood. It is much higher than the surrounding plains, and could be successfully defended by a small force and yet have access to other points of value within the territory. This will force them to come past us, or try to cross the ridge at a point farther north. We could hold the area for some time, could see for miles in every direction, and could move quickly to intersect our enemy should they advance to our flanks. It would be a superlative location, given our current vulnerable state."

Ione was astounded. He had already learned with his own eyes that Lendum was a gifted battlefield leader. The gods had blessed him with the ability to inspire and motivate men to risk their lives for a cause. Now it seemed that he also had as intuitive sense for tactics and strategy. The ridge Lendum suggested was Noga Tine, the hill of the spine, and from its precipice, one could see over the vast plains to the south, east and west. Andesha would find it difficult to sneak around without their knowledge. They would be forced to come at them directly, which was a happenstance that Ione found incredibly appealing. He wanted no more surprises. He looked at Lendum with profound deference. His reasoning was so sound that Ione thought all of the other courses he was considering foolish.

"Any more suggestions?" he asked, though he had already decided. The other captains did not speak. "So be it. We will depart at once. Make ready to move with as much speed as we can. I want to command that ridge in two days."

⇒ ⇐

The war continued. Because of the superior position of Ione's forces at Noga Tine, Andesha could make no further gains into the region, especially the mine at Noveton, without risking great loss. Eventually, reinforcements arrived for both sides, giving greater strength to the belligerents, but at the same time making the possibility of appalling casualties even more likely. The stalemate continued into the winter, when both kingdoms agreed to a weather-induced truce that was to last until the first of March. Both kings used the time to dig their heels in further and tighten their grip on the rope. By the time the frosts began to thaw, each nation had in excess of twenty thousand soldiers in the Bould. Most of them were volunteers, but a few of the men of Andesha were conscripts, a grim example of things to come.

After only a few months of war, thousands had been lost to battle, disease, and injury. The loss of life and limb, though grievous, was not the only cost to bear. In Andesha, gold was drying up in the royal treasury. Grindal increased his taxations, and there was some grumbling from the populace, but the people mostly took it in stride, seeing it as a necessary sacrifice for security and national honor. Commodities grew scarce, as coal, soap, meat, cheese and butter became almost unknown, except at the front. It was common for a man facing poverty to enlist only to receive solid food and decent clothing. The skies became black from the workings of the blacksmith forges, as the production of steel blades, armor and horseshoes outpaced that of nails, tools and cutlery. Some gear of war came from Nefala, where the craft in metal goods had the highest praise, but it was prohibitively expensive, and as the months passed by and the war dragged on, the neighbors of the combatants became increasingly more aloof. It seemed that the paramount issue was to avoid involvement at all costs.

In Gladue, the cost of the war was easier to manage. Jonas controlled the mine, and with the able direction of the twisted Motte, the king was capable of financing all of his military undertakings without raising taxes and creating popular unrest. Jonas traded salt for food and goods, sold salt directly to the people for gold, and used it preserve meat intended for the soldiers at the front. All acute observers deemed Gladue to be in the best position to win the war if they were allowed time to discourage their enemy, and given that they could maintain control of the mine. Motte did all that he could to boost the confidence of the king to a dangerous level, and when March 1st arrived, Gladue immediately began a series of assaults throughout the territory. Skirmishes erupted at a dozen localities, as the countries fought for any tactical site that would give an edge. Forces of Gladue marched on Egel to the north, Elur to the south, and finally the all-important site of Tine Vort. By the sixteenth of July, all of the major assaults had retreated, but the casualties were astounding for Grindal, who had fewer men to spare. His attempt to counterattack at Noga Tine was foolhardy, and by the end of year 1108 and the beginning of the second winter armistice, the same stalemate descended across the region. All that had changed was the number of dead.

Meanwhile, Lendum's career as a soldier was giving him benefits that he had not foreseen: glory and renown. Lendum took part in several of the major engagements of 1108, and in each one, he proved his worth and valor. After the battle of Elur, where Lendum ran headlong into a squad of archers while arrows flew all around him, rumor grew that he was invincible, and that his troops were immune to death. Indeed, it did seem that a certain grace fell upon those fortunate enough to be under his direction. Very few went to the unknown under his command. Soldiers clamored incessantly for transfers to his company, or at least to the battalion of which his company was a part, even though this meant certain combat. Ione put Lendum wherever the fighting was the thickest, and after his performance at Elur, he promoted Lendum again, making him a regimental commander answerable directly to him. Lendum accepted the honor with his usual poise.

At the second Battle of Tine Vort, Lendum again distinguished himself as having unshakable nerves and courage. The mass of brown-dressed men swarmed up the hill, but Lendum refused to yield. He bore his sword with righteous zeal, and the company that followed him was infused with the raw courage of his display. The other companies of Gladue did not prove as stubborn, and cracks appeared in the lines of defense. Ione feared that his command was in danger of perishing. He did not reckon on the contagious spirit of his young regimental commander. Once the battle turned ill, Lendum defied orders to retreat and kept his company against the enemy, preventing the withdrawal from becoming a rout. Whispers said that Lendum slew forty men that day, but that was not the full tale. The number was closer to sixty, and he endured no wound of any kind. Likewise, only five of the five-hundred in the rearguard perished. His legend grew proportionally to his deeds. By the middle of July 1108, Lendum was back at Noga Tine, resting and awaiting new orders.

On the night of thirtieth of July, Lendum was sleeping soundly in his tent when the sound of a drawn sword roused him. He sat up quickly, and even in the darkness, he could see Trand, sitting comfortably with his legs crossed and Lendum's sword across his lap.

"Greetings, Lendum. Once again we are well met." Lendum did not respond. He rubbed his eyes, blinking like a newborn. "I see that the gift of Amarut was well given. You have wielded this blade to great fame. Your name is now spoken in the same breath as Tarsus, the great demon slayer and protector of the treasure. Does it do you proud to know that you are held in such esteem?"

Lendum scoffed. "I am not proud to be so held," he answered, lighting a nearby lamp. Bright light snuffed out the gloom. "In fact, I feel close to nothing at all. This war is nothing to me but a means to avenge those I have lost. When it is over, I don't know what I shall do with myself."

"Delude yourself if you must, but do not try to delude me," Trand said in a sad tone. "I know you have seen much that is horrible, and for that you have my profound sympathy. However, to pretend you feel nothing is self-deception. Every night your pillow is wet with tears shed in anguish for the fallen."

Lendum stirred uncomfortably. He wanted to respond, but could think of nothing to say.

"Why do you have my sword?' Lendum asked abruptly, changing the subject.

"I was just checking the integrity of the steel," he answered, running his thumb along the edge of the blade. "It seems to be in very good shape indeed, considering the use you have gotten from it."

"Corce maintains it for me. I named him my First Lieutenant."

"He does good work, and has shown steadfastness, has he not? What a change from the boy you met in Tibar nearly a year ago. He has risen to meet all of his responsibilities, an admirable feat for anyone. I hope he does not happen upon a challenge that will prove too big for him."

"He is brave, no doubt," Lendum agreed. "I've witnessed no skittishness on his part since we first encountered each other on the march."

"He has found an able model upon which to base his actions, as have many in this war. Take care that you do not bite off too much for your men to chew." Trand brought the edge of the sword to his lips, and whispered in an odd tongue for a moment. Before Lendum's amazed gaze the blade began to glow a pale white. Then the color shifted to red, green, and finally blue. The sword hummed with barely restrained energy, sounding like the pained bawl of a bough about to break. Suddenly Trand stopped speaking, the weapon regained its normal, dull hue, and all was silent. Trand slid the sword back into its scabbard, and then placed it gingerly against the mannequin that wore Lendum's armor, where it always rested when not on his hip.

"What did you do?" Lendum asked after Trand regained his seat, his lanky legs once again crossed and comfortable.

"I made your sword ready for another bout with a determined enemy. You need not worry about where or when. It will handle that itself."

"Speaking in riddles requires me to make shrew guesses, and I have neither the patience nor the ability to concentrate at the moment. I was sleeping soundly before you woke me, if you remember."

"I remember," said Trand with a faint grin on his lips. "And I apologize for that discourtesy. You need not solve any riddles. Your sword has been imbued with power that will manifest itself when the time is right."

Lendum was silent for a moment, and then his eyes grew wide with apprehension. His mouth became a gaping hole in the middle of his gaunt face, worn thin from his trying labor. "The battle," he finally said "Near Tine Vort last year, before I received my rank. My sword made a bright flash of light that disoriented our enemy. That was you?"

"Yes," replied Trand matter-of-factly.

"None of the other soldiers seemed to notice, so I said nothing of it, and for a time I doubted that I saw it myself. You did it at Tibar, didn't you; when we last saw each other?"

"Yes," said Trand again.

Lendum hopped out of bed and stood tall. "Why did you do that?" he screamed, enraged. "If you have no confidence in me, then why did you choose me to do this duty, or whatever it is? Now my accomplishments are tainted because you interfered!"

"If I had not," Trand said evenly, "then you and all that followed you would now be dead, trodden into the ground by thunderous horse's hooves." Trand then stood, and he seemed tall, menacing and perilous in the small tent. His voice was deep and seemed to boom in Lendum's ears.

The folds of his black cloak shimmered with restrained power. "You seem overly concerned with how you are perceived for one that sees this conflict as only a means to achieve your revenge. Could it be that your reputation carries more weight in your own mind than you admit?" Lendum did not respond, but Trand had put his finger on a profound truth that Lendum had not considered. He *did* enjoy his status, and the respect and admiration he received from his peers and subordinates. He felt suddenly ashamed, not only because he thought himself, shallow, but also because Trand had been so quick to see through his veneer of selflessness and expose the truth in his heart. He lowered his head in his disgrace, but Trand was not yet prepared to end his critique. He had more ire to vent. "As for your other question, I didn't *choose* you at all. I may appear to be all-knowing, but it is not so. I am told where to go and who to persuade by one greater than I, but the will of my master does not command me to endure hostility and scorn from one such as you. I am not a freelance enabler of deeds, walking the earth in the hopes that bold little orphan boys will do my bidding because I can astonish them with the curiosities I carry in the folds of my cloak. I follow the instructions of my master, as we all must, and I will suffer no arrogance from anyone for doing my solemn duty!"

Lendum backed away from Trand until the back of his knees hit his cot, and he plopped onto it like a child's doll. He was afraid, afraid for the first time in Trand's presence. All at once, the wizard was revealed in his faculty and majesty, a being of immense strength that was much, much more than he ever seemed. To look at him was to see the rage of a hurricane and the doggedness of the mountains. Lendum quaked and pulled his knees to his chest, backing as far away as he could, lest Trand touch him and render him lifeless. Trand took a step closer. "Whether or not I have faith in you is irrelevant, but if you must know, I *do* believe in you. You have courage, that is clear, but your courage stems from the belief that you have nothing more to lose. Bravery and imprudence make a poor foundation upon which to build a man."

Lendum was now on the verge of tears. "What more have I?" he almost screamed in his agony. "My home, my family, my youth! All gone! My innocence, my hopes, my ambitions are all now void! There is nothing left to take!"

Trand now knelt before Lendum and placed a warm hand on his shoulder. The touch was so similar to his father's that Lendum felt like crying. Yet his shaking subsided, and he could feel calm returning to his soul. When Trand spoke, his voice was gentle and soothing again, flowing like music.

"You cannot know that, my boy," he said in a fatherly tone "The gift of youth is the gift of hope. For though you have nothing now, you cannot be certain that you shall never have anything again. You may yet find something in this world that you love, and that you would be loathe to lose, and would die to protect. Do not forget that hope is something to possess in itself. You always have hope. That, they can never take from you."

Lendum looked directly into Trand's dark eyes, and saw nothing but sincerity and wisdom. He realized that he had been a fool. Revenge was not something to pine for, to seek, and to cling to like a precious jewel. He did have more to cherish than he had reckoned, and the comfort from that realization brought something that he had missed for over a year; it brought a modicum of peace.

"Thank you, friend Trand. I am in your debt."

Trand's smile suddenly grew broad and joyous again. "Nonsense!" he exclaimed, slapping Lendum sharply on his knee in a playful manner. "Don't you recall? I am doing my duty, same as you. I hardly deserve thanks for doing nothing more than performing my assignment." Trand stood and arched his back, making a cracking sound in the process. "Now I must be off. There will be no rest for poor Trand, the bane of the creatures of Sindus and the friend of all good men. Indeed, who has time for rest in these days of woe?" He turned for the flap, his cloak trailing out behind him like a kite tail. All at once he turned.

"Tell me, do you have orders to march north?"

Lendum cocked an eyebrow. "Are you saying that you don't already know?"

Trand simply gave his signature smile, teeth glistening.

"No, not as yet," he answered. "Should I be expecting such orders?"

"Yes, you should. When you do, you should endeavor to secure as much salt for your men as possible. Several pounds each, if you can manage it. You will find it useful, when you go north." With that, he left, gone like a shadow at noon.

ADORATION AND A BEAR'S TOOTH

On the fifteenth of August 1108, two weeks after Trand's nighttime visit, Andesha attacked Noga Tine. The effort was valiant, but in vain. Quereus directed the assault, though he was against it from the beginning. His mentor had taught him to *never* attack an enemy that had the higher ground. History was full of examples were that adage held true, and Quereus had seen nothing in his experience that could refute the advice. However, King Grindal ordered him to assault the hill, so he did his best to obey. Ten thousand brown-clad warriors, most on foot by this time due to the shortage of horses, stormed the slopes testing the strength of the lines of defense.

At one point, the line of Gladue wavered, but Lendum, again without orders, rallied the men and led a furious counterattack that forced the invaders back down the hill. At the apex of his charge, his screaming was so utterly without humanity that his own men quaked at the sound of it. Blood and gore covered his uniform and made his face ghastly and barbaric, but in the moment it bothered him not at all. He was not himself when he fought, and when he felt the change coming upon him while he was in the field, the calculating coldness that covered him with comfort, he surrendered wholly to it. Allowing the war-loving monster to take full control of his faculties seemed to make all of his deeds acceptable, as if he were somehow absolved during the time of battle. He felt no remorse when he wielded his blade. The regret came later, in the quiet hours, when all of the blood was washed away, and he was once again nothing more than Lendum son of Fordrun. However, as the bold warriors of Quereus charged the hill at Noga Tine, Lendum surrendered to his beast once again, and his fury was fearful to behold. He moved with a grace and elegance that did not seem possible when one considered the damage he caused. Corce saw him run headlong into a squad of six men that had breached the line, and Lendum killed them all. The last was the most gruesome. Lendum removed both of the man's arms with two smooth strokes and then run the man through his throat until the hilt of his long sword was under the poor soul's jaw. The men of Andesha that witnessed that horrid spectacle instinctively withdrew out of sheer terror. After two hours and two thousand dead, Quereus called a retreat. The final battle of the year was over.

Two weeks later Ione summoned Lendum to his quarters. A leaning shack with a permanent air stood in place of the canvas dwelling. Noga Tine was no longer nothing more than a convenient point to hold position. It was an outpost, and the spot from which Gladue now directed all of it operations in the Bould. Lendum had chosen wisely.

When he arrived to answer the summons, Ione was eating a light meal. It was the noon hour, and all over the hill, the men were relaxed and joyous, despite the earlier bloodletting. The men sensed that the war was going well for them. It was unlikely that any more orders would come before the winter truce, so the killing was likely done until the spring. Happy songs filled the sunlit air.

Ione did not speak when he saw Lendum, but instead handed him a letter bearing the royal seal. Tentatively Lendum took the correspondence, a little worried at what it might contain. A letter with the royal seal could only come from the court of King Jonas. What could a noble want with a foot soldier like Lendum? He was not sure, but he could think of nothing good.

Once opened, Lendum learned that the letter did not come from a noble, but from the king himself. He demanded Lendum's presence in the capitol at once, but gave no explanation for the visit or the reason for the urgency. Ione read the letter as well, immediately excused Lendum from all duty, and transferred all of his troops to the command of Captains Bereus and Cane for the time being. Ione expressed regret, and the sincere hope that Lendum would be back soon, hopefully before the spring. "I believe that no man is indispensable," he said, "but you have come as close to that as I think possible. Try not to be gone too long, if you please."

Lendum left the following day. Corce went with him, hand picked by Lendum to be his escort. Traveling in the Bould alone in the best of times was ill advised, so Lendum asked his friend to come with him. Corce agreed, though he did not really want to leave the front. He relished his responsibilities, and no one was more surprised at this development that he.

The journey to Ashtone took thirteen days. When Lendum and Corce entered the city, they found a much excited people. Banners hung from every window. Children danced in the streets, and men and women went about their business with a giddiness that bordered on euphoria. Apparently, after two years of grisly war the spirits of the people remained high. In fact, they seemed to have prospered. Lendum noticed more goods on the streets for sale or barter and more willing consumers dickering for the best prices.

Upon reaching the castle and announcing his arrival, Lendum learned that the king was in council and did not have time to meet until the fifteenth, two days away. Lendum, feeling a little put out, thanked the guard anyway and went off in search of an old friend, Timo. He invited Corce to join him, but Corce declared that he wanted nothing more at the moment than a tall ale and a place to rest his feet.

"I'll meet you at the Bear's Tooth Inn," he said. "I'm going to get a hot bite to eat, and then sit motionless in the parlor, nursing a rich drink. I've earned it, I reckon."

Lendum promised to meet his friend later, and said goodbye. He then returned to the stables, and found his beloved horse still in the same stall. Timo was visibly excited to see his master, stamping his forelegs and bucking his head vigorously. "Easy, boy. Don't hurt yourself," Lendum said, laughing and stroking his neck. He had not enjoyed pure laughter in so long that the feeling was alien to him.

He spent more than an hour with Timo, feeding him ripe apples and brushing his silky mane. The grooming was done out of love rather than necessity, for Lendum was most pleased to see that Timo had been well cared for in his absence. The horse's coat was shiny and his eyes were much clearer than Lendum remembered. He even appeared to have gained weight, and increased in vigor.

Soon Lendum felt his weariness from his journey, and resigned to join Corce at the Bear's Tooth. "Goodbye, friend. It was good to see you again. Do not fret. I will be by again tomorrow, and whenever I leave this place to return to my duties, you shall come with me, if you want. I'm now allowed to have my own horse, though we will surely be going into the gravest peril." Timo snorted and nodded his head, signaling the affirmative. The horse rubbed his muzzle against Lendum's cheek, a gesture that was poignant in its tenderness.

Lendum took his leave, and walked through the streets to the Bear's Tooth Inn. He was anxious to see it, for it had a good reputation, and was full of history, being in business since the days of the current proprietor's great-grandfather. There he would get food and drink, lodging, and rest.

He would also find something that he would love, would be loathe to lose, and would die to protect.

⇒ ⇐

The Bear's Tooth stood out sharply from the other buildings surrounding it. While most of the construction of Ashtone was done with the gray stone quarried at the far-off Yosami Mountains on the southeastern borders of Gladue, the Bear's Tooth was built from more locally found stones; limestone that shone brilliantly white once polished. A small edifice compared to the others nearby, the Bear's Tooth was a newer construction, less than one hundred years old, and it was a place frequented by visitors with means, official delegates, foreign emissaries, and, like Lendum, officers on leave. As Lendum approached, he realized that the inn had earned its name honestly. It did appear to be an immense tooth jutting from a sea of grayness.

He entered with no hesitation. The large dining hall was already half-full, even at the 3 o'clock hour. Talk was raucous and jolly, tongues loosened by prosperous times and good ale. The heads of various game animals hung on the walls, watching with a tranquil silence. The largest of all was the enormous black bear that stood menacingly in the corner in all of its glory. These animals were common in the mountains of Aegea, though they normally avoided men if they could. This specimen was the largest yet found, though surely others even larger roamed the earth. Folks called him Tindolino; the big hill boy. His lips curled back to reveal fearsome teeth, his paws spread as if to attack.

With no more than a quick glance, Lendum spotted Corce, doing precisely what he knew he would be doing; playing cards. Corce had parlayed his meager army wages into a fortune while in the king's service by fleecing his comrades of their wages. When their money was gone, Corce was not averse to accepting jewels, small knives, polishing oils, scarves, or anything else of value. He had adjusted to the life of a soldier, and had proven proficient in his duties. Nevertheless, his true love and passion remained Queens and Aces.

Corce did not notice Lendum enter, and he knew better than to disturb his friend in the middle of a game. He found an empty table on the far side of the hall and took a seat, propping his feet up in another chair. He crossed his arms before his chest, and fell asleep almost at once, so deeply that the chatter of conversation and clatter of dishes did nothing to disrupt his slumber.

She was nineteen years old, and a soft-spoken orphan of very poor but proud folks. Her father had shoed horses and built crates for a living, and her mother, though loving and tender, had been too often in poor health to do the work of the home. She had two older twin brothers, meaning that the housework fell on her alone, but she bore it as best she could, and complained not at all. When her parents died she found work at the Bear's Tooth, and she enjoyed it very much, because it gave her a chance to meet so many interesting people, to hear exciting news, and to serve handsome men like the one that now slept soundly before her. Her brothers were both gone to war, having volunteered the previous year. She knew not where they were, when they would be back, or even if they were alive. She was utterly alone.

"Commander?" she said, her voice low enough to be completely inaudible over the din. "Commander, may I help you?" Lendum did not stir. Delicately she extended her hand, lightly taking hold of his shoulder and shaking him with extreme care, as if he were as fragile as glass. "Commander?" she said again. Her voice was a coo.

Lendum opened his eyes, and before him stood a lady of the gods. Golden hair draped her shoulders, while silken, wispy bangs caressed her thin eyebrows. She had green eyes, with irises so large that her eyelids eclipsed them from above and below. The corners of her mouth were turned upward in a perpetual grin, raising her cheeks high and radiating happiness no matter what weight the world placed upon her. Her nose was straight and narrow, turned up ever so slightly at the tip so that her upper lip was separated from lower, exposing sparkling white teeth that were just a tad crooked. She clasped her hands together before her in a delicate manner, though they were rough from her labor and stained with the relentless service of food and beverage. Her emerald-colored dress revealed her forearms, which were milky and thin, leading up to svelte shoulders that were lovely in their simplicity. She was the most beautiful creature Lendum had ever seen in his life, and the sight of her struck him dumb. He stammered, but no words could he utter. Clumsily he tried to get to his feet, to bow or salute or do something to communicate greetings, but his boots became entangled in the chair. In his efforts to free himself he knocked it over, causing a terrible racket and causing the girl to jump with sudden shock.

"Sorry...I'm sorry," he finally managed to say, trying to remove his feet from the back of the chair. Once his feet were free, he stood rapidly, not realizing that the sheath of his sword and the chair were intertwined.

When it overturned, making another great noise, Lendum could feel his face begin to blush. The girl just stared, her hands pressed over her mouth in surprise. Lendum quickly set to placing both chairs upright, and in a humorous attempt to make amends, he bowed low to the girl, saying, "My apologies, Miss. I am Lendum Cetus, here to serve you."

The girl removed her hands from her face, and when Lendum saw the wry smile that was fetching and bemused, he realized with horror what he had said.

"What I mean," he stuttered, "is that I am at your service, not that I am here to serve you, obviously." A sheen of warm sweat broke out and quickly spread across his brow. His heart was thumping wildly, and it took tremendous energy to keep his hands from shaking. He almost laughed at the madness of the situation. He had endured painful tragedies, served with valor in numerous engagements, and killed scores of his determined enemy. Now the sight of a servant girl left him foolish and awkward. He did not even know her name. "Begging your pardon, Miss, but how shall I address you?" he asked, unwittingly wiping sweat from his forehead.

"You may call me Elisa, if it pleases you," she answered, her tone as melodious as a songbird. She gave a little curtsey that was warm and polite, easing the tension somewhat. She had undoubtedly encountered much behavior that was inappropriate during the course of her duties, so she had no problem ignoring the social complexities brought forth by this patron. A hint of the amused smile remained on her lips. "Is there something I can get you, Commander? A drink, perhaps?" She ran her hand through her thin hair in an absentminded way as she spoke.

"Yes, an ale would be lovely," he answered with a little more aplomb. "Also, I will need lodging for at least two days, perhaps longer. Is that possible?"

"I think so, yes. I will check with the master to be sure."

"Thank you, Lady Elisa," said Lendum, bowing again. "You have been most gracious."

Elisa snickered. "You're welcome, Commander Lendum. Please, sit and be comfortable. Excessive bowing can be tiring for even the sturdiest of folks."

Lendum smiled shamefacedly, a little embarrassed that Elisa had been so quick to notice his nervousness. He obediently sat down, and Elisa went to fetch his beverage.

Lendum used his few moments of solitude to try to compose himself. He took several deep breaths, and after a minute, he was calm. The clamoring of the falling chairs had aroused much interest, even from Corce, but that was subsiding, as the dining hall resumed its regular sound of overlapping voices.

"What happened to me?" Lendum wondered to himself. "I was bewitched and made a simpleton by the mere sight of her. Never have I felt so enthralled." Daringly, Lendum lifted his eyes from the table, and gazed toward the bar where Elisa was loading several mugs of ale onto a tray. She really was quite enchanting to his eye. Her every fiber seemed perfect. She moved with an inherent kind of playfulness, as a child set to do a chore they find entertaining. Her dress was teal, frayed at the edges but well fitting, and it matched the ribbon she had tied in her hair. She wore no jewelry, save for a band of gold that hung from a chain around her slender neck. Everything about her was comely, and Lendum swallowed hard as she approached his table.

"Here's your drink, Commander. I hope that it suits you," she said, and Lendum quivered at the sound of her voice.

"Thank you, Elisa." Hurriedly he took a large gulp, both to sample the drink and to settle his nerves. "It is delicious!" he exclaimed, wiping his mouth with his sleeve. He put the drink down on the table, using more force than was necessary. A mouthful of ale sloshed out and splashed on the table. "I'm so sorry," he blurted out.

Elisa pulled a towel from the pocket of her soiled apron and wiped it up, waving off the apology as she did so. "Think nothing of it," she said. "Happens all the time, I can assure you."

"How about supper?" Lendum interjected.

"Well, it's a little early now. I believe roast mutton is being prepared for this night. If you would return at 6 o'clock, then the master should have everything ready."

"No, I mean…" Lendum swallowed again. His tongue had left him. "I mean, would you like to join *me* for supper?" He looked into her eyes, fighting a fear rising in his chest that was greater than any he had felt on the battlefield. If she said no, he believed his heart would be crushed, never to beat the same way again.

Elisa placed her hands on her hips, cocking her head to one side. The wry smile reappeared. "Mother warned me not to get involved with soldiers. 'They're good enough, but their constant peril makes them short-sighted', she would say. 'They tend to act before they think, for each day could be their last.'

"How does that make me any different from any other man?" he asked.

"Peril can be found anywhere, not only in the king's service. A woodsman can be crushed by his tree, and the wrangler trampled by his steed. Are they to be deemed better suitors than I?"

Elisa laughed aloud, throwing her head back in her mirth. Several of the other patrons took notice, but quickly returned to their business. "So," she said, "now you're a suitor, are you?" She laughed again, a joyous sound that made Lendum smile in spite of himself. "I'm sorely tempted to say yes, now that I know that you are silver-tongued as well as handsome."

Lendum grinned so wide that every tooth was exposed. "Say yes, then, and perhaps you can learn if I am truly silver-tongued, or if I am an impostor, worthy of your mother's warning."

Elisa looked at him, her smile fading. "I think that I would enjoy sharing a meal with you," she began, "but sadly my work here will keep me busy until 10 o'clock, maybe later."

"I don't mind waiting for you," Lendum said quickly, "no matter the hour. In fact, the longer I wait, the more I will be famished, for food and for talk."

Elisa considered a moment. Trusting this man was not really an issue. She found him intriguing, not only because of his wholesome character, but because he was evidently recently returned from the front, and a long talk with one such as him could yield a great deal of interesting news. Besides, she did fancy the boy. He could not be much older than she was, if he was at all. A large portion of his story was written in the lines of his face, which looked somewhat sad even when he smiled. She decided that there was much to gain from spending time with him, and almost no risk whatsoever. Little did she know that she risked everything.

"Very well, Commander," she said. "I shall sup with you this evening. Come back at ten, and be prompt. I shan't wait for you if you're tardy."

Lendum stood and bowed low, much to her amusement. "Lady Elisa, you honor me. If I could be shown a room where I could rest before our meeting, I would be grateful."

Elisa giggled like a little girl. "See the master at the bar. He can see to your room. Until tonight, Commander Lendum." She resumed her duties, much more thrilled than her exterior displayed.

The master of the Bear's Tooth showed Lendum to his lodging, a quaint little room on the third floor that had a good view to the south. He lay on the soft bed, to overcome with emotion to sleep. He already knew that furthermore his heart was no longer his own.

Elisa need not have worried about Lendum being late. He arrived a full hour early, looking very bright-eyed and more groomed than he had been in months. He had trimmed his hair and whiskers, and washed his face so vigorously that red marks were still evident from the scrubbing. He took a seat at one of the smaller tables, sipping at a pint, waiting patiently for her to join him. She passed his table now and again, and with each opportunity, Lendum filled his eyes with her beauty.

Lendum spent his time playing Queens and Aces with himself, attempting to become adept enough to best Corce, if that was possible. He tried to concentrate on his cards, but the task was difficult, for every time Elisa passed near him she drew his eye, and he would find it difficult to turn his gaze back to the table. The time he waited was actually very little, a little more than an hour, but it seemed an eternity.

At last, Lendum saw Elisa approaching without her apron, and with two heaping plates of food. Although she was certainly very tired with numerous aches and pains, her face bore a lovely smile of genuine pleasure. Lendum hopped to his feet, careful not to overturn his chair.

Elisa set the plates on the table. "Sit down and eat. You must be starving."

"I must be, but strangely, I am not," Lendum said. "I don't know why, but food is the last thing on my mind." Then he added, "You look very well."

Elisa blew away a few stray hairs that had wandered before her eyes, and took her seat with a heavy sigh. "I look precisely the same as I did a few hours ago when we first met," she retorted. "In fact, I almost assuredly look *worse* now than I did."

"Perhaps," he said taking his own seat, "but you looked well then, too" She made a soft grin that made his heart jump.

"Thank you," she finally said. "Now eat, whether you want to or not, for I'm going to have a go at it, and to avoid the appearance of rudeness, I won't do it alone." The shadows cast by the lamps in the now-empty dining hall fell across her face, making her appear weary, but still very beautiful. Her high cheeks rolled into little spheres whenever she spoke.

Lendum picked up his fork. "As you wish, my lady."

Elisa smiled and began to eat. Lendum at first tried to maintain an air of exaggerated decorum by taking small bites, chewing thoroughly, wiping his mouth with his napkin, and then repeating the entire process.

Once he saw the way Elisa ate, he relaxed considerably. She was not rude, but she was clearly very hungry, and saw no reason to restrain herself to impress her fellow diner. Lendum began to eat more lavishly. The meat was a little tough, but the vegetables were delicious, and his appetite returned to him.

After several minutes of uninterrupted eating, Elisa said, "You introduced yourself as Lendum Cetus before. Did I hear you right?"

"Yes," he answered after swallowing a mouthful of ale. "I am Lendum Cetus."

Elisa cocked an eyebrow. "*The* Lendum Cetus?" she asked with a touch of disbelief.

Lendum was a little confused. "I suppose," he answered, still unsure what she meant. "I know of no other."

"The Lendum Cetus that saved Commander Ione near Tine Vort last year? The one that held the line at Noga Tine against the famous Marshal Quereus just weeks ago? *That* Lendum Cetus?"

Lendum lowered his head. He felt ashamed, though he could never explain to anyone why he should be. "Yes," he answered. "I am he."

Elisa sat back in her chair, both hands placed flat on the table. Her eyes were wide with excitement. "Great Tor!" she exclaimed in incredulity. "You're a hero! It's rumored that you have slain one hundred of our enemy with the very sword that you wear now!" She clapped her hands together very childishly. "Who would believe it? I'm having dinner with a legend!"

Lendum smiled sheepishly, a little put off by such praise. "I'm neither a hero nor a legend," he said quietly, and a little sadly. "I'm a soldier that does his duty, nothing more."

"But you are a great soldier, worthy of glory and renown, if the tales be true," she replied in a more subdued tone. "Are the tales true?' she asked, her voice barely a whisper.

Lendum sighed deeply before responding, pushing his plate away. His appetite had left him once more. "I was at Tine Vort, and Noga Tine, and many other places besides. As for the tale of my blade, I know not the number of the dead, but there have been many." He paused and then added, "Very many." A look of sorrow swept across his face, and Elisa felt her heart break.

She reached across the table and took his hand. Her grip was strong, yet gentle, and the softness of her touch engulfed Lendum in thoughts, feelings and memories that he had shut out for far too long. The death of his mother, run though as she begged for mercy, came to his mind as real as his own flesh.

He could see the faces of all the men he had killed, most certainly guilty of no wrongdoing, other than to be in the line of his vengeance when his fury ran hot. His revenge itself, once deemed of extreme importance, began to take on the guise of foolishness, the absurd folly of a stubborn boy. There, in the capitol of Gladue, in the empty dining hall of the Bear's Tooth Inn, with the beautiful Elisa holding his hand and looking into his moistening eyes with compassion, Lendum felt that all of his previous efforts were an enormous waste. Why had he desired revenge so? Why had he pursued something so ugly, when so much beauty still existed in the world? In that moment, far from the war and the death and the suffering, he could no longer be certain what he wanted. His heart was torn with ambivalence.

A single tear ran from his eye. Elisa brushed it away with her thumb.

"Forgive me, Lendum," she said. "I'm sorry I've upset you so."

He did not answer, but waved the apology away.

"Don't fret," she continued, trying to soothe him. "You are young and brave, and have no reason to be ashamed."

"My deeds are not what shame me," he said, fighting his sobs. "Only my motives. Blindly I have sought revenge against one that did me great injury, and have used the king's service as a cloak to achieve my own ends. In so doing, I have sullied myself, and the adoration of ones such as yourself only increases the magnitude of my betrayal."

Elisa placed a warm hand to his face. "Do not punish yourself unjustly," she said. "Many have suffered great loss in this war. Our goods are plentiful, and during the day people go about with shining faces, for they feel no physical want or oppressive burden. But sometimes at night, I hear the wailing of widows and orphans. They all cry out for Andeshan blood. How many have forsaken their homes for the same reasons as you? How many of those that are feeble and old wish that they could? My own brothers are gone to war, not forced, but willingly, only to secure the honor of our country, and avenge our abuses. Do you hold them in the same contempt in which you hold yourself?"

Lendum placed his hand over hers, and shivered. The joy of touch, of simple human contact, was something he had not experienced since his parting embrace from Amarut more than two years before. "No," he finally answered. "I do not. They are honorable men if they serve the crown. I feel no bitterness towards them."

Elisa smiled. "Be happy then that your exploits bring comfort to those that cannot seek to avenge their fallen themselves; the mothers, the wives, the children," she paused. "The sisters."

Lendum felt his heart melt as he realized her anguish and uncertainty. She had comforted him even though she herself was in need of comfort. He looked into her eyes, captivated, and saw a strength there that could not falter. A feeling of submission to her will came over Lendum, and he did not resist. From that moment on, he would love her and no other.

They talked for many hours, mostly about the war, but soon the conversation grew more personal, and Lendum felt the urge to tell her the truth, the whole truth, about him and his family. However, his sense of prudence kept him reserved. Perhaps he should keep his most intimate secrets to himself for the time being. In the end, he felt that his history was something best left for another time.

In the small hours of the morning, Elisa yawned, despite her keen interest. Lendum offered to walk her home, and she agreed. The held hands as they walked in silence, the chilly air making a fog of their breaths. The stars shone down with their heavenly brilliance, guiding them on their way through the narrow streets, blessing this meeting with the acceptance of the gods. At the doorstep of her humble boarding house, Lendum intimated that he would very much like to see her again, and that he was free all of the coming day. Elisa said yes, though they must meet in the morning, for her work at the Bear's Tooth began at the noon hour. Lendum agreed to meet her in the dining hall, and he would walk with her through the city, seeing the sights that had evaded him during his last visit to the city. She said good night, kissing him on the cheek before disappearing behind her door.

Walking back to he inn Lendum had more energy than he would have thought possible. He literally skipped through the streets, his lighthearted feet making harsh clicks against the cobblestones. With dawning clarity, he realized that what he was feeling was happiness. A pure, impermeable happiness flooded his entire being, the most fulfilling and overwhelming happiness he had yet known in his life. The anticipation of her hand upon his cheek, the sound of her tender words, and the thrill of seeing her features again was all he needed to face the next day, and every day after.

That night sleep came slowly, but when it did, it embraced Lendum like an old friend, and his rest was undisturbed.

⇒ ⇐

King Grindal dismissed all of his advisors for the day, military and domestic alike. He would see his visitor alone. The hour was just after noon, and already the ruler of Andesha was weary with endless troubles and perpetual requisitions. He wanted nothing more than to lie down and sleep, but there was no time for that now. A distinguished guest had requested an audience, and it would not be prudent to keep him waiting. The guest, who could cause so much misery for the monarch, he would see at once.

The young king's lifestyle was one of flamboyant splendor. He would wear only the most luxurious cloth, he would eat only gourmet foods, and the furnishings of his living quarters were universally exquisite, imported, and very, very expensive. However, this room was much different from the grand hall where he normally held court. The room was small, barely twenty feet on a side, and the walls were bare, gray rock. No tapestries, no portraits of long dead kings of old, not even windows were in this room. It was altogether bleak. There was not even a fireplace to keep the chill at bay, and during the winter months, ice would routinely form along the cold stone. Only two lamps fought against the dimness, and one table sat in the center of the dull floor, surrounded by four identical chairs, unadorned and ordinary. This was the secret room where the king took his most important counsel. Only a handful of men even knew of this room's existence, and fewer still could claim the dubious honor of standing before the king within it. Men invited to the secret room felt a sense of impending dread. Ill news was often delivered within the frigid chamber, and the king was often the one that made austere announcements. However, the one that stood before the king on that day was not destined to hear ill news, but to share it, and it was the king appeared disturbed and unsettled.

"Welcome," Grindal said in a voice that did not sound like his own. "Would you care to sit?" he asked.

Trand stood silently a moment, his eyes boring holes into Grindal's soul. "No, I think I shall stand, thank you." Trand had his long, black cloak wrapped tightly around his torso, so that he looked like a pillar of onyx. The contrast it made with his pale face made him seem lifeless.

"Very well," Grindal responded with resignation. He took a seat himself, feeling like a child prior to punishment. Trand towered over him stoically, unmoving, unflinching. "Why have you come here on this day?"

"I have come," he began, "for the same reason I have always come. I offer reasonable advice where it is most needed." In the tiny space, Trand seemed to grow taller. "You have much to answer for, my good king."

"You would hold me entirely responsible for these events?" Grindal was outraged, but his voice was calm and passive, so not to upset Trand.

"Not entirely, no. However, much of the blame can safely be laid at your feet. For your part in this, you shall make amends."

Grindal swallowed hard. He feared Trand.

"So, you have come to make me pay for my deeds, eh? I did not know that retribution fell into your regular duties."

Trand snickered, but it was humorless. "I?" he asked sarcastically. "Make you? Foolishness. You shall pay me naught, for the debt you owe is not due to me, but to your people, and to all of Aegea."

"But you have something in mind, do you not?"

"Yes, I do." said Trand. "It is an easy thing, and at the same time very difficult. Do it and you will be ridiculed and mocked for the remainder of your reign, but you will be in good favor with the gods, and your conscience will be clear. Do it not, and you will be buried in shame, despite your steadfastness and drive, and all you have will be destroyed. Will you hear my proposal?"

Grindal twisted in his chair, suddenly very uncomfortable. He could not imagine what Trand had in mind, but almost certainly, it would be unpleasant. A part of him, a large part, said to send Trand away and not listen to anything he had to say. Trand would leave, if asked to leave, and if Grindal banned him from the borders of Andesha, Trand would obey that as well, for though Trand was obviously a creature great in power and wisdom, he was ultimately obligated to endure the will of men, no matter what he himself might want.

Nevertheless, Grindal was weary, heartsick and desperate. He had met with Quereus just that morning, and all of the reports were bad. He still controlled the western half of the Bould, but that was of little value, since most of the people had fled their homesteads and the area now produced almost nothing. All of his military campaigns had ended in reversals, or outright defeat. Casualties were astounding: Eighteen hundred at Elur, two thousand at Egel, fifteen hundred at Tine Vort, and two thousand at Noga Tine. The total dead now numbered more than ten thousand, and the end was nowhere in sight. Already Grindal had suspended all activity by the army, content to mark time, rebuild his forces, and allow his country to lick its wounds until the winter armistice. He had plans for a massive spring offensive that would be large enough to finally overwhelm his enemy and bring victory to his pride, but the plans would require full conscription, and Grindal was scared to resort to that measure. His people were already suffering. Food was scarce, taxes were high, and those at the extremes of society were beginning to grumble, and refuse to comply with his edicts. Perhaps Trand could offer an escape, a way to yield an exit and still maintain some dignity for his royal house.

Grindal looked at Trand, who was waiting patiently. "You have always been a friend to this kingdom, as well as to all of the kingdoms of men. I will not do you the disservice of ignoring your advice out of hand, nor do you the discourtesy of refusing to give ear to your words. I will hear your proposal."

Trand, with no hesitation, said, "Stop fighting."

Grindal raised his eyebrows, cocking his crownless head to one side. He anticipated more words, but when none were forthcoming, he asked, "Is that all? Surely you have more conditions than that."

Trand laughed boisterously. "'Is that all?' he asks, as if I have requested a beverage in a tavern." Trand snickered some more. "Yes, good Grindal. That is all I ask. Stop fighting, withdraw your forces, and admit your defeat."

"Admit defeat?" Grindal asked incredulously. "I control nearly half of the territory, and if peace were declared today I would be fair in annexing that portion to my kingdom."

"Jonas will never allow it," Trand responded.

"Am I not entitled to the laurels my brave men have won for this kingdom?" said Grindal, getting to his feet. The mention of his rival's name roused his ire. "Why do you insist that I yield to Jonas?"

"Because you are losing," Trand said matter-of-factly.

Grindal paused a moment, licking his lips. It was hard to argue with that. Finally, he said, "I have plans for the spring. We shall overwhelm Gladue and the Bould could be mine in its entirety. I may yet win."

"You shall not," Trand said, unblinking. "Even if you soundly defeat Gladue, and give your cousin his comeuppance, all your efforts will be in vain."

Grindal began to pace the floor, making circles in his half of the stone floor. He was not sure what Trand meant exactly, but he was certain that he could take the mysterious wanderer at his word. If Trand said that he would lose, then most likely that would happen.

"I could convene the Council of Kings," he suggested. "Perhaps we can agree to return the Bould to its previous state, and deny Gladue any spoils. The other kingdoms could force Jonas to comply."

"You can try, but it is hopeless," said Trand, who now pulled a chair and sat. "They would not intervene to stop the war before, and they will not do so now. If anything, they would intervene on Jonas' behalf, against you. They will not alienate the free trade of salt that has been so beneficial to their kingdoms. Your only choice remains to continue fighting, or stop fighting."

"But I cannot simply yield the victory to Jonas!" Grindal nearly screamed. "Why should I not be allowed to keep that which I have won?"

Trand rolled his eyes. "Pride shall be the downfall of the world of men," he hissed in a hushed tone. "You wish to fight not for your people, or your kingdom, or even for glory. You seek only to protect your fragile self-perception."

"That's a lie!" Grindal bellowed, his rage overtaking him. He pointed at Trand and addressed him as he would a subordinate. "You accuse me of letting my people suffer for my vanity! My charge is to protect the honor of my realm! The Bould is mine! I declared it, and I will at least keep what I have earned!"

"Your level of outrage speaks louder than your denials," Trand said evenly.

Grindal calmed himself with a great deal of effort, loosing his energy by clenching and unclenching his fists. "We shall see what the Council decides," he said. His breaths wheezed under the weight of his anger. "I believe they will be more sympathetic to my goals than your own narrow perceptions allow."

Trand stood slowly, and wrapped his cloak around himself once again. "Do as you will," he said, and turned and left. Grindal stayed a few more moments, letting his temper cool. Later, he would be astonished at the memory of him yelling at Trand at the top of his voice, and being so short-tempered.

The next day, six parties left Anboe, each destined for a different capitol of Aegea. They rode with all possible speed, carrying urgent messages from their sovereign to all the kings of the world, pleading for the King's Council to meet to discuss the possibility of peace in the Bould. With them rode the hope of the entire continent, for the collaboration of men would be necessary to end the destructive conflict and bring peace to the world.

⇒ ⇐

Meanwhile, Lendum was discovering feelings in the deepest part of his soul that he had never suspected. Elisa was taking possession of him with the most gentle of movements: a stroke of his cheek, a slight turn of her head to move her hair, or a thoughtless touch of his shoulder when she laughed. Each moment brought pleasure that would eventually lead to unspeakable internal torment.

The morning after they met, Lendum and Elisa shared a very simple breakfast of juice and oatmeal before going out to walk through some of the city. Elisa proved a good guide, not only explaining what the buildings housed, but also she was quite knowledgeable of their history. She talked almost non-stop, describing the architecture styles, the king that commissioned the building, the reason for the construction, the year it was built, and so on. Lendum listened intently, fascinated. In truth, Elisa could have been discussing gardening techniques or the craft of a fletcher and Lendum would have been equally spellbound.

They strolled to the stables, where Elisa was delighted to meet Timo. The horse was lively and energetic, and Lendum suggested that they go for a ride together, to see and share the beautiful day and at the same time allow Timo some exercise. Elisa was ecstatic about the prospect. They saddled Timo, and then they both climbed on, Elisa behind Lendum, her arms clasped tightly around his waist, her exhales striking the tender spot beneath his right ear. They rode out of the city gates, down the road toward the Bould, and then turned left into the fields, riding as fast as Timo could manage. Elisa's hair trailed out behind her, and at times, she shouted into the wind from pure excitement. She squeezed Lendum tighter.

After a time they came to a little stand of trees, where the grasses of late summer were tall and rich. Timo instinctively checked his pace, and the riders dismounted, marveling at the complete silence and profound solitude of this place. Timo began chomping on the luxurious grasses, enjoying the respite he had earned from stable hay with his morning's labor. Hand in hand, Lendum and Elisa walked leisurely through the trees. Suddenly she turned, and without a word, she kissed him full on the mouth. The kiss was Lendum's very first, the most memorable, and an instant he would always desire to experience again. He closed his eyes, surrendering to her embrace, trying with all of his power to record every detail of this perfect moment. Soon it was gone. When he opened his eyes, Elisa stood there, smiling awkwardly. Obviously, her own impulsiveness embarrassed her.

"Seems you were right," she said quietly. "Not only soldiers are short-sighted, acting before they think." She grew very serious all at once. "If you should tell your friends that I yielded my resolve so easily, I shan't forgive you."

Lendum took her hand. She was trembling, ever so slightly. "I will not tell a soul," he assured her. "I also had a wise mother, and she would say, 'Respect a lady, and it will bring honor to you both.' You need not fear. In my mind, these lips are no longer my own." Lendum could feel her hand relax. Her face formed into one of such confident beauty that Lendum felt his being become even more enchained to her wishes.

"I should be getting back," she said with reluctance. "I must be at the Bear's Tooth soon." She paused, biting her lip. "When can I see you again, Commander? Tomorrow, perhaps?"

Lendum looked deep into her eyes, feeling great regret. In his enthusiasm, he had completely forgotten his duty. Indeed, he had scarcely thought of anything but Elisa since he first laid eyes on her. Unwillingly, he replied, "I do not know. I am only away from the front because His Highness summoned me. Once I meet with him, he could send me back at once." With heart-wrenching pain he added, "In fact, I fully expect to depart before the noon hour tomorrow."

A look of absolute sorrow washed over Elisa's face making all of her features droop, as if deflated. The sight broke Lendum's heart, while at the same time comforting him. He already knew that he loved her. Now it was clear that she loved him as well. A single tear formed in the corner of her eye, and when it spilled out, flowing along the edge of her nose, Lendum stopped it with his thumb.

"Lady, do not weep. In mere hours, you have taken my callous heart and reshaped it into something beautiful. You have given hope to a hopeless man, and in payment of this heavy debt, I pledge my heart to you. Come what may, Lendum of Gladue is now your willing servant, and once our lord releases me, I will be by your side, whether it is tomorrow, or many years from now, or in the unknown."

Elisa did not speak, but embraced Lendum fiercely, as if taking possession of what he had given her. He held her in his arms, feeling the life and love within her, knowing that it was probable that he may never have this experience again.

⇒ ⇐

The next day was the fifteenth of September, and while Trand waited patiently for an audience with Grindal, Lendum and Corce were permitted into the palace to meet with their lord. Corce was visibly afraid. He had developed into an honorable man, confident in the skills of his labor, but the pomp and gallantry that surrounded the King was outside the limits of his experience, and he feared anything foreign to him. His hands shook, he had fresh sweat along his brow, and he stammered when he spoke, the words garbled and nonsensical. Lendum was also in fear, but not of the King. At this point, Lendum feared no man whatsoever. He only feared the words this particular man might utter, commanding him to do a duty that would sunder him from his newfound love.

Once admitted, a guard led them through the palace, without whose guidance they would have become quickly and hopelessly lost. After a brisk walk of some ten minutes with many twists and turns, they found themselves in a long hallway, lined with tall torches and covered with elegant red carpeting. Statues of men in helms and battle dress stood at regular intervals on both sides of the hallway, sentries reminding those that tread this length that they were in the presence of greatness and royalty. The guard led them to the end of the hall, where massive doors or oak, carved with runes of the language of Gladue and characters of the tongue of Tor, closed off a great stone archway. In both languages, the words announced, "For the honor and glory of this nation we sacrifice all that we are, and all that we shall ever have, and all that we love." Lendum at first thought that a very heavy burden to lay upon a visitor a monarch, but them he remembered something that Trand had said in his kitchen years ago. The wise wanderer had said that Kings were slaves to their realms. The inscriptions were not meant for the visitors to the King, but for the King himself. Corce thought nothing of the inscriptions, other than they were handsome to the eye. He could speak both languages fluently, but he could read and write in neither.

The guard unbolted the latch and the door opened wide, swinging noiselessly on its huge brass hinges. The guard motioned for them to enter, saying, "Mind your tongues. Thoughtless words can have severe consequences." Lendum nodded in acknowledgment of the warning, thinking the advice to be very sound, then entered the room, with Corce close behind. The door swung shut, and Lendum could hear the bolt slide back into place, sealing them in.

Once again, Lendum was beside himself with amazement. Never before had he seen a room as exquisite as this one. Jonas' throne room was shaped like an octagon, with broad steps running the perimeter of the room, so that as one entered, he felt as if he were lowering himself into a large bowl. Lendum could see equally impressive doors to his left and his right. He turned to see Corce, who was literally awestruck, his mouth agape. Lendum cleared his throat to get his attention, and then tapped his own chin, a gesture meant to tell Corce to shut his mouth. Corce did so.

Thick, red carpeting lay under their feet, leading down the steps into the center of the room. Lendum took a tentative step forward, and then another, until his was within the room fully. The carpet was crossed at the bottom of the bowl, making a giant X on the floor, leading to the three doors and lastly to the throne itself. Immense columns stood where the carpet was absent, reaching high to the ceiling, beveling into a mirror image of the floor. The columns themselves had been fashioned into likenesses of the four goddesses of human virtue, rendered with a skill that no longer existed in the world. Lendum recognized Nisha, the goddess of justice, and Avena, the goddess of peace, but the names of the other two escaped him. The room was incredibly bright, partly due to the two large windows on each side of the throne, but mostly because the stone that made the walls, the columns, the floor and the throne pedestal was polished white marble, quarried far away and transported with great expense to this regal capitol built on the plains. Everything about this room spoke of opulence and tremendous importance. Standing there made Lendum feel very small, and of little significance.

Presently, a man approached. He was very old, from the look of him, and he carried a staff of ebony, with a milky white jewel set into its pinnacle, the surface of which seemed to shift and boil like the clouds. He wore flowing red robes, the same hue as the carpeting, and he shuffled as he walked, leaning heavily on his staff. He had a neatly trimmed beard, but his head was bald, covered with a small cap of red cloth. Once he was before them, he gave a salute, which Lendum and Corce returned at once. Then the man spoke.

"I am Motte, chief advisor to His Majesty King Jonas II of Gladue. Why have you come?"

"I am Commander Lendum Cetus, officer of the Lion regiment of the Third Battalion. This is Corce Norwood, my First Lieutenant. Our lord summoned me. I know not the reason for my summons."

Motte looked long at Corce. "You were summoned, it is true," Motte said to Lendum, but not looking at him. "But this one was not. What the King would say, he will say to you alone. This one may wait outside." At once, the door behind them unlatched and swung open, and there stood the guard that had escorted them through the palace. Corce looked at Lendum, and Lendum nodded. Corce turned and exited the way he had come, more relieved than he could ever express. The large door shut again, with only a whisper of sound to mark its closing.

"Come," Motte said. "His Majesty waits."

Lendum followed Motte, who walked very slowly. However, it was not long before the throne itself came into view, and there sat Jonas, King of Gladue. His golden crown sat on his head, encrusted with hundreds of tiny red jewels, sparkling like fire. His throne sat on a pedestal over a dozen wide steps, so that the legs of the mighty chair were over Lendum's head. The very first step was actually a wooden rail, polished shiny over the long years by thousands of kneeling subjects. Lendum knelt himself at the rail, bringing his right hand to his breast and saying, "Hail! Jonas, King of Gladue and my sovereign. I, Lendum Cetus, have come as you have ordered."

Jonas stood and began descending the steps toward his able commander. "Rise," he said, "and let me see into the face of the one that has brought such glory to my realm."

Lendum got to his feet, and was a little surprised to learn that his ruler was shorter than he, and not much older. As if reading his mind, Jonas said, "I, also, expected someone older. The exploits that have reached my ear tell of bravery rare in one as young as yourself." Jonas smiled, revealing a mouthful of crooked, discolored teeth. His face was covered with a thick layer of white makeup that tried in vain to conceal the numerous scars that had disfigured his skin, the result of large blemishes that plagued him still. Motte, who stood to the King's left, smirked slightly. The jewel in his staff swirled with opaque whiteness.

"Can you guess why I have summoned you?" Jonas asked. The nostrils of his large, red nose flared with his inquiry.

"I know not, my lord," answered Lendum succinctly.

The king nodded and began to ascend the steps to the right of the throne, towards one of the massive windows. Motte followed the king, shuffling as best he could, and he motioned that Lendum should do the same.

"I am told," Jonas said as he walked, "that a great deal of the success we have enjoyed in this war is largely due to your efforts. Is it not so?"

"I think not, my lord," Lendum responded. "Victory must be shared by many, for the sacrifices of many are required. An army is more a centipede than a serpent."

Jonas chuckled at the analogy. "True," he agreed, "but even centipedes must have a head; otherwise there is nothing to coordinate so many limbs.

When all the limbs work together, we win battles, and while all may share in the victory, history remembers the leader. Do you understand?"

"Yes, my lord." Lendum understood, but a large part of him disagreed. He did not say so however.

"I summoned you, commander, because I believe that you will be of supreme importance in our ultimate victory." At the top step, near the stone sill of the great window, Jonas turned, placing his hands on his hips. Motte assumed his place at the king's side, as eager to please and loyal as any lapdog. "You've already proven yourself a superlative leader," the king continued. "That is a great asset in itself, to be sure. In addition to that, your *reputation* is of no less value. Men are willing to serve under your command. The transfer requests are endless, even from those who at present endure no great danger. There are those that would rather face the steel of the enemy than stay here in comfort and safety, guarding this city, and every new volunteer asks to be in your company. Were you aware of this?"

"No, my lord." Lendum felt a little embarrassed by this, as he had when he had dinner with Elisa, but he struggled not to show it.

"I have decided to use these two great advantages to bring about the utter defeat of our rival, and secure the Bould for our nation for all time." Jonas turned his back to Lendum, looking out of the window. The late morning sun shone through, casting soft, yellow light across Lendum's boots.

"You shall not return to the front this year," said Jonas. "You shall winter here, and in the spring you shall lead the newly formed Fourth Battalion to the Bould, and Andesha will be undone."

Lendum could hardly believe his ears. Motte was smiling broadly, showing rows of jagged teeth. "My lord," Lendum said after a moment, "am I to be named Marshal?"

"Yes you are, the commander of the greatest army this world has seen in millennia. Twenty-six full companies, totaling nearly forty-thousand swords. Andesha will be overwhelmed."

For a moment, Lendum felt that his lord was quite insane. He chose his words carefully. "Begging your pardon, sire, but it will take some time to assemble so great a force. Do you think they will be ready before the spring?"

Jonas turned his face from the window, but not his body. "Their state of readiness will be your responsibility," said the king in a low voice. "As for the men themselves, they are already mustered, outfitted, and formed. They await only your instruction."

Lendum was taken aback. Motte's smile seemed to grow even wider, apparently overjoyed at Lendum's discomfiture. The young commander swallowed hard, and when he tried to speak, no words came. His throat was suddenly very dry. He swallowed again and merely muttered, "My lord?"

"Come and see," said Jonas. Lendum walked up the remaining steps until he could see out the window. Once there, he had his bearings immediately. He was looking northeast, over the plains of Lemane. In the distance, he could just barely make out the Yosami Mountains, glittering like icicles.

Nearer, just outside the walls of the city, lay another city of small tents. Thousands upon thousands of domes of white canvas covered the landscape in neat little rows and columns, like a vast field of mushrooms. All around, men in green toiled, performed drills, exercised, sparred, or otherwise engaged in soldiery. Horses pulled wagons full of provisions. Commanders went about loudly shouting orders, occasionally brought to Lendum's ears by a rising wind. Lendum had never seen so many warriors assembled on one spot. These were his troops. He was the marshal of this, the Fourth Battalion of Gladue. A sense of power fell over him, which he found difficult to squash. For no discernible reason, he thought of Trand. Almost certainly, he had foreseen this development, and had desired it.

"Do you accept this post, Commander?" asked Jonas. "If so, you will winter here, quartered in the palace court, to prepare these troops for the coming campaign. If not, you may return to the front at once, with no shame, as commander of the Lion Regiment of third Battalion. What say you?"

Lendum fought the urge to accept immediately. This opportunity gave him the means to achieve his greatest desires. Not only could he seek his revenge with an entire army of ardent followers, but also he could stay in Ashtone for months, and thus avoid being parted from Elisa, at least for a while. The opposing aims of his heart were at once reconciled, and he did not appear to lose one whilst gaining the other. He could pursue his love and his vengeance, capable of seizing both with one outstretched hand.

Lendum turned to face his king, and then knelt before him. "I accept this charge, humbly, my lord. Trust you have bestowed, and my death will take me before I betray that trust." Jonas laid his hand on Lendum's head, in symbol of anointing. Motte, out of this King's sight, sneered as if disgusted.

"Rise, Lord Marshal of Gladue, and go forth in honor, love and justice, that we may have peace." Lendum regained his feet. When he looked at Motte, the crooked smile had returned.

"Go and see to your belongings. The guard outside will show you to your quarters within the palace grounds. On the morrow, you will be decorated, and you shall meet your regimental commanders, and then begin to make Fourth Battalion into an army."

"Yes, my lord." Lendum turned to Motte. "Good day to you, sir," he said to him merely to be polite.

"Congratulations, Marshal," Motte said in a wheezing voice. "I know I shall be proud of what you achieve."

There was nothing rude about the comment, but Lendum found the words ominous nevertheless. Lendum gave a perfunctory nod, and then turned to leave, suddenly very eager to be out of the room.

"Lord Marshal," said the king, stopping Lendum in his tracks. "I hope I need not tell you that your charge is one of extreme secrecy, and to speak of it to anyone outside your command amounts to treason."

"I understand, my lord," Lendum replied, feeling the threat but registering no fear.

"Good," said Jonas. "Then on your way."

Lendum left the throne room. After being shown his quarters at the palace court, he departed for the Bear's Tooth to give Elisa the news that they had more time together.

⸺ ⸺

Quereus was, primarily, a soldier. He was an excellent judge of battlefields, horses, armor, and weapons. He could read maps, he could read terrain, and he could read the morale of his troops. He was less adroit, through both experience and his innate manner, at reading individual people. Up to this point, his career had advanced because he had received orders and then carried them out with alacrity. Now, he had to deal with the conflicted orders that came from the king himself, and he could not fathom the logic, or the lack thereof, that had generated such orders. He stepped gingerly, trying to be both humble and exact, though the task seemed beyond his meager abilities.

"I beg your pardon, my lord, but how many men did you say?"

Grindal's face seemed contorted into a perpetual sneer. A huge vein had swollen in his temple, and with every pulse of life-giving blood, the vessel throbbed so violently that the king's crown rocked almost imperceptibly on his head. His hands gripped the armrests of his throne with such force that his whitened fingers seemed to melt into the stone.

"Fifty-thousand!" Grindal screamed, so loudly that the other men in the hall lowered their eyes and backed away. "I want fifty-thousand ready for battle come spring!"

"But my lord, just this morning you ordered our armies to cease operations for the season, and this very day you have sent envoys to the other kingdoms to convene the King's Council in the hope of securing peace. Why do you also…"

Grindal abruptly stood, plucked to crown from his head and slung it wildly at Quereus. He missed terribly however, and it struck the stone wall beyond. Dislodged jewels clattered on the floor, a fortune scattered within the cracks.

"That word!" Grindal shrieked, his voice shrill with rage. "That damnable, damnable word! I shall not hear it again! Not ever again!"

Quereus, for the first time in his long years of service, feared that his sovereign was mad. "My lord, what word angers you so?"

"Why!" He shouted in response. "Why, why, why, why, why! It grates on my ears like a balling baby! I will not hear it again! You dare question me? You question my judgment? My motives? I will not tolerate it! Never again!"

Quereus, breathing deeply, tried to remain calm. He was not entirely above groveling, but he wanted to avoid doing it if possible. "My apologies Sire," he said in his most submissive tone. "To achieve such an ambitious number we shall need to resort to conscription, and even then…"

"Then conscript them!" Grindal yelled childishly.

"And," Quereus continued, "even if we raise that number, our armories could not hope to clothe and arm so many."

"Then clothe them in sackcloth, and arm them with clubs and pitchforks! Let their nails grow into talons and file their teeth into fangs! Just get me fifty-thousand men!"

"As you wish, my lord." Quereus was convinced that he was conversing with a lunatic, but what could he do? "What range shall we set for the conscription?"

"Fourteen to sixty," the king answered, sitting back down in his throne. The men in the room, military or otherwise, looked at their king and each other in disbelief. A servant boy scurried over and retrieved the thrown crown, bringing it back to Grindal with deference. Grindal waved him away, seeing that the crown was bent and broken.

Quereus did not want to antagonize Grindal further, but these orders were grossly irresponsible. He had never been squeamish about sending men to die. Soldiers drew their wages from that labor. Could he lead an army of boys and old men? Ordering such a group to charge could only mean robbing one of the life they have yet to live, and the other of the leisure they have earned.

"My lord, such conscription will strip our lands bare. You will rob both cradle and grave."

"Then I am a thief," Grindal said quietly, feeling exhausted after his tirade. The war was having a telling effect on his body and mind. His normally bright eyes were sunken, and deep lines etched his face, which was gaunt and pallid. Concentrating was difficult, for his mind felt pulled in too many directions at once. The last two years had aged him ten. "Go see to it, Marshal. You have five months."

Quereus bowed to his king, and then exited, a row of commanders following in his wake. The other councilors took their leave as well. Many worried that the conscription decree would snag them as well as their sons.

= =

During the two weeks following his promotion, Lendum trained vigorously with his men. He came to know his commanders by name, and he learned the capabilities of each of his regiments. He rarely chose to stay in the quarters provided by the crown, preferring to sleep in a tent amongst his troops to become familiar with them. By not setting himself apart, as some leaders are prone to do, he earned great respect, both from his subordinates and from the common soldiers. In a very short time, the reputation he had earned with his sword in the Bould was reaffirmed, and his men grew to love him, to follow his orders with enthusiasm, and to trust his judgment.

Lendum spent all day with his men, but he spent all of his evenings with Elisa. He had dinner with her every night, and they talked for many hours. Eventually, he came to tell her the truth about his past, and she wept for his suffering. She came to love him even more, for in his heart he was a good man, able and strong, and yet tender to her. In his presence, she felt beautiful and vital, as if nothing in the wide world existed except her. The moments they shared were unrivaled bliss.

On the first of October, Jonas summoned Lendum. He went to the palace, and found his way to the throne room unescorted. Corce, now the chief officer in Lendum's staff, went with him as well, less nervous than he had been on his first visit. Both young officers wore their full uniforms, their helms tucked under their left arms, polished and shining like mirrors.

At the door of the throne room, Corce once again waited outside, avoiding the King's sight. Lendum entered alone, the single guard opening the door, and then silently closing it again after Lendum was inside.

Once he stood before the king, he knelt, and after hailing his sovereign, Jonas began at once to deliver interesting news.

"It seems," he began, "that my cousin doubts his chances, and has requested the kings of the earth to meet to discuss the prospects of peace." A wry smile sat on his lips, inwardly amused at the thought of Grindal twisting in an agony of misgiving and misery.

Lendum's eyebrows rose instinctively, betraying his surprise. Motte stood silently to the king's left, hunched like a bird of prey. His face showed no reaction at all. He watched Lendum intently.

"The Council is scheduled to begin on the first of January," Jonas said. "I would depart for Farshton during the first week of December, allowing time for the winter travel."

The king paused again, waiting. Lendum suspected that Jonas desired some kind of response, but he could think of absolutely nothing to say.

"Should I attend, Lord Marshal Lendum? The envoys await my answer."

"That," Lendum finally replied, "I think is a matter best decided by Your Majesty."

"I will decide," said Jonas curtly. "What I am requesting is an opinion. What do you think?"

Lendum thought a moment. He was unprepared for this eventuality. Thus far, his business had been the making of war, not peace, and taking orders from a king was far less taxing than advising one. Tenseness wormed into his stomach as he mentally juggled the possibilities. If the king went to Farshton, and could end the war through negotiation without forgoing his original ends, the country and its people could benefit, and he could pursue a life with Elisa, though he would lose his chance for revenge. If he did not go to the council, then many more men would undoubtedly die, the suffering would continue indefinitely, and he could lose Elisa, but his lust for vengeance could be sated. He quickly realized that the misery of the land outweighed his personal desires, no matter how much his heart may crave them.

Finally, he responded, "I think that if Your Majesty can accomplish his ends without further bloodshed, then that possibility should be pursued."

Motte rolled his eyes like a child, clearly disagreeing with Lendum.

"Even if it means the end of your command?" asked Jonas. "Without the war, Fourth Battalion is superfluous, and it will be disbanded with all haste once these hostilities are concluded."

"My personal wants are nothing compared to the well-being of the realm," Lendum said promptly. "I fear not for my future, because I trust that my liege will remember the service that I have rendered in his name."

"Well spoken, and your faith in me is honorable and well-received." The king stood and walked down the steps of the pedestal until he was standing before Lendum, eye to eye. Motte followed like a mongrel.

"I will go to Farshton, and try my best to balance our gains and our potential losses. If I am successful, then we will have peace, and the spoils of our great efforts will be ours with no more sacrifices. If I am not successful, then the spoils will still be ours, but more labor must be done. Continue with your charge, Lord Marshal, to be prepared for the worst, while we hope for the best."

The king dismissed Lendum, and after telling Corce the news that peace may well be at hand, he reminded him that the work of forming Fourth Battalion into a formidable fighting force would continue. Most of the recruits were young and naïve, though hale and eager, and they had much to learn about combat before they would be ready to meet an adversary on the field.

Therefore, the possibility of peace had affected Lendum's duties not at all. As autumn slipped into winter, the resolve of the men of Fourth Battalion hardened, and they became a little concerned that peace would be declared before they had a chance to prove themselves. By the first of December, when Jonas and his party departed for Farshton, a severe snow blanketed the ground. Lendum suspended daily training until the conclusion of the Council. His reasons were that the weather was inhospitable, and that potential peace with the enemy made future training moot. In reality, the men were growing beyond control. They longed for challengers with which to test their steel, and they thirsted for blood and triumph. Jonas had selected the correct leader for his army. Lendum had made Fourth Battalion a beast, craving war, and silently detesting peace. Woe to the enemy that had to face them.

═ ═

On the eighth of December, Lendum had dinner with Elisa, and at that dinner, he proposed. She was happy, happier than she had ever been, but a single shred of doubt clung to her heart.

"I would love to be your wife," the wisps of her thin hair covering her shoulders, "but I am selfish. I would have my husband be entirely my own. Will not your pledge to the king interfere to the point of sundering us?"

"I have pledged my service, but my heart belongs not to the king, nor to me. My heart is yours and has been since I first saw you. All I can promise you is my love and devotion, and pray that that is enough."

Elisa, full of hope and joy, relented, casting her doubts aside. They were married on the twelfth of December in the Temple of Avena, the Goddess of the Sorna that personified all things beautiful. Lendum had reached out and daringly seized that which he loved, hoping that he would never again be alone, or experience loss, tragedy, of grief. For a blessed time he was happy, as he had been before he fell into the mine of salt. He knew no anger, no hatred, and no fear, save the fear of losing his beloved.

Yet deep in his heart, blackness festered that needed only a gentle reminder to regain its full fury. The memory of his elderly mother, slaughtered in the dust like an animal, had not been wholly forgotten. The gift of his wife's love offered merely a reprieve from the pain, not genuine solace. The relief was glorious, but unfortunately, would be tragically brief.

THE KING'S COUNCIL

Farshton was an ancient city. Located in the heart of the kingdom of Rubia, at the very center of Aegea, legend held that it sat on the very spot where man first walked the earth. Kings often met each other in Farshton, and both of the previous Councils of Kings had been held there, it being the most accessible location for all those attending. The Rubians were an intensely religious people, and they still held the annual festival of Tor with pious devotion. Flocks of humble worshipers would crowd into the plaza of the temple of Tor, there to make sacrifices, pay homage, give thanks, and pray for the speedy return of their deity. The city itself was nestled into the foothills of the majestic Yosami Mountains, a long range that formed the backbone of the continent, running from sea to sea. The mountains ran diagonally across the lands, from southwest to northeast, and separated the northern nations from the southern. Andesha, Gladue, Rubia and Anafaline lay in the north. Nefala, Tolone and Hashana lay in the south. At this council, the heads of all nations would be present.

As the first of January neared, winter released its power, and heavy snowfall covered the landscape for many miles around the city. Many feared that some of the southern kings would be obliged to postpone, if not cancel outright. Indeed, some whispered that calling a Council of Kings was unnecessary for a reason as regional as the War of the Bould. King's Councils were exceedingly rare. Despite the view that the war was too trivial for a council, the kings of Aegea were reluctant to decline the invitation because of the uncommonness of the occasion. Any king that attended a council of such esteemed men could cement a valuable cornerstone in the foundation of their legacy. In the end, all the kings attended, though Duras of Nefala arrived late. He had foolishly attempted to cross the mountains, trapping his party for three days in the massive snowdrifts. His recklessness cost the lives of two of his escorts, and nearly cost him his own, but he was too hardy a man to let himself be bested by snow. The other kings of the south, Lindus of Tolone and Alcoa of Hashana, elected to arrive by way of water, sailing along the southern coasts before ascending the river. Thus, they endured fewer hazards, and entered the city fresh and with their full delegations. The council was delayed two days to allow Duras time to honor the memory of those that had died in his service.

On the third of January, all of the kings of the world met in the glorious upper citadel of Farshton. With them came their various councilors, military advisors, pages, couriers, and for some, their sons, the heirs of their kingdoms. In addition, there was Ronuse, the high priest of the temple of Tor, who would act as mediator and control the agenda. There was also a man named Thortus, and his son Andus, men in attendance as honored observers only. Finally, seated at the high table looking as disinterested as can be imagined, was Trand, dressed in his usual black garb.

As the noon hour approached, the kings of Aegea took their seats at the thick stone table, their associates seated in chairs behind them. When the noon bell sounded, Ronuse stood, and the chatter of the room ceased, becoming altogether quiet. A middle-aged man of about forty years, Ronuse was experienced at dealing with kings. Nevertheless, he was at that moment quite vexed, faced with the duty of monitoring this monumental meeting. The previous Council had taken place nearly five-hundred years before, and there was no one to guide him or offer advice on how to proceed. When he was informed of the coming council, Ronuse and two of his subordinates spent nearly a week searching the archives, looking for basic procedures for council etiquette. Once found, the script was so archaic that Ronuse was required to seek out a lore master to decipher its meaning. Now, with the proper instructions near to hand, he was ready to begin.

"Greetings to all," he said in a loud voice. He spread his hands welcomingly. "My sincere thanks to all that have braved the journey to come to this city, and I pray that the gods of the Sorna guide us, and give us wisdom to solve the problems of the world that our people may spend their lives in blessed peace."

There were a few shouts of 'Hear hear', and some stamping of feet, but largely the room remained somber. Trand did not move, or even look up. He examined his fingernails.

"It is the great strength of men," Ronuse continued, "that despite the differences of our convictions, in our time of need we seek each other out, that we should find wisdom from our combined perspectives. Hail to the kings of the earth!"

There was some applause, but not much. The occasion was too serious to allow for a great deal of merriment. Ronuse appeared disappointed by the lackluster response, but he pressed on.

"Now, let each king step forth and be counted, that his words may be recorded and heard by this council."

Then each king stood in turn, introducing himself and each member of his house. Then the kings introduced their advisors and councilors. This was ceremony, and quite time consuming, for more than fifty men sat together at this meeting, and introducing every man by name took more than an hour. However, it was necessary. Few of the men present knew each other, and the debate was likely to be long and heated. Some familiarity at the table could cool passions and make things run smoother.

Once all of the introductions were made, Ronuse stood again, his gray-speckled beard laid out like a bib on his chest. "It is tradition," he stated, "that the king that made the call be the first to state his intentions. King Grindal, are you prepared to make your initial statements, or do you wish to defer?"

King Grindal stood, looking very calm and rested. His sleep had been troubled of late, but a hearty serving of Rubian wine had made the past night's slumber both long and invigorating. Seven servants and advisors sat behind Grindal, including Quereus, appearing immaculate in his shining mail and earthen-brown cape. His marvelous exterior concealed a turbulent interior. This council was the last hope he had of avoiding a horrendous debacle. Even now, Andeshan men were being plucked from their homes to feed the machine of war that would be unleashed should this meeting prove vain. Quereus said a prayer that Tor might enlighten his sovereign.

Grindal smiled at the room. "Thank you, Lord High Priest Ronuse. I am prepared to make my statement." He left his seat, walking around the table as he spoke. "My fellow kings, my most indemonstrable gratitude for being here today. I am ashamed to admit that, though I am the lord of a great nation and a capable people, my ability to solve certain dilemmas has come up lacking. I am in need of assistance, and I fear that only this council can provide it." Grindal made sweeping arm gestures as he spoke, punctuating each phrase with the movements of his delicate hands. His words were smooth, genuine, and compelling. Most of his audience paid him rapt attention, eager to hear each syllable. Jonas made notations on a parchment, smugly doing other business while his rival made his case. Trand actually yawned.

"As you know," Grindal said, continuing his circuit around the large, round table, "for two years now a state of war has existed between my kingdom and the kingdom of Gladue. This war, through a lack of foresight on my part and others," he said, looking at Jonas, "has become a horrible beast, terrible in its effect and unthinkable in its proportions. I sought out this council, in the hope that all of the kingdoms of Aegea could be brought to bear, thus ending this conflict, and restoring the peace that was enjoyed for so long in the contested area of the Bould."

Grindal's prepared speech fell on receptive ears. He enchanted the room with his talk.

"As a humble man," he said, "I am willing to accept my portion of the blame for this tragedy of misunderstanding, and am also willing to discuss any option one of the great kings present could be able to put forth." Grindal completed his circle around the table, and retook his place, putting his palms on the cold, stone surface before his seat. "My ego, admittedly, has already made many widows and orphans. I beg you; help me conclude this matter that no more need suffer." With that he sat, finished for the time being. His speech had been well delivered, concise, and very believable. Grindal's display shocked Quereus. It was so at odds with the insanity he had seen just weeks before. Only Jonas and Trand remained unmoved, their indifference tattooed in their expressions.

Duras of Nefala rapped the table with his mug, asking for recognition. Once Ronuse gave him the floor, he stood, his long, braided beard swinging like a pendulum. "King Grindal speaks with humility, and that is good. He has admitted fault, and seeks the aid of this council to end the war. To clarify, does this also mean that he admits defeat?"

"Absolutely not!" Grindal replied sharply. "My troops currently control nearly half of the Bould, and could continue fighting for a long time, thought that is not something I desire. I would have the war end today, with no more men dying or displaced. That is my goal. My worry is not that our efforts may prove vain, but rather that my adversary will be too selfish to allow any kind of concession." If Jonas took offense at this minor insult, he did not show it.

Duras replied, "Well, my understanding is that the matter has already been decided, in this very room, though it was long ago. The second council placed the Bould under joint occupation, and I see no reason why we cannot simply return the Bould to those terms."

"We cannot return to those terms," said Jonas, finally taking an interest, "because Gladue will not consent to another such arrangement. I have declared by edict that the Bould is now the sovereign territory of my kingdom, and every realm represented here, save Andesha, gave recognition through inactivity. The Bould is mine in its entirety, and I will eject any trespasser with prejudice." Motte, seated near the king, smiled with approval. His staff rested against the hollow of his shoulder, gripped tightly with both hands. The white jewel shone faintly, frothy and boiling. He had advised the king that with victory so imminent, conceding one inch of the territory was foolhardy.

Lindus of Tolone was recognized, and the aged king stood with the aid of his son Silvius. "King Jonas, your arguments are faulty, for many reasons. One king alone cannot undo what the second council did here. Breaking a solemn oath, and then using that betrayal to legitimize what you have done is beneath royalty. Besides, the seizure of the territory and the subsequent war has not only injured those that hail from Andesha and Gladue. *All* nations had colonists in the area, many of whom have been forced to flee and lose everything. Your claim to protect the citizens of the Bould appears hollow. It's evident that the breaking of the treaty and the encroachment made by both sides was done because of the Noveton mine."

"Motives are irrelevant when the subject is legality," Jonas retorted. He was by far the youngest king present, and he addressed the council in an arrogant tone that was not at all appreciated. "By my interpretation, Gladue voluntarily entered the agreement to jointly settle the Bould, and now it has voluntarily withdrawn from it."

"That agreement was only reached because of the unanimity of the seven kingdoms," Lindus replied. "Unanimity is required to undo it."

"That is your stance, your Highness," said Jonas. "Not mine."

"It is not only his stance!" cried out Duras, out of turn. The break in good manners upset Ronuse, but he did not try to restrain Duras. "I happen to agree, and many of my people have returned to my lands with tales of woe, having lost both their homes and their faith. I hold you responsible, Highness, and if you have any dignity you will make amends here today. Not just to me, but to every kingdom you have wronged with your rashness."

"I am not solely to blame for this," said Jonas childishly. "Grindal also broke the precious agreement that you claim to cherish."

"Grindal called this council, and he has publicly shown his remorse, an action that is humbling in its bravery," Duras replied. "What have you done, other than to fill this grand hall with swagger and display your gross apathy?" The more passionate Duras became, the more Ronuse squirmed in his chair. Duras did not notice. "Do you think that the kings of the earth will permit this to go on indefinitely? Do you believe you can best all of Aegea?"

Jonas eyed Duras sternly. He did not flinch, because he knew that he had a powerful bargaining chip. "What I believe," he said coolly, "is that we will never have the opportunity to know." Motte had also advised Jonas that the other kings would never intervene in the war, because they had all benefited from a rich trade in salt from the Noveton mine. To make war would cut off this vital resource, an eventuality that was unlikely to happen. It was a shrewd guess, because Duras, his bluff called, sat back down in disgust.

Ronuse took a deep breath, and let it out with relief. Duras was known as a fair man, but he was also renowned as having a fearsome temper, and quick to come to blows. He had controlled himself, thus far, and Ronuse was grateful for that blessing. Gingerly, he got back to his feet. "Gentlemen," he said contritely, "I think it would be best to make suggestions that would apply only to the present and future." He looked at each king, sweeping his eyes around the room. The lamps on the columns burned brightly, the flames dancing wildly with each draft of air. "To bicker and cast blame over the past can only lead to bitterness and deadlock."

"Hark!" shouted Trand abruptly, making half of the room jump. "I think I just heard the voice of reason, the first yet today."

"You have an opinion on this matter, wise wanderer?" asked Ronuse with genuine respect.

"An opinion?" said Trand with thick rhetoric. "Why, yes! I believe I do, thought it is already known to all of the crowned heads here. However, I will state it again, should anyone wish to hear it."

With a wave of his hand, Ronuse yielded the floor, sitting down as he did so.

"Everything that has transpired is a travesty," said Trand, still seated. In fact, he seemed most comfortable, with his legs crossed and his hands folded in his lap. From the look of him, he seemed to be discussing nothing more important than the weather. "Most blame the combatants entirely, but my indictment is wider, including every member of this council." There was some mumbling and grumbling, but no one interrupted. "My opinion is simple and concise: The belligerents should stop the war now, returning the Bould to its pre-war status. And if they do not," he paused, letting the brief silence build suspense, "then they should be made to."

Trand's utterance made the room erupt with angry talk. Ronuse quickly stood, spreading his hands, as if he could silence the council with elaborate gestures. After some time the chatter did subside, and Ronuse was visibly disturbed.

"Trand," Ronuse asked, "are you suggesting that we bring *more* nations into the war? That seems contrary to the goal of ending it."

"I can understand that point of view, but it is fallacious in the extreme. King Duras has already spoken the wisdom of it; neither Andesha nor Gladue can overcome all the armies of the world. If they refuse to comply with a directive issued by this council, then force should be applied to make it happen."

Ronuse looked at Grindal, and then Jonas. Grindal squirmed in his seat, but Jonas seemed as unconcerned as ever. Clearly, a return to pre-war days was unlikely. He decided to embark on a new course that would hear other options and have them debated at length.

"Are there any other suggestions?" he asked hopefully. A silence as profound as death filled the room. Outside the large, shuttered windows, the winds swirled and whistled, searching for a way in. Heavy drapes covered every inch, stunting the winter's chill.

King Alco, the ruler of Hashana, finally stood. An imposing yet personable man, his rule was something of a joke, since his realm was little more than a commonwealth of Tolone, but he was nonetheless treated with much respect, for his people bore the brunt of the malice of Sindus to save the lives of others. He wore a narrow circlet of silver to acknowledge his station, but otherwise he appeared as a common soldier, which was the manner of his people. In Hashana, to be a soldier was to be a citizen, and there was no higher honor than combat. Even priests of the forgotten tongues of the forest were of lower status than the infantry of the realm. Alco prized the art of war above all else, yet these events, men fighting other men, was unseemly. He desired a cessation of hostilities, so the strength of men could be refocused where it belonged; to the east.

"If there can be no return to the days of peaceful coexistence, then can there be no discussion of partition to appease both nations? Surely the spoils can be divided along the lines where the strength of each kingdom now holds sway."

Ronuse raised his eyebrows. "A reasonable compromise, to my mind," he said. "What say you, King Grindal?"

Grindal slowly got to his feet. His fur coal hung loosely around his shoulders, indisputable evidence of his recent weight loss. "I am willing to accept such an arrangement, provided my nation is treated equitably."

Presently, Ronuse motioned for his aide, who brought a large roll of canvas to the table. He unrolled it, and a large map of the Bould unfurled across the stone surface, intricate in its detail, made especially for this occasion.

Jonas, unbelievably, seemed to acquiesce with his silence. Hope swelled in the hearts of the council members. Perhaps a solution was possible.

Discussions began. Grindal, with the help of Quereus, drew a line in chalk where he wanted the partition to divide the area. It was a modest claim, giving Gladue the lion's share of the Bould, including the Noveton mine. Jonas, the twisted Motte whispering in his ear, made several trivial objections, pointing out a half-dozen places where the line should be altered in his favor; the Alana Plains, the corner of the Kapa Pines, and the west bank of the aptly named Narrow River. They argued the merits of each objection and came ultimately to the same end. Neither king was willing to yield the point to the other. The debate became so heated that after two full hours Ronuse called a break to let tongues relax and tempers cool.

When the council continued, the talks were more civilized, but no more productive. Jonas continued to reject each proposal for petty reasons, and Grindal would hear of nothing that altered the original line. When Jonas finally demanded that the Andeshan side be demilitarized, the talks threatened to break down completely.

"What?" Grindal screamed, certain that he had not heard correctly. "You would have me strip my area bare, to be conquered at your leisure? What king here would agree to such a refusal to protect his land and people?"

The question had been rhetorical, but every king at the table, excluding Jonas, was as aghast as Grindal. Heads shook vehemently at the thought. "I fail to see how I could be more accommodating or conscientious," he continued, his rage unabated. "Either you accept this line," he said, pointing vigorously at the map, "or we concede the area, as was originally put forth. Otherwise, that has all been for naught, and we shall fight this war to its conclusion."

The council members sat in silence, frightened. Ronuse wanted desperately to halt this chain of events, but knew that any effort would be fruitless. An ultimatum lay on the table, the very thing that he had most feared, and now all eyes lay on Jonas, whose behavior so far had been so impetuous and aloof that his response was a surprise to no one.

Jonas rose from his seat, smirking as if he found something humorous. Motte dutifully rose behind him, fully anticipating the reaction of his monarch. "My strength in the Bould is unmatched, and I should enjoy a more favorable bargaining position than my opponent." The ensemble of powerful men sat breathless, helpless, knowing that the council was already over, and in vain. "It should be I, not Grindal that dictates terms." He brought both hands to his chest, slapping himself as he spoke each word. "The Bould is *mine*, and if *I* see fit to *allow* Andesha to maintain rule over *any* portion of it, then Grindal should be grateful and pleased that he has *anything* to justify the death of so many of his faithful servants."

Grindal stood, infuriated, his hand on the hilt of his sword. "Speak not of the fallen!" he shouted, filling the air of the hall with his rage. "So mighty you are! So full of pomp, yet you fail to show even a sliver of decency to any member of this council!" Grindal, mindless in his anger, drew his blade, the metallic grinding as the weapon emerged from its sheath very loud in the silent chamber. In a short moment the civil king had transformed into a persona that Quereus readily recognized; a barbarian, consumed by his ire and wholly without control of himself. "A very succinct lesson in manners is long overdue!" He took two steps toward Jonas, his eyes filled with murderous intent. The other men gave way, either from shock at this development, or from a baser instinct that condoned violence toward the young king.

Finally, Trand intervened.

He stood suddenly, and leapt like a cat onto the table. Thought it was cut from a six-inch thick slab of stone, it seemed to sway, buckling under his heels as if it were willow wood. Bright light erupted from his hands, blinding every eye and leaving each man speechless, enveloped in awe. The moment of pause was enough to allow reason to reenter the chamber.

"There will be no blood spilled here, my good king," he said quietly. Grindal blinked stupidly, as if waking from a dream. "Your proposals, as you were told, have been rejected. Adding murder to your list of deeds does nothing to improve your case." Grindal absently sheathed his sword, the motions of his arms lethargic and mechanical.

"As for you, King Jonas of Gladue, I fear for you. You were handed great opportunities, yet you spurned them, and your comeuppance will be grievous. Arrogance must be earned, not inherited, and your insults are both unnecessary and inflammatory." Jonas now had a chance to become enraged, but he controlled himself, unwilling to cross Trand. "You have ignored the eagle, in order to follow the serpent. If you leave this room now with nothing but your pride, you will never again have a chance to repent your deeds. Your reign will be short indeed, and coming generations will note only its wastefulness and folly." Trand held the audience captivated, projecting a power and majesty unequalled in the world. His eyes burned like fire, and each member of the council could feel the steady vibration of the room, thumping rhythmically with each beat of the wizard's heart.

Jonas, the eager Motte by his side, scarcely hesitated. He pulled the fabric of his fabulous, green cloak tightly around his shoulders. "My part in this council is done. I will depart tomorrow." He turned to Grindal. "Know that the armistice will end in March, and be prepared to defend yourself. You will withdraw, if you have any love for your people."

Grindal threw is hands up in disgust, and turned his back, unable to stomach the sight of Jonas for another second. Jonas spun on his heel and left the room, a string of advisors following him. The third council was over, without even a full day's debate, and without taking a vote. The other kings, who had expected more civility for such an occasion, sat dumbfounded. They had failed to end the war.

⇒ ⇐

The next morning dawned bright and fair, yet cold, and as the party of King Duras stood near the eastern gate of Farshton making the final preparations to depart, their breaths hung around their bearded faces like a veil. All of the other departing kings had gathered at the western gate, closer to the lake, to make their way either to the northern road through the plains, or to the river. Duras alone, stubborn as ever, was determined to test the pass through the Yosami range once again. The clear skies encouraged him, and, as was characteristic of his people, he believed the true foolishness lay in traveling hundreds of needless miles around an obstacle, instead of overcoming the obstacle itself. The men of Nefala were grim in battle, steadfast in duty, and relentless in the face of adversity. They never knew despair and feared death not at all, believing that once on the other side they could know endless warfare without suffering. It was their greatest joy.

The king was squatting, going through the contents of his knapsack. A fur-lined leather cap was pressed down tightly over his ears, making him appear shorter than he already was. A single band of gold, unadorned by any jewel, encircled the cap, stitched finely into the leather, the only visible sign that distinguished him as king. His walking staff rested on his shoulder as he rummaged through his things, the only aid he would have as he crossed the mountains. Duras believed, as did most of countrymen, that riding a beast was demeaning to the beast and the rider. The men of Nefala would often use oxen to pull the mighty, felled trees of Greatwood into the clearing, or to pull plows to till their fields, but the idea of riding a horse was as alien as living at the bottom of a lake. Nefala, alone among the kingdoms, had no royal stables, and Duras even sent important messages on foot by speedy runners.

Therefore, Duras was preparing to depart, with no servant to carry his provisions, and no beast of burden to ease his journey. Thus, Trand found him, on his haunches at the gate of Farshton as if he were any other traveler.

"Hail! Duras, Lord of Nefala!" he said in greeting.

"Trand!" replied Duras with joy, deftly getting to his feet. He came forward and embraced the wizard heartily. Trand returned the hug with gladness. "You've come to see and old fool on his way, eh? I'm honored that you've taken the time."

"No fool do I see," he said, barely concealing his grin. "And in truth, my hope was not to speed you on your way, but to join you, if you would grant me that."

"Indeed?" said Duras. "I would be most pleased. I assume you wish to share a little talk regarding the past council?"

"Heavens, no!" Trand exclaimed, shaking his head. "That debacle was as useless as a glass hobnail, and doomed from the beginning." He gave a warm smile. "My desire was to have a little holiday; a break from my endless business, at least while the road lay beneath our feet. The warmer climes of Tra Gorome would be a welcome experience after seeing all of this bleakness. A long walk, and a long talk, shared by old friends, could go a long way to refreshing my soul."

Duras placed a gloved hand on Trand's shoulder. "That would suit me fine," he said, and smiled with gratitude. Duras openly liked Trand, despite the fact that he was often the deliverer of bad news, and despite the fact that he often was critical of Duras or anyone else that disagreed with him. Duras had known him for decades, and he had the uncanny ability to see Trand's acute observations as advice rather than personal attacks. Duras attributed much of his life's accrued wisdom to his friendship with Trand, and he had already introduced his heir to him, in the hope that his son would be as receptive to his counsel as he had been. So far, the endeavor had yet to bear fruit, but given time and a nurturing hand, Duras knew that he could bequeath the relationship to his son just as he would the crown. "We were just about to depart. Are you ready, or do you need time?"

Wordlessly Trand placed two fingers in his mouth and whistled shrilly. Presently the sound of hoof beats came to Duras' ears, and from the fields near the foothills of the mountains came Dampe, Trand's mysterious steed. The animal galloped toward the city gate, snow rising like clouds of steam from his stately flanks. He checked his pace near the entrance to the city and came right to Trand, nuzzling into his shoulder with affection. Trand patted his muzzle, whispering in a strange tongue, and then took the reins in his hand, aware that he would walk rather than ride on this journey.

"After you, Your Highness."

Duras hoisted his pack and exited the mighty gate, side by side with Trand, the rest of the party following closely, heading up into the mountains.

⟹ ⟸

From the center of the continent, the news of the failed council spread quickly in all directions. Surprise was the most common reaction, north, south and west. In the east, however, there was joy. Sindus knew of it almost instantly. He had many eyes in his service, and his reach had grown in tandem with his power during the long period of neglect he had enjoyed. His flocks of Kaitos had become legion, and thousands of bloodthirsty rokul had been hatched and armed, wanting nothing more than to deliver destruction and chaos at the behest of their dark master.

Soon he would be ready. The immortal Sindus, once a god of the Norsa, now diminished, had laid his trap. The kingdoms of men, upon whose encroachments were built the slope from which he had slipped from grace, were now going to feel his unquenchable wrath, and know that the hatred of the east, though silent and unmoving, never sleeps.

THE MARCH OF FOURTH BATTALION

Jonas approached his capital city on the fifteenth of January. Due largely to the efforts of the devious Motte, he was met by throngs of enthusiastic subjects, who had already heard Motte's twisted version of events from riders sent ahead to foretell of the king's arrival. They threw flowers before the king's horse, and shouted his name in unison, chanting like mindless children. Jonas had never known such adulation, and he never would again. The people of Gladue earnestly believed that their king had defied the entire council, refusing to be browbeaten into concessions that would strip the country of its hard-won gains. The war would go on, with even greater support from the common folk. They hailed Jonas as a hero.

Once in his throne room, Jonas summoned Lendum, and demanded to know the status of Fourth Battalion. Lendum's report was concise and warmed the king's heart: The men were ready, even desperate, for war. All regiments were fully equipped, and proficient in their duties. They required nothing more than the order to march, and they would receive the order without a moment's trepidation.

"Excellent!" Jonas exclaimed, almost giddy with delight. His smile made his pockmarks even deeper. "The order is given. Marshal, you shall depart from Ashtone on the first of March. And what's more, I shall come with you."

This surprised Lendum, but he merely said, "Very well, my lord," and spoke no more of it. Motte was so distressed by the news that his face twisted, making new lines appear on his face. The sweat on his spotted forehead glistened.

Once Lendum had been dismissed, Motte said, "My lord, are you certain it is wise to go to the Bould? The peril is great, and the benefits do not outweigh the risks."

Jonas ignored such warnings. "I grow weary of hearing tales of this land that I have never myself seen." He plopped himself onto his cushioned throne, suddenly very tired. "I want to see the land, Motte. I want to see the mine that has yielded such great wealth." Motte's face did not relax, but remained distorted from concern. The look was so comical that Jonas chuckled. "Easy, old friend," he said, as if speaking to a younger person rather than to someone many years his senior. "I shan't be near the actual fighting, not without an heir to carry on my line. I am young, but have not as yet embraced such recklessness."

The odd stone in Motte's staff stirred more vigorously than usual. As carefully as can be conceived, he brought it closer to his ear, as if listening. All at once, his face changed from one of grave concern to one of pleasantness and unstoppable willingness to please. His lips parted in a wide grin, showing his worn teeth. "His Majesty knows best, of course."

Jonas nodded in agreement, but the smile of his councilor troubled him. It was unsettling, though he could think of no reason why it should be.

⇒ ⇐

Lendum entered his quarters just as the sun was setting, ambivalent about his meeting with the king. There was now no doubt; he was going back to the Bould, back to war, and His Highness was coming with him. The war did not bother him, outside of the prickly business of informing his adoring wife. In fact, a good portion of his being was relieved to know that he could once again bear his weapon against his hated enemy, dealing retribution for the verdict he had passed on Andesha. His only reservation was leaving Elisa, whom he cherished above all others. Since they had met, he had not gone even a single day without seeing her, and their whirlwind courtship now seemed in the distant past, though it had been barely a month since they had married. She was a part of him, and he would miss her as much as he would his arm or his eyes. The thought of leaving her was in itself a torment.

Lendum's quarters were located off the palace courtyard, in a ring of dwellings built specifically to house those highest in the king's service. They were not extravagant homes, but they were well constructed, warm and dry, and decorated moderately. The furnishings were utilitarian, and though the interior was designed with thriftiness in mind, it was still the nicest house Lendum had been able to call his own. It did not *feel* like home; not like the wooden-framed house he had shared with his father and mother, where the roof sometimes leaked and the perpetual battle against pests and vermin continued year round. Nevertheless, it was the place where he wanted to be at the end of his day, so he could share a meal with Elisa, rest in the shelter of her love, and let the day's worries wash off him.

When he opened the door, she was there, dressed in her lovely teal green dress, setting the table for supper. "You're early," she said. "I wasn't expecting you to come in from the field for another hour at least."

Lendum unbuckled his sword from his hip, placing it in the corner next to his new armor, which he had only worn once, at his promotion ceremony. "I didn't come from the field. I was in the city. In the palace, actually." He sat down at the table, his strength suddenly vanished under the magnificent weight of what he was about to say. "The king has returned," he said, subdued. "I was summoned at once."

Elisa fell into the chair next to him, her hands pressed over her mouth in an expression Lendum could not read. Was she frightened, expecting the worst? Did she hope against all logic and rumor that the war was finished? He could not guess, and had not the power to ask her. So he simply said, "I am returning to the front come March."

She crossed her arms before her, curling her lip. "So," she said, "off to war you go, my husband for not even a season." Her words were huffy, as a child that has been denied a second piece of candy.

"We knew that this could happen," he said, trying to comfort her. "I am sworn, and cannot honorably forgo my charge."

"I've no problem with you doing your duty," she said, standing unexpectedly, out at the elbows. "I'd think less of you if you did shirk a task on my behalf. My problem is the illusion you present. You *want* the war to go on."

"I've no desire at all to leave you," he cried, suddenly defensive.

"Of course not." Her cheeks flushed a little. "You love me, and I have no doubt of that, but you love your duty too. You want to punish the men that caused you such hurt, and you are willing to leave me behind to do it."

Lendum's ears burned red as his temper rose, but he said nothing.

"I've heard you," she continued. "You no longer sleep alone, husband. You cry out in your slumber, and your anguish breaks my heart. The anger and pain you suppress every day flows like a river while you dream, released when the dam of your consciousness is broken."

"If I find him," he replied, very quietly, "then all will be put to rest. My family can seek peace, once I put down the man that ended their lives."

"You don't even know his name!" she blurted out, hands waving wildly. "He may have been recalled, or fled! He could be walking in the unknown already, out of your reach! Why do you insist on pursuing something that could prove impossible to achieve?"

Lendum answered, "Because I must."

Elisa sat down again, exasperated, burying her face in her hands. She began to weep. Lendum tentatively reached out and placed a warm hand on her knee. She did not pull away.

"My love, you are right about me, and I am sorry. I do not know how to reconcile the two great passions of my heart. But since I must go to war, I may as well seek my vengeance as well. Staying here, with you, is something I also desire, but that is not an option for me, at present. We must be parted for a while."

"Removed from me, your hatred will overwhelm your judgment, and it will be the death of you." She wiped at her tears, circles of moisture spreading wherever they touched the fabric of her dress.

"I may die," he finally said, "but it will not be from rashness or folly."

"Take me with you," she said.

Lendum sat back, dumfounded. "What?"

"When you go to the Bould, take me with you. Do not make me spend what little time we have parted from you. Do not leave me here, waiting to become a widow."

"The peril is too great," he said, "and should you be harmed the guilt would cripple me for life."

"Don't speak to me of peril," she said sharply. "I ask no more from you than you ask of me."

"I cannot take whomever I wish to war with me."

Elisa laughed incredulously. "You are a field marshal, the highest rank that can be granted. Concessions are made for men of your stature, I know. The wives of officers travel with them wherever they go, and at the expense of the crown."

Lendum opened his mouth, but Elisa cut off his protest.

"Already you have exercised your discretion, by making your friend Corce your aide-de-camp, though others of more experience were available, and perhaps more deserving."

"Corce is a brave, able soldier, and has proven his worth before my own eyes many times."

"That may be, but you miss the point, my dear. You are answerable only to the king, and I do not think he will deny you the company of your wife, even in a war-torn area like the Bould."

Lendum searched his mind feverishly, seeking something, anything, that could counter her persuasion, but he found nothing. She was correct, as she so often was. He resigned to allow her this request, even though he thought it madness, because he could think of no reason to say no.

"Very well," he said. "I will speak to the king about this, and his word will be final."

Elisa looked at him, her still-moist eyes penetrating his soul. She placed her hand on his cheek, feeling the roughness of his whiskers. "Thank you," she said. Lendum thought it was bizarre that she would thank him for conceding to carry her into such danger. "Now, unless you've lost your appetite, let's have a bite together."

They ate their supper, frugal as usual, and they spoke pleasantly to each other, the argument between them already forgotten.

Over the next two weeks, Lendum trained Fourth Battalion intermittently, with each regiment having one day of training followed by two days off. Each evening when he would return home, Elisa would ask if he had talked to the king. Always he said no, and she would then remind him of his promise. He needed no reminding. He scarcely thought of nothing else.

During the first week of February, the weather warmed noticeably and, finally, significant hours of sunshine melted away the last remnants of the winter's snow. Lendum resumed the drilling of his entire force, marching and sparring and collecting supplies. The time was nigh. He finally went to Jonas.

The king was most interested in anything concerning Fourth Battalion. No detail was too trifling. He asked about the shoes of the horses and the wood of the arrow shafts. He wanted to know all about the men's endurance. Could they manage twenty miles a day? Twenty-one? Twenty-two? Were the rations of sufficient value? How many horses were there? Questions streamed out of Jonas faster than Lendum could answer them. The day was fast approaching. He was as excited as a child. Motte seemed equally giddy, yet more restrained.

Finally, Lendum found an opportunity to ask his own question. Jonas leaned close, his interest as keen as a razor.

"My lord, my wife requests permission to accompany me to the Bould."

Jonas threw back his head and laughed, a joyous sounding bundle of mirth that caught Lendum unawares. "That's all?" he exclaimed, once his chortling subsided. "Tor help me! I expected something of supreme import, seeing how grave your face was." Lendum managed a weak smile, insincere. To him, this *was* a matter of great import. Nothing mattered more. "Of course she can come. She may reside at our fortress at Noveton while you are away engaging the enemy."

"Fortress, my lord?"

"Yes. I have built a castle in the Bould. It is a modest structure, to be sure, but still formidable to keep any army of Andesha at bay. I will be there myself, and while you are away fighting the war, I will guarantee her safety."

Lendum tried to imagine a castle sitting on the land that used to be his home. The thought was infuriating, but also comforted him. Elisa would be out of harm's way, secluded behind the very walls that protected the king himself. No other place in the Bould could be safer, and this knowledge eased the tightness around his heart.

Lendum thanked Jonas, and when the king released him, he began to walk home. The late afternoon sun was quite warm, and the early spring gave a faint smell of freshness, gave luster to each tuft of grass that squeezed between the cobbles, and augmented each rare sound of songbirds. Though nearly everything around him lay cold and bare, life was emerging, heralding the coming of a new season. Lendum was glad of it. He breathed deeply, taking in all of the smells of the dying winter. It was sweet and satisfying.

Nearly at his door, he heard a voice on the air, distant but unmistakably calling his name. "Lord Marshal!" it cried, full of urgency. Lendum turned to see a courier, running as fast as his legs would allow, his leather shoes making slapping noises against the stones. The boy ran right up to Lendum and made a comical salute, trying to gasp all of the air he could at the same time. Lendum returned the salute, squelching the laughter rising in his throat.

"Lord Marshal, I have a message for you. It is very serious, I was told." He handed Lendum a parchment, elaborately folded and sealed with wax. The imprint on the seal was in a script Lendum did not recognize, and could not read.

"Who sent this?" he asked, curious.

The boy was taken aback, surprised that Lendum did not know. "My lord, I know not, I am sure. It was passed to me by a runner from the south."

"*Where* was it sent from, then?"

"From the halls of King Duras of Nefala, my lord."

Lendum's face betrayed his shock. He knew no one from Nefala, certainly not King Duras. To his knowledge, he had never even *seen* anyone that hailed from that realm. Who in the wide world could be sending him a message from Nefala?

Suddenly, Lendum had a vision, a memory come back to him, years old; the kitchen of their home in the Bould, the smell of bacon hanging in the air, and a wayward wanderer recounting news to fill their hungry ears. *"I have stood in the great hall of all the seven kingdoms of Aegea, and have shared thoughts with some of the greatest minds of our world, even though I have no hearth or bed to call my own."*

The message was from Trand.

Lendum was now very eager to get away. He thanked the courier, handing him a copper piece as he did so. The boy was delighted, grinning from ear to ear, and scurried off in the direction he had come. Lendum proceeded into his house, entering as silently as he could, but he knocked the hilt of his sword against the jamb as he crossed the threshold.

"Dear, is that you?" Elisa called out from the bedroom.

"Yes," he answered, his voice cracking from his excitement. His hands were shaking, so nervous that he could barely hold onto the letter that he so desperately wanted to read. "Give me a moment, please." He sped into the washroom, knowing that if she saw his face she would know immediately that he was hiding something. He had not told of about his dealings with Trand, not to keep a secret, but rather because the subject of Trand was delicate to say the least. He was not frightened to tell her, and he was certain that at some point he would relate to her every detail that he could recall. However, that time was not now. Not while this letter lay in his palm, probably full of wisdom, guidance, and most importantly, knowledge of the future. He shut the door and latched it, sitting down next to the washbasin. He turned the letter over in his hands, running his fingers over the seal, feeling the rough texture of the embossed characters before finally breaking it with his thumb. Carefully he unfolded the yellow paper to see a flowing script, written cleverly in the tongue of Andesha, practically guaranteeing that no one but he in this entire country could read it.

My dear boy, it began.

I hope you are doing well and are not too overburdened by your duties. It grieves me that I cannot be there with you now, but prudence demands that I be here in the south, though I am aware that you also could use my help. Alas, it seems that even I cannot come up with an answer to the problem of being in two places at once. Therefore, in lieu of the personal visit that you probably need and undoubtedly deserve, I have dispatched this correspondence, which, if my figuring is correct, should reach you during the first few days of February, barring the intervention of the gods or the incompetence of men.

First, let me congratulate you on your promotion, which you have earned through your bravery and your natural ability to lead. You have become exactly what the world needs you to be, and I could not be more pleased. Let me urge you to stay the course, for your actions will decide the outcome of this war. I fully expect all to be done before midsummer, possibly even earlier.

After this line, Lendum breathed a deep sigh of relief. The end was in sight. He continued reading.

Secondly, a bit of warning. All of the happenings of the world transpire due to the decisions of men. As you know, small things that would be mere trifles to the bulk of the wide world, can have massive consequences. Be wary! The stories are endless that recount how men have let their passions dominate their wills, and the results cost them more than they could bear. Do not be among them. You know better than most how a decision to move to a new home, or electing to use the contents of a mine, can change the course of the whole world. Remember your duty, and the actions you take will protect all that you hold dear.

Lastly, I want to relate that I myself, despite my strongest desires, cannot see the full outcome of this matter. I have been granted the knowledge that it will end, and soon, but beyond that, I am blind. My ability to foresee has inexplicably failed me, and at such a critical time. A power has aligned itself against me, and I am helpless to stop it, or even discern its origin. Such is the way of the gods. Heed all that I have told you. Go north with courage. Do not forget the salt. It could prove useful, more useful than bow or blade.

I think that I shall see you soon. If I do not, then you shall never see me again. Therefore, I will end this by saying goodbye, and add that my sincere hope is that I can someday sit with you in peace, sharing stories and drinking ale, remembering our times of danger with jokes and laughter.

With affection, Trand

Slowly, and with great reverence, Lendum refolded the letter and placed it under his shirt, next to his heart. He felt greatly comforted, though Trand had actually been quite vague, and had answered very few questions. It was enough to know that he had not been forgotten, and that the war would soon be over, largely through his efforts.

He exited the washroom, and sought out his darling wife, kissing her deeply as a greeting. He plunged his hands into her silky hair, absorbing her scent and thinking how wonderful it was to be home.

⇒ ⇐

As the first of March approached, responsibilities buried Lendum. Fourth Battalion, the pride and great hope of Gladue, was fully assembled along the western road of the city, every helm polished, every blade honed to a razor's edge. Lendum felt the anxiousness of his men, and his being was partially infused with their willingness and excitement. He felt too big for his skin, the thrill of coming battle washing over him and filling his soul. The brave men of Fourth Battalion, soldiers all, purposeful and valiant, were prepared to kill for their king, and prepared to die for their commander.

The opening morning of March, though overcast and dreary, was nonetheless greeted with enthusiasm. Men stretched as far as the eye could see, grouped into companies of hundreds and regiments of thousands, the banners riding high and whipping in the cool spring breezes. Hundreds of onlookers flanked the formations, in awe of its size, its might, and its incalculable ability to mete out destruction. Fourth Battalion stood rigidly at attention, its energy bound like a coiled spring, needing only a nod to unleash its potential.

Lendum sat on his trusty horse Timo, in full battle armor, the medallion of Field Marshal placed directly onto his chest plate. He was at the very head of the column, Corce next to him in the saddle of a magnificent animal he had purchased with the proceeds of his gambling enterprise. They were viewing the men, but not critically.

"It's different, seeing them in rows and columns, isn't it, sir?" Corce asked.

"Yes," Lendum agreed. The city walls were very far away. Somewhere in the rear with the supplies and luggage, there was a wagon that he could not see at this distance, but he knew it was there. The wagon was painted black, had an A-shaped canvas top, and had the same emblem along its side that graced his armor. Within were all of the possessions he intended to bring with him; extra weapons, another set of uniforms and armor, food and water, and more precious than all the rest, Elisa. She would not ride with him, and he would see her only during the dark hours, after all the men were bedded down for the night. The previous evening he had tried to convince her to remain behind, and forgo the danger and risk, but she would have none of it. She was going, come what may.

Jonas was also present, riding a large white horse, surrounded by his royal guard. The king likewise wore his full armor, a mail shirt that covered his head, and the crown. A short cavalry sword hung from his hip, and he had a fine dagger hidden away in his left gauntlet. He looked almost fearsome, although most realized, Lendum included, that the odds of His Majesty doing any actual fighting were slim.

Presently, Jonas brought his horse forward and gave a well-rehearsed speech espousing the virtues of men and the glory and honor of solemn duty. Actually, Motte had arranged the words, who also sat in the saddle nearby, looking old and fragile, but also fully alert. The speech was finely crafted and well delivered, but they lacked any depth of feeling or rousing bits of phrasing. When Jonas concluded, instead of the uproarious response he had expected, he received only scattered bits of applause, most of it coming from the civilian spectators. The young king was visibly disappointed. He turned to Lendum.

"Let's go, Marshal. Give the order."

Lendum drew his sword, and holding it as high as his arm could reach, he cried out, "To war! To victory! To our enemy's end!"

The noise from the resulting chorus of voices was deafening. Motte's horse bucked from fright, almost throwing him from the saddle. Spear shafts struck shield, feet stamped the hard ground, and an incoherent garble of songs, screams, and zealous speech converged to form an audible mess that was somehow pleasing to the ear. Jonas was uncomfortable. He realized at that moment that his army was not really his at all, and if Lendum had ordered them to collect the king's head as a trophy, they would have been all too happy to oblige.

Lendum nodded to the trumpet heralds, who blew a short blast. Slowly, like the segments of an immeasurably long worm, Fourth Battalion began to move. Lendum and Corce moved to the side of the road, leaving the king and Motte alone at the head of the column. The Marshal saluted each company as they passed by, and privately he was brimming with pride. Every face he saw was grim and determined, lust for battle in each eye. They moved with no hesitation, knowing that they would kill or be killed, and indifferent to which actually transpired. Lendum had done his job well. From a mass of farmers, brewers, tailors and butchers, he had created a legion of professional soldiers, fearing death no more than the bite of a fly. They knew their business, and they emanated an overt confidence that was contagious.

"Magnificent," Lendum heard Corce say, watching the men file by.

Lendum felt his own confidence rise at the sight of them. Why not? The morale of his soldiers was high because they believed that no force existed in the world that could best them. All at once, Lendum began to have similar thoughts. Their victory would be swift, complete, and irreversible.

After an hour, Lendum spurred Timo into a quick trot, getting back to the head of the column

Quereus had one blessing for which he was extremely thankful; his king would not accompany him on his march. From that point, however, his good fortune abruptly ended. Grindal had given very specific orders, and had forbidden Quereus to deviate from them in any way, essentially demoting him from Chief Commander to court page. The men under his command were starkly different from those that now came to meet him. Underfed, poorly armed, insufficiently trained, and worst of all, frightened, they plodded along the road to Tine Vort as men condemned. Supplies were low; the rations were small, and often spoiled. The horses at his disposal were thin and aged, startled by any noise, and unaccustomed to the saddle, having spent most of their lives attached to a plow or buggy. In a very real way, the lack of proper horses was the bitterest pill for Quereus to swallow. To be Andeshan was to be on a proud horse, not a tired old nag with worn teeth and saggy withers.

The faces of Quereus' men were downcast, shoulders slumped and arms dangling like meat hung from a hook. Quereus was amazed at how many balding scalps he could see in his 'army'. Most of the soldiers not bald were freckled and covered with blemishes, their faces beardless and afraid. Grandfathers were marching to war with their grandsons.

"How did we come to this?" Quereus wondered to himself. "So much has gone amiss, and now we make a stroke that will surely be another catastrophe. What can be done?" As the men filed by, he cursed himself for his weakness. He wanted desperately to be the kind of leader that his people needed: a champion that could inspire average folks to accomplish the extraordinary. Alas, such strength eluded him. He could wield a weapon with skill. Was this huddled mass of commoners a weapon? He thought not. He had become a shepherd, and across the river, the land was full of ravenous wolves.

It came to Quereus suddenly that he hated Grindal. What manner of king would demand so much from his people, with no perceptible return for their sacrifice? So much had already been lost, and Grindal's only cry had been more, more, more! The people were on the edge of rebellion, and once this campaign had shot its bolt, pandemonium would ensue.

Quereus thought that a rebellion was precisely what was needed. Many would die, certainly, but many were about to die anyway, and the imminent deaths would yield nothing. The conflict would go on, a gaping chasm into which Grindal would send even more hapless men and boys. At least a revolt would cause death that would remove the tyrant from power, ending the quagmire in the Bould and delivering peace. Could Quereus lead them? Did he have the gumption to stop stubbornly dividing his loyalty between the king and the country, and dedicate himself wholly to his people? He did not know, but he thought not. Some would label him a rebel, a traitor, and an opportunist. Others would see him as a hero, a patriot, a procurer of freedom. Which was true? The semantics made his head ache.

"Forward, men!" he cried out, more to quiet his own thoughts than anything else. "The villains of Gladue await our judgment!"

The pace of the men increased somewhat, but the faces remained downward, shielding eyes from the late afternoon sun. Quereus looked at his shadow, a long, beastly thing that reflected a grotesque rendering of his shape. It was oddly a little like he truly felt.

This would be his final campaign. No more marches would there be for Marshal Quereus of Andesha. If he survived, which he believed unlikely, he would return to Anboe, and skewer Grindal to his throne. Then he would suffer whatever came. Either he would be praised as the savior of his country or he would stretch from the gallows as a regicidal traitor. In either case, he would finally know peace.

━ ━

Prince Mindus was widely admired as a very able heir to the throne. Those that had regular business around the palace at Tra Gorome had watched him grow up to be a strong and trustworthy man. Some called him brave. Others called him fearless. Still others called him reckless. Whatever he was, he had acquired the characteristic honestly, and it came to him as naturally as his breaths.

Once, when only four years of age, his governess discovered he was missing. Everyone in the palace, including the king and queen, tore the place apart looking for him. He was finally found walking along the *edge* of the parapet on the southern wall, trying to knock gulls out of the sky with stones. Beneath the young prince's bare toes was a sheer drop of almost one hundred feet. The waves of the sea crashed loudly against the rocks, a relentless power that did not scare the young prince in the least.

The incident horrified the queen, but Duras dismissed it as a quirk of all children, not likely to happen again once his reason began to govern his impulses. Indeed, what childhood does not contain a story of a child naively having a brush with death through thoughtless action? However, as the boy matured into a man, it became obvious that his behavior was no quirk of childhood. Every act he performed, regardless of how meaningless, he did without any consideration for his own safety. The men of Nefala were renowned for this trait. Most of the cultures of Aegea thought it honorable to die in service of the crown, but the people of Nefala thought it honorable to die in any endeavor whatsoever. Nefalian lumberjacks perished nearly every day, but they managed to topple the largest and most valuable trees. Nefalian blacksmiths went blind after a lifetime enduring the tremendous heat of their forges, but they unquestionably made the finest steel in the world, solid and pure. There was glory in sacrificing flesh and bone for optimum results. Mindus, even more so than his compatriots, embraced this tenet.

During his time of service, when all the men of Aegea are sent to the east to guard against the encroachments of Nactadale, Mindus was stationed in Hashana, close to the eaves of the Rachwood. Not content to wait for the enemy to reveal themselves, he sought them out, often hunting for hours at a time, looking for the three-toed tracks of the rokul and pursuing them all the way back to their holes. He would plunge into the dark caverns, often killing the monsters in darkness, and then haul the carcasses back into the daylight, where he would carefully skin the hide from the bodies, whistling as he did so. Rokul skins were soft and delicate, and made fine leather if one had the right skill.

He did so for the entire two years of his service, almost daily. The men of Hashana, unrivaled in valor, thought the stalwart prince to be mad, or bent on self-destruction, or both. In truth, he was neither. He was simply the pinnacle of his people's beliefs, their future leader, and the supreme example of what all Nefalian men desired to be. In their eyes, he was perfect.

It was because of this fearlessness and lack of self-regard that the first impulse Mindus had on that day was to kill Trand.

On an abnormally warm day in February, Mindus stood on the east lawn, sweating heavily, the sinewy flesh of his arms and legs standing out from his exertion. He was sparring with the off-duty men of the guard, honing his skills in the most enjoyable way he knew. He wielded a mighty war hammer that weighed several dozen pounds, but he handled it as if it were nothing more than a common woodsman's axe. It was not his preferred weapon, but the halberd he normally used was too lethal to employ in this type of play. One slip could be enough to decapitate a man; such was the prince's strength.

The hour was ten o'clock, and the breezes coming from the sea were at once warm and cooling. Mindus took each of the men in turn, swinging his hammer with a skill unmatched, until he spotted his opening and laid a blow to an unguarded part of his opponent's vitals. He tempered his strokes, not intending to harm anyone, but still, he knocked many men to the ground with his power. He would then turn to the next, and then the next, never yielding to weariness or growing bored.

That was how the page found him, engaged in mock combat. The boy waited patiently for the sparring to end, knowing better than to interrupt the prince in the middle of a battle.

After besting the latest challenger, Mindus placed the head of hammer on the ground, crossing his forearms over the handle and leaning forward. The muscles along his bare spine bulged like a double row if molehills.

"What is it, boy?" he asked. His breathing was regular.

"My Lord," the page said, bowing, "King Duras summons you to his chambers. He would speak with you."

Without a word Mindus stood, strapping his hammer to the thin belt across his back. He left the lawn, walking to the palace dutifully, nearly naked, and a little annoyed. His father always interrupted his training it seemed, but to be fair, Mindus did little other than train, so the king was likely to disturb his fighting no matter when he summoned him. The king had not called on him much recently, as his father had been locked away with that conjuror Trand since the council, discussing Tor only knew what. However, infrequency did not lessen the agitation he felt.

Mindus crossed the lawn speedily, wanting to take care of whatever his father wanted quickly so he could resume his fighting. He walked past the sandstone pillars, past the granite image of the royal anvil, past the seven banners of the seven provinces of the realm whipping in the high breezes. He had already decided that he had spent the men of the east lawn, so he would seek new combatants on the north lawn once the business with the king was finished. His heart leapt at the thought of fresh soldiers against which to test himself. He walked faster in his glee.

After a very brisk ten-minute walk through the halls of the palace, he came to the entrance to the king's anteroom. He knocked vigorously.

"Father, it is I," he cried out, a bellowing that echoed through the stone hallways with dark timbre.

No answer came.

Thinking that the king may be in his bedchamber and unable to hear, Mindus thoughtlessly opened the door, and was shocked at what he saw.

Despite the warmth of the day, huge flames burned brightly in the fireplace. Large shards of glass littered the hearth and floor, reflecting the redness of the blaze and glowing like rubies. Trand stood on the far side of the room, wrapped in his black cloak, looking more like a gargoyle than a man. Between Trand and Mindus, on the high oaken chair where he loved to drink his ale, sat Duras, Lord of Nefala. The king had his eyes open, but there were no other signs of life. His hands lay limp in his lap, cradled loosely in the folds of his breeches. His feet dangled from his legs, slipped off the top step of his tall chair. The dazzling light from the fire filled the normally darkened room, where Mindus had so often spent evenings with his father, discussing the finer points of national rule, the older wanting nothing more than to pass on his knowledge to the younger. Now it seemed that would never occur again, for Mindus believed his father dead. The color of his face is what convinced him. No living man could be so ashen and sickly looking.

In moments, Mindus had surveyed the scene and drawn his conclusions of what had transpired. In a twinkling his hammer was back in his hands, the steel caps on the wooden head on fire with the awesome light.

"What have you done, Wizard?" he demanded of Trand. Trand did not answer. He gave no sign at all. He was as still as death itself.

Mindus advanced, fully intending to kill him. He drew his hammer back, wanting to remove the conjuror's head with a single, bloody strike. The foolishness of this desire did not register with him. Trying to kill Trand was like trying to bury air. Fortunately for the prince, in that moment the king spoke.

"Put it down, boy."

Mindus jumped, and nearly brought his weapon to bear on his father instead, for the tiniest instant believing he had heard from a spirit.

"Our guest has done me no harm," said Duras. "Apologize to him, that this house can remain one of courtesy."

Immediately, Mindus stayed his weapon, and said, "Apologies, guest." He bowed to Trand. Trand nodded in acknowledgment, but said nothing, which Mindus found a little odd.

"Now thank our guest, for through his graces you are to receive that which your heart has always desired," Duras said.

"But father," he stammered, "I do not know what it is that…"

"Do it!" Duras commanded, spitting and balling his hands into fists. "Do it, and be as gracious as you can!"

Mindus dropped his hammer, where it clattered on the floor like a sack of dry bones. He sped to Trand with almost indecent haste, dropping to one knee at his feet, lowering his head in a sign of humble vulnerability.

"My most sincere gratitude for what you have provided me," he said, which was a very polite thing to say, though he knew not what he had received. "I offer you my life, in exchange for this boon." In Nefalian tradition, there was no greater offer of thanks than the pledge of life. Mindus gave the pledge with great reluctance. His father had commanded him, so he had obeyed. If there was one man in the world Mindus feared, it was his father. He remained in his submissive posture, waiting for Trand's response.

Trand gazed downward at the tender, exposed flesh of the neck. He would have been fully justified in severing the prince's head from his shoulders, because now the life of Mindus belonged to him. However, he did not do so. Instead, he placed his hand on the prince's scalp, feeling the wetness of sweat as he buried his fingers in the course, dark hair. "Rise, good prince, and know that our account has been settled, and I accept your pledge in good faith and peace."

Mindus got to his feet, suddenly very angry that he now owed his life to Trand. He suppressed his tongue however, for his father's sake. The confusion he was experiencing dulled his rage somewhat, but this series of events had sparked his indignation, and it rumbled just beneath the surface. His brow was deeply furrowed, three deep ridges above his emerald eyes. His nostrils flared with each breath, flexing and releasing above curled lips.

"Come, son, and sit close to me, that we can speak together."

Mindus tore his gaze from Trand, and went to his father, sitting on the topmost stair of His Majesty's chair, placing his arms across his father's knee. Duras leaned forward painfully, apparently quite weak, and braced himself against his only son's broad shoulder.

The king began to speak. As he spoke, the lines in the forehead of the prince became less deep, the tension easing slowly until the skin was smooth. A boyish grin spread across his face, eventually exposing every tooth in his head. Mindus reached up blindly, groping until he found his father's hand and squeezed it tightly, lest he scream and shout with uncontrollable emotion.

When Duras had finished his talk, Mindus rose and went to Trand, who had not moved. Once again, he knelt and renewed his promise, with absolutely no reservation and complete earnestness.

Trand, once again, humbly received the vow.

⇒ ⇐

Fourth Battalion reached the Tundish River late in the afternoon on the ninth of March, two days ahead of schedule. The army camped on the Gladue side, and early on the tenth, they began the arduous work of crossing the river. The bottleneck created by the bridge allowed no more than ten to walk abreast, forcing each company to pass one at a time. Otherwise, the wooden and stone span would collapse under the weight of so much flesh and bone. They carried out the task with speed and maximum efficiency, but even so, the crossing took most of the day. They camped that night on the Bould side, just outside Ghar.

The morning of then eleventh was undeniably a spring morn. The air was cool, but not cold, and radiant sunshine warmed the faces all. "The gods favor us," Jonas remarked to Lendum. "They provide us with a glorious day to speed our progress. All will be well." Lendum politely agreed, but knew otherwise. All, everywhere in the Bould, were enjoying whatever weather they happened to enjoy.

The army headed northwest, making a straight line for the newly christened town of Noveton. Lendum did not know how to feel about having the center of settlement of the newest province of Gladue named after his family. Was it an honor, immortalized as the discoverer of such a great horde of wealth? Was it an insult, the pathetic attempt of a thieving monarch to assuage his guilty conscience? Most likely, it was merely an act of convenience. Folks had been calling the area Noveton before the invasion, so they were calling it Noveton now. Still, Lendum felt angry and thrilled, sad and wistful. He buried all of his feelings, where they joined the other myriad of emotions, festering, as irritating as a canker.

Lendum was amazed at the changes he saw to the land that had formerly been his home. The most obvious change was the ground upon which he traveled. Where once only unmarked wilderness covered the entire area, now the makings of a road were well underway. The grasses and sagebrush were trampled flat by thousands of soldiers and hundreds of supply carts. Had he not known where he was going, it would have mattered very little. The path cut out of the wild led directly to their destination, with very little deviation, and no forks whatsoever. He reckoned that more people now stood on the soil of the Bould than had ever been there before. Many, many more, like his father, and hopefully his mother, brothers and sisters, lay here, taking their final rest within this tiny, war-ravaged region of the world.

"Remember us," he heard his father's voice say. The memory jarred him. Some time had passed since he had heard it, and it was at the same time blissful and excruciating. "Punish the fiend that took your family from you, so you can finally know peace."

Lendum shook his head, trying to eject the unwelcome thoughts. He turned his attention to his men, in the hope that he could deny himself even his conscious mind. Timo snorted sadly, as if he sympathized with his master's anguish.

The march lasted six days. Lendum kept himself as busy as possible, distracting himself from his internal struggle. On the sixteenth, just as the sun passed overhead, erasing all of the shadows of the men, Lendum saw something that was both familiar and utterly foreign. Noveton, the town named after his father, lay in the valley before him. The little stream, by which he would fish and play, letting the cool water run between his toes on the hottest days, ran its course just as he remembered. Everything else was altogether different. The grove of pecan trees, that had provided welcome shade as well as sustenance, were gone, only a polka-dot pattern of burnt-out stumps remaining to mark their former places. All along the valley, rectangles of bare earth lay like graves among the grasses, where the homes of his family once stood. No timber remained from the fence his father had built, its planks and struts long since burned or scavenged. The only evidence of his family's years of hard work was the water wheel, which no longer turned the stone of a grinding stone, but instead worked the giant bellows of a blacksmith, making the king's steel. Smoke belched to the sky, and the clang, clang, clang of hammer against anvil was audible from where he stood.

Most different of all, and most impressive, was the hastily built Fort Noveton. Even at this distance, Lendum could see that the structure was almost thrown together, mostly wooden frames that supported a rock wall. The stones were improperly cut and mortared at queer angles, making the wall appear like a patchwork quilt. Still, the walls were more than fifteen feet high, and the fort measured one hundred yards on a side, covering an area that would protect the entrance to the mine, as well as house several companies of soldiers and all the materials needed to endure a prolonged siege. Even now, Lendum could see men scurrying about, strengthening the wall here and there, making it even more forbidding, and permanent.

"Surprised?" the king asked, apparently pleased with Lendum's shocked expression. "I ordered the construction to commence as soon as the mine was safely in our hands. It is not yet complete, but the men are doing more all the time. Soon it will be impregnable." He laughed suddenly, a raucous sound that made Lendum's stomach turn. "The homesteader that discovered this spot built a fence of wood. Wood! Can you imagine? It was destroyed in a matter of minutes, burned and snapped like a bundle of dry twigs." Jonas laughed again, and Lendum's hand strayed unconsciously to the hilt of his sword, led there by his anger, which by this time was almost a separate being.

Just then, the gate of the fort opened, and a contingent of six soldiers on horseback rode out to meet them. At their head was none other than Ione, who Lendum was very pleased to see, and not just because of their friendship. He smiled a little, and he dismissed the king's statements as the portentous ramblings of pampered royalty. His hand left the hilt.

Presently Ione approached, and saluted his former subordinate, against whom he held no bitterness. "Greetings, Your Highness," he said to the king. "I hope you will find everything to be as you ordered. We are honored by your visit."

"Commander Ione, it has been far too long. Are my quarters prepared?"

"Yes, indeed, my lord. Captain Cane, escort His Majesty to his quarters. I am sure that he would like to rest after such a journey, before touring the works."

"Yes, sir," Cane replied, and dutifully spurred his horse, leading back to the fort. The king followed, along with a dozen members of his personal guard and, as always, Motte, who trailed behind, bouncing in the saddle like an adolescent.

When the king's party was gone, Ione said, "It's good to see you, Marshal. I was delighted when I heard. Your exceptional service has been rewarded."

"I don't know if *exceptional* is the proper word," Lendum joked. "More often than not I only followed your lead, and played my part." Lendum liked Ione, and though he now outranked him, he recognized that it was more a series of fortunate events that led to his promotion over him rather than his merit. Ione was a fine military commander and Lendum greatly respected his courage, his ability, and above all, his opinion. "I see that my orders were received."

"Yes, sir. Four days ago." Lendum had sent a rider ahead of the army while they were camped at Ghar. "Noga Tine has been stripped of all but fifty men. They are maintaining the pickets, making all manner of noise, and keeping several fires burning at night. Hopefully, that will be enough to keep Andesha away."

Lendum nodded, pleased. His plan was to use the ruse at Noga Tine to allow those men to swell his own forces. He would strike hard, with all his strength gathered; at the spot he was convinced his enemy was weakest. "Where are your men?" he asked, looking around.

"To the north, camped in a dell about a mile distant. There was no room to station them here. This valley is too cramped."

"Yes, it is," Lendum agreed. "How many men do you command?"

"Six thousand, sir. One thousand are garrisoned here, the rest in the north."

"Well friend, for the rest of the day you command forty and six thousand. I want you to march Fourth Battalion to the encampment, and see to it that they are organized. Fold your men into the main army, for when we set out, we shall all go, minus the troops left behind to protect the king."

Ione grinned, as only a happy soldier can. "Yes sir, Marshal."

"Try to return ere six o'clock. You shall dine with the king tonight and hear the strategy revealed in full."

Ione saluted, and then approached the men of the massive host without hesitation, giving the order to march. Slowly the files of men began to move again, heading northward. Lendum spurred Timo, turning the horse and heading to the rear of the column, where his wife waited. Corce followed him.

Once at the buggy, Lendum dismounted and handed Corce the reins. "Ride on the fort," he said, "and see to it that the horse is groomed and fed. Then you are dismissed until supper. Remember! Six o'clock, and don't be late!" Corce departed, leading Timo away.

Lendum got inside the buggy, and once out of the sight of his men, he embraced his wife fiercely, fighting the tears that he knew would inevitably come. He was home, at the resting place of his father's bones, though it was no longer a place of solace.

The interior of Fort Noveton was Spartan. Everything there was unadorned, simple and necessary. The fort was nearly a perfect square, turned so each one of its corners pointed in a cardinal direction. The only gate was situated in the center of the southwest wall, and as Lendum drove the buggy inside, he could perceive that the walls to his front and left were bracketed with several crate-like dwellings, stacked end to end like boxes on a shelf. The roofs of the houses served as a catwalk, permitting soldiers to see over the wall. Over the houses in the center of the northeastern wall flew the banner of Gladue, marking the site as the temporary residence of the king. To his right, Lendum saw hundreds and hundreds of barrels, stacked five high, almost exceeding the height of the wall itself. Each barrel bore the stamp of Gladue, and though they were not labeled, Lendum knew that they were all packed full of salt, ready to spread throughout the empire and all of Aegea. The precious mineral was both feeding the machine of war and buying the hostile acceptance of the other kingdoms. Who would intervene, and create an embargo of this most valued resource? Lendum put a hand to his breast, feeling the crumpled letter from Trand that he still bore there.

"Don't forget to take the salt!" he had warned, and Lendum was resolved to do it, though he could still not fathom why. Trand demanded that much be accepted by blind faith, but he had been accurate so far, and Lendum would do what he requested, with good reasons or with none.

Next to the barrels, and surrounded by several busy men in plain clothes, was the mine itself. The opening was significantly widened, and a ring of stones were built up to help support wooden beams and a pulley, but it was still essentially nothing more than a hole in the ground. The hole was the same that had swallowed him years ago, yielding its secret as the opening act of this entire bloody mess; the same hole that held him in seclusion while the crops burned and his family began to rot. The sight of it made Lendum nauseous, and he closed his eyes tightly, shoving his tongue into the roof of his mouth, trying to calm his flopping stomach. The horror of those days, trapped in the belly of the earth, a child, scared, cold, and alone, came upon him like a storm. He began to quiver. Only the gentle squeeze of his wife's hand brought him back to the present. Through her understanding and compassion, he was a man again, and when he opened his eyes, the evil seemed only a dream.

A soldier showed Lendum to the house that would be his. Only one room, holding nothing but a bed and a table, it reminded Lendum of the room he had shared with some of his nephews it the early days of his youth. Though it was small, the room was clean, and the washbasin on the table was filled full with fragrant water, smelling of lilac. Lendum sat on the bed, suddenly very weary. The ceiling creaked loudly as a heavy-heeled soldier made his rounds over their heads.

Elisa lit the one lamp, which was more than sufficient to engulf the tiny room with light. Lendum squinted stubbornly against the brightness. His head began to throb, putting additional pressure on his eyes.

"Are you alright, dear?" asked Elisa, feeling his forehead.

"I'm fine," he lied. "Only tired." He opened his eyes, and shadow shrouded her face, the lamp beyond casting a perfect corona around her feminine form, making an exquisite silhouette of loveliness. Lendum smiled, despite feeling so wretched.

He could not see her expression, so he did not notice when her eyes grew round, and her mouth dropped open. "Lendum," she gasped. "Look. There. On the wall."

He turned his head, and there, basking in the luminous offering of the lamp, words were carved into the wood of the wall. Lendum got up on his elbows, so thunderstruck that he could not speak. Tentatively he reached up, feeling the grain of the wood and the grooves of the characters, tracing them with his fingers, sure that when he removed his hand they would be gone, only a delusion brought forth by bittersweet memories so traumatic as to leave him addled.

The words remained, etched into the wall by a small knife, a permanent fixture for as long as the wood could endure the world. In the differing scripts of three tongues were written only two words.

Lendum Noveton.

Lendum Noveton. Lendum Noveton.

"I did this," he told her, feeling the words again with his fingertips.

"After father built the wall, I would carve words into the planks, to practice my lessons." It did not seem possible that these writings should still exist. How could the childish scribbling from another lifetime have survived, while everything else had perished? All of his misery came flooding back, drowning him in a torrent of pain. "This wood was salvaged to build this house." He laughed suddenly, even as he began to cry. "What a coincidence this is!" he said between his sobs and guffaws. "This wood protected me once before and now I return to have it protect me again! How marvelous!" He began to weep, his ability to endure his anguish utterly spent. Elisa cradled him against her breast, choosing not to offer clumsy words of comfort. She was crying as well.

She held him like that for a long time in silence, until his weariness overcame his grief.

The dinner with the king that evening was actually a very small affair. Jonas, Motte, Lendum and Ione were the principle men in attendance. Captains Larsh and Cane, the senior officers in Ione's staff, were also present, as well as Corce, who Lendum now relied on heavily to handle the day-to-day business of the Fourth Battalion. Besides the servant boy that presented the meal, no one else was in the humble room, which held the top military men of the realm. Even the meal itself was frugal, especially for a king. Raw green leaves of lettuce with fresh radishes, loaves of black bread, and dark wine that had come from Tolone; no meat, no cheese, and no butter. There was plenty of salt, however.

After the meager meal, the business of the war began. The servant cleared the table, and Corce produced a map of the Bould, laying it before he king.

"Gentlemen," Jonas said, getting to his feet, "We are come to the end. In the coming weeks this conflict will be concluded, and the ultimate victory will be ours." He smiled boyishly, showing a bit of lettuce stuck in his teeth. "I have provided you with a magnificent army, and I would hear suggestions as to how it can best be deployed to achieve our ends."

All around the room, the officers all agreed on the best course of action; move directly to Tine Vort with all haste and smash the army of Andesha, seizing the bridge at that town. That would end the war, removing the bulk of the enemy's strength and preventing any more from returning from that route. The peripheral forces at Elur and Egel could then be destroyed piecemeal, allowed to flee, or starved into submission. Gladue could claim the entirety of the Bould by right of conquest.

There was only one dissenting opinion. Motte argued against such a frontal attack. "Why go to Tine Vort directly, knowing that the greatest portion of our enemy's strength lie in wait for us there? This army, though large beyond reckoning, is untested in battle, and it could prove a calamity to demand so much from them at their very first outing."

Lendum was offended. He did not like Motte very much in any event, but to have this aged jackal doubt his beloved men was almost too much to stomach. "The troops are ready, Motte. The size of the obstacle will be of no consequence."

Motte sniffed, and shrugged his shoulders, a clear sign of his misgivings.

"Then what would you have us do?" asked Lendum, barely keeping the mocking out of his tone. The other officers smiled, ever so slightly. They each had a strong dislike for Motte, and could not understand why he was at this council or even in the Bould at all, for that matter. The king's trust in him was inexplicable.

"Marshal, we should strike where they would never expect." His hand extended a twisted, gnarled finger, the joints nearly crippled with age. He traced along a valley in the north, a tight space that was long and of little breadth, which led from the open fields of the east to the rolling plains of the west. "We should go this way, and bloody our men at Egel. Then we can turn south and make the larger battle at Tine Vort, assured that no force lies behind us."

"You're an imbecile," Corce blurted out, and then jerked his hand up over his mouth, astonished at what he had said. Motte's face twisted into one of such pure anger that he no longer looked like a man. His lips curled up, revealing his teeth, and he hissed like a serpent about to strike. For just a moment, he appeared as monstrous as he actually was.

"What I think he meant to say," said Ione diplomatically, "was that your proposal takes us a stone's throw from Charwood."

Motte, with great effort, tore his venomous gaze away from Corce. "What of it?" he snapped. "I did not say go *into* the forest. The route skirts along the edge. The risk is minimal."

"I think the risk is greater than you believe," Ione retorted, "and even if it is not, then minimal risk is still greater than no risk at all. We should avoid the forest at all costs."

Jonas glanced around the room, to see the faces of every officer. Each nodded in turn, agreeing with Ione. Lendum, who felt that Ione had said all that was required, merely nodded his assent.

"Can it be," Jonas asked, "that all of these valiant men are afraid of the goblins and phantoms of Charwood? There is nothing there, nor has there been for ages. The beasts are dead, and only the memories of the tales remain. I think Motte is right. We need not fear Charwood. The gods will protect us, as they have during this full ordeal."

"My lord," began Ione, "begging your pardon, but your youth has skewed your vision. The beasts are not dead. I myself have slain them, during the time of your father, and not within the forest, of even in sight of it, but as far as *ten leagues away* from their sanctuary. We could pass through the proposed route undetected, but do not presume that nothing exists there at all. That forest is evil, and woe will come to any that approach it with apathy."

"Rubbish," Motte sneered. "These past three years, not one soldier has reported seeing a single sign of these creatures you speak of. Not a hole or claw or tooth has been found."

"But I still see no reason to venture in the valley," Lendum said. "We can move to Egel as you suggest without coming to the forest at all. What is the point of assuming such risk? I see no possible return for it."

"The Marshal sees no reason to venture in the valley," said Motte, taking his turn to mock. "The return for our risk is the element of surprise. The pass will shield us from all eyes, and we will come upon Andesha as a storm. The opportunity to come upon our enemy unawares granted by this route outweighs any conceivable danger."

Jonas sat in his chair, brow furrowed, fingers drumming loudly on the table. He was inwardly fuming at being called a youth by Ione, though he was indeed very young, and without any military experience. He had ascended the throne before his time of service had come due, and thus had never been in the army. He had no practical knowledge of tactics or strategy, had never fought a foe in combat, and had certainly never seen a rokul. If he had, he would at that moment felt less impetuous: less eager to ignore all of his tenured officers.

"I am convinced," he finally said, "that the reasoning of Motte is sound." The shoulders of the officers slumped noticeably. "Tomorrow you shall begin your march to the northern valley, and come upon Egel as soon as may be. How many days will you require to reach your objective, Marshal?"

Lendum studied the map carefully before answering, rubbing his square chin thoughtfully. He had never been to that part of the Bould, and no member of this army had ever operated there. It was virtually uninhabited, and no one but the international border guard even existed that could provide any information greater than what Lendum had before him. The scouting reports were equally dubious. No man of Gladue had been within twenty miles of the valley in question, which was so remote that that it had not even been named. That would change however, and soon.

"If the weather continues to be kind," he said, "I believe that we could make the valley in six days, Egel in thirteen. We know little of the terrain, and it may prove treacherous. We could engage the enemy at Egel in a fortnight, if we are fortunate."

"That would be splendid!" the king remarked. "How many men do you intend to leave at Noveton?"

"Already one thousand are garrisoned here, my lord. I had no intention of increasing that number."

Jonas nodded, pleased. His smile was broad, which oddly made him uglier. "So be it. I agree that there is no need for more."

Jonas stood, stretching his back as if weary from some tiresome labor. Motte also stood, still looking at Corce with unconcealed hatred. "Gentlemen, we should retire," said the king. "Tomorrow brings us to the last leg, and I know we all welcome the end of our toil." Lendum said nothing, and gave no sign. The king's endless pomp was growing tedious. He was thankful when he was finally released.

He walked with Corce across the fort, heading for their own lodgings. The bright stars of the night sky twinkled beautifully. "A little loose with your tongue, were you not?" asked Lendum, and then he nudged Corce in the ribs. "Say less than you think, and then you are wise. My father used to say that, and as I get older, it rings more true. You tested the wrath of a powerful man, dear friend."

"What can I say," Corce said with a mischievous grin. "My tendencies are to tell the truth, which is admirable, I reckon. Pandering to authority in the face of foolishness is beneath me."

"Telling the truth is fine, but you don't have to be so blunt about it." Lendum laughed at the memory. "Calling old Motte an imbecile! Your father would be torn between his pride and his panic. Motte has the power to stretch your neck, if you should get too uppity."

"Someone should stretch his, so he can be as tall as the rest of us." Corce hunched his shoulders and shuffled along, a rather good imitation of the elderly councilor. Lendum chuckled at the jest, slapping Corce on the shoulder playfully.

"Thank Tor for you, dear Corce," he said. "Your lightheartedness has made my unenviable duty a bearable burden."

"Just doing my part, Marshal. Any who does less is not a man."

They came to their tiny quarters. In the dark, Lendum saw his wife sitting outside their door, her knees pulled to her chest, waiting for him. Once she saw him, she sprang to her feet and ran to him, arms wide.

"Lendum! Lendum!" she shouted. "You won't believe it!"

"What is it?" he said, catching her in his arms. He could smell her hair, fresh and intoxicating.

"My brothers! They are here! I spoke to the quartermaster's wife over supper, and she has seen the twins, both in the same unit, and has heard their names! She says that they have joined the force over the ridge to the north!" She was so excited that she was shouting everything that she spoke.

"Calm down, dearest. Did she know which unit?"

"No," she replied, chapfallen, "but she did know that they came from Noga Tine, just before our arrival."

Lendum sent Corce to find Ione. Promptly he returned. Ione was still in his full uniform. Lendum would not have been surprised if he slept in it.

Ione did indeed know the twin brothers, Dalius and Talius, and could speak well of their bravery. Elisa's green eyes reflected joy and pride.

"Commander," said Lendum, "I am ordering the immediate transfer of these two men to the Noveton garrison. Please make them aware of this at once, and bring them here as soon as may be. Speak not of the reasons! I want this meeting to be as merry as it deserves."

Ione saluted and was off. He rode his black horse, and led another by the reins. During his absence, Elisa talked incessantly, and fidgeted with nervous energy. Lendum listened with commendable patience. He was as happy for his wife as he could be. He held her soft hand and listened to her tell stories of her beloved brothers, not interrupting. The time passed slowly, but he did not mind. Her elation was contagious.

The hour was nine o'clock before Ione returned. The twins were sharing the second horse, and when they came upon Lendum, all three dismounted quickly, standing at attention and saluting. Lendum returned the salute and asked, "Commander Ione, are these the men I requested?"

"Yes, sir," he answered.

"That will be all Commander. Thank you very much."

Ione regained the saddle and was off at a trot, leaving the two soldiers alone with their Marshal. They appeared nervous and most befuddled.

"Which one of you is called Dalius?" Lendum asked.

"I am Dalius, Sir," said the one on the right. Lendum moved to stand right before his face.

"Do you know why you have been summoned before me, soldier?"

Dalius swallowed hard. "No, sir. I do not." A bead of sweat emerged from the band of his infantry helmet, flowing across his temple before being lost in his beard.

"You are here," said Lendum with a glimmer in his eye, "so I can do this." He then hugged Dalius fiercely, much to his astonishment. Dalius remained at attention, afraid to do anything. Talius cocked an eyebrow at the sight, very perplexed.

Lendum relinquished his embrace and laughed for joy. "Fear not!" he exclaimed. "I have a surprise for you that I hope will erase any apprehension you may have. Come out, my dear!"

The door of the tiny house opened, and out stepped Elisa. The three men saw her, and all thought that they had never seen anything more breathtakingly beautiful in their lives. Without thinking, the brothers went to their sister, holding her tightly and showering her with sentiments. She held them too, one arm around each of their necks, pecking their cheeks whilst trying to answer their barrage of questions.

After several moments of this exchange, the brothers remembered that they were soldiers, and that none other than a Marshal of the realm stood before them. Quickly they regained posture, apologetic that they had forgotten their duty.

"Forgive us, Marshal," spoke Talius. "We were wrong to move before you released us."

"Your apology is not necessary. I hereby grant you one week's leave to be with family, and when you resume your duty, it shall be as the guard of this lady. You are transferred from Fourth Battalion, to avoid the obvious conflict you now have."

"Conflict, sir?" asked Dalius.

"Of course. You cannot serve directly under me. What would happen if I were forced to send you to die? I would be a bad commander, and an even worse brother-in-law."

The brothers looked at Elisa, who simply shrugged her shoulders. "I'd like to meet my husband, brothers."

A moment of silence ensued, when both brothers were too flabbergasted to speak. Finally, Dalius, more of a joker than his brother, said, "What happened, sister? Could you not woo the king himself, so you settled for a Marshal?"

They all laughed merrily, and then Lendum invited them into their tiny home, where some hours were spent talking, telling tales, reminiscing about days long gone. Lendum felt better than he had in years. He counted himself lucky to have found love with his beautiful wife. Now he also had a family, and that night, the last that he would spend at Noveton, would be the last true happiness that he would ever know in his life.

＝ ＝

Lendum rose well before dawn, despite the late hour of the previous evening. He had business to attend to before the world awoke.

The quartermaster of Fort Noveton was responsible for more than the supplies and gear of war. He was also in charge of accounting all of the production of the mine, and in truth, the mine occupied most of his time. So much had been extracted, and yet from the explorations they knew that they had barely scratched the surface. It was almost obscene, taking so much wealth from the earth, offering only blood in return. The man was dreaming when Lendum rapped on the door, waking him with a start.

"Who is it?" he gasped, his throat gurgling with leftover sleep.

"Marshal Lendum. Open up, please."

From within, Lendum could hear fumbling and mumbling, but soon the door opened, and a short, balding man with a round belly stood there, his remaining hair comically unruly. Spindly arms and legs stood out in stark contrast to his thick frame. The purple color of his nightgown made his look like an overripe grape.

"What do you want, Marshal?"

"I need twenty barrels of salt transferred to Fourth Battalion immediately."

The quartermaster laughed. He was not actually in the army, and felt no need to show Lendum any kind of respect. To the quartermaster, Lendum was nothing more than another arrogant boy that had won the king's favor for a time. Soldiers like Lendum came and went all the time, but he held the purse strings. He was a fixture everyone relied on, and he answered to the king alone.

"This produce belongs to His Majesty," he said simply.

"King Jonas will authorize the transfer. My men need it. Now."

"Why does the king not come himself?" he asked, sure that he had stumped the Marshal with this point. He wanted to return to bed.

"His Majesty is occupied by many matters, the least of which is dealing with you. He has not the time to personally direct every willful little man that would dare argue with a Marshal of the Realm."

"You don't scare me, Marshal of the Realm," he responded with mocking distain. "I don't answer to you, and am responsible for the very thing that you would take. I shall not give it up. Not to you." He crossed his arms before his chest, indicating the finality of his decision.

"You don't answer to me, eh?" Lendum asked. The quartermaster shook his head vigorously, like a child refusing his medicine.

"A pity," said Lendum, "because these two men *do* answer to me." Corce and Ione stepped out of the darkness, swords at the ready. "You will do as I request, or these men will take you into custody. I do not think you will enjoy your ultimate destination should you refuse."

The quartermaster now looked frightened. He kneaded his hands together, knuckles popping loudly. "The barrels weigh two hundred pounds each. You cannot expect me to move them all!" he protested.

"Don't be an idiot! You do not have to move *any* of them. I just need you to make them invisible. Fix your records, to account for them, so to speak."

The quartermaster licked his lips, considering. Finally, he said, "Fine. I will do it. Just leave me alone. I am not looking to be strung up. Great Tor! Do I hate this place! I wish the Bould were at the bottom of the sea!"

Lendum did not respond to that. "Good night, sir." He motioned to Ione, who came forth with six strong lads and a long cart pulled by two horses, emerging from the shadows like ghosts. In a matter of minutes, they had the twenty barrels of salt loaded and left the fort, turning north toward the encampment.

Lendum left Ione and returned to his little home, where he ate a meager breakfast with his wife; taking in every moment with her like a drowning man takes in air. He would be away from her for many days, at least a month, and probably much longer. He could not conceive of a life without her.

At first light, he kissed her goodbye on the threshold of their tiny hovel. He had asked her to join him at the encampment so she could view the departure of the army, but she declined, saying, "I save my farewells for you alone."

He pulled her close to him, whispering in her ear. "If trouble should come, do not trust in walls of stone, or men with steel. You flee. Grab a horse and head east to the river, and take your brothers with you. Go on foot if you must."

"I will not leave you here alone. I will wait for you to return to me."

"That would be foolish, if the enemy should come," he said. "Despite the king's conceit, this fort cannot withstand a determined attack for long."

"I will wait for you," she replied stubbornly, and that was the end of it.

Lendum kissed her once more, and then turned away, mounting Timo with one smooth motion. The horse really was a remarkable animal. He was now much stronger and smarter than he would have ever believed when he had first seen him in the corral at Amarut's homestead. Timo snorted with impatience, eager to be underway.

"You are everything I cherish," he said to her, and with a wave he rode off, ready to command the army of Gladue and lead them to their fate. The crisp morning air trailed his green cape out behind him as he rode away from her, unsoiled and majestic.

"I wish that were true," she whispered to herself once he was gone, and she closed the door.

THE PASS OF GRAVES

The king was there to offer his blessing before the march. Lendum, Ione and Corce endured it, at once recognizing its necessity and futility. More disturbing was Motte, who wore a traveling cloak and a sheath with a short sword. Lendum prayed that the leech was not coming with them. Unfortunately, he was.

"He will be my eyes and ears on your journey, recording the actions of your men with poetic verse that will be passed down to the generations not yet born. The glory of Fourth Battalion will live forever!"

"I cannot vouch for his safety, and would prefer to not be bound to one that cannot defend himself against the peril that we shall surely face."

"Motte is skilled in the arts of war, as well as gifted in tactics and strategy," Jonas replied. "Our fortunes in this war are as much due to his counsel as to your sword."

"Very well," Lendum said, deferring to his monarch for the last time. "Farewell, Your Majesty."

"I pray the gods show you favor, Marshal Lendum."

The standard was unfurled, and the herald took up his horn, blowing a long blast. Fourth Battalion began to move northward. Spearheads shimmered in the sunlight, rocking like pendulums as the shafts moved against muscled shoulders. Hundreds of company banners whipped wildly in the spring breezes. Tens of thousands of heavy feet crushed the long grasses of the unsettled Bould into the earth. Nearly one thousand horses, bearing officers and scouts, rode outside the lines, shouting encouragement and keeping the men in rank. Fourth Battalion moved like a perfectly geared machine, every foot in step, ready down to the last polished brass buckle.

The progress was good. They covered many miles of flat, dry plains under bright sunshine on the first day, seeing no sign of man or beast. The weather continued to bless them on the second day, but the landscape grew steeper and rockier, as they neared the ridges that would form the southern slopes of the valley through which they intended to pass. However, they still covered many miles despite the more difficult terrain, the endurance of the soldiers being of such a high level due to Lendum's excellent training. They camped that night forty miles from Noveton.

During the night, the gods betrayed them. Strong winds began to blow in from the east, and as the morning light broke the back of the night, the men could see the rain in the distance that would soon drench them. The air grew cool, and when the large droplets began to fall in heavy sheets, there was no way to fight off the cold. Tiny rivers flowed down the slope of the ridge to their left, displacing mud and debris, making even careful walking treacherous. The lines crept along as best they could, but every face was downcast, and the frigid wind and wet threatened to stop the men altogether. The rain lessened at nightfall, but the drizzling mist continued throughout the night, and most of the next day. Fires were impossible, and men shivered away their energy as they ate cold and unsatisfying rations.

The fifth day dawned clear, the fury of the storm finally spent. Lendum welcomed the warm sunlight, and thought the ground was still muddy, Fourth Battalion resumed their quick pace, eager to make up for lost time. There was already a sense of accomplishment, having weathered a storm that threatened to stop them entirely. There were no injuries, and up to that moment, no one was sick, except for Motte, who had grown quite ill. He shivered and shook uncontrollably, yet sweat poured out of him. When he spoke his voice was little more than a hoarse croak, and he sneezed and coughed incessantly. Lendum tried on several occasions top send him back to Noveton, but he refused to comply adamantly.

"I am bound to fulfill the will of my master, Marshal. Same as you."

Lendum let the matter be, though he kept Motte a safe distance from the men.

At midday on the sixth day, Lendum could see more darkness on the horizon to the north.

"Another storm is on its way," he said to Ione.

"Nay," he answered, his voice low and unsettled. Lendum thought he sounded frightened, but could not believe that Ione was afraid of anything. "That is no storm, sir. That is the foul reek that hangs over the Smoke Mountains. The haze never moves, never lessens. We are close now, very close..." He would say no more.

Indeed, within three hours Lendum could perceive the tree line of the ominous Charwood Forest. Even now, in the bosom of spring, when all was alive and bursting with new growth, the forest seemed a dead thing. No trace of green could be detected, and though the trees were still miles away, one could *feel* the death within it, as if were nothing but an empty shell of what it once was, full of evil squatters that cared not at all for their adopted home. In the beginning, Charwood was a lovely place, exceedingly clean and beautiful, full of life and loved by Tor. Beasts and birds found home and sustenance under its eaves, and men were drawn to its resources. That was the chief reason for the schism between men and servants of Tor. Tor had reserved the forests of the east for the Norsa, but when men blatantly ignored the ban and encroached on Charwood, the undergods rebelled and fell into evil, turning the beauty and grace of the forest into a place of iniquity and mischievousness. The forest was a fitting domain for the dark master that now waited patiently for men to walk into his snare.

The effect of the forest on the men was plain. They grew curiously quiet as they grew nearer, afraid that something could hear their voices, their footsteps, and their very thoughts. The horses became antsy and difficult to manage. A feeling of dread descended on the army.

By nightfall, they had reached the mouth of the valley. Lendum ordered triple the men for the night watch. Though very weary, rest for all came with trouble. The quiet of the night was broken over and again by the startled screams of men, their minds deceived into believing nightmares so horrible that waking up, even on the vestibule of the province of the dark lord himself, was deemed a blessing.

⇒ ⇐

On the morning of the twenty-third of March, Fourth Battalion entered what came to be known as the Pass of Graves. An old riverbed, now dry due to the unstoppable forces of nature, provided an avenue through which the men could march with a renewed vigor. Indeed, the pace of the soldiers was greater than it had been since the outset, so desperate they were to put this valley behind them. From the entrance to the exit was three day's journey. Most resolved to make the trip in only two days. Lendum sent a squad of six scouts ahead, ordering them to ascertain the conditions of the path they were to traverse. Lendum, like his men, hoped to limit his time in this cursed valley as much as possible.

With each step, the cliffs on either side grew taller, more forbidding. On their right, the trees of Charwood stuck their boughs out over the valley, as if trying to seal them in. The valley itself seemed to close behind them, choking off an escape.

"I have never felt so oppressed in the open," said Corce, who was more claustrophobic than most, though he handled his fear estimably. "It's as if I am wrapped head to toe in wool blankets, or *enclosed* somehow. My chest is tight."

Ione said nothing. He alone knew the fright that Charwood could induce. He had felt it before.

The height of the cliffs reached their apex, some one-hundred feet above them. Sheer walls of jagged rock stretched over their heads. The proximity of the realm of Sindus had spread death over this thin portion of the Bould. No grass lined the valley. No wildflowers or insects were evident. Not even a weed grew amongst the cracks of the dry rocks. The smell of the arid lands was strangely rank, like decay, even though there was nothing that was rotting. The floor of the valley, which at most had been about a half-mile across, constricted to less than four-hundred yards. Fourth Battalion squeezed its ranks closer together, each man feeling the shoulders of the man next to him. Clouds of throat-choking dust rose into the air from thousands of shuffling feet. The cliffs blocked the pleasant rays of the sun, and each man could enjoy its skin-tingling warmth only during the noon hour. After it passage, the army had to endure the march in shadow.

As night approached, the army came upon a wondrous sight. A small grove of cedar trees, perhaps one-hundred or more, grew in a thin line near the base of the left side of the valley, as far from the trees of Charwood as could be. The fresh smell of the trees was a welcome addition to the experience of the pass, pleasing and refreshing, a glorious reprieve from the dread that enclosed the valley. Lendum decided to camp near the grove, despite the few hours of daylight that remained to them. It was unlikely that they would happen upon a more fortuitous spot, and the men deserved at least one night near something that could take their minds off their peril. The small grove of trees provided a more welcome place to rest than anything else they had yet encountered in this valley, and Lendum counted it a gift from the gods that they had found them at all. He would not them pass unused.

That night passed in awkward silence. Fires burned fiercely, protecting the front and rear of the army with intense heat. The howling of wolves came from the east, robbing many men of their much-deserved rest. Lendum himself slept fitfully, tossing and turning within his tent, troubled by dreams that would jar him awake, panting and sweating feverishly. He could never remember what he had dreamed, but he knew they were gruesome images, terrible with power. Always he would try to sleep again, and always he would reawaken, gasping for air and clutching at his blanket until his knuckles were white. When Corce came to his tent to inform him that the scouts had returned, he was relieved that he no longer had to dare slumber, thought the early return of the squad meant almost certainly that they bore bad news.

He met them outside his tent, where Ione and Corce joined him. Ione appeared as fresh as he always did, frosty and alert, but Corce was still half-asleep. He yawned over and again, his mouth cavernous. He had crust in his eyes. Motte was not present. Lendum had not seen fit to make him part of this meeting.

As the scouts approached, bathed in firelight, Lendum could tell that they were excited, and a little fearful.

"Why are you returned?" Lendum asked. "I did not expect you until midday tomorrow at the earliest."

The leader of the squad removed his helmet. "My lord, a great host of our enemy approaches." The scout was a young man with bad teeth. Hair hung in his eyes. "They are in the valley, barely forty miles distant, camped down for the night."

"How many?" Lendum asked.

"My lord, I know not. Their numbers are beyond my reckoning. Many thousands, at the least. Perhaps enough to match our own."

"Horses?"

"Not many. Not standard for Andesha, at any rate."

Lendum thought a moment. He wondered if so many men had ever been gathered together at one spot before. Probably not. "Are they aware of our presence?"

The scout shifted his eyes earthward, a clear sign of guilt. "Sadly, yes, my lord. We watched them for some time, but they found us out. They tried to pursue us, but we evaded them, and stayed nearby until they stopped for the night. Then we returned to deliver this news."

Lendum rubbed his face broodingly. For once, the immediate answer eluded him. He did not want to engage an enemy in this accursed valley, with no room to maneuver and no place to take cover. Should they turn and leave, and face them on the plains? That could give them a tactical advantage, but also allowed the enemy access to the east of the Bould, perilously close to Noveton. The mission of destroying Andesha and the responsibility of protecting his men collided in his mind, a seemingly inevitable conflict that made a reasonable decision impossible. Finally, he asked, "Scout, what is the character of the valley ahead? Does its width change?"

"Well, no my lord. It runs straight for another twenty leagues, in the same manner as we see here. No twists or turns, and no major obstacles to stop our advance."

"Very well," said Lendum. "There remains about four hours until dawn. You and your squad rest now, and take some refreshment. You have done well."

The scouts took their leave, and went to follow their most welcome orders. Lendum turned to enter his tent.

"Marshal?" asked Ione. "What do you plan to do?"

"For now, nothing. Let the men sleep while they can. Bring me a fresh rider, and then you may retire until daybreak."

Ione was very distressed by his commander's apparent apathy. "Should we not prepare for assault? They could come upon us at any moment."

"Not tonight," Lendum said softly. "Fetch me a rider, the speediest we have, and then go to your bed. You need not fear any combat to come upon us unawares."

Ione nodded, oddly reassured. Men did not just follow Lendum's orders blindly. Somehow, through the power of his own voice, men *believed* what they were told. Ione left to summon a rider.

⇒ ⇐

In the morning, Quereus ordered the march to continue. This was the morning of the third day since entering the valley, and he felt more wretched with every step. Somewhere ahead, he now knew, was the wolf, and the lamb was calmly walking into its gaping jaws. He continued to hope that all would be well, but it was a child's hope, a hope he clung to like a tattered blanket. After only ten minutes, a captain raised an alarm. Quereus lifted his eyes to see a single rider, galloping hard down the center of the valley, a white banner held high in the breeze. The rider came without any caution, trusting that the flag he bore would protect him from any violence. Quereus called a halt and dismounted, waiting patiently for what he assumed was a message from the opposing commander.

The rider rode very close, waiting until the last few dozen yards before reining in his horse. He dismounted fluidly, and asked in a loud tone, "Who leads here?"

"I, the First Marshal of Andesha," Quereus responded.

The rider immediately strode over and knelt before him. "My thanks for hearing me, Lord Marshal. I was bidden by my lord to give you this message." He stretched out his arm. In his open palm lay a rolled piece of parchment.

Quereus took the message with no hesitation. Once it was in his possession, the rider jumped up and remounted his horse. "Good day to you, sir," he said, and then spurred his horse, returning the way he had come. He was gone before Quereus could respond.

Slowly, carefully, Quereus unrolled the tiny scroll, and was surprised and very pleased to see a message written in his native tongue. His adversary was at least learned in a culture that was not his own, and that was all to the good. He began to read.

Sir,

My army approaches you even now. Within a day, we could be facing each other, preparing to engage in combat. No doubt, your men are fatigued, footsore, and famished. Though I serve a king that demands that his goals be met, how those goals are achieved are largely at my discretion. Therefore, since I see no glory to be gained from issuing orders that could lead to senseless and needless slaughter, I pledge to you that you need not fear any attack from any member of my host, until we have had a chance for parley, or, of course, you set upon us first. I trust that my faith is not misplaced, and that you agree to hold your forces at bay until such time as conflict become inevitable, should that time arrive.

The blessings of the Sorna,

Lendum Cetus

First Marshal of Gladue

Were he not in the sight of his men, Quereus might have leapt for joy, or wept, or both. His opponent was a reasonable man, and that gave him more hope than he deserved. He looked up to see the rider of Gladue, now a mere speck, grow even smaller in the distance, until he was gone. He placed the parchment in his saddlebag, meaning to keep it as a cherished souvenir of this otherwise horrible experience, and he jumped into the saddle, patting his beloved horse's withers. He gave the forward command with his hand, unwilling to speak for fear that his voice would break and betray the magnitude of his emotion. There was a chance, one chance, that he could spare his men horror of an unspeakable battle and probable death.

He would grasp that chance with both hands, seizing like a treasure at the end of some grueling quest.

He led his men deeper into the valley.

⇒ ⇐

Both armies converged in the evening. Once they were in sight of each other, both commanders ordered a halt. The last rays of the sun disappeared from the world, and night covered the valley like a grim veil. The soldiers lit large fires, and the men on both sides were remarkably cheerful, a festive atmosphere permeating the enormous camps. Lighthearted men sang songs into the night, because regardless of what came tomorrow, there toil was done. There would be no more marching, save the possibility of marching home. The morning would end the war, for good or ill, because Andesha could muster no more strength. Once the force of Andesha present in the Pass of Graves was spent, there could be no more resistance. Gladue would have the victory by attrition if peace could not be achieved by negotiation.

Lendum was as good as his word. He ordered his men to stand down completely. He sent no scouts, refrained from any skirmishes, and even forbade his men leaving the watch perimeter. He rested as he could, as did every man on both sides, husbanding their strength for the coming day.

⇒ ⇐

There was no sight like this in the long history of Aegea. More than ninety-thousand souls stood in this confined little vale, facing each other as a prelude to what could be the greatest battle ever fought.

At the head of Fourth Battalion, mounted on their powerful steeds, were Lendum, with Corce to his right, and Ione to his left. Corce held aloft the white banner, a signal of Lendum's willingness to discuss terms with his opponent. Motte sat behind them, his raspy breathing very loud in the eerie silence. Lendum could hear him sniffling in a most annoying way every few seconds. He paid it little attention. Two-hundred yards away, a sea of brown-clothed men blocked their westward passage. The reports from his scouts had been quite accurate. The army of Andesha had numbers at least to match their own, perhaps many more. It was difficult to be sure, due to the narrowness of the pass.

Corce whistled beside him. "This could get ugly, Marshal," he said. "How did Andesha muster so many so quickly? We could have a hard time here, should we come to blows."

"I think not," said Ione. "Their numbers may be greater than our own, but they are still outmatched. Look closely. I see not a glint of steel anywhere in their front line."

Lendum scanned the soldiers he faced and saw that Ione was right: very little armor, almost no helmets, and no chain mail. Many of the men carried nothing more than sharpened sticks, useless against a chest plate. There were far fewer horses than one would expect from a nation with such a tradition of masterful cavalry. Furthermore, the *feel* of the men he faced was so miserable that he pitied them. Any fight would be a massacre, and the dry riverbed would flow once again, only with blood. Andeshan blood.

"Well," said Corce, "the birds are confident." He gestured overhead, where Lendum could barely see black specks circling high above. His eyes were not as good as Corce's, so he guessed that he was seeing crows or vultures or some other opportunistic birds waiting tolerantly for a chance to gorge themselves on the flesh of foolhardy men.

"What day is today?" Lendum asked suddenly.

Corce thought for a moment, counting on his fingers. "March twenty-fifth," he finally answered.

"Hmm," said Lendum. "Today is my birthday. The fact had completely escaped me until this moment. Do you think that brings me good fortune?"

"I don't know the minds of the gods," Corce replied, "but I would say no. I'm not a superstitious fellow."

"Nor I," said Lendum. "I cannot unleash our strength against them, not unless they make it impossible for me to do otherwise. They are clearly unable to stand against us. Hopefully, their commander is a reasonable man, willing to take heed."

"We shall soon know," said Ione. "They are coming out." A contingent of three, bearing the flag of parley rode majestic horses towards Lendum and his army. "Shall we go to meet them?"

"Yes, let's go," said Lendum, and he lightly spurred Timo. The horse, however, refused to move. Instead of kicking or yelling at the animal like most men would have done, Lendum leaned close to the horse's ear, whispering. "What is it, boy?"

Timo made no sound, but turned his head, his alert eyes looking backward at Motte. That was when Lendum realized that the sickly advisor to the king intended to join them in the discussions.

"You stay here, Motte," Lendum ordered.

"You cannot deny my participation in the talks, Marshal," he wheezed. The glowing orb of his staff seemed to swirl faster as his irritation grew. "The king would be most displeased if he knew you left me out of any discussion."

"Then I must rely on His Majesty's mercy," Lendum responded. He motioned for a captain to come forward. "If this man tries to come forward, restrain him. Shackle him, if you must."

Motte was beside himself with rage. "How dare you issue such an order!" he croaked. The jewel of his staff spun like a cyclone, shifting colors, finally coming to a deep crimson that matched his ire. "I will not tolerate being treated like a common criminal!"

"You will, if you violate my command," Lendum said calmly. "You will remain here, because I do not trust your tongue. Already we are in a situation that could end tragically due to your advice, councilor. I will not permit you to make it worse by enabling your folly."

Finally, Motte dismounted, grumbling under his breath. "This will end poorly for you, Marshal. My master will see to it that you suffer for your insults." He shuffled away, following the captain that held his horse's reins.

"Let's go," Lendum repeated, and Timo went forward without any urging. Corce and Ione followed, the pure white flag of truce caught in the morning breeze.

The six soldiers met between the two armies. Thought the army of Andesha was poorly equipped, its representative officers had resplendent uniforms. The leader, a thinly bearded man with a straight nose and pronounced chin saluted before saying, "I am Quereus, First Marshal of Andesha, commander of this and all armies of His Highness King Grindal."

"I am Lendum, Lord Marshal of Gladue. I am honored to meet you, Quereus. I have faced you before, and your name is spoken with respect among my men." Lendum then introduced Ione and Corce, which made Quereus a little embarrassed. He had forgotten to show the same courtesy because of his nervousness. He quickly corrected the oversight, and the slight was soon forgotten.

"I want to thank you, Marshal, for the message you sent," said Quereus.

"Receiving it reminded me that there are still gentlemen in the world, despite the blood that has been spilled."

"You are most welcome, and thank you for receiving it with such grace. My faith seems to have been well placed, for a less honorable enemy could have used it to great advantage, were he so inclined."

"You're welcome," Quereus replied. A moment of awkward silence passed, bereft of any words. No one was quite sure what to say. At last, Quereus asked, "Marshal, could we speak together in private?"

"Of course," Lendum replied, and quickly dismounted. Quereus did likewise, and together they walked several paces away, to a point where no one could overhear their palaver.

Quereus began, "Marshal, I am going to be as honest with you as I can be. So honest, in fact, that my very words will be sedition, if not outright treason."

"Say what you will, but pray do not hobble yourself rashly. Your king will hold you accountable, no doubt, for anything you say here."

Quereus nodded, heeding the warning. "My king has descended into madness, and my own considerations have long been of no consequence," he said sadly. He bit his lip, as if under a great pain. "This duty is all that I have, Marshal. I have never married; I have no children, no family. I've never even taken steps to have my own home, opting to live in the palace to better serve my soldiers. My love and soul belongs only to Andesha, and the men that toil under her yoke. Until now it has been a burden I bore with pride, but my conscience has stripped any joy I once had." He looked at his men, lined up evenly, clearly amateurs to an untrained eye. "You seem to be a man of great restraint, a superb gentleman, and I would beseech you to show these men mercy, if you have any power to do so."

Lendum's heart broke. This man was sacrificing himself to save his troops. The act was so selfless, so full of despair, that the gods would weep.

"My men are wholly unprepared for battle," he continued. "They seep fear from every pore, and carry themselves with a posture so docile that nothing more could be expected of them than to calmly walk to their doom. Look at them, I beg you."

Lendum did as he was bid. It was needless, because he had already chosen to spare this army, provided Quereus would agree to leave the Bould and never return. He did not have the spirit to stamp out a mass of men so incapable of defending themselves. The men he saw were lifeless, passive, and carried their weapons in such a transparently unskilled manner. To charge against them would not at all be heroic. It would be cowardly.

Then he saw him.

He sat on his horse, on the right side of the line, the tall feather jutting from his helm, fluttering in the light wind. Even from a distance, Lendum could see the opaque eye; the horrid, diseased thing that the man displayed to the whole world, unwilling to cover it with a simple piece of cloth. As Lendum watched, the man yawned, apparently disinterested with these doings. His apathy infuriated Lendum as nothing else could have. All at once, Lendum felt his compassion evaporating. The coldness, so familiar, came upon him and covered his being like a comfortable garment. In that moment, he knew that he would kill every member of the enemy's host just for the thin opportunity to punish that man. Quereus took a step backward, so sudden was the change in Lendum's expression and demeanor.

"Marshal, are you alright?" he asked, afraid.

"What would you ask of me?" Lendum said, unable to tear his eyes from his mother's murderer.

"Only that you allow us to depart in peace. You can escort us to the river, where we will leave, along with any other troops under my command, and I will formally yield the Bould to you and your sovereign. The war will end, and these men can return to their homes, wearied from the long walk, but otherwise unharmed."

Lendum seemed not to have heard the request. "Who is that man? The one with the tall plume and the bad eye?"

Quereus looked, squinting hard to focus his eyes that had become rigid with age. "That is Captain Ecmus," he answered. "He is one of the few veterans at my disposal. He has seen a great deal of combat, both here in the Bould and along our frontier against the agents of Sindus."

"He is a murdering dog, nothing more," said Lendum, his voice carrying the point of a dagger.

"Marshal?"

Lendum turned to face Quereus, and the glint in his eye was so chilling that Quereus took another step backward, fearful. "I accept your proposal," Lendum said, "with one condition. You must deliver this Captain Ecmus to my lines ere you depart. Do this, and you have my word that that all your men shall live to see another day. Do it not, and I will have every one of them killed before the noon hour. What say you?"

Quereus swallowed. He was unable to process this abrupt change in his adversary. "What has Captain Ecmus done to deserve your wrath?" he asked.

"That is of no consequence. He is a criminal of the worst kind and I will deal with him myself."

"I am afraid that it is a matter of great consequence," Quereus replied. "If there has been some wrongdoing, then tell me, and I will punish him after the manner of our own country. I cannot in good conscience yield him to you, even to save so many others. The act would be dishonorable."

"Then there is nothing more for us to discuss," said Lendum evenly.

"Marshal, I beg you. Do not do this. I have proven myself an honorable man, worthy of your trust. Allow me to handle the punishment of the guilty, and forgo your own vendetta. You will be creating untold suffering for countless women and children in my homeland should you refuse."

Lendum knew the offer was a reasonable one. Elisa would have urged him to comply. Trand would have told him to accept. His own mother would have insisted on his moderation. Yet these thoughts barely registered in his mind. At the very apex of the conflict, at that most critical moment, his desire for vengeance was superior to any other imperative. His duty to his men, his responsibility to his country, the intense love he felt for his wife; they all faded to trifling insignificance. He would slay the man himself, and quiet for all time the pleading of his soul for revenge. Nothing else mattered.

"Give him up, Marshal Quereus, or return to your lines."

"I'm sorry. I cannot do what you ask under these terms."

"So be it," Lendum said, and walked speedily back to his horse, leaving Quereus shocked and alone.

Lendum jumped in the saddle, and without a word to his subordinates, he rode at a gallop back to Fourth Battalion, drawing his sword as he came. The men interpreted the brandishing of steel correctly, and likewise readied their weapons, so eager for blood that they screamed and shouted, bellowing like men possessed. Lendum reached the line, and raising his sword high, proclaimed, "The enemy awaits you! Forward! Stamp them out!" The infantry ran forward, snarling like ravenous dogs. Men held their weapons high, the sharp steel hungry for flesh to rend. Lendum turned Timo, and plunged at his enemy, making a straight line at the hated Captain Ecmus of Andesha.

Quereus also went back to his lines, but his men greeted him with less enthusiasm. The noise of Fourth Battalion roared across the valley, forcing the men of Andesha to cover their ears and quake with fright.

"Come, men!" he shouted. "The time has come to test our mettle and punish the trespassers that have fouled our soil!" The infantry of Gladue were already running towards them, every throat erupting with a screeching din. Quereus knew he was going to die, along with most or all of the good men that had followed him so trustingly into this chasm of death. His movement as he drew his sword was lethargic, almost disconnected, as if in a dream. The hesitation on his part was so great that he had just given the order to advance when the first of the foot soldiers of Gladue smashed into his line, making a terrible cascade of blood and innocent flesh. Quereus could see his men torn to pieces from the onslaught, ripped apart with vicious strokes that made the lines disintegrate before his very eyes. Men turned and fled, trampling each other in their blind haste to escape, but there would be no escape that day for any man that bore a weapon for Andesha. Obstacles blocked the route of escape. There were others, besides Lendum, who craved revenge above all else.

Lendum could see his quarry. He rode as hard as the trusty Timo could carry him, a squadron of his loyal troops following him without any prompting. As he closed in, the world evaporated to its most intricate state, leaving nothing but the clearest essence upon which to focus. Colors were vibrant. His ears organized the clamor of hoof beats and screams into understandable coherence. The sweat on his back, kissed by the spring winds, was more real than any he had felt before. Timo galloped beneath him, intuitively carrying his master where he wanted to go.

Some of the braver, more experienced men of Andesha came forward to meet him, hoping to strike Lendum down and turn their fortunes by leaving Gladue bereft of their hallowed leader. Lendum cut them down in stride without even losing his balance, a masterful display of warfare that made the witnesses of his skill quake with fright. Arrows flew all around him, but none found their mark, fired in either panic or incompetence. Lendum made no effort to avoid the missiles. They buzzed in his ears as they passed him by, but the noise barely registered. He was on a mission, and nothing would deter him.

The man was before him; Captain Ecmus, he now knew. Murderer. Criminal. He was a man unworthy of life, of honor, of prominence. Lendum would take away all that he had, just as he had taken away all that Lendum had. All of the blame, the pain, and the hatred were at that moment congealed and honed into a single point of concentrated judgment, the tip of which was so sharp and lethal that nothing could stand before it.

The battle was joined all around him, furious. The screams of maimed and dying men filled the air with ghastly resonance. Dozens of men lay on the dusty earth, hewn to the death by swords, spears and brutal gauntlets. They were not dying for king or for country, for the Bould, or even for the Noveton mine. They were dying so Lendum Noveton, son of Fordrun, could have his vengeance.

Captain Ecmus rode toward Lendum, leading his company, their courses bringing them together. Timo did not slow at all, but instead slammed into the other horse, knocking the riders to the ground. The men gained their feet quickly, and then joined in single combat. The battle waxed and waned for several minutes, for both men were exceptional soldiers, comfortable in their weaponry, enjoying an experience and skill that few in the world could boast. The men of Gladue and Andesha that had accompanied their leaders ceased their fighting and watched their commanders, chanting support for the men that they had come to love over the years of turmoil and sorrow. They cheered and hollered, pumping their fists and slamming their hilts against their shields, creating a racket that sounded for like a crowd of arena spectators rather than a contingent of belligerent soldiers.

The stalemate began to shift in Lendum's favor. Ecmus began to tire, panting for each breath and aching from burning muscles with each parry and thrust. Lendum, fueled by his abhorrence and contempt, had more endurance than he had never known before. He had waited so long for this chance, and he seized his opportunity with hands of iron. He fought with callous disregard, for he felt that once he had meted out his reprisal, the world could end and he would still be at peace. At last, he saw an opening, and he laid a stroke to Ecmus's thigh, maiming him. He fell to his knees, his sword still held loosely in his right hand.

He looked up with his one good eye, gasping for what would be his last breaths. "Why do you wait?" he asked. His free hand covered his wound, the blood seeping from between his fingers. "Finish it, and send me to meet Miro."

"Not for you, villain," Lendum said, holding the unwavering point of his blade at the throat of his downed tormentor. "I send you to those that will see that your time of peace will not be peaceful at all. I curse you, for all eternity."

Ecmus closed his eyes tightly, waiting. And Lendum, who had sought only this moment for so long that the desire was a portion of his soul, garnered all of his considerable strength, and brought his sword down across the skull of his enemy with such force that the helm was split in two.

Lendum let the sword fall from his hands. He reached up to the heavens, and screeched towards the clouds in an inhuman voice, relinquishing all of his anguish and grief to the gods. Suddenly feeble, he fell to his knees as his loyal men battled all around him. Lendum was removed from the vicious tearing of flesh and breaking of bone. The intense clarity he had known while riding down his foe was now absent, and all of the happenings around seemed nothing more than a hallucination. Then something answered his scream from the skies, and the earth shook.

= =

Ione noticed them first, even before anyone had heard the chilling scream.

Andesha was in full retreat, after only minutes of battle. Officers tried to maintain the lines, but the men simply did not have the discipline of professional soldiers. They were afraid, so they fled. The soldiers of Gladue were actually having some difficulty finding any prey to strike down.

Ione was still in the saddle. He had not bloodied his weapon, because he had not had the opportunity. Fourth Battalion came forth like a storm, slamming into their enemy with no prompting from their commanders. Marshal Lendum had rode away in madness, for what reason he knew not, so the direction of the battle had fallen on him. Very little direction was required, however. The enemy was before them, and there were only two choices: advance or retreat. The high cliffs and narrowness of the valley made maneuvering impossible, and the only result was appalling slaughter.

The lines of Gladue pressed forward. Ione, on the left side of the valley, was about to call a halt. The battle was over. Andesha had already lost any capacity to resist, and they were fleeing chaotically, leaving weapons, supplies, and anything else they carried. To continue to kill unarmed, hapless and retreating men was beneath him.

Before he could signal the trumpeter to sound the halt, a shadow passed over him. He tried to look up, but the sun's glare hid everything in the sky from him. However, he did notice the tree line over the cliffs. The blackness of the Charwood was enduring, even in broad daylight, but he thought he detected movement among the forbidding boughs. Creatures darted between the trees; ugly, black monsters with slimy skin and dead eyes.

Rokul. Many rokul.

Ione gazed in astonishment. His horse bucked under him, jittery. "To the right!" he yelled, reining his horse. "Enemy to the right!" His voice was lost in the wake of a low bellowing that filled the whole valley with despair. Sand skipped along the stones as the raucous sound shook the very ground. Men covered their ears and ran wildly, wanting more that anything for the noise to cease.

Ione recognized the sound. He alone present that day in the Pass of Graves had heard it before, and he was most distressed to hear it again. They were undone, he knew. This chasm was a trap. Rokul had cut off their escape, set upon them from the cliffs, and horrible, demonic, kaitos filled the skies.

"Fall back!" he ordered fruitlessly. "Fall back! Escape to the rear!" No one heard him, no matter how shrilly he screamed.

Then he felt a tremendous pressure on his shoulders, the hot pain of his flesh tearing, and he was lifted from his saddle, never to be seen again.

⇒ ⇐

The screams brought Lendum back from his stupor. Ecmus lay lifeless before him, crumpled on the ground like discarded paper. He had completely forgotten about the battle that raged all around him. His sword lay on the ground, glittering like jewelry amid the dirt and debris. He reached for it just as a black-feathered arrow struck the earth before him. He looked up to see hundreds of black mountain rokul descending the sheer rock face head-first, while a legion of others launched bolts into the mass of men below. The sight stunned him. There were so many, so many. It did not seem possible.

A soft nudge in his back interrupted his thoughts. He turned to see

Timo, as loyal and calm as ever, his head lowered so his master could more easily get in the saddle. Quickly Lendum retrieved his sword and leapt onto the horse's back, pulling sharply at the reins to turn the animal around. Once in the saddle, Lendum surveyed a scene of total chaos. The army of Andesha was decimated. What was left of it had fled, but now thousands of rokul beset them. They attacked with no self-regard, often taking the time to feast upon the fallen.

Fourth Battalion was doing better, but not much. They were holding their formations, and were repelling the rokul that came down the rock face, but they were unhinged, without a leader. Arrows fell relentlessly, raining down deadly hurt on anything in their path. Lendum grabbed the round shield at Timo's flank and held it aloft. He rode hard, weaving through his men while urging them to retreat. "Leave the valley!" he ordered. "Back to the plains! Run!" An arrow struck his shield, knocking him askew. With some difficulty, he regained his balance and rode on.

In time, he was in front of his retreating soldiers. He stole a glance around, and was very pleased to see Corce near him. His helmet was gone, and his freckled face has hidden behind smeared blood and grime, but he appeared unhurt, and in control of himself. "Where's Ione?" Lendum asked him, breathing hard.

"Gone, taken right off his horse by one of those flying things! Great Tor! What are they?"

"Kaitos!" Lendum answered. "We must get out of this valley! I want every archer we have to concentrate their fire on the trees, and have Eagle Company act as rearguard. We must buy some time!"

Corce nodded and went to carry out his orders. Just then, a heavy blow to his shield, too heavy to be an arrow, knocked Lendum to the ground. Rocks chewed his skin and dented his armor as he rolled across the unforgiving terrain. The impact knocked the air from his lungs. He recovered quickly however, struggling to grasp for his weapons and ignoring his pain. He got to his feet in time to see one of the dragon people, a kaito, land before him, folding its delicate wings behind its back. Nearly seven feet tall, they were the fiercest, most deadly, and cruelest beings in the service of Sindus. Sharp talons projected from his hands and feet, and a circle of five curved horns crowned the hairless head. Thick, dark scales served as armor for this creature, covering all of its body except for the abdomen, which was bright red, delicate, and vulnerable. Kaitos wore strong chest plates over this area; otherwise, even a glancing blow to the midsection could mean death.

The kaito stared at Lendum with hateful intent, but did not advance on him, or try to engulf him with the fire that they produced in their bellies. The long, curved, jagged blade that it carried pointed toward the ground, a menacing weapon held in a non-threatening manner. The creature gurgled in its throat, making sounds that sounded like air escaping from a bog. Lendum, sword and shield in hand, realized that the monster was trying to speak.

The kaito pulled back its lips, revealing long fangs that were as pointed as its nose. "Who do you ssserve?" it hissed, contorting its face in disgust because it was speaking the language of Tor.

"King Jonas of Gladue," Lendum answered, not reducing his guard.

"Joh, nass. Glah, dooo, ehh," said the kaito thoughtfully, annunciating each syllable with precision. It spat. "Ssserve Sssindusss?" it asked.

"Never!" Lendum screamed.

"Die!" the kaito retorted. It sucked air from a fleshy flap at its throat, and then belched flames. Lendum crouched, compressing his body into a small enough package to fit behind his shield. Fire flickered all around him, singeing his hair and ears, sending up the foul stench of burning flesh to his nose.

The fire burned itself out, and when he peeked over the rim of his shield, the kaito was gone, flying off to the forest.

"Enemy to the front!" someone shouted.

Lendum turned to face the corridor of the valley, from the direction in which they had come. Thousands of rokul raced towards them like ants, their forked tongues tasting the air as they came, shifting their serpentine necks back and forth with every step. Still arrows fell from above and still more rokul came down the cliffs, jumping with abandon into the troops to bite and slash and claw. A sea of dark flesh and jagged steel flowed around Lendum's brave troops. Fourth Battalion was in danger of being overwhelmed.

"You cannot win, Marshal."

Lendum turned to see none other than Motte, sitting on his horse, the distinctive red cape he always wore wrapped loosely around his shoulders. He was pallid, but sat upright, and seemed quite unconcerned that everything was unraveling about them. "I told you, Marshal that this would end poorly for you. Alas for Lendum Noveton!" He spurred his horse, and rode at full gallop toward the approaching host of rokul. Lendum watched him go, mouth agape, not believing that the old man possessed such courage. His surprise was so complete that he did not notice that Motte had just used his proper name.

"He would rather die now," he thought, "than wait for the torture and mutilation that must surely come later once we are utterly crushed." For one brief, fleeting moment, Lendum admired the aged councilor, facing the unknown unflinchingly.

As Motte approached the line, however, a curious thing happened. The rokul did not attack him, or try to stop him. The line split like a torn seam, and allowed Motte to pass unmolested. Then the seam closed again, and the rokul continued to come, bellowing and hissing and shouting curses in their nefarious tongue.

"We are betrayed," Lendum said to no one. "We have been led into this trap, and I aided in the plot."

The rokul continued to charge.

≕ ≔

Sindus had been very cautious and cunning, as he was prone to do. Seducing Motte, as the event proved, was the easiest part. The man was old, decrepit, corrupt, and terrified of dying. Once Sindus convinced him that he could delay the journey into the unknown, Motte became his willing servant, a window into the very hall of a king. Deep in the council of Jonas, Sindus need only wait for the war to bring the armies of men to his doorstep. They were such pitiful things, these men of Aegea. Their halls were so grand, their egos so inflated, their pride so developed. Yet they were blind to their own frailties, weak and stupid. He resented them thoroughly, for his former master had shown them more consideration. Now they would pay.

For years, the dark lord of Nactadale had been hording his strength, bringing together a force to destroy the kingdoms along his borders. After his long wait, he could loose his minions on the luckless armies of men, and they had nowhere to run, nowhere to hide, and no hope of aid. The Bould would be his.

≕ ≔

Quereus had given up. He was no longer the leader of an army. He was no longer the leader of anything. Everywhere he looked men simply ran away, without order, without reason, and without regard for anything other than survival. The onslaught of Gladue had put cracks in his lines, but the arrival of the rokul had shattered what was left of his host. These monsters, which most of the wholesome village folk knew only from bedtime stories and fireside tales, were too much to endure. They ran heedless of danger, so ensconced in their panic that many ran toward the rokul rather than away.

Quereus fled as well, shouting the retreat as loudly as his lungs would allow. The harsh twang of the bowstrings overhead continued unabated. An arrow fell into the neck of his beloved steed, and it fell awkwardly, dead before it struck the earth. Quereus was injured in the fall, breaking a rib and bruising his thigh deeply, but his main concern was for the animal. He crawled to it, stroking its blood-soaked mane with affection, and he wept. Even in the midst of so much peril, he took a solemn moment to mourn his companion, his sturdy comrade, his friend. For fifteen years, this horse had carried him wherever he led, without hesitation, and without a single misstep.

"Goodbye, dear friend," he whispered through his tears. "Forgive me."

Quereus struggled to his feet, sword in hand. The pain was excruciating, but he bore it with nothing more than a grimace. He could see that most of his men were now running back the way that they had come, westward. So many of the simple folk that had marched into the valley would never walk again. Dead littered the ground like autumn leaves. Rokul streamed down the cliffs, striking at any man they found, living or otherwise. A terrible reek began to fill the valley: a mixture of blood and vomit and filth.

"Treasure of the earth," Quereus said to no one, "woven into the bones of the land, with a cost so high that men will curse their needs and wants." He shook his head vigorously, clearing his head and trying to focus his thoughts. His wits came back to him, and his desire to live finally trumped all other instincts. At the very least, he would make a stand, killing any enemy he encountered, so others may escape. That was his duty. He hobbled towards his fleeing men.

Three rokul beset him from the right. Even in his weakened condition, exhausted and wounded, he dispatched them quickly and easily, with motions efficient and effortless. His sword meted out death like lightening. Other men saw this spectacle and turned to fight with him, suddenly ashamed of their cowardice and flight. An unorganized rearguard developed, holding the enemy at bay somewhat while some of the simpler folk sought escape. Quereus urged them on.

"Fight, my boys! Fight for your lives!" The power of battle was on him, and in his hysteria, he actually began to laugh. His sword arced and stabbed, raining destruction wherever it struck, sending up a mist of black blood and a barrage of severed limbs. Dead rokul began to pile all around him, an inelegant testament to his prowess in battle. Their dark, lifeless eyes stared at nothing.

For several minutes, Quereus fought. He suffered a scratch that ruined his left eye, and a bite on his left forearm that was deep and throbbing, but he refused to yield. Every minute he continued to stand is one more minute that his folk had to seek safety. Blood flowed freely down his face, making a widening patch of darkness on his tunic. Several of the experienced men that struggled alongside him had fallen, but many more continued to fight, often with hurts as serious as those of Quereus.

Then he noticed something odd. The number of men around him seemed to be increasing. He looked past the gaggle of scared men and was appalled to see his folk rushing back toward him, back into the valley. Straining his one good eye, he saw the reason. Brown-skinned wood rokul, the venomous variety of the evil that now engulfed him, were advancing on them along the valley floor. Dozens of kaitos came with them, standing a full two feet over their counterparts, walking with a wide-legged gait that seemed to shake the very ground.

Quereus sighed deeply. They were trapped, no way out. All of his men were going to die. *He* was going to die, a victim of the trickery of Sindus.

Before his fear could overcome his valor, Quereus hoisted his sword and ran at his advancing enemy. He screamed like a man possessed, and in truth, he was no longer himself. His life was forfeit, and the only power he had left was the power to choose how he would meet Miro. He reached the lines and began to attack the agents of Sindus, felling several of the wood rokul before he felt a bite on the back of his neck. Then another bite, and another, and another, pumped a massive amount poison into his veins. His sword fell from his hand, falling amongst the dead like a treasure amid refuse. As the venom flowed through his body, Quereus could sense his mind disconnecting from his flesh, leaving his carcass for whatever came along. The pain of his wounds lessened, and a queer feeling of peace fell over him, making his last thought even more spiteful.

"I wish I could have killed Grindal," he thought, and then all was darkness.

≡ ≡

Lendum thought feverishly. Fourth Battalion was still in one piece, a formidable army, but substantially weakened. To his left, every bowman he had launched arrows upward into the trees, often blindly. The forest was so dense and dark that few targets were visible. To his rear, Eagle Company was holding the rokul at bay with shield and spear, giving their Marshal precious seconds, but they could not hold indefinitely. The black rokul of the mountains were mindless, coming wave after wave, regardless of casualties. Overhead, kaitos circled and dove, plucking men off the ground and breathing fire into the ranks. A few of the flying beasts had been shot from the sky, but more often that not the bolts that found their targets were deflected away by armor or impenetrable scales.

To the front, thousands of rokul came, running as fast as they could. In seconds, they would smash into his lines, and then it would be over. Lendum watched them come. Their movements were mesmerizing. They swayed as they ran, almost like birds. Their skin was so dark and shiny, reflecting the rays of the sun, as if the daylight itself found them reprehensible. They looked slimy and wet, a mass of tar flowing along the dead river.

"Their skin is moist, sensitive," he thought, and all at once, he understood. He reached into his shirt and felt the corner of Trand's letter, quietly thanking the wizard.

"Spearmen, form up!" he ordered. The front line came together, spears leveled at the advancing enemy, shields interlocking like the links of a chain. The men behind the front line covered their heads with their shields, blocking the fire and arrows.

The rokul host came on, their flattened heads bobbing as they ran. Very soon now.

Corce was near. Lendum yelled to him. Corce in turn yelled orders to the other officers.

So close now. Two dozen yards. The earth shook. Lendum hoped that he was not a fool to trust in his mysterious friend.

Lendum raised his sword, shouting, "Long live Gladue!" A blinding flash came from his blade, just as it had outside of Tine Vort, in a year that seemed a lifetime ago. The advancing rokul stopped in their tracks, screeching and clawing at their eyes in great pain. There was a brief reprieve from the aerial assault, as the rokul in the trees could not see their targets.

Lendum wasted not a single second. "Charge!" he screamed, and Fourth Battalion surged forth as if slung from a sling. Hundreds of rokul were slain, skewered by heavy shaft, and the ground became slippery with their blood. The line continued to push, spears working all along the formation like heavy pistons, each thrust piercing the tender bodies of their enemy. Before the rokul could recover from the initial onslaught, several thousand were slaughtered, evening the odds for Gladue somewhat.

However, the rokul did recover, and came forward again with renewed ferocity. Now the phalanx of the front line was on the defensive. The archers of the enemy resumed their volleys. The floor of the valley was a massive pincushion. Fourth Battalion was beset on all sides, stymied and taking casualties.

"Corce!" Lendum shouted. "Now! Do it now!"

Corce shouted orders, and the men of Lendum's command began to throw the contents of their packs at the enemy.

Lendum could remember his long walk through the passage of the mine. He was so afraid of coming upon these very creatures under the earth, away from light or any kind of aid. He was just a boy then, and knew nothing at all about rokul. If he had, he would have known that the mountain breed of rokul would never have been in that corridor. They love dark places under the earth, but they would have shunned that passage at all costs. They had no cognizant reasoning, but they did understand pain, and being in that tunnel would have caused them terrible suffering. They would have avoided that cave for the same reason a man will not walk into a raging fire: because it burns.

The men were throwing handfuls of salt at their enemy.

Every rokul that was touched by the white grains began bellowing in agony. The salt bore through their skin like slivers of glass, instantly liquefying the meat off their bones in a most gruesome fashion. Their attacking ceased at once. Seeing what was occurring made some turn and flee, despite the certain doom they would face at the hands of their master.

Lendum again seized the initiative. "Charge!" he screamed. "Push them out!" Again, the soldiers of Gladue brought their spears to bear, tearing flesh and breaking bone, splintering the enemy to pieces. Cascades of white salt arced overhead, destroying everything they touched. Lendum himself came into the fray, wielding his weapon with deadly artistry, making a mockery of the mighty host of Sindus.

Several kaitos landed. They were not afraid of the salt, or anything else. They vomited fire from their mouths into the line, with minimum effect. The shields of Gladue were solid, and broad. Lendum came forth with righteous zeal. He removed the head of one kaito, and literally hacked another in half. Nothing could stand before him. The line continued to move forward, determined. Fear was not an issue. The enemy was between them and the exit from the valley. They would have continued to fight if Sindus himself stood before them.

Most of the rokul had turned from the battle, leaving their kaito superiors to face the fury alone. They ran down the valley or ascended the cliffs, seeking the sanctuary of the trees. The kaitos divided themselves between fighting the men and punishing their scattering foot soldiers. They were as likely to kill one as the other. The host of Sindus was in total disarray; the rokul were all but gone, with only the kaitos, still fearsome, remaining to carry out their master's will.

Lendum ordered his archers to turn their fire to the kaitos. Hundreds of arrows sped through the sky, a barrage so thick and devastating that that even the protective skin of the kaitos were not immune. Most took to the skies after the first volley. Those that remained were finished with sharpened steel.

Lendum could scarcely believe it. The enemy had retreated. The kaitos had left. Even the constant bombardment from the trees had ceased. All he could see were the rokul that had escaped eastward through the valley. He let his guard relax somewhat. He was weary from the battle, and all at once, he could feel it. He was sore everywhere, bruised and battered, bleeding from a dozen minor cuts and scratches, but otherwise whole.

Corce came up on horseback, leading the faithful Timo by the reins. He also appeared uninjured, though the black blood of rokul had joined the blood and gunk smeared on his face. He looked like a goblin. Lendum supposed that his sword could tell quite a tale.

"Your ride, Marshal," he said jokingly, handing over the reins. "I've just come from the rearguard. There is another host to the west. Wood rokul; not susceptible to the salt, I reckon. They are massacring the remnants of Andesha, but they will be on us next, and soon."

Lendum nodded in agreement. He had already decided to leave at once, even if they did not have any more threats in the pass. He intended to pursue the enemy out of the valley, for that business remained unfinished.

He wanted Motte.

"Give what horses we have to the wounded. Sorry, friend, but you and I will go on foot. I hope that is not too great an inconvenience for you."

Corce smiled broadly, showing the mess between his teeth. He seemed happy. "Yes, sir. I can manage. Let's get out of here."

Fourth Battalion quickly got ready to move. Less than a mile away, the screams of the men of Andesha echoed across the floor of the valley as they gave up their lives.

The army began to march, double time. Their target was on the move, and Lendum meant to have them. The rokul could possibly escape his wrath, because they were swift on foot, or could scale the cliffs like spiders, but Motte was no rokul. He was only a man: an old, sickly man that was incapable of swift travel. He would have no choice but to traverse the entire length of the valley, and that could take whole day, even on horseback. Lendum would have him, and then he would pay for his treachery.

Fourth Battalion moved quickly, despite their fatigue and anguish for the fallen. Of the forty and six thousand that had entered the valley, ten thousand had breathed their last in the Pass of Graves. Every man from Andesha was dead or dying. Countless rokul lay dead, plus hundreds of kaitos, the latter being a more grievous loss for Sindus. Rokul could bear a weapon after two years of life, but kaitos required five moltings to mature, taking decades. The ranks of his most able lieutenants would be thin for some time to come. No single day in the history of Aegea could claim to have experienced so much death than the day of the battle of the Pass of Graves. The losses for all concerned were atrocious.

Lendum had no time to mourn the fallen. He ran, leading his men, following the claw marks of his prey. On and on he pushed himself, setting a ridiculous pace, until his muscles burned and his lungs cried out for air. Yet he would not rest or even reduce his speed. The need was urgent. As he chased one host, another was chasing him. He was at once the hunter and the hunted, and he guessed, correctly, that this defeat would not dissuade Sindus.

THE FINAL STROKE

Spring had come fully to the Bould. The nights were still cool, crisp and invigorating, but each day dawned bright and fair, bringing pleasant warmth that encouraged new growth. Leaves struggled to escape from the tree limbs, and fresh wildflowers dotted the landscape, daffodils and dandelions, adding agreeable smells to the scenery and accents to the yellow-green grass. New life sprung everywhere.

This particular morning was even more lovely than most. Rains had come the day before, washing the lands, and the rising sun revealed a pristine country that was clean and fragrant, perfect. The skies were completely blue, without a wisp of cloud. Elisa thought that Lendum's eyes were the same shade of blue as the sky, a deep sapphire that still made her breathless, even at the memory. She sighed in her longing.

Lendum had been gone four days. Each morning she had risen early, eaten, and after completing whatever tasks she had, she walked to the rise overlooking Fort Noveton, facing north. There, with the valley at her back, she would spread a blanket over the grass, and in the warm sunshine she would sit, gazing northward, watching the horizon, hoping to see her husband returning to her. The broad swath of trampled grass was still evident, marking where the awesome Fourth Battalion had camped and then marched away, seeking the enemy.

Dalius found her, just as he knew he would. She sat alone, knees pulled to her chest. Her hair danced in the light breezes. Since Lendum had departed she had fallen into a deep melancholy, and neither brother had had any success in consoling her. Seeing his little sister in such distress made Dalius feel helpless and weak, yet he continued to try to comfort her, despite the hopelessness of the gesture.

He sat down next to her, taking her hand and squeezing it gently. "Sitting here for hours on end will not cause your dearest to return to you any sooner," he said softly. "It is likely a fortnight will pass before his campaign is complete, at which time he will still be forty leagues away. He could be gone a month, or longer."

"I know," she replied sadly. "I've nothing else to do. All of the doings within the fort are so mind numbingly tedious. How long can I watch men load salt into barrels or see the walls of that structure get higher and thicker? No, dear Dalius. I sleep, I eat, and I wait for my husband. There are no other diversions here."

"So you plan to just sit here day after day? Your brothers are here, and we love you. Can you not find any comfort from our presence? Your desire for solitude is understandable, but needless, and it brings you pain."

"My pain would be mine, no matter where I may be," she answered. "I knew that loneliness would be the price I would pay for coming here. If I desired companionship, I would have remained in Ashtone."

"If you would hurt anywhere, why did you come?"

She looked at him, smiling dryly. "The price I am paying bought me another week with my husband. I would pay it again, and again, many times over. And, I might add, I have a reunion with my brothers, who now get to watch over me rather than wander the wild seeking out danger. It is a bargain, actually, to get so much for giving so little."

Dalius smiled. "You love Lendum very much, and I am very pleased to see you every day. I count it a blessing that I barely deserve. Please, will you not consider leaving this place? There is only danger here, and if you were lost Talius and I would be wretched with grief."

She caressed his face with her long fingers. "Nay, brother. I am here for as long as my husband is, regardless of what may come. I will not leave without him."

He brought her hand to his mouth and kissed it. "So be it, dear sister." He laughed suddenly. "Even as a child you were the most stubborn of us all. Now you are a woman, vibrant and beautiful, residing alongside the king of our country, and still you are stubborn. It eases my heart, in a way, to know that there are some things that never change."

"I agree, just as I know that my brothers will watch over me, no matter what, and condone my stubbornness by honoring my decisions."

They shared a quiet moment together, brother and sister, each immersed in their own thoughts, remembering cherished memories. A cool breeze blew from the northeast, bringing an odd sound with it. Dalius cocked his head, straining his ears. As he listened, his eyes grew wide with trepidation, and he could feel his heart begin to pump hard in his chest.

He leapt to his feet, searching the country.

"What is it?" she asked, suddenly afraid.

"Something is coming. I know not what, but it is large. Listen!"

She tried, but all she could hear was the wind in her ears. Then a light swishing sound came to her, like grasses swaying back and forth in a heavy breeze, and then a rhythmic stamping. She looked northeast, into the wind, and was horrified to see black creatures sprinkled across the landscape. From their vantage on the hill, the monsters were small, like ants in the distance, and they were running towards them, so quickly that they would close the distance between them in mere minutes.

"Oh, my dear Lendum," Elisa said, and began to cry.

"Come," Dalius shouted, taking her arm. "Make haste!"

They ran back to the fort.

⇒ ⇐

"Marshal, we must rest," Corce said through gasping breaths. They had been running for six hours, and dusk was upon them. Fourth Battalion was nearly spent. The long journey from Gladue, the day's battle, and the relentless pursuit of their enemy brought a degree of weariness that none of them had felt before. They had seen no sign of the enemy, either to the front or to the rear, but Lendum knew they were close. He could feel them, resting on his neck like impending doom.

Lendum surveyed his surroundings at a glance. He knew that his men desperately needed rest, but nothing here provided any protection. The valley was flat and smooth, without any deviation to the left or right. The cliffs did not overhang, and only tattered tufts of tangled grasses grew anywhere. To stop here meant death, for the brown rokul were coming, and though the cooler temperatures of night would slow their advance, they would still not hesitate to attack them on sight, even in their lethargic state.

"We must keep going," he said to Corce, even as he ran. "If we are set upon here, in the open, it will be the end of us."

"We cannot run all the way back to the plains without stopping!" Corce implored.

Lendum had an idea. "We don't need to run all the way; just a little further." Corce did not respond. There was no sense arguing when Lendum had already made up his mind.

They continued running. Darkness descended in full, and only the stars lit their path. A few of the men lit lamps or torches, casting light that was as weak and sporadic as the starlight itself. The pace slackened due to the darkness and indescribable fatigue. For two hours after sundown, Fourth Battalion continued its murderous march. Finally, mercifully, Lendum called a halt. Men literally collapsed, almost unable to breathe. Their commander allowed them a terribly brief reprieve however. Lendum had come to the spot he had been hoping to reach: the cedar grove. He ordered the trees felled at once, and spread the width of the valley, blocking the way they had come. The work went forth with good speed, because this final task would allow them some rest, if only for a few hours.

Lendum circulated his ranks, checking morale, tending the wounded, offering words of congratulations and encouragement.

"This is it, men!" he shouted. "Soon we shall have blessed sleep! Don't yield to your flesh now, while we are so close to victory!"

Soon they had enough felled trees to block off the western half of the valley, and they were promptly set ablaze. The fragrant smoke from the burning cedar was pleasant and invigorating, giving the men an unexpected boost of vitality. They piled logs and branches high, until the flames roared in excess of ten feet. The heat alone was sufficient to keep even the most determined enemy away.

Lendum set a watch, and then allowed his men to sleep as they could; four hours, he had decided. No more than that. Men fell over where they stood, lying like dead things, too exhausted even to eat. Lendum himself did not sleep, however. He maintained his vigilance, convinced that when the time came to leave this place, it would come suddenly, and with little time to act. He would be alert when that time came; his men depended on him. His weary body and mind would have to wait for another time. He paced the fire line, adding fuel and stoking the flames wherever they were weak. He worked tending the wounded, doing whatever he could. Many of the injuries were mortal, and the sufferers waited only for the walk with Miro. Others had lost an eye or a limb, and once the wound was treated, their life was no longer in jeopardy, though their pain was great and left them longing for death.

After two hours, Lendum called for a change in the watch. Men came to relieve those on duty, amazingly without complaint or grumbling. Lendum was exceedingly proud of his men. They were honorable in every sense, willing to sacrifice their basic needs for the good of the whole.

It was in the middle of the third hour that Lendum heard the sound he had been dreading: approaching steps. Even over the roar of the fire, he could hear them: several thousands at the least, and coming fast. In the distance, the heinous noise of snarling kaitos echoed through the valley. The enemy was upon them. Their time of rest, brief though it had been, was over.

"On your feet, Fourth!" Lendum screamed. "The enemy is here! Up, and make ready to move!" All around men sprang up as if after a full night's slumber, gathering their belongings and falling into formation, ready to begin the run anew. Lendum ordered all of the remaining fuel to be cast onto the raging fire, to keep the monsters at bay as long as possible, hopefully long enough to buy the time required to escape. As this was done, the first arrows began to arc over the flames, aimed blindly. Lendum fancied that he could see red eyes beyond the fire, barely hidden in the forbidding darkness. Evil hissing reached his ears, sounds so loathsome and full of hate that he wanted to cry out.

"Move!" he yelled, running towards the front. "Run with everything you have! They are here! Retreat!"

Fourth Battalion began to run again, much faster this time. The idea of the minions of Sindus right in their heels gave them extra incentive. Over his shoulder, Lendum watched the flames shrink as they moved away, and prayed that they would continue burning long enough.

⇒ ⇐

After three hours of running, the sun's first rays of the day eclipsed the horizon, and they were most welcome. Lendum was astounded to see how far they had come in less than twenty-four hours. The end of the valley was in sight. What the corps had covered in two days going in they had covered in one day coming out, a distance of almost fifteen leagues. It was truly a remarkable achievement.

Even more remarkable was the speck of red Lendum could see far ahead. "Corce, that dot of red I see; is that what I think it is?"

Corce shielded his eyes from the rising sun. "If you think that is our friendly councilor Motte, then yes, that is he. He is bouncing around somewhat haphazardly." As he spoke, Motte exited the valley and turned right, heading toward Noveton. "I think he is asleep in the saddle. He must be exhausted, the poor chap."

Lendum found that funny, but he did not laugh. He had been contemplating another brief halt now that the sun was up, but he put it out of his mind. He wanted that traitor. He wanted to place him before the king and let him explain himself. Better yet, he would just give him to the men of his command. Motte had betrayed them, and they could devise a fitting punishment, he was sure. After what they had endured, no reprisal would be deemed unjust.

"Send a squad of horsemen after him," he ordered. "Bring him back here."

Corce issued the orders, and six horsemen left the formation, chasing their prey. Meanwhile, Fourth Battalion kept running. The cliffs on either side got lower and lower with every footfall, bringing them closer to the open plains. The trees of Charwood loomed menacingly on the left, a constant reminder of their peril.

Soon the plains opened before them. They turned south, heading for Noveton. All of the men felt their spirits rise, and new energy fueled their limbs. They believed that the worst was over. Just then, an alarm cry came from the rear. The army of forest rokul was closing fast, barely one thousand yards away. They would be able to engage Fourth Battalion in a matter of minutes.

Lendum saw the scouts returning and, much to his dismay, Motte was not with them. "Where is Motte?" he shouted as he ran. "Surely that aged fiend did not elude you!" His voice was harsh, from both his frustration and his labored breathing.

"Nay, sir. An army of mountain rokul, coming from the south, overtook him. They are less than a mile from that ridge." The scout had very round eyes, and the expression on his face told him everything he needed to know. He called a halt. A host coming from the south meant that they were coming from Noveton. Lendum feared the worst.

Corce put his hands on his knees, sucking air into his burning lungs as fast as he could. "So," he said, "once again we are between the hammer and the anvil."

"Begging your pardon, sir," said the scout, "but if we are between the hammer and the anvil, then so are they."

"What do you mean?" Lendum demanded.

"The mountain rokul that approach from the south are not coming to attack. They are in retreat. A great army of men pursue them."

Corce and Lendum exchanged a quick glance. They both knew that no force of Gladue existed outside their own. "Who are the men?" Lendum asked.

"I'm not sure, sir. I could not see the banners at such a distance. But I could see the blue uniforms that seem to be of Rubia adorning half of the host, and the other half carries the massive halberds that only the men of Nefala choose to wield."

Lendum smiled despite his ragged condition. He knew not what forces had conspired to bring him aid at this moment, but he was most grateful for it. Besides coming to the aid of Fourth Battalion, perhaps this unexplained army of men had been in time to save his beautiful Elisa. If so, he would kiss the feet of her saviors, and sacrifice everything he had to honor Tor.

"How many men approach?"

"Many thousands, sir. A force that would be more than match for our own."

"Then we shall rely on them to handle the mountain rokul, while we concentrate on the wood rokul to our rear." He whistled sharply, and Timo came forth, bearing two wounded soldiers. Lendum helped them dismount then climbed onto the saddle, once again on the back of his reliable friend. The first of the mountain rokul crested the hill before them, a horrid blackness in the clear light of day. They paused suddenly, surprised to find even more men between them and the safe haven of the forest. Lendum used their hesitation to full effect.

"Spread out!" he cried, raising his sword high. "Cut off their escape! Let none of them live to see another day!"

In a mass, Fourth Battalion surged along the base of the hill with what was left of their strength. The dazed rokul, unable to advance further, succumbed to their fright and scattered in all directions, seeking any outlet not plugged with angry steel. Lendum sent Corce to the rear to organize the men that would face the forest rokul, the cries of which were now fully audible. Fourth Battalion was about to make its stand, its last battle ever.

Lendum led his men in a slow walk up the hill, gradually closing the space his enemy had to maneuver. He came to the top of the ridge, slashing at any rokul that came within his reach. From his vantage, he could see an awe-inspiring sight; two full armies of men, side by side, chasing their foes at a full run. He could see that his scout had been correct. The men in blue did indeed bear the standard of Rubia, while the men in dark leather and black beards hailed from Nefala. They numbered at least sixty thousand, and between them and Fourth Battalion swarmed rokul innumerable. "Every hole in the mountains must be empty," Lendum thought. He never would have believed that Sindus had so many servants at his disposal.

Lendum's men spread out in an arc, hemming in the mass of scampering rokul. Lendum led the charge. The men of Gladue slew everything in their path. The kaitos were curiously absent, apparently willing to leave their subordinates to their fate. While Lendum's men acted as a dam, the armies of Rubia and Nefala rushed on, a flood of furious retribution. Lendum could now see their faces. The large men of Nefala, with bulbous noses and ruddy cheeks, sang joyous melodies even as they ran, filled with childish elation at the thought of the coming battle. The blonde men of Rubia, composed and brilliant in their indigo tunics and polished armor, held a disciplined line as they advanced, spearheads leveled to do deadly hurt.

Between these two hosts, sitting tall on his snow-white steed Dampe, rode none other than Trand. He bore a short, broad-bladed sword, and he came forth with righteousness.

"Come to my rescue again, I see," Lendum said to no one. "Shall I ever be out of your debt, I wonder?"

The three armies converged on the enemy.

Trand, gifted with some knowledge of the future, had shown this very scene to King Duras. The sight of so many rokul was much for the king to bear, and he bore a great deal of guilt for his stubbornness to intercede between Gladue and Andesha. His refusal had caused this eventuality to come to pass. He knew that he had no choice but to become involved in the war.

"A war between men is detestable, but no real concern of mine," he said to Trand. "But this image you show me, if it is true, then...then..." He trailed off, unable to believe that so many monsters still lived in the world. "Any servant of Sindus," he continued, "is an enemy of Nefala, no matter where they are in the world. My son will lead our army there immediately. We will not allow the treachery of Sindus to pass unpunished."

Mindus was not at all hesitant. In a way, this duty was a calling that he had craved all of his life. He had slain many rokul, it was true, but to face *legions* of them, locked in a titanic battle, was a pleasure he feared he would never be able to enjoy. His labor matched his jubilation. He set out from Tra Gorome in only three days, marching north to the Yosami Mountain pass. From there he would travel around Lake Farsh, crossing into Gladue, before entering the Bould. Then he would have his battle. Trand set out before him, bound for Farshton.

Poce, king of Rubia, was no more difficult to persuade. He had been spoiling for a fight ever since Jonas had befouled the meeting hall of his palace with his impudence. When Trand arrived and related the news of the coming actions of Sindus, Poce was all too happy to offer his aid. Mindus arrived two weeks later with his host, and the king and the prince agreed to work in tandem, marching side by side to war.

"But who shall lead?" asked Mindus. "I care not, as long as I have living rokul to hew."

"What about you, Trand?" asked Poce

"What about me?" Trand said. "Is there something else you require?"

"What would you need to go to war with us?" asked Mindus humbly.

Trand smiled as only he could. "There is only one thing I need; a sword."

Mindus drew his own sword, a mere secondary weapon to him, but still deadly and very heavy for an average man. He knelt before Trand, presenting to him the sword with both hands. "I beg you to accept this weapon, and join us in our campaign. Your presence would be a strength beyond anything our enemy could produce."

Trand put out his hand, grasping the hilt. "I don't know if that is true, but you shall certainly have what strength I have at your disposal." He lifted the sword from Mindus' grip, twirling the sharpened blade with perfect balance, as if it were no more than a broken bough from a willow tree. "A fine blade this is, with a gimlet point that will surely withstand trials longer than the world will last. Nefalian steel has no equal in Aegea! I accept this gracious gift, and swear to fight alongside you for as long as you choose to do so."

The next day was the twenty-sixth of February, a sunny day that witnessed two great armies marching together, bound for Noveton. Trand led them to the Bould, riding his tireless horse, and secretly he hoped that the mighty effort would not be too late.

⇒ ⇐

The battle was epic. The men of Rubia, renowned throughout Aegea for their skill in archery, were as good as their reputation. They fired ceaselessly, both on foot and from the saddle, with deadly precision. The Nefalian army, led by the incomparable Prince Mindus, waded into their enemy, slaying several rokul with a single swing of their hefty weapons. Fourth Battalion did their part, preventing the enemy from escaping, but the newly arrived allies dispatched the bulk of the black rokul. The men of Gladue were spent, suffering from ailments, wounds, weariness of spirit and absolute exhaustion. Many of the men, Lendum included, had not eaten or slept in the past two days. Finding the strength to fight at all was a marvel worthy of song. Lendum rode the length of the arc and back again, aiding wherever the line was weak or beginning to falter. In the end Fourth Battalion yielded not a single inch, as Marshal Lendum lived up to his name in leadership. In two hours, the black rokul of the mountains were completely annihilated, leaving only the forest rokul in the valley to do the bidding of Sindus.

With no prompting whatsoever, the three armies of men turned their hostility to the remaining rokul of the valley. The brown-skinned beasts of the forest proved more fell than their black-skinned cousins of the mountains, putting up a furious resistance in the face of impossible odds. Nevertheless, when all was done, they were routed. They fled into the trees or back into the valley from whence they came, spitting curses and venom as they sped away. The men of Aegea did not pursue them, though Mindus was difficult to restrain. Most were pleased to have taken the field, more than content with their victory without risking further harm by running back into that unholy valley. For generations, the Pass of Graves was considered haunted, and men did not tread there, lest they disturb the numerous dead that walked the valley in spirit, searching for a peace that would never come, their bodies defiled and their bones laying bare to the elements. The valley became a place of unspeakable evil.

Lendum surveyed the scene around him. A great battle had ended, and the kingdoms of men were victorious, but almost no one of Fourth Battalion was celebrating. Their reaction to the glorious encounter with the minions of Nactadale was heartrending. The Nefalians were singing, and the Rubians were dutifully reforming their ranks, but Lendum's men stood in a daze, unsure what to do. Most simply sat down, their weapons across their legs, unable to move anymore. They blinked at the sun through a haze of tears like newborns, crying silently, without the power even to wail. Lendum let them be for now. He had not the heart to issue a single order to his valiant men. They deserved a reprieve, and he was determined to let them have it while he was able.

Lendum stuck his sword into the ground, and fell to one knee. He felt so hot and thirsty. He removed his helmet, and the cool breezes of March that swept across the plains caressed his sweat-soaked hair, bringing indescribable comfort. His legs and arms ached. His lungs felt scarred and made his breathing raspy. His heart was broken from the loss if so many of his brave men. He refused to acknowledge any of that pain, concentrating all that was left of his mind on the satisfaction of the light winds.

Captain Cane, the intrepid leader of Eagle Company, found him. The actions of that company had been instrumental in their survival, and they had paid a heavy price so the rest of Fourth Battalion might live. Lendum had already decided that he would decorate Cane for his remarkable effort, once they returned to Ashtone.

"Marshal, are you fine? Do you require medicines?" he asked.

"No, I am fine; whole, as it were," he answered. "How are you, Captain?"

"I have suffered no injuries, but many of my troops have."

"What happened with Motte? Was he captured?"

"No, my lord. He was slain, by the rokul it seems. We found his body slashed and broken. There are, well, pieces of him missing."

Lendum nodded thoughtfully. "So be it. It is a fitting end for him."

"Yes, sir." Cane fidgeted, nervous. He was averse to report what came next.

Lendum noticed his discomfiture. "What is it, Captain?" he asked. A moment passed in which the pained screams of wounded men filled the air. Cane looked down on his commander, his face full of all of the signs that he was a messenger bearing ill tidings. His shoulders were slumped, and he held his head low. He held his helmet in his hands before him, distracted by its weight. It was a curious thing, that a man with such physical prowess could appear so frail and meek.

"My lord," stammered Cane, "your chief of staff walks with Miro."

Lendum, who by this time had anticipated such news, nearly swooned, and fell onto his rear. His hands hung loosely in his lap. "Corce fell," he said quietly, only to himself.

"Yes, my lord. The line wavered, and then broke. Rokul got behind us, but Chief Corce led a squad into the breach, sealing the break. He was slain, but he saved a great many of us. It was the most courageous act I have ever seen with my own eyes."

"Mmm," Lendum responded, no longer really listening. Ione was lost already, having suffered tortures that he could not dare to imagine. Now Corce was also slain, his constant companion and good friend, the contagious laugh that he enjoyed so much silenced forever. Thousands more of his loyal men were also dead, or unspeakably maimed. Many were in misery so Lendum Noveton could have his revenge. Guilt fell upon him like a drenching rain and, coupled with his grief, nearly got the best of him. A single tear left his eye, running down the crease of his nose, leaving a clean line of skin amongst the filth of battle that covered his face. Cane wordlessly took his leave, bowing as he did so. The sight of his commander in such distress was too much to endure.

Lendum sat there for several minutes, trapped in his own thoughts. He wondered what he could have done differently, replaying the events of the last few days repeatedly in his mind. He had been willing to let Andesha go, until he had seen Ecmus. What had come over him? Was his anger such that it had become a separate entity, able to come forward as it chose to claim his body and wits? He reached down deep, searching for that feeling again, but he found nothing, nothing at all. It seemed that his actions had at least quieted that demon, but the cost had been high. He wondered anew if he could absorb the full price, once he had rested and regained his full faculties. Would he look back at this with regret? Would the honor he had won with his sword be tarnished by the intense anger that governed his will? Would he feel shame rather than pride when he thought of his accomplishments?

Lendum thought that he would.

He buried his face in his hands, the soft leather of his gauntlets saturated with the metallic smell of blood. He wanted to weep, but there were no tears. He lacked the even might to grieve.

All at once, Lendum was draped in shadow. He looked up to see a giant man before him, thickly bearded and clothed entirely in brown leather, to which steel plates had been attached over his shoulders and chest. The black vileness of rokul blood splattered him from head to toe. He carried a large axe in his left hand, which was still clearly very sharp, even though numerous rokul had surely met their end due to its infallible edge. Lendum was astonished to see that the man was smiling.

"Are you the commander of Gladue?" the man asked, his smiled faltering not at all.

"I am the Marshal, yes," Lendum managed to say.

"I am Prince Mindus of Nefala," the man said, face beaming. "Are you wounded, Marshal?" The man extended his right hand, offering to help Lendum to his feet. Lendum now saw that a terrible burn covered the Prince's arm. Blackened skin began at his shoulder, and extended almost to his wrist. Craters of exposed flesh pockmarked the length of his arm, and even though the wound was generously smeared with some kind of strange-smelling salve, the pain must have been enormous. It was a wonder that the man was up and walking, much less smiling as gleefully as a child.

"I am fine," said Lendum, taking the man's outstretched hand. The power of that diminished arm jerked him from the ground and onto his feet. "Your arm? Does it not pain you?"

"Not too much," Mindus responded with nonchalance. "Fortunately for me, I came to war with the possessor of more medicine than anyone in the world. He reduced my pain to a point that I could manage, and has kept me from infection these four days. I would have succumbed to it without him."

"I would imagine so," Lendum said, still amazed. "I know that I would be made useless by such a hurt."

"But rest assured," Mindus continued, "that the foul beast that harmed me will never harm another." Reaching into his satchel, he pulled out the skullcap of a kaito, all five horns still intact. Lendum found it to be a gruesome thing, but Mindus seemed overjoyed to possess it. "Once home I shall fashion this thing into a necklace of great beauty. No king of my people has ever ascended the throne without one since the Rebellion. Now I shall be counted as worthy as my sires!" He slapped his knee, laughing loudly. "I feared that my legacy would be mocked, but now I can be mentioned as great a king as my father. I am most pleased!" he said, putting the scalp back into his pack. "Have you seen Trand?" he asked once his trophy was stowed.

"No, I have not." He honestly was not sure if he wanted to see him. He feared what the wizard would say.

"Well, he desires to see you. With your permission, he has charged me with tending to your dead, so that their bodies are not exposed to the animals of Sindus once we depart. Trand said that you and your men would not be fit to do the task yourselves."

Lendum merely nodded. "Thank you, your Highness. I am grateful for your help. Where can I find Trand?"

"He is there," he said, pointing northward towards the blue-clad army. "He takes council with King Poce, lord of Rubia."

"Thank you, good prince. I owe you a debt, as do all of my men."

Mindus shook Lendum's hand and left to see to the fallen, still smiling.

Lendum looked in the direction Mindus had pointed, and was crestfallen to see that several hundred yards separated him from the men of Rubia. The distance may as well have been many leagues, given his worn condition. Walking that short spell seemed impossible. His arms were full of lead, and the grief of his spirit made even rudimentary walking a painful burden.

Timo nudged him from behind, startling him from his thoughts. The animal had a limp, and Lendum was distressed to find a black-shafted arrow jutting from the horse's rump. The leather cover had limited the arrow's penetration, so the wound was not very deep, but already signs of infection were present; a red tinge around the puncture and the disgusting seepage of pus.

"My dear boy, are you also to fall prey to my madness?" Lendum whispered through clenched teeth. "How long have you been like this? Have you suffered in silence for over a day?" Lendum removed his glove and ran his fingers over the shaft, feeling the heinous, pitted surface "Hold still, friend. This will hurt." With a mighty pull, Lendum jerked the arrow from the tender flesh, slinging the projectile away as if it were revolting to touch. Timo whinnied harshly and bucked his head, but did not kick or try to run away. Lendum stroked his friend's mane, trying to calm him. "Shh. Easy, boy. It's over now."

Timo lowered his head, expecting Lendum to rise to the saddle, but Lendum said, "No, friend. You are lame from your injury. Though I am tired nearly to the death, I shall not ride you again until you heal. Come. We will walk together. Perhaps Trand has some knowledge of horses and can help you."

Lendum took the reins and led the horse toward the army of Rubia. The trek was almost a quest in itself. The horse took staggered steps, hobbled by its wound. Lendum moved just as slowly, as if each step froze his foot to the earth and required tremendous effort to pull it free again. The journey took more than five minutes, and when Lendum finally got close to Trand, he sat down on the ground, and Timo likewise knelt to the earth, simply unable to go any further.

Trand was deep in discussions with who Lendum assumed to be King Poce. The king was an aged man with deep wrinkles around his eyes and a long, fully grown beard, but he was still hale, and used no walking staff. He wore full battle armor, and the blood of the enemy soiled his clothes. Lendum knew almost nothing of the king of Rubia, but he was clearly no coward.

Lendum wondered then, where was Jonas? These armies presumably passed by Noveton during their march north. Did Jonas not see fit to join them on their mission to secure the salvation of Fourth Battalion? Was he so much a coward that he would not pry himself from his protective walls even in the company of so many able warriors? The disdain he felt in that moment for his sovereign made his stomach turn.

However, if Jonas was still safe at Noveton, that meant that Elisa was as well. The king was young and impulsive, but not so despicable as to leave a helpless lady alone to face her fate. Elisa was stubborn, but she would obey direct commands from the king. Perhaps they had already left the Bould, leaving the danger and death behind them.

Ah! His precious Elisa! Now that his revenge was sated, his love for her found new room to grow in his heart. He would trade everything he had to touch her flaxen cheek or hear her soft voice say his name. The sight of her smile would be a treasure invaluable. Now that the war was over, and he believed that it was, he would resign his commission, and they would spend their lives together in a quiet corner of the realm, passing each day as if it were the last they had. He knew that if she were all that he could ever call his own, he would be happy. He could not imagine a life without her.

Presently King Poce turned on his heel, walking away with purpose and giving orders as he did so. Trand came directly to Lendum, squatting before him as agile as ever. His clothes remained spotlessly clean, despite the rokul he had killed and the leagues that had passed beneath his boot heels.

"Trand, I…," but Trand cut him off by shoving a leather flask in his face.

"Drink this," he commanded. His face was kindly, but behind his eyes laid venomous rage, barely concealed by the façade.

"My horse, he's…"

"Shut up and drink it. I will see to the animal, after I see to you. I should tend the beast first. At least he can be counted to act with some modicum of reason." Lendum lowered his head like a whipped dog. He brought the flask to his nose and sniffed it. It had a sweet aroma, so he turned it up, taking a huge gulp.

He nearly spat it back out. The taste was bitterer than anything he had had before. The flavor was detestable. Trand snickered at the contorted grimace.

"Doesn't sit well, does it? No matter. Finish it. Even fools at these times need all of the strength they can muster." Trand walked as nimbly as a spider on his haunches to the horse, lifting the leather guard from the wounded rump. He examined the wound briefly, and then reached into his cloak, producing a small clay jar filled with some kind of greenish cream. He dipped his index finger deeply into the jar and pulled out a gob of the stuff, and slathered it all over the wound. Timo jumped a little at the contact, but he did not pull away. Trand then got another heaping clump of the salve, and without any warning plunged his finger all the way up to the last knuckle in the horse's puncture. Timo peeled back his lips, revealing all of his yellow-tinged teeth, and let loose with a deafening whinny that forced Lendum to cover his ears. Timo stamped his forelegs on the ground in agony, shaking his head, but still he did not try to leap up and get away. On some intuitive level, the beast knew that Trand was helping him, and that the pain was unavoidable and necessary.

Once he was satisfied, Trand removed his finger, and Timo quieted down at once. "Only my finger caused him pain," he said. "The ointment itself is quite soothing. It will ease his suffering, and kill off the sickness that was already beginning to spread. He will be perfectly fine in time."

Indeed, Timo got up suddenly, kicking out his rear leg several times as if trying to loosen a sore muscle. He trotted around a few times, with only the slightest limp in his gait, and then leisurely began to eat grass. He seemed healed already.

"Amazing," said Lendum. He was still holding the flask, putting off finishing it as long as possible. "I feared that he was lost to me."

"You need not worry about Timo. No matter what you have lost, he will be yours for many years to come."

"What do you mean?" Lendum asked.

"Drink it, and then we can talk."

Realizing that he would receive no answers until he had done what Trand wanted, Lendum turned up the flask and downed every drop in several large gulps. The taste made him gag, but he choked it down. He handed Trand the empty flask, coughing and sputtering.

"Good," said Trand, retrieving the flask and placing it back in the folds of his cloak. Lendum continued his fit of coughing. "So it seems that even dullards can take their medicine when they must."

Lendum finally got his hacking under control. The fluid in his belly grew warm, and seemed to branch off throughout his body, filling every muscle with renewed vigor. His strength returned to him, and his drowsiness faded away. Without assistance, he regained his feet, and he felt taller and more robust. Even his hair felt full of energy. The wizard's powers of healing were truly extraordinary.

Lendum did not compliment him on his skills, or even thank him. Trand's words hurt and confused him.

"Why do you speak to me so?" he asked, looking Trand in the eye. "My men have done very well. The war is over."

"Where are the men of Andesha?" Trand asked, crossing his arms before him.

"They are in yonder valley. Since the forest rokul set upon us this very day, I must assume that the army of Andesha is no more."

"Army?" Trand asked with sarcasm. "You use that term rather loosely, do you not? Did they appear an army to you?"

Lendum remembered the disheveled appearance of the ranks, the lack of steel, and the overwhelming feeling of confusion and fear that radiated from the host of his enemy. No, they did not appear to be an army. They looked a great deal like what they were: a mass of farmers with pitchforks and clubs.

"What does it matter?" Lendum said, suddenly very defensive. "Gladue is victorious, and the Bould is ours. The killing can stop now."

Trand rubbed his forehead with his long fingers, seemingly very perturbed. "I care not for Gladue, or her king. My goal was to end the war, but only to hold the power of Sindus in check, and spare countless lives." He knelt to the earth, gathering a handful of soil into his palm. "My duty is to humanity, not this worthless land. What is the value of what I hold in my hand? What is the value of this entire region? Would you sacrifice one of your men to secure this area? Ten? One hundred? I am pleased that peace has been achieved, but I would rather it had been without the slaughter of thousands of innocents."

"They were slaughtered by the rokul, not by me," Lendum protested.

"Really? Would you defend your actions by placing the blame on the dark lord? Your attack was the signal Sindus needed to unleash his servants," Trand answered, very sadly. "Do you believe the dark lord would loose his strength on two great bodies of men that were not quarrelling? Besides, you had many opportunities to prevent this catastrophe before it came to a boil. You could have argued with Jonas about going north. You could have slowed your march. Even one day would have been sufficient. Your lust for revenge overcame all else, and now the blood of untold dead stains your hands. I hope your vengeance is fulfilling, because in your pursuit of it you have abandoned all else."

Lendum felt his heart rise into his throat. He felt sure what Trand meant, but his mind refused to acknowledge it. "What are you saying?" he finally asked, quivering all over.

"Noveton has been destroyed, Lendum. There is nothing now in the world that bears your name but you alone."

"No," Lendum managed to say. Then he almost lost consciousness, his knees buckling beneath him. Trand grasped him fiercely by the arm, his fingers as tight as a vise, and kept him on his feet.

"It is true. We passed there four days ago, and came upon the rokul while they reveled in their evil deeds. They fled at the sight of us, and we set out after them at once, but the fort was overrun. There is little hope that anyone survived."

Lendum shook his head, refusing to hear the terrible news. Tears streamed out of him, and he wailed in a low tone that was beastly.

"You cannot yield to your grief now. There is much work to do here, and your position demands that you see it done."

Lendum struggled against the steely grip, quite uselessly. "Release me!" he hissed. "I must go to her! She may yet live!"

"If you go there, you will harvest nothing but more anguish. I beg you, wait until your heroic men are at rest, and let your passions cool."

"I feel constant anguish, and I see little reason to suffer in ignorance. I would rather endure my pain knowing the truth beyond all doubt."

Trand's face finally broke, and expressed pity. "As you wish," he said, and released Lendum's arm. "I will go with you," he added thoughtfully. "I am needed here, for there are many wounded that may yet walk with Miro, but no one should face what you will alone. And you are alone, my boy."

Trand whistled twice, and the horses, Dampe and Timo, came trotting up together. Lendum climbed on his horse's back, and then spurred him on. Trand rode Dampe majestically, matching Timo's stride. They headed south swiftly, toward the ruined fortress of Noveton, where the Lendum would deliver the final stroke of the War of the Bould.

⇒ ⇐

Trand and Lendum rode all that day at a trot. Lendum, desperate to get back, kept urging Timo to move faster, but the horse refused to quicken its pace. He was still tender from his injury, and knew that his master should not be traveling so strenuously. Mercifully, Trand was quiet. Lendum had feared that the conjuror would regale him with lore laced with hidden wisdom, but the fear was groundless. Trand was actually being very respectful. Though he knew it not, Lendum had already begun his time of sorrow.

As evening came nigh, Timo slowed to a walk, prompting Dampe to do so as well. The stars shone brightly in the clear sky as the darkness descended in full, and the horses came to a halt.

"Come on, boy," Lendum pleaded, kicking harder than usual. "We can go a bit further. There is good starlight tonight." His voice was broken on the edge of tears.

"Lendum, you should sleep," Trand suggested softly. "Your weariness and hunger can only be suppressed by an elixir, not eliminated, and only then for a while. Going for as long as you have without rest can kill you."

"I can't stop!" he screamed. "She wouldn't stop, so neither will I!"

"Lendum, your beloved has passed. She awaits you in the unknown."

"You don't know that!" His voice carried far over the plains. "She could only be hurt, or hiding! She could have fled before the siege! I told her to flee, if trouble should come! She could already be out of the Bould!" Spittle leaked onto his chin from his tirade. In the pale starlight, the gauntness of his face made him seem barely alive, a wretched and wasted thing not long for the world.

Trand nodded his assent, though he acquiesced reluctantly. He produced his flask and passed it to Lendum, who took it wordlessly and drank it as if it were perfectly brewed ale. He passed it back to Trand, and the wizard deftly returned it to his cloak.

"None for you?" Lendum asked.

"No. I never imbibe my own concoctions."

"Are you not weary? You must feel sleep coming over you as I do."

Trand grinned slightly, and even in the darkness, Lendum could see the glimmer in his eye. "I can sleep," he answered. "I do quite often, though for me it is mostly a tool to pass the time. A hobby, if you will." The wizard's teeth were very white in the gloom. "Come; let us put my potion to good use. Many miles lie before us."

The horses resumed their pace, trotting steadily into the night.

⇒ ⇐

They could see the smoke at daylight of the third day. Fort Noveton was still smoldering. Lendum, looking nothing like himself, was nearly at the end of his rope. Huge, black circles hung from his eyes, and his emaciated frame had grown so feeble that he had cast off his armor the day before to lighten his load and ease his toil. His remaining garments were tattered and blood-splattered, and they stank. He had the look of a lowly peasant rather than the most powerful commander in the entire kingdom.

As they approached the single gate, they could see that a portion of the wall was smashed. The large stones that littered the ground were scratched by blade and claw, making the depraved characters of the tongue of Sindus. They were an abomination to the eye. Trand could understand the writing, but Lendum could not. He was certain that he did not want to know what it said.

The timbers of the gate were splintered and broken, and lay in a heap near the entrance. Lazy tendrils of smoke still rose from the blackened wood, signaling to all that could see that the fort was no more. Hundreds of hideous three-toed tracks crossed each other in every direction, a haphazard series of markings that gave no indication of order or reason. Near the burning debris, a crude banner of the dark kingdom of Nactadale stood out like a blister. The banner was a setting sun of dark crimson, half-consumed by a field of black, impressed onto a field of white. As they passed the banner, Lendum paid it no mind, but Trand plucked it from the ground and flung it onto the smoking ruin of the gate. It quickly succumbed to the heat and erupted into flames.

Once inside, the scene that greeted them was ghastly. Hundreds of men lay dead, along with even more festering rokul. A rancid stench hung in the air, the putrid reek of tons of rotting flesh. The battle had been great. No doubt, there was incredible valor and honorable sacrifice at the battle of Noveton, but no one lived to tell the tale or sing the songs of glory about the fallen. Everyone was dead.

With dread Lendum turned his gaze towards the tiny room he had shared with his wife for all of a day. From the gate, he could see that there seemed to be an inordinate number of decaying rokul collected near the door of his hovel, baking in the sun and attracting vermin. Waving flies from his face, Lendum took a few tentative steps in that direction, Trand very close behind him. As his paces brought him closer, Lendum recognized the twin brothers of his wife, the new family he had come to know for only a single night. They lay on the ground near the entrance of the small room, dozens of rokul strewn around them. They had put up a furious defense, more so than the others had, for they had fought for more than national pride. They had fought not only for their very lives, but for a cherished loved one only paces away. Alas, they had come up lacking, and now they walked in the unknown.

Then he saw her. He could perceive the beautiful teal green of her dress; the clothing that made her seem so lovely to his eye. She lay across the threshold, her blonde hair covering her face, trailing from the doorway and just barely touching the ground.

"Elisa!" Lendum shouted. "Elisa!" He made to go to her, but Trand quickly restrained him, holding him tightly across the chest.

"No, Lendum. You do not want to view her this way."

Lendum's face contorted to one of pure torment, to the point that he no longer seemed a man. He squirmed in Trand's grip, but the struggle was weak and futile. He fell to his knees, and loosed his sorrow to the heavens with a long wail that made the gods weep.

"Nooooo!" he cried out loudly, his voice disintegrating into a sound that was barely human. "Not again! Not again! Are these lands cursed? Do the gods have no mercy?" Trand embraced him tightly, because there was no one else that could do so, or could understand so completely why it was necessary.

Just then, a voice cried out behind them, far away. "Help! Help me, please!" it cried, muffled as if through a thick wall. "Help! I'm starving!"

"Come," Trand said. "Someone here yet lives." He hoisted Lendum to his feet, and nearly carried him across the courtyard of the fort toward the sound of the cries. They came at last to the entrance to the mine, where there were very few rokul tracks. They had avoided this area, not surprisingly.

"Down here!" the voice cried out. "I am trapped! Please! Help me out!"

Trand set Lendum on the ground as if he were a baby. He was still sobbing and sniffling. Trand searched the area around him until his eyes set upon a short coil of rope. He grabbed it up and expertly flung it into the mouth of the mine. For a few seconds it hung loosely, and then it grew taut, and Trand began to pull hand over hand, until up from the interior of the earth came none other than Jonas, King of Gladue.

The king looked terrible. His lips were dried and cracked, and wilted skin hung from his face. His eyes were glassy, clouded and bereft of feeling. His clothing was dirty, but intact, and Lendum quickly noted that the king had not a drop of blood anywhere on him, nor any injury that was evident.

"Trand!" Jonas exclaimed once he saw the face of his rescuer. "Bless you, old chap! I have been in that filthy hole for days. It was foul!" His entire face seemed shriveled, and it was apparent that the king had drunk some of the water of the stream, despite the saltiness. His warts stood out farther than usual, making him even uglier.

Jonas saw Lendum sitting on the ground before him. At first, he did not recognize his First Marshal, but after a few seconds amazement blossomed on his hideous face. "Marshal! What are you doing here? Has the battle been won already?"

Lendum slowly got to his feet. "Has the battle been won?" he repeated quietly, his tone full of poison. "My wife lay dead within your sight, and you ask me of the battle?"

"I'm sorry," Jonas said. "Her death was regrettable, but nothing could have been done to prevent it. We were completely outmatched."

"You guaranteed her safety," Lendum said, walking nearer. "You promised me she would be protected, and when the time came to honor your word you did nothing."

"Are you blind, man?" Jonas asked, backing away slightly. Lendum's voice was calm, yet crazed, and the king was a little frightened. "Nothing could be done. They beset us from all sides. It was horrifying! No help could be given from any quarter."

"You hid," Lendum said plainly. "You ran away and hid in a hole like a weasel, and let your brave men and innocents die alone. You let my beloved die, alone." His voice was cold, even.

"But I would have been killed," Jonas protested, holding up his hands. "I cannot die. The kingdom needs me."

Lendum drew his sword. "Kingdoms don't need their kings. Kings need their kingdoms. You ask others to give what you refuse to give yourself. You are a coward." Lendum stepped closer, his fingers tightening and loosening around the hilt in preparation.

Jonas saw his doom in Lendum's eyes. "Trand, stop him!" he pleaded.

Trand laughed. "I would, my lord," he said mockingly, "but he has yet to say anything with which I disagree. His case is solid, as it were. You have usurped countless lives to acquire the hole near your very feet. You have stolen and killed for wealth. You have listened to faulty counsel from a treasonous beast. Judgment comes to all, and pampered royalty are no exception."

"You lie! This was not as sordid as you make it sound. I have stolen nothing! My conquest of this area was legal, not criminal."

"You stole this land, Jonas," Lendum said. "I was there when your envoy demanded its possession, and when he was refused, troops came and took what you wanted. That is thievery, no matter how well you wrap your intentions in legal niceties."

"You were not there," Jonas protested.

"You say that because you believe that all who stood against you are now dead, but it is not so. I survived. My name in Lendum Noveton, and my father gained this homestead from your father. This is legally my land, not yours, and I think that I shall now take back what is mine."

Jonas' face became one of unconcealed fear. "Stop! I order you to stop, Marshal!" Lendum kept coming. Murder was in his eye: murder and judgment. "Please, you can not do this! I am the lord of Gladue!"

"Not anymore," Lendum replied, and he thrust his blade deep into the king's chest. Jonas gurgled, and blood ran from the corners of his mouth. He grasped uselessly at the blade, unable to remove either the steel or the pain from his torso. After what seemed a blessedly short time, he collapsed, his final breath escaping with a labored hiss. The sword slipped from Lendum's grip. Never again would he level a strike with a weapon.

Lendum fell to his knees. Weariness seized him with both hands, and he fell over on his side. He curled up like a child and slept on the hard ground, dead to the world. He slept for a long time, deeply and without dreams.

Trand let him be. He turned to the ugly business of tending to the dead. He went first to Elisa, so Lendum would not see her disfigurement when he awoke.

CONSEQUENCES AND CONCLUSIONS

So ended the War of the Bould. News of the defeat reached Andesha in due time. There were no riders, no messengers on foot, and no word of mouth to pass along to Anboe, but fishermen along the Shae made grisly discoveries that confirmed some of the worst fears. They found bodies of brown-clad men all along the banks of the river. Some of the corpses were missing limbs, or the head. Some had bites taken from them, the flesh used to refresh the horrible monsters of the east. No living men that marched into the Bould behind Quereus were ever seen again, but body parts and fragments of tattered clothing were found for weeks afterward.

Once the people knew and believed the truth, the insurrection erupted. Grindal's days were numbered, and as he came to understand this, he holed himself up inside the palace, refusing to see anyone, trying to rule behind locked doors. His rule was without any authority however. His military was decimated, robbed of its most effective and loyal leadership. His councilors, who had suffered indignity over the years from the king's foul temper, were no longer at his beck and call, and refused to carry out the orders of His Highness. The populace, who had yielded so much on the promise of a glorious return, were embittered, and saw more honor in disobeying than in compliance. Grindal had lost the power of compulsion.

When the people stormed the palace, they met no resistance. Grindal had ordered the palace guard to repel anyone that tried to breach the walls, but instead, they bound their king, and hand delivered him to the mob. Prince Tundal, the king's younger brother and heir to the throne, did not actively participate in the rebellion, and he wept in private for his brother's fate, but he did not intervene, and quietly gave his tacit approval.

Rebels constructed a gallows in the heart of Anboe. They carried Grindal to the top, denying him even his last few steps. As they placed the halter around his neck, he heard his subjects heckling him and cursing his name, blaming him for monumental losses and accusing him of all manner of corruption and vile deeds. The words stung him, cutting him like a thousand tiny knives. When the trap was finally sprung, he was grateful that he was about to be granted silence.

＝ ＝

The newly crowned King Tundal of Andesha assumed power while his brother's body was still warm, and immediately took steps to yield the entire area in dispute to his rival nation. The Bould became the sovereign territory of Gladue, and a treaty of peace was eventually signed by all of the crowned heads of Aegea, recognizing the uncontested victory of Gladue.

Jonas, like Grindal, had no son and no brothers either. Rule of Gladue passed for a time to his younger sister, Dine, who became the first sitting queen of that country. Her rule was a short one, however. Some month's after the war's conclusion, Tundal arranged the marriage of his younger brother to the sitting queen, thereby creating another brother-brother dynasty between the two kingdoms. Ironically, the struggle and ultimate failure to acquire the territory that had cost Grindal so much came to be under the rule of his family in the end. Such is the nature of war and bloodlines.

In the east, Sindus was pleased. The optimum goal had eluded him by unforeseen efforts, but still, the plan had yielded a great deal of death and destruction, and now the kingdoms along his northern border were hastily trying to rebuild their defenses. He had lost many kaitos, it was true (in Nefala *the War of the Bould* would ever after be referred to as *the Kaitos War*), but many, many more men had lost their lives, and he still had rokul uncountable in his service. He believed he could replenish his numbers faster than the realms of men, and then he would begin the chaos anew, and then again, and again, until all the world lay under his heel.

＝ ＝

In the summer following the death of Jonas, a lone rider approached a small cottage in the western half of the Bould. This land was now Gladue, though the soil was no different, and the skies still maintained the same shade of blue. The flowers continued to grow as they had for countless years, and the rivers flowed in the same direction they had since the beginning of time. The land itself had not changed in any way whatsoever. Thousands had died and nothing had changed but the color on the map.

The war was over now, and on this sunny day in August the weather was fair, though a little hot. The horse came to the cottage with a leisurely pace, unhurried in any way. The hour was close to noon, and the rider knew that the occupant was home. Flowers bloomed from a dozen clay pots along the front porch, the drapes covering the windows were tied back, and the windows themselves were opened wide, letting the cool breezes eradicate the stifling heat within the dwelling.

The rider checked his horse at the little cobblestone walkway and sat there a moment, taking in the sight of the home. It was as perfect as he remembered it to be, neat and tidy, with scarcely a blade of grass out of place. The rider sighed deeply, wishing more than anything that he could be transported back to the time he had first set eyes on this house. He would do so much differently; so many choices he would alter, but it could not be so. Men are blessed that can look forward, and it is a curse that they can look back, and remember.

The rider dismounted slowly, hearing the soft creak of leather straining under his weight. He retrieved the item he intended to deliver, and started along the short path, his boot heels clicking lightly along the stones.

At the door, he traced the characters etched into the wood, feeling the texture, as ignorant of their meaning now as he had been then. He thought that the tongues of men were beautiful things, and amazed him. That so many abstract concepts could be expressed with nothing more than the sounds of the throat was a remarkable achievement. He knew nothing of the characters carved into the door, but soon, he hoped, he would understand all of it. He had a knack for languages, and there was little else he could do with his time.

Tentatively, he rapped on the door three times. From within he heard a bustling, and rapid footsteps that grew louder as the occupant accosted the entrance.

Amarut opened the door.

She appeared a little older, and she squinted more than he recalled, but she emitted the same aura of happiness, of unrestrained glee, that she always had. She clapped her hands to her cheeks in surprise, then she began to bounce in place, her joy growing to the point that she might burst.

"Hello, Bould-mother," Lendum said. His body had recovered from his ordeal, and he was fit and whole, but his face was incalculably sad.

Amarut began clapping her hands in excitement. "You're alive!" she exclaimed, nearly yelling. "You've survived the war!" Her cheeks flushed from her display.

"Yes, I yet live. I have come to return this." He extended to her the sword, still in its sheath. The blade was polished, the scabbard cleaned, and the edge was as keen as the day he had received it. Overall, he was returning it in the same condition in which it had been lent.

Amarut did not take it. She suddenly grew somber. "But I made a give of it. Is it not rude to return something that was given in love?"

"I have used this to terrible effect, and be comforted that I only stand before you now because I carried this gift these past years. Now, I need it no longer, and beg you to release me from it. Never again, I believe, will it be my duty to bear a weapon." He held the sword out again, and this time she took it, her plump fingers cradling the blade as he let it go.

"I have nothing," he said abruptly. He was unspeakably forlorn, but he did not cry. He had no more tears left in him.

"We always have something," she said softly, looking up at him.

"I had something once, and it was taken. I despaired, but then I found something else, something wonderful, and in my rashness, I threw it away. There is no one to blame but myself." His guilt was heavy, for he had not only lost Elisa. Corce, and Ione too, both good men that had been confidants and the only friends he could count in the world, were lost forever. Everyone he had known or cared about was gone. He carried the pain of thousands of unnamed mothers and fathers, orphans and widows. The weight would crush even the most remorseless man.

Amarut placed a warm hand to his cheek, and Lendum turned to it, feeling the unmistakable and inexplicable love within the touch.

"Where will you go?" she asked tenderly.

"I do not know. I have no home. I do not feel any ties to Andesha or Gladue. I am a Bould-son, but where in the Bould can I rest my head? I have no where to go."

"You will always have this place, son," she said, a tear escaping.

Lendum only nodded, too emotionally drained to speak. Amarut placed a hand on his strong shoulder and ushered him indoors, where everything was clean and comfortable, and the smells were always sweet and soothing. Lendum would live here, never fully relieved of his grief, never fully removed from his shame. This was his home now, but it would never feel like home, for his guilt would never allow it.

The door closed behind him, the latch clicking softly. Outside, the grass continued to grow, and the sun's rays shone down on all, blessing the earth with heavenly light.

A WORD FROM THE AUTHOR

Greetings, dear reader.

My sincere thanks for reading my little tale, and I certainly hope that you enjoyed reading it as much as I enjoyed writing it. No one could have been more surprised by what transpired in the lands of the Bould than I, because when I began I had no clear idea where it was going. Perhaps all authors feel this way, but the story never really felt in my control. This was my first endeavor at writing a tale of this length, and it was an adventure to say the least. In any event, I had great fun, and I look forward to embarking on the journey again.

This story came to me out of nowhere. I can hardly believe that I wrote it, because it embraces a genre that I do not myself enjoy. I have always preferred stories of crime dramas and sneaky attorneys, not wizards and dark lords. Fantasy novels are great, but by and large I would rather read an actual history book. I have done what I can to give this book the feel of history; of true events that took place long ago. I don't know how successful I have been in that regard, but I do know that when I reread my words weeks after I wrote them, I was pleased. This book is a window into a world that contains marvels yet untold. There are brief mentions of things to come, and things that have long since passed, and rest assured that it is my goal to tell the tale in full, and explore the entire map of Aegea with heroes and villains, scoundrels and monsters. The history of Aegea since Tor is imprisoned covers almost 1200 years, and there are many epics to be uncovered.

I want to stress that this work of fiction is meant solely to entertain the reader. I know that there are authors that use their craft to present their viewpoints or perhaps put forth some sort of agenda. I don't begrudge them that, because it is, on the whole, and effective means to implement change. I do use symbolism in my writing, but I stop short of any kind of allegory. Any connections drawn between my characters and actual people, living or dead, is purely a function of the imagination of the reader, not myself. I've nothing against representation per se, but I find allegory to be rather tedious, and less fun to read than a work of pure fiction. Therefore, I take pains to avoid similarities between my characters and any famous person. Instead, I give my characters quirks of personality that remind me of people that I actually know. It just seems more real to me that way, and it is much more entertaining that way as well.

I want to thank my wife, Ruty, and my kids McKenzie and Patrick. They inspired me at every turn, and gave me viewpoints that I could never had come up with myself. I also want to thank Keith and Andrea, whose feedback was invaluable to the ultimate result. To Terry and LT, I miss you guys, and hope we will keep in touch in the coming months.

Once again, thank you, Reader, for your time. Maybe soon we can talk again, and we can find ourselves roaming the untamed lands of Aegea, bound for more adventure and surprises.

Until next time,
Robert Thomason